Proof of Intent

WILLIAM J. COUGHLIN

Proof of Intent

WALTER SORRELLS

THOMAS DUNNE BOOKS
ST. MARTIN'S PRESS ✒ NEW YORK

THOMAS DUNNE BOOKS
An imprint of St. Martin's Press.

www.stmartins.com

ISBN 0-312-28066-1

First Edition: November 2002

10 9 8 7 6 5 4 3 2 1

Acknowledgments

I would like to thank Mary Kelly and John Walke of the Prosecuting Attorney's Office of St. Clair County, Michigan, for the generous gift of their time and legal insight.

Also thanks to Van Pearlberg, assistant district attorney of Cobb County, Georgia, who has been helpful to me on many legal and law enforcement issues over the years. I've taken a couple of liberties with legal procedure in this novel. The blame for this naturally falls on me and not on the legal professionals who have assisted me along the way.

To Jane Rayburn, I appreciated the fine tour. You have a big future as a tour guide if the journalism thing doesn't work out.

Personal thanks to Patti Hughes and Ruth Coughlin for reasons that will be obvious to both of them.

PRELIMINARIES

One

ATER THE ADDRESS would become familiar to everyone in America, a phrase on everyone's lips. Just like "the Rockingham estate" or "the compound at Waco." But at the time 221 Riverside Boulevard in Pickeral Point, Michigan, was just a big house I'd never visited before, dark and unfamiliar at that dead hour of the night.

And so at first I didn't see him. As I'd been instructed on the phone, I had come in the back door. The moon was throwing a white patch on the dark floor.

As my eyes adjusted, a dark blob in the middle of the large empty room slowly resolved itself into the form of Miles Dane. He was sitting on his haunches, head bowed, eyes shut, lips moving silently. Meditating, maybe? He wore a robe of liquid white silk.

He didn't look at me, didn't stir, just sat there with his lips moving, something glistening on his face. I figured, okay, maybe the guy was a flake—but since he was a potentially big client, too, I'd wait. Even if it was a couple minutes past four o'clock in the morning.

After a moment or two the moon went behind a cloud. Miles Dane stood abruptly and walked across the straw mat floor, through a doorway and down a long, dark hallway. I followed. He was a short man, with the physical vigor and build of a wrestler.

We walked silently through his large living room, up a flight of deeply carpeted stairs, down a long hallway, into a bedroom with an expensive view of the river.

"There," he said, pointing.

"What?" I thought he was pointing out the picture window. The dark, mottled water looked like hammered lead.

"No, Charley. *There.*"

Then I saw her. She lay in the bed as though sleeping. The moon came out from behind the cloud and a pale light washed the floor, revealing both her ruined face and the black blood that suddenly seemed to be everywhere.

EVEN BEFORE SEEING the woman lying dead in her bed, it had been a bad night. I'd been woken at around two o'clock that same morning by a disturbing call from my daughter, Lisa, and then been unable to sleep, lying there in bed torturing myself about the mistakes I'd made in my life. Just as I'd decided the night was a dead loss, that I might as well get dressed and read a book for a while, I'd gotten the puzzling call from Miles Dane.

You probably know Miles Dane. He's the most famous writer in Pickeral Point, Michigan—which, to be fair, is not saying a whale of a lot. But still. One of his early novels, *The Bust*, had been made into a movie starring Charles Bronson back in the early seventies, and he's been on the best-seller list off and on ever since. Though from what I gathered, lately it's been more off than on.

I had met Miles several times over the years. He hung around the county courthouse occasionally to do research for his novels, and had taken me to lunch once to ask me some technical details about murder prosecutions. We said hello to each other in the grocery store or bookstore every once in a while. But other than that, we were pretty much strangers.

Miles is one of those writers who ended up being famous as much for being famous as for anything to do with his work. The square jaw, the bantam rooster build, the black clothes, the black cowboy boots, the omnipresent shoulder holster. And, of course, the eyes: They were gray and piercing, somehow managing to seem both haunted and threatening at the same time. He did well on the talk shows back in the days when Johnny Carson had still sandwiched the occasional writer in between the starlets and the ballplayers and the funny guys from the zoo. He said inflammatory things about women and minorities to magazine writers. He drove Italian cars into trees. He got into the occasional well-publicized fistfight, and always came out of the police station looking great for the waiting cameras.

I always thought his books were a little pretentious. The hero was generally some kind of compromised semicriminal with a name like Donnie or Dwayne who went around thrashing people and then talking like he'd read too much Kierkegaard. But Miles kept the pages turning, I'll give him that, throwing Donnie or Dwayne into one scary predicament after another. While the first books were alright, the last few I'd read seemed to verge on self-parody.

But then, what do I know about writing? I'm just a small-town lawyer, scraping by.

H AVE YOU CALLED the police?" I said.

Miles Dane had slid down the wall and was hunkered on the floor, where he began panting like a dog.

"Miles?"

When his breathing finally settled down, he shook his head slowly, no.

"It's your wife?"

He nodded, then put his face in his hands.

"I'll make the call," I said.

"Diana," he said. "Her name is Diana."

T HE CITY FATHERS of Pickeral Point have been uncharacteristically wise when it comes to shepherding the police department. The latest chief they hired, Elvin Bower, is a good man. They pay him well, and he hires good people. Over the years the detectives in the department have been drawn from the ranks of Detroit homicide cop retirees. I've had my share of run-ins with them, but I've never questioned their professionalism.

The first policeman to show up at Miles Dane's house was a uniformed kid of at least twelve. I told him not to worry about the body, just to call for his supervisor and the city detective, then to start stringing crime scene tape. He gratefully did as he was told. The new town detective, a woman with the unfortunate name of Chantall Denkerberg, showed up about fifteen minutes later. I'd had no dealings with her, but she'd cracked a very complicated murder-for-hire case in Detroit that had made national headlines a couple of years back and came to the department with a reputation as a hotshot.

"Charley Sloan," I said, sticking out my hand. "I'm Mr. Dane's attorney."

Denkerberg's eyebrows rose slightly. She was a tall, handsome woman of about fifty, her severe black pageboy punctuated by a white streak over the left ear. Blue coat, blue skirt, white blouse buttoned to the neck and starched hard.

It wasn't the usual thing for a detective to roll up on a crime scene and have a lawyer there to greet them. I expected her to ask why I was there, but instead she just said, "You touch anything?"

"No, I didn't."

"Do you know what happened?"

"Mrs. Dane appears to have been beaten to death in her bedroom." I chose my words carefully, doing my best to keep my answer as vague as possible. "As you might expect, my client is very distressed and hasn't articulated what he knows very clearly."

"Anything he wants to get off his chest before I start conducting my examination of the scene?"

"If what you're implying, Detective, is *did he do it?*—the answer is no."

"Then sit tight. I'd like you and Mr. Dane to stay in the living room. Please instruct him to stay there until I come in."

"Don't you need to see the body?" I said.

Denkerberg smiled blandly. "Amateurs always stampede straight for the body. I, however, proceed methodically."

She took a 35mm camera out of a shoulder bag and began walking unhurriedly across the lawn, pausing to take pictures of every door and window, peering closely at the ground.

———

I WENT BACK inside and sat on the couch. The room was beautifully decorated, with a spare, Japanese flavor. A large, richly colored book of woodblock prints lay in front of me on the coffee table, open to a picture of a Japanese courtesan playing a shamisen, one bare breast and a wisp of pubic hair visible beneath her loose kimono. Behind her a man peeped around the corner of the room, a comical leer on his face—and from the coquettish expression on the courtesan's face, it seemed likely she was not unaware of the voyeur's presence. I considered picking up the book for a closer look at the odd picture, but then decided it would be best not to touch anything. Miles sat across from me, still wearing his spotless white silk dressing gown.

"So," I said, "have you collected yourself enough to tell me what happened?"

He stared across the room for a while, his face empty.

"I work at night," he said finally. "I was in my office at the other end of the house. I was getting a little tired, and the juices weren't flowing, so I decided to go to bed. I brushed my teeth, put on my robe and pajamas, then I opened the door to check on her . . ." His hands moved feebly in his lap.

"There's no blood on your robe. You didn't touch her?"

He frowned, half-quizzical, half-irritated. "You saw her, for godsake!" he said. "What would have been the point?"

Logically speaking, he was right: She had been beaten so badly there probably had been precious little question she was dead. But still, it seemed odd to me. The natural human reaction when you see an injured loved one is to approach them, to see if there is anything you can do to help, no matter how remote the chance of success.

"Okay," I said. "And you didn't hear anything while you were working?"

"I play music when I'm working. Play it pretty loud, actually. Helps me get where I need to be so I can wring out the primal juices." He said it like it was a line he'd rehearsed for a bad play.

"So you didn't hear anything."

"Nothing but Beethoven. *The Tempest.* Piano Sonata number 17."

"Mind my asking why you called me before you called the police?"

He studied me with his haunted gray eyes. "Are you joking?"

"No, I'm not, Miles."

"Well, the answer to your question is, because they're going to crucify me."

"Why would they do that?"

"I'm a student of crime, Charley: the husband is always the first suspect. Right? Plus, hell, you know who I am, what my reputation is. That new guy? That jerk-off fair-haired boy whom the good people of our county voted into the prosecutor's office last year? He's gonna take one look at me and figure this is the best chance he'll ever get of being on Court TV."

"Not if there's no evidence against you." I didn't mention that the new prosecuting attorney was a friend of mine, a man who could be trusted not to pursue anybody who didn't look like he deserved it.

He fixed his eyes on me like he was trying to stare me down. "You just watch."

We sat for a while in silence.

"They're going to ask about your relationship. Were there any problems there that I should know about?"

His eyes suddenly filled with tears. "I loved my wife more than anything else on this planet. We had a thing so strong you wouldn't believe."

"There were no affairs? No conspicuous arguments? No late-night calls to the police?"

He eyed me for a while. "How many times have you been married, Charley?"

"Three."

"Good marriages?"

"The worst imaginable."

His eyes softened, and he smiled at me with a look of pity in his eyes. "Then I guess you'd have no idea what it's like," he said. "Devoting your whole life to one person, loving completely and being loved completely in return?"

I didn't know quite what to say to that. So I just sat there and waited for Detective Denkerberg to come talk to my client. Miles was right: I'm forty-seven years old, and I'd never known the thing he was talking about. Forty-seven years old, and I was only just now feeling my way toward a life where such a thing seemed like a realistic possibility.

Suddenly he came over to me and put his arm around my shoulder—as though *I* were the one who'd just suffered an unimaginable tragedy.

Two

THE SUN WAS just coming up as Miles turned a large, unusually shaped key, unlocking the massive door of the office in the back of his house. The lock was exceptionally sturdy, with a bolt as big around as a banana, and the door itself was made of two-inch-thick mahogany. I'd seen bank vaults that looked like sissies next to that door.

As soon as we walked into the room, I nearly turned around and walked out. One wall of the office consisted of a large window with a spectacular view of the harsh white sun as it rose over a glittering St. Clair River, the slow-moving half-mile-wide body of water that separates Michigan from Canada. There was nothing wrong with the view. But the other three walls were a problem: They were covered with weapons. Everything from expensive English shotguns and hunting rifles, to antique cavalry sabers and Japanese swords, to cudgels, to a bewildering array of martial arts weapons. It looked like the *sanctum sanctorum* of a man who was preparing to invade a small West African nation. Talk about a poorly chosen place for a murder suspect to let himself be interviewed by the police.

Denkerberg looked around the room with obvious interest. She was a good four inches taller than Miles, I noticed. "Quite a collection," she said.

"Yeah, I had all this stuff appraised last year. Well over a hundred grand, you believe that?" Miles said loftily. "That's why I keep the door locked."

I suddenly felt a prickling on the back of my neck. It wasn't just the weapons. Something seemed to have changed in Miles's countenance the second Denkerberg had entered the room. It was as though a mask had dropped over his face: Suddenly he seemed a harder, tougher man than the one who had led me to his dead wife. Miles had a reputation—in the press, at least—for belligerence. And friction was the last thing this interview needed.

I cleared my throat. "Shall we get started?"

Miles and I sat on the couch, but Denkerberg continued to circle the room, hands behind her back, examining every item carefully. Each weapon was perched on its own small pair of wooden hooks—each hook, from the look of it, custom-made from mahogany to fit the individual weapon and to match the room's wooden paneling. Under each rack was a small brass plate detailing the weapon's particulars.

Denkerberg finally sat down, crossing her long legs primly. She took a pack of Tiparillos out of her purse, stuck one in her mouth, clamping the plastic holder between her teeth. She reminded me of a hateful nun from back in my parochial school days, Sister Herman Marie, who was always whacking me in the back of the head with her prayer book when I fumbled in catechism practice. You stumbled over a couple words, then KA-WHACK!

"I'm deeply sorry about your wife, Mr. Dane," the detective said, lighting the Tiparillo. "And I know this is a difficult time for you. But if we're going to find the person who committed this horrible thing, I'll need to speak with you while your impressions are still fresh." She examined Miles Dane's face with frank curiosity. The writer might as well have been wearing a kabuki mask for all the expression he showed. The vulnerability he'd shown just minutes earlier seemed to have entirely evaporated. "First, Mr. Dane, if you'd tell me what happened tonight. Everything you saw, everything you heard. When you're done I'll ask you some more questions."

Miles looked at me and blinked. "I'm not being thin-skinned, am I? I mean, this is my house. Isn't it customary these days to ask before you fire up tobacco products in other people's houses?"

"I'm sorry," Denkerberg said, not sounding sorry at all. "I wasn't thinking."

Miles's eyes widened. "Oh, no. I don't mind in the slightest. I just was a little surprised you didn't ask." He smiled without warmth as he fixed his cold gray eyes on the detective.

I rested two fingers gently on the back of his forearm. "I'm sure the detective didn't mean anything by it. She's got a lot on her mind."

"Not a problem," Denkerberg said, drawing on the Tiparillo. "Mr. Dane?"

"Some people describe the writing process as being something like entering a fugue state," Miles said. "If you're not a writer, you probably don't know what I'm talking about. But at a certain point the characters on the page seem to get up and start walking around on their own. Once that happens the writer's job is almost like taking dictation. But that doesn't mean a writer just sits on his ass. Ever learn shorthand, Ms. Denkerberg? Taking dictation requires a great, great deal of concentration."

"I can imagine," Denkerberg murmured.

"I write at night." Miles's face had changed subtly once he started speaking, taking on a pugnacious look, like a drunk who was hoping to get in a fight with somebody. "I require complete and utter quiet, so I located this office at the far end of the house."

This caught me by surprise. Why had he told me he was blasting Beethoven when his wife died? Denkerberg must have caught me frowning because she said, "Something to add, Counselor?"

"Pardon?" I said vaguely. "What? Oh, no, sorry I was just . . . I sort of drifted off for a moment there." I smiled pleasantly. Over the years I've perfected the art of acting marginally competent. It's an act that fits with my rumpled clothes and scuffed wing tips, my forgettable face, my cheap haircut. But it *is* an act.

"Anyway," Miles said, apparently irritated at the interruption in his narrative, "I started working at around midnight. I only work at night. I don't see how writers get anything done during the day. I'm suspicious of these sanctimonious jerks who always go on about how much they accomplish bright and early in the morning. Seems like some kind of character flaw to me.

"Anyway. Me, I'm lucky. I never have writer's block. My view, writer's block is an excuse for chumps and dilettantes who don't like working. You don't want to be a writer, hell, go dig ditches, be a secretary, whatever. But don't whine to me about writer's block." He glared at the detective as though expecting some kind of objection. When Denkerberg continued to sit silently, pulling on her Tiparillo, Miles continued.

"So I'd written about eight pages by around three-thirty. Goddamn good work, too, if I may say so myself. The juices were really flowing. Then I heard something."

The room was silent for a while. I noticed that Denkerberg wasn't looking at Miles. Her gaze was fixed on the wall. I followed the direction her Tiparillo was pointing, saw that one of the weapon racks was empty. There was a brass plate next to the two mahogany hooks, but nothing rested on them. I wondered if she found any significance in that.

"What did you hear?" Denkerberg said finally.

"A noise," Miles snapped.

"A noise." She didn't say it with any particular inflection, but still there was that vaguely accusatory Sister Herman Marie quality about the way she said it.

"What." Miles didn't seem to like her tone. "A *noise*. A *noise*, that's all."

Derkerberg raised her eyebrows slightly. "As an accomplished author, I'm sure you appreciate the need for precise description. 'Noise' is a rather vague term."

"How should I know? I'm in the middle of a gripping scene, characters stomping around in my brain, then suddenly something reaches in, some kind of goddamn noise, and yanks me out of what I'm doing."

"But you don't know what kind of noise?"

"What did I just tell you?" The room was silent for a long time. "A sharp noise, maybe? Somewhere between a crack and a bang? I don't know! But it was inside the house. That's about all I can say for certain. So I got up to see what the noise was. My wife is usually asleep this time of night, so I wanted to make sure she was okay."

"Any reason to think, based on this noise, that she *wouldn't* be okay?" Denkerberg said.

Miles glared at her. "Are you questioning my story?"

"I'm just trying to establish the whys and wherefores, Mr. Dane."

Miles looked at me, raised his eyebrows sarcastically. "Ah! The whys and *wherefores*! Now I understand."

"Miles," I said softly, "let's not get off track. I know you've received a terrible shock here, that you're angry and distraught. But let's just focus on helping Detective Denkerberg do her job."

Miles shrugged. "Yeah, well, what it was, the noise made me nervous. I don't know. Like something wasn't right. Hell, it could have been a million things. I just wanted to make sure she was safe."

"Were you concerned it might have been an intruder?"

"Well, yeah, I mean, it crossed my mind. You hear a funny noise in the middle of the night, it could be a lot of things."

"So what happened next?"

"I went down the hall toward the living room. Then I heard it again."

"The noise."

"Yeah. Like a crack. Or a bump. Only this time it sounded more, I don't know, like splintering wood or something."

I felt a tingle running under my skin. I didn't like this at all, didn't like the way this was going, not one bit.

"Where was it coming from?" Denkerberg said. "This noise."

"Upstairs." He stopped, and his face went blank.

The room was silent again. I didn't watch my client's face. Instead I watched Denkerberg. I noticed her gaze had drifted up to the empty weapon rack again.

Miles continued. "That's when I saw him."

I nodded slightly, as though I'd heard this all before. I hoped Denkerberg didn't pick up on my consternation. Or my sudden urge to strangle my client. I was about three seconds away from terminating the interview. Which one was the lie—the story he'd told me earlier or the one he was telling now? I could feel a cool sweat sprouting on my forehead.

"Saw who?" the detective said.

"The man in the hallway."

In the movies lawyers are always storming into rooms and demanding that detectives terminate interviews. Sometimes that has to be done, of course; but in real life getting pushy with detectives is pretty much an invitation to get your client charged with something.

I began coughing. Miles and Denkerberg looked at me, both seemingly annoyed at the interruption. My coughing segued into a sort of choking, hacking croak.

"Water," I gasped.

Denkerberg looked understandably skeptical.

I kept hacking away, putting my hands over my throat.

"Here." Miles stood. "I'll get you some water."

I shook my head sharply, pointed at Denkerberg. "Her. Don't want . . . you disturbing . . . the scene . . ." I gasped and spluttered some more.

Denkerberg didn't move.

"Please." I pointed at her. "Get . . ."

She scowled. "Glasses in the kitchen, Mr. Dane?"

He nodded.

As soon as she was out of the room, I hopped up, closed the door, and cranked the massive bolt, locking the door.

"What in the world do you think you're doing, Miles?" I said.

He looked at me blankly, all innocence.

"Let's put aside the fact that you've been needlessly and childishly antagonizing that woman from the word go," I said. "More importantly, Miles, I asked you very specifically if you knew what happened." My voice was low but hard. "You said no. I asked if you heard anything. No, you were blasting Beethoven's seventeenth piano sonata on your stereo. I asked if you saw anybody. No, you were working. Now all of a sudden, there's thumping and bumping and some mysterious figure in the hallway. Don't tell me you were confused, distraught, whatever. That won't wash."

Miles didn't say anything, just stared straight up in the air.

"So which is it, Miles? Was there a guy or not?"

"There was a guy."

"You saw the man who killed your wife."

"Yes. I did."

"Then why did you lie to me earlier?"

He looked at the floor, sighed. "When you hear the whole story, the way it really happened? It's going to sound improbable, stupid. I almost wasn't going to tell the truth at all. I hadn't decided at that point."

I studied his face, but I couldn't get a sense of whether he was lying or not. "If I get a whiff of stink here," I said finally, "if I get even a hint that you're lying, I *will* stand up and I *will* walk out of this room, and that will be the last time you see me. Do you understand me?"

Miles nodded.

"Everything you've done so far looks self-incriminating. Just the fact that I had to interrupt this interrogation in such an obvious and silly way looks extremely, extremely, extremely bad. But I wouldn't have done it if I weren't concerned that you were about to do something wildly stupid. Are we on the same page here?"

"Now hold on just a—" Miles stood up and jabbed his finger in my face.

I grabbed his finger and twisted. He sat down hard. "No, *you* look here, Miles. You need to think very hard about what you're going to do next. You need to be certain that what you're going to say is absolutely truthful. Okay? If you say it was quiet but your neighbor says he couldn't sleep because Horowitz's Steinway is blasting out your window at two thousand decibels, that's a problem. If you tell Denkerberg you were writing, but your computer says that you haven't saved a new file in three days, that's a problem. If you say you didn't touch your wife's body, and they find a bloody glove stuffed in the back of your sock drawer, that's a problem. Understood?"

"Yeah, but—"

"Shut up! I'm not interested in *yeah but*. Sit down in that chair, and think. Silently. For precisely two minutes. If at the end of those two minutes you have even a shadow of a doubt about whether each and every event that you are about to describe might be controvertible by other facts in even the smallest detail, then I'm going to tell Detective Denkerberg that you are very distraught and emotional and that you need medical care and that this interview is hereby terminated."

"Now Charley—" He started to rise out of the chair.

"*Sit!*"

We stayed there, eyes locked for a few seconds. When the fire cooled a little in his eyes, I stepped back. He blew out a long breath, then stared up at the ceiling.

Denkerberg knocked sharply on the door. I didn't open it. She knocked again.

"You ready?" I said.

"Go ahead," he said softly.

"And for godsake do your best not to antagonize her."

Miles nodded, looking at the ground like a chastened schoolboy.

I OPENED THE door, called the detective back in. "Sorry about that, Detective. I'm actually feeling much better now." I rubbed my throat. "As it happened, once the choking passed, I realized there were a couple of housekeeping issues between me and my client that I'd meant to clear out of the way before our talk, but in all the haste and confusion, I had forgotten to address them. I hope you won't hold it against me." I tried out my biggest smile on the detective.

She ignored me, her eyes fixed on Miles's face. "There was a man in the hallway," she said.

Miles nodded. "That's right. I don't know if you looked closely, but it's a curved stairway. So you sort of come around the corner, then you're in the upstairs hallway. Anyway, I came around and there he was. I guess I just froze." He frowned thoughtfully. "No, that's not right. Actually, I ducked back behind the wall. My first thought was, you know, what if he has a gun? Then I heard him running down the hallway, then I heard this smash. Like glass breaking. After that I guess I just got mad and stopped worrying about my own safety, because I came back out and ran after him. But he was gone. I looked out the smashed window in the back bedroom, and I saw—I guess I'd call him a shadowy figure. And he's hauling ass off toward the road. Then I started shouting my wife's name. She didn't answer, so I ran into my bedroom. And there she—"

Suddenly Miles broke down, put his face in his hands, and began to weep. By this point I had started feeling skeptical about virtually every word he'd said—but his grief looked entirely convincing to me.

When Miles finally seemed to have collected himself, Denkerberg said, "This man. What did he look like?"

Miles's face hardened. "I wish I could say. It was dark up there."

"But it was definitely a man."

"Yeah. I could tell by the way he moved. He didn't move like a woman."

"Is there anything else you can tell me? Height? Build? Race? Scars? Tattoos? Eye color?"

Miles shook his head.

"Was he carrying a weapon?"

"I don't know."

Denkerberg took some notes, then looked up. "Were you?"

"Was I what?"

"Carrying a weapon?"

Miles seemed to hesitate. "No," he said finally.

"You're sitting in a room full of weapons. You hear a strange noise, something that you suspect might have been an intruder, you rush toward the noise . . ." She squinted curiously at Miles for a moment. "And yet you don't take a weapon?"

Miles's face was blank for a moment, then his eyes narrowed. "Are you implying something?"

"Like I said before, whys and wherefores. My job is to tie down every single detail."

"Well I wasn't carrying a weapon. Like I said earlier, my first thought was that my wife might have slipped and fallen."

"Didn't even grab something small? A knife? A stick?"

Miles shook his head.

Denkerberg nodded, then pointed her Bic pen at the empty rack on the wall. "What's usually in that rack?"

Miles looked up, blinked, then looked slightly confused. "On the wall?"

"That rack. There's an empty rack." Denkerberg stood, walked over to the two wooden hooks, then peered at the label on the small brass plate next to it. "It says it's a bokken."

"It's pronounced BO-ken, not bock-in. B-O-K-K-E-N. A bokken is a wooden sword used by Japanese swordsmen—kenjutsu practitioners. That one is Gabon ebony, hand-carved by Toshio Nakamitsu, the most famous craftsman of wooden weapons in modern Japan."

"What does it look like?"

"Basically it's a black stick. A curved piece of wood, shaped roughly like a samurai sword."

"What happened to it?"

Miles shrugged. "Seems like it's been gone a while."

"Did you loan it to somebody? Lose it? Break it?"

Miles kept staring at the empty space on the wall, a vague expression on his face. "I don't know where it is."

"Stolen?"

"I don't know. Hard keeping track of all this stuff."

Denkerberg looked skeptical. "You keep the door locked at all times to protect your valuable collection, how could you lose it?"

There was a long silence.

"Okay, now that I think about it, I believe it *was* here yesterday."

More silence.

"Maybe he . . ." Miles frowned. "I went to the bathroom right before I heard the noise. This son of a bitch must have snuck in here and taken it off the wall while I was in the toilet."

Denkerberg took some notes, then looked up. "My experience tells me that thieves look for four things. In descending order: cash, guns, jewelry, electronics."

Miles's jaw clenched.

"You're the author of all these famous crime novels—I assume part of what you do requires you to be able to put yourself in the mind of a criminal?"

"So?"

Denkerberg gave him a hard look. "So imagine that you're a sneak thief, a common burglar. Probably stealing to pay for your next drug hit. You come in to the house, I don't know, through a window or something. You walk into this room. What's the first thing you grab?"

Miles didn't say anything.

The detective pointed at a beautiful double-barreled shotgun hanging over Miles's desk. "I'm not a burglar, I admit. But nevertheless my eye is drawn to that, Mr. Dane. Tell me about it."

"It's a Purdy. A twenty-gauge English best gun."

"*Best* gun?"

"That's the terminology they use in the English gun trade to describe the highest quality custom-made shotguns."

Denkerberg strolled over to it. "Boy, that's a pretty thing. Look at the detail in that little hunting scene engraved on the side. Pheasants flying through the air and such." She leaned closer. "My heavens, that sure looks like gold inlay, too."

"It's gold, yes."

Denkerberg wrinkled her nose. "What's a gun like this worth?"

"Seventy, eighty grand," Miles said softly.

"My heavens!" she said again. Sister Herman Marie's favorite expletive, as I recall. Denkerberg turned to Miles. "Okay, let's try this again. You're an imaginary crook, looking to make a quick score. You walk into this room. Do you grab the eighty-thousand-dollar gold-inlaid shotgun? Or the black stick?"

Miles shrugged. "Look. I got up to go to the bathroom a couple times. Let's say the perp sneaks in here at three in the morning while I'm in the john. Naturally, that time of night, he thinks everybody's in bed—until he hears the toilet flush. So he goes, *Oh, shit! There's somebody in here! What am I gonna do?* He's frantic, he's in a rush, no time to think, he just reaches out and grabs the closest weapon to his hand and runs out the door."

"Hm." Denkerberg squinted skeptically. I could see she didn't buy it. I wasn't sure I did either. "Alright, Mr. Dane, I know this is unpleasant, but could you tell me about discovering your wife? What happened then?"

Miles slumped backward into the soft cushions. His eyes slowly closed. "I don't know," he said finally, his voice coming out in a hoarse whisper. "My legs just got all weak, and I couldn't stand up."

"Did you touch your wife?"

"No."

"You didn't check her vital signs?"

Miles's eyes opened. "Check her *vital* signs! Jesus! Have a heart, lady. She was dead as a doornail. Any fool could see that. You've seen her! My God! I couldn't touch her when she was that way!"

"Easy, easy," I said softly.

"And how long did you sit there, Mr. Dane?"

He shrugged.

"Mr. Dane."

"How should I know? Five minutes?"

"You had no urge to pursue the murderer?"

"I already told you. He was gone by then."

Denkerberg nodded. She jotted down some more notes, stubbed out her Tiparillo. "Can you think of anyone who would want to do a thing like this to your wife, sir? Enemies, anything like that?"

Miles looked at me incredulously, then gave me a sardonic, angry smile. "Enemies? Jesus H. Christ, lady! She's not some goombah from the Gambino crime family. A scumbag thief broke in and killed her. This is not a mystery."

"Is there anything else really pressing, Detective?" I said quickly. "As you can see, Mr. Dane is having a tough time keeping it together. I may need to get a physician to take a look at him, maybe give him a little something so he can get some rest."

I had the impression that if Detective Denkerberg had been carrying a prayer book, she'd have given me a good lick in the back of the head.

"One last question, Mr. Dane. How long between the time you discovered your wife and the time you called Mr. Sloan?"

"Ten minutes? Five? Two?"

"And he got here . . ."

"Like twenty minutes later."

"And the police got here . . ."

"Ten minutes after that. Around four."

"So from the time of her death until the time we got here was less than forty-five minutes?"

Miles Dane looked at her for a moment, then looked away. "Could have been longer," he said vaguely. "Could have been longer."

Three

A s i eased Miles into the cab I'd called to take him to a room over at the Pickeral Point Inn, I said, "From here on out, you don't talk to the police outside of my presence. Understood?"

"Absolutely. I understand."

"And absolutely no talking to reporters."

"Sure."

"Don't even discuss the case with your best friend. Given who you are, this thing is likely to go nuts in about five minutes. We'll need to manage it very, very delicately. Okay?"

"I heard you the first time." He was sounding testy now.

"Good. Mouth shut. We'll talk later."

Pickeral Point, Michigan—where I've made my home for the better part of a decade—is a small town about an hour north of Detroit. It's the county seat of Kerry County, a small, axe-head-shaped jurisdiction that hugs the St. Clair River, reaching from some of Detroit's eastern-most suburbs up into farm country. Keep driving north and you end up in the "thumb" of Michigan that sticks out into Lake Huron. Pick-eral Point has a row of big houses on the river, mostly owned by people who made lots of money working in Detroit and are now taking it easy; it has a salt factory, a boat factory, a mile-long boardwalk, and the usual collection of civic buildings befitting its place as county seat; and it has a view of the river only slightly spoiled by the row of oil refineries and chemical plants on its Canadian bank. When the wind is right, we don't smell Canada.

The big freighters on the river—like most everything else—pass us by. That's why I came here. When I left Detroit a few years back, I'd had about enough excitement for one lifetime. Pickeral Point is a quiet, pleasant, solid, modest, earnest little town—the kind of place where nothing much happens. But it's close enough to Detroit that word of things gets out pretty quickly. I suspected that within a few days Miles Dane was going to be a big red pushpin on the map of newsrooms all over America.

I just hoped Miles wouldn't chum the waters.

AFTER THE CAB had taken Miles off to the hotel, I caught up with Detective Denkerberg, who was talking to the forensic technician outside the house. "Did you find the missing stick?" I said pleasantly. "The bokken or whatever it's called?"

Detective Denkerberg eyed me for a moment. "We're still looking, Mr. Sloan," she said finally.

I gave her my card. "If you need to chat with Mr. Dane again, call me first." I gave her a big smile. "Just for efficiency's sake, of course."

"Of course," she said dryly.

Four

I AM A drunk. Off the sauce for seven years now, but once a drunk, always a drunk. Sadly, my daughter Lisa has the same disease coursing through her veins that I do.

Lisa had figured out that she had a problem a lot earlier in her life than I had. She'd worked the program, she'd gone to the meetings, she'd done everything right. I figured if a contrary old guy like me could stay on the wagon for seven years after having spent several decades as a drunk, then surely it wouldn't be so hard for Lisa. She was a wonderful girl, with most of her mother's best traits and none of her bad ones. Except the drinking, maybe. She'd been on the program for four years now. It seemed like she ought to be out of the woods.

But a drunk is never out of the woods.

Lisa had called me—collect—from New York at two o'clock in the morning, just an hour and a half before Miles phoned. The throbbing music and loud conversation in the background told me she was in a bar. And her slurred, maudlin speech told me she was plowed.

She had told me that she was quitting law school. It was her last year at Columbia, a hell of a time to be washing out of something she'd put that much effort into, or that she'd done that well at. She'd been a top student, law review, clerked for a big Wall Street firm. And now suddenly this? It didn't make sense.

So I did my paternal duty, told her to go home, get some sleep, find a meeting first thing tomorrow, then buckle down and finish up.

"No, Daddy," she wailed. "You don't understand. I haven't even gone to class for the past month. It's over. I'm already done. I'm cooked."

I have to mention a little bit about our history here. My first wife, Lisa's mother, left me when Lisa was three years old. Both of us were drinking heavily at the time, and the breakup was about as far from amicable as it could get. After Lisa's mother moved to California, I didn't see Lisa anymore. My own life was a mess, I remarried, my law practice was busy, my drinking was gradually consuming me, and so I simply walked away from my parental obligations to my daughter. I didn't see Lisa again until after she graduated from college. I can offer no excuse for this. But it's what happened.

In the past few years, Lisa had come back into my life, working for my firm one summer after college, visiting for holidays, and so on. But in many ways we still verged on being strangers.

That said, all parents—even the miserable ones like me—have the highest hopes for their children. My daughter was attractive, smart, determined. I figured the Ivy League law school was just another step toward some sort of ideal life I'd imagined for her. And I admit, I wanted to believe that my bad behavior hadn't hobbled her for life, that some kind of fairy-tale life might await her despite my many failings as a father.

So that phone call—coming out of the blue as it did—made me feel like I'd been kicked in the heart. It made me feel cheap and ineffectual, a failure at the one thing in life that really counted.

"Still," I had said weakly. "Sweetheart, it's the last year. Everybody takes it easy toward the end. There's plenty of time. Just buckle down and . . ."

There was some coughing and fumbling on the other end. Finally, Lisa said, "I was hoping you'd understand, Dad. I was hoping I'd get your blessing."

"Blessing?" I said angrily. "For what? Bless you, my child, for embracing failure? Bless you, my child, for being a drunk and a quitter. Something along those lines?"

Long pause. "Screw it," she said finally. "I don't even know why I called. Like you were ever any kind of father anyway."

More fumbling noises. It took me a moment to figure out that she'd simply dropped the phone, walked away, letting it swing on its tether.

Like you were ever any kind of father anyway. The things that hurt the worst are usually the things that are the most true. I sat there for a while listening to the bar noises, the unfamiliar dance music that sounded like it had been written by some thuggish machine and not by a human being—and my chest was filled with a nameless, hollow yearning. A yearning for what, I wasn't sure. Maybe I wanted to save her. All I can say for certain is that I had done my child a terrible wrong and that I had a lot to make up for.

Then again, there are wrongs so large that you can never really make up for them. But I felt I had to try.

I HAD A pretty sure instinct that the Miles Dane investigation was going to get hot, fast. There was a lot of work to be done if I was going to keep Miles Dane from getting burned by that heat. So I probably should have gone straight to the office and gotten started on the case.

But I didn't. Just then, Miles Dane didn't seem like much of a priority. By ten o'clock I was on a plane to New York.

Five

I HAD NEVER been to Lisa's place in Manhattan, but I knew the address. After catching the bus into Manhattan from La Guardia, I took the C train up to 103rd Street, hiked over just past West End Avenue, and rang the bell outside the seedy-looking foyer of her apartment. The run-down condition of the place gave me a feeling of foreboding.

I had pushed the button three times before an irritated female voice finally came out of the speaker. "*What?*"

"Lisa?" I said.

"She's not here." Her roommate, I assumed. I'd spoken to her a couple of times on the phone, but we'd never had anything you could have described as being an actual conversation.

"It's Lisa's father," I said. "May I come up?"

"Who?"

"Her father. Please let me up."

There was a pause. "Why? She's not here."

My daughter's roommate was beginning to annoy me. "For crying out loud, just open the door."

There was another long pause. Finally, the door let out an angry buzz.

I knocked on Lisa's ugly brown door, Apartment 4D, after climbing an absurd number of stairs. I had to knock several times before a long, grudging series of clicking noises signaled that several locks were being opened. Then the door creaked open about an inch and a half.

"Yes?" One red-rimmed eye glowered suspiciously at me. The chain was still on the door.

"I was Lisa's father when I pressed the buzzer about three minutes ago. It may surprise you to find out that climbing four flights of stairs has not changed that fact. Do you mind if I come in and wait?"

The red-rimmed eye blinked. "For what?"

"For Lisa to come back."

There was a loud television going in the background. "She's not coming back."

"What do you mean?"

"You didn't know? She quit school. Left town last night."

"What!" My hope started draining out of me. "Where did she go? Back to California? To her mother's?"

"How should I know?"

"Look, young lady," I said. "I just flew all the way out here from Michigan. Am I being too Midwestern to hope that you might open the door so we don't have to conduct this conversation through an inch-wide crack?"

"I wasn't aware we were having a conversation." The eye continued to stare mulishly at me. "Lisa is not in New York. She's gone. Deal with it, man."

The door shut in my face.

Repeated banging on the door resulted only in the TV inside the room being turned up even louder.

If Lisa had left for California, odds were that she was going back to stay with her mother. There was nothing more for me to do in New York. I went back down to the street and called the airport to see if I could catch an earlier flight back to Detroit. The listless voice on the phone told me that if I really wanted to, I could try standby . . . but all the flights for the rest of the day were overbooked.

I hung up, walked down the street trying to figure out what to do next. After a while I passed a large chain bookstore. A thought occurred to me; I went inside and asked the young man at the information desk if he could help me find some books by Miles Dane.

"Who?" he said.

I repeated the name. He pecked at the keys on his computer, then shrugged. "Most of his stuff looks like it's out of print. No, wait, his latest couple books are over at our warehouse. We could order one, you know, if you really want it."

"That's alright."

"You might check out the Strand, downtown. They got all kind of old junk down there," he said.

I did as he suggested.

The person I asked at the Strand—a huge, wonderful, ramshackle bookstore in the Village—was a great deal more helpful. He was about my age, with gray hair hanging down to his shoulders, a black turtleneck, clunky black boots—the perpetual graduate student look.

"Oh, yeah!" he said. "Love Miles Dane! The old collector titles are flying out of the store right now. You must have heard the news, huh? Looks like he just whacked his wife."

So I was right. The news had already made it out of Michigan. And by the sound of it, Miles was already being touted by the media as the chief suspect.

"Absolutely untrue," I said. "She was killed, but he had nothing to do with it."

He frowned at me for a moment. "Well, whatever. Anyway, we've got a very rare first of *Busted Knuckles*. Not cheap, but, hey, pristine dust jacket and everything. And a really cool story, too. Very underrated. That one came out right after he shot that guy."

"Whoa, whoa, whoa!" I said, my stomach suddenly rising into my throat. "He *what*?"

"Yeah. You didn't know about that? Must have been like '91, '92? He shot his editor at Padgett Books."

My heart started sinking. "Did this person die?"

"Nah, nah, I think he just winged him or something. The guy didn't even press charges."

I turned and started walking out of the store.

"Hey, man," he called. "What about that copy of *Busted Knuckles*?"

Six

I CALLED PADGETT Books and, after being shuffled around to a number of people, got through to a woman named Meredith Kline, who had a patrician English accent. After I'd explained who I was, she allowed that, yes, there had been an "incident" some years back involving my client. She seemed disinclined to talk about it, so I said, "I'll be right over. It won't take a minute, but I really need to get your statement on this matter."

Half an hour later I was taking an elevator up to the offices of the Padgett/Reinbeck/Dart Group International, PLC. According to the sign on the heavy glass door, the company owned what had once been about fifteen independent publishing companies, of which Padgett Books was obviously the flagship operation. A glass case next to the door of the spartan reception area contained a large display of Padgett's recently published books.

"I really don't have a great deal to say," Meredith Kline told me. "Other than what I told you on the phone." She was a lovely young woman with chestnut hair and a very short black skirt and a man's black plastic digital watch, which she had conspicuously consulted at least five times between the reception area and her office. Her fingernails were chewed to the quick.

"Look, I wasn't here at the time of the, um, incident," she told me. "Miles is a legacy author for me."

"What's that mean?"

Meredith Kline clicked her chewed-up fingertips on her desk. "He's been on our list for a long time. He was very very successful back in the day, but now . . . Well, I sort of inherited him. He sends us manuscripts once a year and we slap a cover on them and put them out." She shrugged. "But his work doesn't do well anymore. He's an artifact of an earlier age, if you know what I mean."

"I'm not sure I do."

"He's a tough guy. Broads and dames, yadda yadda yadda. Tough guys are out."

"Oh. Who's in?"

"Women, mainly. Softer, richer, denser material. Character-driven vehicles. Bigger concepts." She said this airily, like I should be intensely impressed at her *savoir faire*.

I smiled politely. "So do you know who he actually shot?"

She looked at me curiously. "Oh, he didn't shoot a *person* I don't think. He just shot a hole in the wall." Another deep, profound consultation with the cheap watch. "We still have the hole." She smiled tightly. "I could show it to you on the way out."

We went back through the rats' maze of cubicles. The door leading out of the reception area was made of greenish glass. Sure enough there was a bullet hole in it. A small rectangle had been etched in the glass, with a tiny label next to it—also etched in the glass in six-point type—which read, HOLE FROM BULLET FIRED BY BEST-SELLING PADGETT AUTHOR MILES DANE.

"Best-selling?" Meredith Kline said, squinting. "Not lately. We really ought to get rid of this. The whole concept is extremely tired."

"So do you know who actually saw this bullet get fired?"

Meredith Kline frowned. "You know something? I'm thinking here. Okay? I'm thinking, and it occurs to me, the editor who acquired Miles back in the Jurassic, he's still here. Daniel Rourke. I bet he's the one who saw it."

"Oh?"

She pointed one black fingernail at the floor. "A few years back, they kind of, ah, shelved him downstairs in our . . ." She lowered her voice slightly. ". . . *paperback* division."

Seven

"DIANA'S DEAD?" DANIEL Rourke's smile of greeting faded.

I nodded. I had introduced myself as Miles's lawyer, then come right to the point.

"Good God." Rourke's face grew blank, and he looked distantly at the wall.

Rourke was a fat man with bright, corrupt-looking blue eyes, a thick mop of white hair, and wild black eyebrows. He must have been well into his seventies. His office was large but windowless, with huge piles of dusty manuscripts and papers lining the walls. A faint smell of mildew hung in the air. Meredith Kline hadn't been kidding: His office was literally in the basement next to the boiler room. A half-empty bottle of Cutty Sark sat on the desk—though whether it was some kind of prop, or whether he was actually drinking from it at two o'clock in the afternoon, I couldn't tell.

"Diana was the most beautiful woman I've ever met," he said after a moment. "Not just physically beautiful. There was a sort of penetrating decency about her." The canny light came back into Rourke's eyes. "Penetrating decency. I think I'll write that down." He scrabbled around in the mound of papers on his desk, scribbled something on an envelope, then tossed it on the floor. "See? Working on my memoirs." He pointed at a pile in the corner. It looked like someone had kicked over a trash can.

"I bet that would make for interesting reading."

Daniel Rourke's blue eyes grew slightly chilly. "You're patronizing an old fat man, aren't you."

"I didn't mean it that way," I said. "Do you mind my asking what your relationship to Miles was?"

"I was his literary mentor. He was my creation." Rourke said it in a tone that was half-grandiose and half-ironic.

"So you were his editor? Or what?"

"I was a wunderkind once." Again his tone hung somewhere between self-aggrandizing and self-mocking. "A publishing prodigy. Did you know I pulled one of the best-selling books of the forties, *Anatomy of a Trial*, out of the slush pile when I was twenty-three? Then I became a young lion. Executive editor at Lippincott at twenty-eight. Then on to Elgin Press, where I became a titan, then on to here, where I entered my *éminence grise* phase. Padgett is the top publisher of commercial fiction in America, and I'm the one who put them there." He laughed brightly. "These days, of course, the children upstairs joke about me and condescend to let me put out a few paperback originals every year, but I'm not taken seriously. I'll never finish my memoirs, and if I did, who would care? Who would publish it? Stories about old writers, my little creations, has-beens like Miles Dane."

"Okay," I said, "but can you tell me about this shooting Miles was involved in?"

But Daniel Rourke seemed to have lost interest in me. "Miles Dane was my greatest invention. When he came to me, he was a nice kid from the Midwest. Short, awkward, bad skin, a little shy. But his work was wonderful. Mean, spiteful, angry stories about small-town losers who did terrible things to each other. Not polished, of course. He's never been polished, never been a stylist of any note.

"I started publishing him in paperback back in the late sixties. That was the end of the great heyday of men's action books. He wrote six books for me there. *Savage Hands, The Ravaged, Ladykiller, Guttersnipe*—some others. They never sold especially well. But I saw that he had . . . there's a sort of indefinable energy in his work, wouldn't you say?"

As I said earlier, I was never a great fan of Miles Dane's books. But there *was* something compelling about them. "Yes. Energy's exactly the right word."

"There you go, patronizing me again."

When I laughed, the old man joined me. He was testing me, feeling me out.

"Television finally killed off the men's action book market in the seventies. But I saw that Miles had the goods to move upmarket. Fatten the books up a little, give them more scope, a hair more presence, bigger concepts. But there was something else. In the late sixties Jacqueline Susann had showed us all what publicity could do. Turn an author into a celebrity, a star. I suggested that Miles think about doing something to change himself. Adopt a sort of persona, you see." Rourke's wild eyebrows shot up and he smiled fondly. "I had no idea how successfully he would pull that off. I got him booked on *The Dick Cavett Show*. You should have seen Cavett's face when Miles walked out there with that shoulder holster. The gun was fake, of course. But who knew?"

I could see why Daniel Rourke had been consigned to the basement. He didn't really seem to live in the present anymore.

"Miles was enormously disciplined about it, too. Once he put this persona on, he hardly ever took it off. In public I'm talking about. It was as though one of those angry tough bastards in his books had come to life inside his skin. Before, he'd been a real sweetheart. Deferential, polite, easygoing. Suddenly, you took him out to a restaurant and anything could happen. He'd abuse the staff, come on to a good-looking gal at the next table, you name it. As soon as you were out of the public eye—ffft!—off it came."

"May I ask you a question, Mr. Rourke?"

Rourke blinked as though he'd forgotten I was there. "By all means, young man."

Young man. I hadn't been called that in a long time. "Miles has not been arrested. I want you to understand that. But it's possible that he might be. If I put you on the stand and asked if you think Miles could have killed his wife, what would your answer be?"

Rourke's little blue eyes examined me for a long time. "Absolutely not. He loved Diana in a way that few men ever love a woman. And I suppose she loved him just as much."

"When did they marry, do you know?"

"Sure. They married when he was about twenty. Right after he'd written *Savage Hands*, his first book. He was bussing tables at some fine old restaurant, and she came in with her mother and her brother. The way Miles told me, they looked at each other, and it just happened. Bang. Like that."

"So she's a New Yorker?"

The shaggy black eyebrows went up again. "You didn't know? She's the *original* New Yorker. She comes out of the old New York WASP elite. Brearley, Bryn Mawr, social register, house in the Hamptons, that whole thing. Her family, the van Blaricums, started out as Dutch slavers, then moved into banking. Don't suppose anybody in that family has worked in a century, though. Naturally they hated Miles. They disowned her or something after she married him."

"Anything else you can tell me about her family?"

"Mother, awful harridan. Father, decent fellow as rich men go. Only met them a time or two. There was a brother, can't remember his name. Robert? Roger? Something. Supercilious character with a grotesquely exaggerated sense of his own self-worth. He kept hounding me to publish a book, ancient Japanese erotica or some tedious thing. One of those rare people you actually *enjoy* sending rejection letters to. Saw a lot of him for a while there. It seemed like he and Diana were awfully close. But then once the family ditched her, he disappeared."

"Tell me about her."

"She was this beautiful, serene, debutante rich girl. First impression, you would have thought she'd never been touched by anything harsh or unpleasant. If that were all there was to her, she would have seemed a little shallow, a little smug maybe. But after you knew her a while—it was almost imperceptible—but there was a sense about her that she had seen real sorrow. It gave that serenity of hers a depth that was . . ." Rourke's eyes grew dark for a moment. "Well. I fell in love with her myself. I was married; she was married; I couldn't do anything about it. But I became almost obsessed with her for a while. Awfully unhealthy thing. My wife saw it in my eyes, and our marriage was never the same." He raised his hands, taking in his shabby, dim shambles of an office.

"She left me a couple of years later, and now this is all I have left."

He gave me his sly little smile, as though what he said was not to be taken seriously.

"Diana, she was everything that was best about the old New York gentry. The lovely manners, the beauty, the grace—a kind of other-worldly quality. No one cares about these things anymore. Good manners? There's no such thing today. It's all middle fingers and shouting today. The world has lost something without people like Diana. We've spent the past century merrily pissing on our aristocracy, and it's too damn bad. The world needs aristocracy. The world needs Diana van Blaricum, and it's too damn bad, it's too damn bad, it's too damn bad."

The old man began to weep silently. After a while he looked up and grunted. "Was there something else you needed?"

"The shooting," I said. "What about the shooting?"

"The shooting *here*?" Rourke's sadness seemed to pass quickly. He studied me with his crafty blue eyes, then laughed sharply. "There was no shooting here."

I frowned. "Then where did the bullet hole up there come from?"

"I told you that Miles Dane is only a mask." His eyes kept twinkling at me.

"So now you're playing with *me*."

He picked up the bottle of Cutty Sark, made as if to pour some of it into a glass. "May I offer you a drink?"

"Thanks, no."

"The shooting, quote unquote, was a publicity stunt." He screwed the top back on the bottle of Cutty Sark and set the bottle down. "Late one night we brought in a sculptor from Hollywood and he carved the 'bullet hole' with some sort of diamond-tipped drill. Looks quite authentic don't you think? Then we called the *Times, Publishers Weekly*, a few others, gave them a 'tip' that this had happened. But it was all fiction." Rourke sighed. "His career was on a bit of a slide by the early nineties. We were hoping to pump things up a little. But . . . In this life, when the sea decides to suck you down, you sink. That's a piece of cheerful wisdom for you to take away with you."

I smiled in what I hoped wouldn't seem a patronizing way. "I've heard there are a number of incidents," I said. "Fights with movie stars. Things like that. Were they all staged?"

Rourke studied my face for a while, then finally sighed. "Of course they were."

"You'd be prepared to testify to that effect?"

"Is he really going to be charged with killing Diana?"

"I don't know the answer to that."

Rourke scowled. "It's ridiculous. Underneath the mask, he's a sweet man. He'd never do a thing like that."

"So you'd testify? If it came to that?"

"Of course."

"Hopefully it won't come to that."

"I'm sure it won't."

I wished I was equally confident.

Eight

SINCE THERE WAS nothing more for me to do in New York, I took an early flight home the next morning. My cell phone rang as soon as I got off the plane in Detroit. It was Miles Dane.

"Charley?" Miles sounded shaken. "I've been trying you and trying you."

"I've been on a plane. What is it, Miles?"

"I think . . . I think I made a mistake."

"*What did you do?*"

"I talked to that woman again. Chantall Denkerberg. The cop."

"Miles, what did I tell you? Talk to nobody without me? Remember that?"

"That's not what I'm saying, Charley," he snapped. "What I'm trying to tell you is she just called and asked if I was going to be home for the rest of the day. I don't think she wants to talk."

"Sit tight, Miles. Keep your mouth shut, stay calm, and I'll be there as soon as I can."

"This is scaring me a little, okay?"

"Sit tight."

Nine

THE LARGEST, MOST expensive houses in Pickeral Point are on Riverside Boulevard. The view of the river that separates Michigan from
Canada is spectacular, the trees are large and old, and the houses are
grandly massive. These days the smallest house on the road would easily
run you a million five.

Riverside Drive is not the sort of place you expect to see squadrons
of police cars, certainly not twice in one week. But as I pulled up in
front of Miles Dane's house, that's what I found.

I jumped out and found Detective Chantall Denkerberg standing
on the street, her hands on her hips, a cigarillo dangling from her lip.
Chief Bower was there, too, along with about fifteen patrol officers.
More ominously, a black panel truck that read S-TAC in gold letters on
the side was parked half a block down from Miles's house. Standing
around the van were six or eight muscular young guys wearing black
BDUs and Kevlar, and carrying machine guns. Great. S-TAC was the
Sheriff's Tactical Unit, recently created by the megalomaniacal new
sheriff of Kerry County. As I was pulling up, the Channel 5 news van
screeched in behind me and began hoisting its satellite dish so they
could broadcast live to the newsroom back in Detroit.

I breezed past Detective Denkerberg and went straight to Chief
Bower.

"What in the name of God is going on here?" I said.

"Hi, Charley." Chief Bower gave me the dry, appraising look that is about the most enthusiastic greeting I can expect from law enforcement people. "Your client seems to have wigged out on us."

"Meaning what?"

"Detective Denkerberg was coming to talk to him, and he assaulted her."

"What do you mean assaulted her?"

"He pulled a gun on her, punched her, and now he's barricaded himself in the house with a weapon."

"Did she come to talk? Or to arrest him?"

Chief Bower briefly avoided my eyes. "We haven't released the crime scene yet. She's well within her rights to come back for a crime scene follow-up."

"And what's up with S-TAC?" I said. "Do you really need those trigger-happy morons here? This isn't even their jurisdiction."

"I requested their assistance," Bower said. "Your client is making threats and waving a pistol."

"I'm extremely upset about this," I said. "I told your pit bull Denkerberg if she wanted to talk to him, to call me."

"Look—"

"Forget it. I'm going in to talk to him."

"You can't go in there," Bower said. "He's got a *gun*."

"So do half the people in this state," I said. Then I smiled pleasantly and started striding across the yard toward the front door. I admit, I don't cut much of a figure, but I do my best. Chin up, big smile on my face. I knew some eager cameraman over in the Channel 5 van was rolling tape by now, so every move I made counted. The spin was starting this very minute. If I went creeping in like I was afraid of being shot, that would show up on the news, making Miles appear to be a dangerous nut.

My rational mind told me I was in no danger, but my heart was beating hard as I knocked on the door. I turned and waved pleasantly at the mob of police, gave them a big cheesy thumbs-up.

After a moment the lock clicked and the door opened. Miles Dane stood there, ashen-faced, hair uncombed, clutching a big Smith & Wesson with a custom grip. Every time I'd seen him before, he had looked taller than his five-foot-six-inch frame; he was enlarged somehow by his physical energy. But now, he looked very small, like something had been drained out of him, causing his body to wither and shrink. I forced my way past him, quickly slammed the door shut. I didn't want any visuals of Miles Dane and his trusty revolver showing up in the media.

"Have you lost it, Miles?" I said.

Miles looked around vaguely. There were bags under his eyes and the skin sagged in the hollows under his cheekbones. "I got . . . I got scared, Charley."

"Well, I'm here, and we're going to work things out. Now put the cannon down for a minute, okay?"

Miles nodded, locked the door, then walked into the living room, where he set the Smith on the coffee table.

"Explain to me *precisely* what happened here," I said.

"I got a call from Denkerberg," Miles said. "About an hour and a half ago. She said she was calling to make sure I was home. I go, 'Obviously I'm home.' She goes, 'Well, don't go anywhere. I need to talk to you.' That's when I called you. If she really needed to talk, she'd have been all peaches and cream. As much as she's capable of it anyway. Plus, she'd have called you first so that you'd be present for the interview."

"So you figured she was coming to arrest you."

Miles nodded miserably.

"What did you do when she got here?"

"She showed up on the doorstep. I told her she couldn't come in. She got real insistent. So I . . . ah, I kind of . . ."

"You pulled your gun."

"Well. Not *actually*. I was wearing my shoulder holster, and I just sort of put . . . I kind of rested my hand on the grip."

I felt like shaking him. "Did she show you a warrant?"

Miles shook his head no.

"Then what?"

"She started to pull her pistol . . ."

"So you punched her?"

"Punched her!" His eyes widened. "Is that what those morons are saying? Give me a break. No, what happened is I could see that she was about to draw down on me—with no legal justification, I might add—so I just sort of reached out the door and shoved her. Just to keep her out of the house. She kind of stumbled back, and I slammed the door."

"And that's it? Next thing you know, we've got *this*?" I waved my hand at the flashing lights and camera crews outside.

Miles shrugged. "I may have yelled a couple things out the window."

"Great. You wave the gun around, too?"

Miles avoided my eyes.

"Miles, Miles, Miles . . ." I sighed loudly.

Miles started pacing up and down.

"Okay, let me think. First, you're sure she didn't show you a warrant?"

"Absolutely not."

I smiled. "What you did, nothing personal, Miles, but this was pretty asinine. Nevertheless, we can salvage this. Give me a minute, okay?"

I went back to the door, walked across the lawn again, smiling pleasantly. Charley Sloan, out for a nice afternoon constitutional. I noticed there were now four TV trucks on the scene. When I reached Chief Bower, I laughed genially. Not for the chief's benefit and certainly not because anything funny had happened, but because I knew I was on camera. Cameras love a friendly face.

"I hope you plan to take disciplinary action against Chantall Denkerberg," I said. My face was jolly, but my tone was not.

"*Excuse* me?" the chief said, eyes narrowing.

"You are aware she tried to force entry into an established and lawful residence without legal authorization?" That wasn't precisely what had happened, but it was close enough. The main thing was that I needed to put the chief on the defensive. "I think probably breaking and entering would be about right. Maybe throw in some battery, just for good measure."

"Give me a break, Sloan. It's a crime scene. She has the right of access."

"Three days ago it was a crime scene. Your own people cleared him to take possession when you were done. Now it's his home again. I don't know what *she's* saying happened, but she had no warrant, and she tried to force her way in there, Chief, and that's against the law. At that point Miles basically just showed her his gun. Didn't draw it, didn't point it, just let her observe that he had it—a right he has, I might add, under protection of the Constitution of the United States of America. Then when she tried to draw down on him, he nudged her backward so he could close the door to his own lawful residence. End of story."

"Bullshit," Bower said. "He was yelling out the window about how he was going to kill anybody who set foot on his lawn."

"Any of these folks have that on tape?" I waved at the TV trucks. I knew they hadn't because I'd seen the first TV truck roll up myself. "If not, it's the word of small-town cop against a world-famous author."

Bower rolled his eyes and turned his head away from me.

"Thought not," I said. "But look, all of that's irrelevant now. Denkerberg came here to talk to my client. If you want to talk to Miles, I'd be more than happy to bring him by the station right this minute. But I got news for you, he's not coming out as long as all the Gestapo stuff is going on out here." I gave a big sweep of my arm, taking in the pumped-up S-TAC boys, the parade of flashing lights, the uniformed police, the TV trucks.

Bower laughed derisively.

"I don't see the humor," I said sharply. "You've got a rogue officer over there who just unlawfully provoked a potentially life-threatening situation with the grieving spouse of a murder victim. Now I'd hate to have to file suit against the city over some silly little misunderstanding like this. Put a leash on the S-TAC guys, send them back to their cage, and Miles will happily come down and chat."

Chief Bower scowled.

"Are you *that* eager to have people talk about Pickeral Point in the same breath as Ruby Ridge and Waco? I give you my word, Chief. Fifteen minutes after the last cop is gone, Miles Dane is standing in your station house. Then it's your move."

"He's agreed to this?"

"Absolutely."

Chief Bower sighed, turned to the patrol sergeant on the scene. "You heard him. Everybody out. Now!"

T HE FIFTEEN MINUTES gave me an opportunity to make a little state-ment to the TV crews, which went live on the moon news. I made sure the cameras were aimed so they could see the S-TAC boys packing up in their black van. I smiled a lot and made a statement about the Pickeral Point police that, while sounding complimentary on its face, had the obvious implication that they were bumbling idiots. I praised their "restraint," in the same breath that I referred to Detective Denk-erberg as "a confused female officer." I may have even used the phrase "storm trooper" once or twice. It was all a bit of a cheap shot. But it also served to put them on notice that if they came after Miles Dane, Charley Sloan wouldn't take it lying down.

Then I went inside 221 Riverside Boulevard, and said, "Okay, Miles, comb your hair and put on a white shirt and a pair of khakis."

"A *white* shirt? I never wear white."

"And I'm telling you, white shirt. Until I say you differently, black has disappeared from your wardrobe."

Ten

WE DROVE TO the police station in my car. For reasons known only to the four members of the city council (all of them, not coincidently, heavily involved in the real estate business), the new Pickeral Point police station had been built way on the western outskirts of town in the middle of a very large field. The field—which had been sold to the city for three times its value, naturally—had once been devoted to the cultivation of soybeans. Since the soybeans were long gone, there was now plenty of room for all the TV trucks to spread out, their antennae thrusting pugnaciously at the sky. They weren't just local stations either, I noticed. CNN and CNBC were both also represented. And if CNN and CNBC were there today, tomorrow it would be national crews from NBC, CBS, ABC, and Fox.

I took Miles by the arm and led him inside the building. Chantall Denkerberg was waiting at the front desk. She had a smear of dirt up the side of her blue suit—presumably from falling down the stairs of Miles's house.

"*Confused*, Mr. Sloan?" she said, smiling coldly and holding a piece of paper in front of my face. I got the feeling she hadn't appreciated my confused-female-officer speech on TV. "Here's an arrest warrant. Is this *confusing* to you?"

I saw in a flash what had happened. She had almost certainly had the warrant in her pocket when she had rolled up at Miles's house. She had gone over there hoping to con him into talking some more. But if he wasn't willing to talk, she had intended to serve the warrant.

Miles saw the piece of folded paper in her hand, stopped, then took a step backward. The color drained out of his face. "No!" he said. "No, I can't—"

He tried to step backward again, but Denkerberg was too fast for him. I don't think Sister Herman Marie had ever slapped a prayer book upside my head as quickly as she leapt on my client. She grabbed him by his dark mane of hair, yanked him over backward, and slung him to the floor. Then she had a knee in his spine, his arm twisted behind his back.

"Confused? Huh? Who's confused now?" she said, twisting his arm a little tighter with each word.

Chief Bower watched from the other side of the room, a smirk on his broad face.

"Miles Dane," Detective Denkerberg whispered, "you are under arrest for the murder of Diana Dane." Then she gave him his Miranda warning while he grunted in pain.

"Is this entirely necessary?" I said to Bower.

"Making little crocodile-tears speeches live on the TV, it cuts both ways."

"You think?"

"It just don't pay, making cops out to be morons," Chief Bower said, still smirking. Then he left the room.

I stood there and tried to look cool. But I didn't feel cool. The police knew something that I didn't. Even as angry as she was, Chantall Denkerberg was a pro; she wouldn't have moved this quickly against Miles without evidence.

What did she have that I didn't know about?

Eleven

THE POLICE MADE it clear to me they wouldn't do me any favors in processing Miles. By the time they got done booking him, it would be too late to get him over to the courthouse for his arraignment.

All of which meant Miles would spend the night in jail. I tried to call in favors hither and yon, hoping to get a special court appearance for him. No dice. The word had gotten around that I'd profaned the High and Holy Church of Law Enforcement on TV—*national* TV, as it turned out, with CNN and CNBC running my entire speech every half hour, right after the China trade agreement story—so I got nothing but irritable stares as I made my rounds in the criminal justice community.

Finally, I gave up and slunk back to my office.

As I WALKED into my office, my secretary, Mrs. Fenton, looked like she was in a snit. "Don't blame me," she said. "I tried."

I wasn't really paying attention to her. "Tried what?" I said vaguely as I walked into my cluttered office.

I had more or less inherited my office from an old lawyer in Pickeral Point who died a few years back. I kept his furniture, the pictures on the walls, everything. Situated at the top of a flight of rusting iron stairs on the second floor of a small brick commercial building just off the town square, it's the sort of place that would put you in mind of an

English gentleman's club fallen on hard times. Heavy wood tables and desks, brass lamps with green shades, red Spanish leather upholstery. The leather is cracked, the wood is chipped, and the prints of pointers and woodcock and pheasants seemed to defy Mrs. Fenton's constant efforts at keeping them plumb and level.

But the place is me. Or at least it's how I like to think of myself. Good solid stuff, a little the worse for wear.

Oh, and there's a view, too. You go past my secretary's desk and into my office, there's a big picture window that takes up one entire wall. It looks over the boardwalk and onto the river. I'd have kept the place just for the view.

It was as I looked out at my view—a big breakbulk freighter was chugging by—that I saw what Mrs. Fenton was in her snit about. Silhouetted against the big window, back turned, was a woman. All I could see of her face was that she had a cigarette hanging from the corner of her mouth, the smoke trailing up around her head. Mrs. Fenton has a thing about cigarette smoke. Out on the river in front of the woman in my office was an echo of that cigarette, trails of toffee-colored mist rising up off the river. A bottle of Ron Rico spiced rum was open on the desk.

"Lisa?" I said.

My daughter turned and looked at me stonily. Lisa, luckily, favors her mother in looks. I may not have married stable women, or nice women, or sober women. But they were all fine-looking girls, I'll give them that. Lisa is about five-two, with long rich brown hair that meets her brow in a widow's peak, a pert nose, a square Irish jaw, large brown eyes, and a lovely smile.

Just then, however, she was not smiling. She wore a pair of jeans that could have stood a wash and a shapeless sweater that hid her body. The last time I'd seen her she was verging on plump. Now she looked wan, undernourished, a good fifteen pounds lighter.

"You look terrible," I said.

"Marvelous to see you, too, Dad." She gave me a bored smile and sat down heavily in my chair.

"You also look plastered."

"Oh just taking a little vacation from sobriety. Off to the islands, don't you know?" Her tone was arch, an ironic put-on, as she took a swig of the awful Ron Rico. She wasn't stumbling drunk or slurring her words, but it was obvious she'd already had a few.

A distant part of my brain wanted to join her, to match her pull for pull. Off to the islands. Let the problems of Lisa Sloan and Miles Dane float away on the same aromatic tide.

"I just flew all the way to New York to find you," I said.

Lisa looked at me curiously. "Really."

I nodded.

"Isn't that quaint. Were you going to save me from myself?"

There are maudlin drunks, there are happy drunks, there are thrill-seeking drunks . . . Apparently, though, Lisa took after her Irish forbears: She was a fighting drunk.

I threw her the keys to my house. "Take a cab back to my place. Sleep it off. When you wake up sober, we'll talk."

She gave me the sarcastic smile again. "I was kind of looking for work. You got anything around here for a law school dropout with a drinking problem?"

The truth was, my practice was already stretched a little thin. And with the Dane business heating up, I really did need some help. But I wasn't going to broach that subject with a drunk woman.

"We can talk about it later."

"You know I'd earn my keep. I've worked for you before."

"When you're sober," I said sharply.

She sighed theatrically. "Oh well. I suppose there's always prostitution."

"Dammit, Lisa . . ." I was about to launch into her, but then I clamped my mouth shut. What was the point? I am of the firm opinion—and this is confirmed by my own experience with a wide variety of wives, girlfriends, law partners, and concerned friends who tried to talk sense into me back when I was drinking—that trying to reason with a drunk person about his or her condition is not just a vast waste of time, but is actually counterproductive. It makes people defensive and angry, which only increases their interest in the bottle.

It's agonizing to watch someone you love do self-destructive things and know that trying to intervene or make decisions for them is the worst thing you can do. But sometimes that's just the way it is.

The phone rang.

"Can you get that, Mrs. Fenton?" I called.

The phone continued to ring. I supposed Mrs. Fenton had discreetly gone off to powder her nose so that Lisa and I could talk in privacy.

"For Pete's sake, Lisa, I've got work to do," I said. I knew I seemed unfeeling, but in her current combative condition, the best thing I could do was get Lisa back to my house in hopes she might go to sleep and wake up in a saner frame of mind. I took the bottle of Ron Rico off the desk, set it on the floor, picked up my ringing phone. "Charley Sloan."

"You that big lawyer?" It was the voice of a young man. "The one off the TV?" I could hear the noise of jail in the background. When you've practiced law as long as I have, you learn to recognize the sound.

"I'm Charley Sloan. Who am I speaking to?"

"Yeah, my name is Leon. I'm down here at the jail. I was wondering if you could come get me out." He sounded very young, if not particularly frightened about his predicament.

"Okay, Leon. Full name."

"Leon James Prouty."

"What have you been charged with, young man?"

"Uh. They said I was doing some midnight landscaping."

"I don't know what that means."

"Like if you was to find a yard where somebody had just did some landscaping, and you was to dig up all the new bushes and throw 'em in a truck, drive off with them? That's what you'd call midnight landscaping."

"So the charge would be grand theft?"

"I guess. Plus, you know how they do, make up a bunch of shit, try to scare you? Criminal trespass, breaking and entering, receiving—so on, so forth."

"You at the city jail?"

"Pickeral Point police station."

"Okay, good. So have you been booked?"

"Yes sir."

"You got money, Leon? I don't work for free."

"How much this gonna cost me?"

I picked a number out of the air, just to see if he was serious. "We could probably get you started for five hundred. If you should happen to go to trial, considerably more."

"Oh. No problem. Can I write you a check?"

"You're making a joke, right?"

"I'll get it from the ATM as soon as you spring me."

A thief with a bank account. What a pleasant novelty. Most of my clients keep their life saings in a fat wad in their front pocket. "I'll be right down," I said. "I trust you haven't given a statement to the police?"

"No sir. I don't say jack to them clowns."

"Keep it that way. I'll be right down."

I hung up the phone and turned to Lisa. "I've got to run. Go back to my house and just sit tight for a while, okay?"

"How about I come with you?"

"Forget it."

"I'll leave the rum here. Huh? What do say?" She smiled coyly.

I didn't feel like negotiating with a drunk, so we walked silently out to my aging Chrysler. Lisa slouched in a small heap next to me, drumming rapidly on her thigh with her fingernails. "Put your seat belt on."

"Yes, Daddy," she said in an ironic tone.

"And when did you start smoking?"

"You know what, Dad? The reason I came here is I was hoping to avoid the judgmental bullshit."

Despite her promise to leave the rum in the office, she'd brought it with her. I reached over, grabbed it, poured it out the window.

"Man!" she said. "You had to do that, didn't you? Mr. Good Parent. Mr. Take Charge."

When she was sober, Lisa was a terrific kid. But right now I didn't like her much. Had I been this impossible back in my drinking days? Undoubtedly. Probably a good deal worse. I am a grandiose drunk. The more I swig, the bigger a man I am, the greater my accomplishments, the smarter I get, the braver, the taller . . . I sneaked a look at my daughter and felt the creeping itch of shame. My fault. Surely this was all my fault.

It was the hook she would always have in me. As long as I felt like I might be able to reclaim her, make up for my mistakes as a father, she'd always have leverage over me, always have the ability to force me into being softer on her than I probably ought to be.

I kept my mouth closed and drove.

When we reached the police station, I said, "Wait here for me." Why I bothered saying that, I don't know. Lisa, of course, got out and followed me into the station.

The lobby of the new Pickeral Point police station has all the latest security features. Outside it's a bland sandstone box, designed to fit in with the aging Art Deco knockoffs that comprise the city and county government buildings on the square. But inside it's all modern: cameras, a receptionist behind bulletproof glass, fancy locks that you have to punch secret codes into. The old station had featured an open front counter and doors you could have jimmied with a credit card. So far as I know, nobody had ever invaded the place, nobody had ever come in waving a gun, nobody had ever planted a bomb. Nevertheless: now, Fort Knox.

"Hi, Regina," I said to the receptionist.

Regina was a chatty type. I make a point to keep on her good side because she knows everything that happens in the law enforcement community and isn't afraid to tell you about it in great detail. "Hi, Charley. Boy, they're hot at you today."

I laughed.

"They already put Mr. Dane on the bus to the county lockup."

"No problem. I've got another client. Leon Prouty."

"That snakehead boy?"

"The who?"

"The snakehead." When she saw I had no idea what she was talking about, she said, "The midnight landscaper, right?"

I nodded, and Regina buzzed me through the door back into the innards of the building. Lisa slipped in with me. "I'm with Mr. Sloan," she said cheerily, as Regina looked ready to object. "I'm Charley's new paralegal."

The duty sergeant eyed me briefly as I came into the booking area, then looked back at the paperwork he was filling out.

"Hi, Fred," I said brightly. "Coming to pick up a prisoner. Leon James Prouty."

"After that wiseass performance on the TV today?" the duty sergeant said. "You can call me Sergeant Ross."

"Aw, come on. They always quote me out of context."

The sergeant ignored me for a while, started ticking things off on a pink form. Tick. Tick. Tick. Giving each line a great deal of study.

"Take your time," I said.

Lisa was pacing up and down. Not only a bellicose drunk, it appeared, but a hyper drunk, too.

The desk sergeant kept pretending to work. The way the room is set up, most of the prisoners are held in a corral behind the desk. If they stand in the right place, they can watch us.

"Hey!" It was a tall thin boy with dyed blond hair and lots of tattoos. "Mr. Sloan? You getting me out?"

"Hang on," I said. "We'll have you out in a jiff."

The sergeant ignored me. Another lawyer came in, Victor Trembly, probably the most despised criminal lawyer this side of Detroit. "Charley, *mi amigo!*" he said in his usual unctuous tone. "How's the big star of the small screen?"

"Victor." I smiled noncommitally.

Victor Trembly rapped on the desk with his gaudy Wayne State ring. "How's she hanging, Fred? Need to pick up a scumbag, excuse me, a *client* by the name of Roe-shawn Beasleyyyyy." He pronounced the name in a broad parody of a black accent, winking at me as he drawled.

"RahShawn Beasley. Right away," the desk sergeant said. "You got his bond and everything?"

"Absolutelayyy, mah brothah."

The desk sergeant pulled some forms out, set them in front of Trembly, then went back and unlocked the door of the corral. A bedraggled-looking black kid came out.

"Just sign here, Mr. Beasley," the desk sergeant said, handing him a clipboard. "Then here, and . . . yeah. Just like you did last time you were here."

The kid slouched over to his lawyer.

"Your personal possessions are in here, Mr. Beasley," the sergeant said, setting a small cardboard box on the counter.

"I'll take that, Fred," Trembly said. He rummaged around in the box, came out with a couple of gold chains, two gold rings, and a gold tooth cap, then tossed the box back on the counter. "Thank you, Roe-Shawn. These will be applied to my fee. Let's shuffle on out of here so you can get back to your *alleged* pharmaceutical sales stand before too much of your daily income has been lost."

Trembly and his client left.

The desk sergeant sat down and went back to his paperwork. Tick. Tick. Tick.

"Hey! Hey! What about me?" It was my client calling from the bullpen.

"Sergeant?" I said. "You intend to let my client out of here sometime today?"

Sergeant Ross looked up at me with a mock-innocent expression on his face. "You still here?"

"Yes, Sergeant Ross, I'm still here. Still waiting on my client."

"Well, see, the thing is, Mr. Sloan, I still have some paperwork to do before his booking is complete. And if I don't get him booked by . . ." He looked at his watch. ". . . by two-thirty, then he won't make it to court today and, gosh, I guess we'll have to send him up to County along with your other client. The one, you may recall, who struck a fellow police officer this morning before pulling his weapon on her? That ring a bell with you?"

"Now, Fred, it didn't happen quite like that."

"My name is Sergeant Ross."

Behind me Lisa was pacing up and down, up and down.

"Cut me a little slack here, Sarge. That poor guy back there had nothing to do with Miles Dane."

"The problem is, you made yourself unpopular around here. Counselor." The sergeant raised his voice so that all the prisoners in the bullpen could hear him. "And when that happens, all your clients suffer. *Maybe your new client would be better served if he hired another lawyer!*"

I raised my hands in surrender. It wasn't two-thirty yet. "Take your time, Sarge." The truth was, Fred Ross could do anything he pleased back there. I figured the best strategy was to let him get his licks in, bust my balls a little, and hope he'd relent. If two-thirty started rolling around, then I'd take the gloves off. But there was no point in getting ahead of myself.

Tick. Tick. Tick. I could see my client watching me with an annoyed expression on his face.

Sergeant Ross flipped to another pink form. Tick. Tick.

Lisa continued pacing up and down.

Tick. Tick. Scribble, scribble. Tick, tick.

Finally Lisa walked over to the counter. "Hey, ASSHOLE!" she yelled. The veins were sticking up in her neck.

The desk sergeant looked at her, wide-eyed.

"Sweetheart," I whispered. "Easy. This is not New York City. Around here you have to go along to—"

"Yes, SERGEANT ASSHOLE, I'm talking to you!" Lisa screamed. She pulled out a cell phone, then yanked her sweater off over her head revealing a ratty T-shirt. She threw her sweater on the ground.

"Lisa!"

Lisa pointed at Leon Prouty. "That is my client. Do you see him, you moron functionary bureaucrat?"

The desk sergeant just stared at her.

Lisa waved her phone. "This is called a cell phone. I am about to use it to call every TV station in the city of goddamn Detroit. I am going to tell them that you are trying to fuck my client, Mr. Prouty, just because my partner, Mr. Sloan, made you look bad today."

She took off her T-shirt, threw it on the floor. Now she was wearing nothing above the waist but a black jogging bra.

"And just to sweeten the pot, you third-rate pencil-pushing miserable excuse for a cop, I'm going to take off all my goddamn clothes and parade my skinny, naked ass up and down in front of this building. You better damn well *believe* that the cameras will show up for that. Are you listening, you moronic witless cretin?"

The stunned desk sergeant looked around for guidance.

Lisa started punching numbers into the cell phone. "I'm dialing! I'm dialing!"

"Now, hold on, miss. Just, look, hey . . ." Fred Ross, I happened to know, was Knights of Columbus, a pillar of the church down at St. Luke's, the whole bit. I don't think he cared about the TV exposure, but somehow the idea of this nice-looking young woman parading naked up and down in front of the police station offended his sense of propriety and decency.

"Hold on, miss," he said. "Hold on. Just, hey, just put your shirt on, we'll get this whole thing squared away."

Back in the bullpen the prisoners were applauding and wolf-whistling. "I want *her*," one of them yelled.

"Yo, yo," another one yelled. "Yo, lady, come back here, reppasent *me*!"

B ACK IN THE car, Lisa looked over at me and grinned. "So," she said, "do I have the job?"

"I have never been so mortified in my life," I said.

Her grin faded, and a shadow of hurt crept into her eyes.

"For chrissake, Lisa, this isn't the Bronx. You don't get things done around here by screaming at people and acting like a maniac."

"I got him out, didn't I?"

"You're lucky you didn't get arrested. And what happens next time? After you've got everybody in the entire police department pissed off at you?"

She stared out the window. After a minute I heard a sob break out of her. I looked over and her shoulders were heaving.

"I don't know what's happening to me," she said. "I don't understand what . . ."

I reached over, tried to put my hand on her shoulder. She squirmed away. I pulled my hand back. Again that inexplicable sense of shame washed over me, of responsibility for her troubles.

Murder cases are unpredictable beasts. They can give you a sense of purpose, energize you, fill you up with hope and direction—or they can drag you down and grind you to dust. If I pulled Lisa into this case, I was taking a terrible risk. I wanted to think that she would rise to the challenge. Best-case scenario, the case could help her turn her life around. But with drunks, you never really know. I was in a bind. The case was about to take over my life. If I was going to be able to do anything for Lisa, I'd have to keep her in sight for a while. For all practical purposes, in sight meant in the case.

"One thing at a time, little one," I said softly. Little one? My God, where had that come from? I'd called her that when she was just a baby, back when I had still been fitfully trying to be her father on a more or less full-time basis.

She kept sobbing softly.

"You came to me because you want my help," I said. "This is what I can do for you. A job, a place to stay."

She didn't answer.

"I could use your help," I said. "But if you want to work for me, you do it clean and you do it sober. Period. You find a meeting, you work the program."

No answer.

"Otherwise, go elsewhere."

For a long time she didn't speak. We drove through Pickeral Point, past the salt factory, past the haggard old Masonic Lodge, and through the touristy downtown shopping district. Finally, as we were about to reach the office, she reached over and grabbed my hand where it rested on the steering wheel. She squeezed hard and didn't let go. My heart leapt like a crazy little bird in my chest.

Sure, I thought. The case. The case will bring us together. The case will make us better, stronger, closer. Murder trial as family therapy. Why not? But in the back of my mind something was saying that anything that morbidly ironic was probably too good to be true.

Twelve

I FOUND LISA waiting in my living room the next morning. There were livid spots on each pale cheek, and her eyes were puffy. But she was clean, her hair was brushed, and she wore a blue power suit and sensible-looking pumps.

"How you feel, little one?" I said.

"Like getting plastered." She gave me a tight smile. "Look, Dad, I'm sorry I acted like such an idiot yesterday. I get stupid when I drink."

"Don't we all." I smiled awkwardly back at her. "Look, I guess you know what I'm embroiled in here," I said after a brief pause. "Miles Dane has just been charged with murder. What's immediately in front of us is trying to get him out on bail. It's going to be a tough sell, frankly. In Michigan it's pretty much out of the question getting bail on a murder charge. But we'll try anyway. After that we need to start investigating. We need to find out what evidence is out there that incriminates him and what we can do to undermine it. This is going to be a full court press. Lots of pressure, lots of exposure, lots of stress, cameras everywhere. We're going to be under a microscope. It'll be like nothing you've ever experienced. So let me ask you again. Are you sure you're up for this?"

She looked out the window for a moment. "Yes," she said finally. "I think I need this."

FIRST I MET with Miles Dane at the courthouse in the cramped conference room next to Courtroom B. Despite the fact that it is used almost exclusively for meetings between defense lawyers and their clients, it is relatively pleasant. No concrete block walls, no toothpaste green institutional paint. There's actually carpet on the floor, and the walls are the same wood paneling as in the courtroom. The only thing that might put you off is that there are no knobs or handles in the doors, and anchored on the floor under one side of the small conference table are two huge steel rings so that prisoners can be shackled to the floor.

Miles was sitting disconsolately in the chair when the bailiff let me in. He was fully shackled and manacled, and the chain between his ankles was indeed looped through the ring in the floor. He wore the standard county-issue orange jumpsuit and orange plastic sandals with white socks.

After the bailiff left, I sat down, set my briefcase on the floor. Lisa sat down beside me. I introduced her to Miles, then said, "How you holding up, pal?"

He shook his head. His eyes were hollow and his dark hair unkempt. "I don't know. I don't know. They put me on suicide watch."

"Should they be worried about that?"

Miles sighed. "I just . . . I just feel like, you know, I had this great run in life—and then the man upstairs said, 'Okay, that's good enough,' and jerked the rug out from under me."

"I don't know what I can tell you," I said. "Other than the usual pointless platitudes. Chin up, that sort of thing."

Miles smiled without warmth.

"Is there anything I can get you? Books, cigarettes, a radio, candy, anything like that?"

"Just get me out of here."

"I'll do what I can, but frankly I'm not hopeful." I explained the near impossibility of his getting out on bail, then opened my briefcase. "There are some issues that I avoided talking about up to this point because I wasn't sure which way the wind would blow. But at this point, unless you decide to plead guilty or unless somebody else pops up saying they committed the crime, this case will almost certainly go to trial. I hate like hell to have to deal with this issue, but we just have to get it out of the way."

"Money," Miles said.

I nodded. "First, I'm sure it's just a clerical thing, but Mrs. Fenton tells me that your retainer check bounced."

Miles looked off into the distance, not speaking.

"Miles?" My eyebrows rose. "Miles, did you knowingly give me a bad check?"

Miles still didn't say anything.

This was unexpected. I had assumed money would not be a problem for a famous writer. "Look, Miles, let me be straight with you here. If I'm going to represent you, we're going to be working together very closely for a very long time. It is absolutely imperative that there be a bond of complete trust between us. If you're experiencing financial difficulties, then I need to know that right this minute so we can figure out a strategy for dealing with your situation."

Still nothing from Miles.

"I'm not a charity, Miles. I have two employees. I have rent to pay. On occasion I even like to eat a square meal. I don't think I should have to explain this to you. Murder trials are terribly expensive. However much of a bargain I like to think it is, my time doesn't come cheap. Plus there will be expert witnesses. They cost money. Every time I make a flip chart or a blowup of an exhibit for trial, it costs sixty bucks. Every time I FedEx a document? Money. Investigators? Money. Photocopying? Money."

Miles put his face in his hands.

"Miles, modesty aside, I am hands down the best criminal defense attorney in this county. But I cannot give you a good defense on the cheap. It's that simple."

Miles finally looked up at me. "How much are we talking?"

"Depends on how long it runs, how many experts I need, how much investigation . . ."

Miles suddenly looked irritated. "Just give me a number!"

"Assuming we go to trial? Absolute, utter rock bottom, seventy-five grand. If we do it right—half a million? Maybe more."

Miles's eyes widened. "You're kidding me! I've just had my wife stolen from me in the most horrible way. And you're saying that the cost to me—a totally, totally, utterly blameless innocent bastard—just to walk away with my freedom, it could run me half a *million* dollars?"

"And that's not counting appellate work," I said dryly.

Miles stared furiously at me. "If I wasn't so goddamn angry, I could weep. This is *wrong*."

"Yes," I said. "But imagine how you'd feel if you were some poor broke guy who came up on the wrong side of town."

He looked at me for a minute, then he started to laugh. He laughed and laughed until tears started running down his face.

"What?" I said.

When he finally stopped laughing, Miles said, "Here's the funny part, Charley. I *am* some poor broke guy who came up on the wrong side of town."

"What about all those best-sellers? All those movies?"

"That was a long, long time ago, pal. You know how much money I made on the domestic sale of my last book? After I paid my agent? Twenty-nine thousand seven hundred and fifty dollars. I made one thousand eight hundred bucks in film residuals, and got royalty checks for six thousand and twelve dollars on old books."

"Savings?"

"*Nada*. Used up long ago."

"House?"

"I've borrowed against the equity in the place twice already."

"Can you go back to the well?"

His eyes widened. "Charley, that's my *house*! You're asking me to hock the title to my house when I know with absolute dead certainty I'll never be able to make enough money again in my life to get out from under the note."

I sat silently.

"Diana and I have been living beyond our means for a long time," Miles said finally. "I've been slowly selling off assets, tightening the belt. Diana's been a good sport about it, but I've finally cut to the bone. I put those two mortgages on the house without telling Diana. I didn't want her to know how bad it had gotten." Tears began trailing out of Miles Dane's eyes.

Finally, Lisa spoke. She was sounding a little choked up, too. "This is about the most depressing and cruel thing I've ever heard in my life, Mr. Dane. But the reality is that if you don't put another mortgage on whatever equity is left in your home, you will get represented by the public defender. My father knows all of them. I'm sure they're nice young people, well-meaning, hardworking. But they have no resources and nowhere near the experience or talent of Charley Sloan, Attorney at Law."

Miles let out a long, slow breath.

Lisa's dark eyes were wet and glowing. "Mr. Dane, this guy may not look like much. He doesn't blow-dry his hair, and his suit could fit better. But make no mistake, sometimes a man ends up at a place in life where Charley Sloan is their last, best hope." Her eyes gleamed. "Mr. Dane? This is that place. And you are that man."

Miles studied her for a minute. Finally, he said, "I got the house appraised a year ago. There's a bunch of repairs and maintenance that I've let slide that have actually caused the place to depreciate. I mean, I've got barely any equity left." He turned to me with a look of awful resignation on his face.

"What about your collection?" I said. "The weapons. You told me that shotgun alone was worth, what, eighty grand?"

Miles stared disconsolately at his fingers. Finally, he blew out a long breath. "What do I have to do?" he said.

I opened my briefcase, took out a power of attorney form, set it in front of him. "Sign right there. I'll do the rest."

AFTER THE MEETING was over, Lisa and I walked silently down the corridor. When we reached the elevator, my daughter said to me, "Well, that was just about the worst thing I've had to do in a long time."

"Welcome to the criminal bar," I said.

She took out a cigarette, put it in her mouth without lighting it.

There was an odd light in her eyes. "You know what, though?" she said. "I'm kind of jazzed."

As I mentioned earlier, in a way, Lisa and I barely knew each other. Other than the summer she'd worked for me a few years earlier, I had spent very little time with her since she was three years old. But still there are things, I guess, that you'll only say to someone who shares the bond of kinship, things too intimate to be spoken outside the circle of one's own blood.

"Yeah," I said softly. "So am I."

She gave me a strange smile—half-regretful, but half-fierce and feral, too.

MARK EVOLA—THE judge who was handling the arraignment—smiled brightly at me as Miles pleaded innocent, and he continued to smile as I made my long and emotional bail pitch about Miles Dane's deep roots in the community and his constitutional rights and the sweet breath of justice and a lot of other high-sounding stuff. Evola's smile hadn't dimmed by one single watt as he said, "Bail denied."

"Your Honor," I thundered, "the state has proferred not one shred of evidence!"

"As you are well aware, that's what probable cause hearings are for, Mr. Sloan. This is not a probable cause hearing."

"Well, I must put you on notice, Your Honor," I added in the same outraged tones, "that I intend to appeal this injustice, if necessary, to the very highest authorities in the land!" It was all bluster of course. I was trying to give Stash Olesky the impression that Miles Dane was willing to spill vast amounts of treasure on this case in order to clear his name. But the truth was, Mrs. Fenton would print out a canned appeal, I'd sign it, and then I'd quietly let the issue die. When you're on a budget—and ultimately every defense lawyer is—you pick your battles. The bail issue was a loser.

"Knock yourself out, Mr. Sloan," Judge Evola said. "I'm setting your client's probable cause hearing for Monday."

Thirteen

I CAME BACK to my office and found my new client Leon Prouty in the reception area having a conversation with Lisa. Leon Prouty looked up and grinned, showing off several missing and rotted teeth. "So, the stripper lawyer is your daughter, huh, Chuck?"

"First," I said frostily, "my friends call me Charley, not Chuck. Young man, you are not my friend. You may call me Mr. Sloan. Second, my daughter is neither a lawyer nor a stripper."

Leon Prouty's snaggle-toothed smile faded. He shrugged sullenly. "Whatever."

"Come into my office. Let's talk about your future. Lisa, feel free to join us." One of the most important things a criminal lawyer has to do with his clients is establish who is the top dog. When a person of criminal disposition thinks they have their attorney on a string—well, God help that poor bastard.

I sat down and waited for Leon and Lisa to come in and make themselves comfortable. "Alright, Mr. Prouty," I said. "While I was over at the police department on another matter, I picked up a copy of your police report. Let me tell you what the police say happened. They say that they received a call from a neighbor regarding a prowler on a recently built spec home out in the Cornish Pointe subdivision. That's quite a high-rent district. The police say they rolled up and found you and what they described as 'three Latino males' on the property. The alleged three Latino males ran away and were never captured. You, on the other hand, were sitting in the cab of a rented Ryder truck. In the back of the truck . . ." I put on my reading glasses. "According to the inventory, the police discovered four ornamental trees, thirty-nine bushes, four cases of tulip bulbs, and approximately half an acre of sod. According to the report, this property had been recently landscaped, and you and these three Latino males were believed to have stripped the entire property and stuck all of this stuff in your rental truck. They valued the materials at roughly five thousand dollars. Does this accord, more or less, with what happened?"

Leon laughed. "Obviously that cop ain't landscaped his yard recently."

"Meaning what?"

"The sod alone's worth five grand, retail. Them big-ass Japanese maples? Eleven hundred a pop, easy. There was ligustrums, roses, a boatload of real nice Cheyenne privets and shit. You're talking twenty-five grand worth of stuff easy. Of course I couldn't of got more than six or seven out of it on the, ah, used landscaping market." He smiled at me as though I would find this as amusing as he apparently did.

"What kind of outcome would make you happy here, Leon?"

Leon Prouty blinked. "Huh? I want you to get me off!"

It was my turn to be amused. "What you just did, Mr. Prouty, was virtually admit to me that you and three confederates attempted to steal twenty-five thousand dollars' worth of property. You were caught red-handed. In your police file, I note that you have been convicted three times already on various property offenses. And you're only twenty-two years old. What this means is that, barring a miracle, the only question here is how much jail time you serve."

Leon Prouty looked over at Lisa, confused. "But she said—"

"Lisa has been my employee for about twenty-four hours. She is not a lawyer. She has virtually no experience with criminal law. If you're looking for legal opinions, ask me."

"Yeah, but . . ."

"If you're willing to roll over on the Mexicans—"

"Shoot, them boys is back in Tijuana by now."

"Then it's a question of pleading it down to something you can live with."

Leon's eyes hardened slightly. "Mr. Sloan, I didn't come to you because I was looking to plead. I want a trial. Expert witnesses, the whole bit."

"Judging by the condition of your teeth, son, I'd guess you can't afford a trial."

Leon looked over at Lisa. "Man, we was getting along real good till the old guy come in. I want *you* to be my lawyer."

Lisa glanced at the floor.

"Mr. Prouty," I said, "how many times do I have to tell you? *I'm* the lawyer. You cannot retain a nonlawyer to represent you in a court of law. And speaking of which, where's that five hundred dollars you said you'd pick up at the ATM?"

"Uh. Well, see I thought I had it in there, but I come up a little light."

I rolled my eyes. "Get the money or get a new lawyer."

He didn't seem especially concerned about this turn of events. He turned to Lisa. "You want to tell him?"

"Tell me what?" I said sharply.

Lisa looked uneasy. "He claims he knows some things. Some things about Miles. He says if we ease up on his bill, he'll tell us what he knows."

I laughed. "Oh, that's a good one. The old I-know-something-about-your-other-client trick."

Leon sucked some air through the gap where one of his teeth had rotted away. "Go ahead. Yuck it up, man."

I crossed my arms. "You want me to stop laughing? Impress me with what you know."

"I want a free ride, man. Right through trial. And none of this pleading guilty crap." Leon Prouty looked at me with a pleased expression on his face.

What if? The kid was probably blowing smoke, but even if he wasn't . . . This was one of those times where the two-hour legal ethics class you snooze through in law school comes slamming into the brick wall of real life. Theoretically a lawyer should keep each client and each case in a magical box, with no point of contact between. Any point of contact is called a conflict of interest and demands that the lawyer trot down to a judge and recuse himself from representing one of the clients. Again—theoretically—I probably should have instructed Leon about the conflict of interest rules that govern my performance before the bar, then explained that I couldn't in good conscience listen to what he had to say.

Theory and practice, of course, are sometimes two different animals. And to split legal hairs, I couldn't actually *know* there was a conflict of interest unless I heard what he knew. "Tell me what you know or get out of my office," I said.

Leon sucked on his bad teeth, then finally said, "Well, without admitting to nothing, it's possible I might have been doing a little midnight landscaping over in the vicinity of Riverside Boulevard about a week ago."

I waited skeptically.

"Again, without getting bogged down in the specifics as to how come I was there, I seen a guy come out that house."

"Which house? Be specific."

"Miles Dane's house! The hell you think I'm talking about, man?"

"A guy. You saw a 'guy.' "

He nodded significantly.

"Can you describe this man?"

"White."

I raised my eyebrows at Lisa. "Hey, it was a *white* man! That rules out all of the two dozen Chinese people that live in Kerry County. Several hundred African-Americans, too."

Leon scowled. "He was wearing a black leather jacket. And he drove a black Lincoln. An old one, maybe '63,'64 somewhere in there. The kind with the suicide doors."

"Suicide doors?"

"You know, where the rear doors open backwards. So if the car rolls forward while you're getting out, it kills you."

"Ah. And when did he leave?"

"Late."

"Like midnight? Like 3 A.M.?"

Leon shrugged. "What, you think I was sitting around checking my watch all night? I was busy."

I sighed. "Leon, look, I appreciate that you don't want to go to jail. But making up stories is not going to help."

Leon scowled. "Man, I know a lot more about Mr. Big Shot Writer than you think."

"I'm sure you do." I stood. "Thank you for coming down. Your court date has been set for November 11. Call the public defender's office, they'll help you out."

Leon turned to Lisa, winked. "Hey, man, I'se just playing with you." He took a fat roll of money out of his pocket, tossed it on the table. He stood up, then watched me as I counted it. Five hundred on the nose.

"I ain't lying, Mr. Sloan. Straight up, I seen what I seen. But you want me to testify, you gonna have to do the right thing far as the rest of my bill goes. I ain't made out of money."

He stalked out, the door banging shut behind him. I snorted dismissively.

Lisa was staring at me. "You aren't going to follow up on what he said?"

"Let me give you the first rule of thumb in the practice of law. The client always lies. It's true in civil law, and it's true in criminal law." I waved my hand toward the door that had just closed behind Leon Prouty. "But it's especially true of people like that."

"Yeah, but that was very specific. The black Lincoln with the rear doors that open backward . . ."

"Of *course* it was specific. Good liars know that the key to a good lie is to fill it with tantalizing details. The only thing missing from his story was a man with a wooden arm."

I guess there must have been something bitter in my tone, because her eyes widened, and she leaned back in her chair as though I was about to hit her.

"You think Miles is guilty, don't you?" she said.

"Put it this way, Stash Olesky is both a careful and an ethical man. He's not like his worthy predecessor, our friend Judge Mark Evola. When Mark was prosecuting attorney, he wasn't above indicting you just because you showed promise of getting the smiling face of Mark Evola on the news—no matter how remote the likelihood of your guilt.

No, if Stash drew up a warrant three days after the crime was committed, then things are not looking good for Miles Dane."

At that moment Mrs. Fenton came in and handed me a folder. "This just came in from Mr. Olesky. He said, 'Tell Charley this is professional courtesy at its finest.' "

I read through the file folder, then handed it to Lisa.

"So they found the murder weapon with his fingerprints on it," she said after she'd finished reading it. "Big deal. It's his stick, of course it has his fingerprints. I don't see how they could they convict on this."

"Yeah," I said. "That's precisely what worries me."

Fourteen

THE PICKERAL POINT town square abuts the river. Its most prominent feature is the Kerry County Courthouse, a large Depression-era box whose sandstone facade alludes in the most perfunctory way to both the Federal style and to Art Deco, without having any of the charm of either. I like the courthouse for precisely this reason: It's pure Pickeral Point. By which I mean the design makes no pretentious declaration about the aims or workings or majesty of "The Law." It's a place where real human beings do the real work of the law—by and large with professionalism and a reasonable dose of humanity and humility.

Ordinarily you can see the river from the front steps of the courthouse. On Monday morning, however, all you could see were the antennae of the various television trucks parked along the boardwalk. Lisa and I bulled through the throng of camera crews and microcassette-recorder-thrusting print journalists, into the courthouse, and up to Courtroom 2B.

The first thing I noticed was the TV camera in the back of the courtroom. I had heard a rumor that Court TV would be broadcasting live—but I didn't believe it until I saw their logo on the side of the camera.

I should have known. When I mentioned the humility of Kerry County's legal professionals, I have to except one man in particular. Judge Mark Evola.

Mark Evola had always considered himself to be larger than Pickeral Point. He loved the limelight. In theory the probable cause hearing was supposed to be held in district court rather than the more senior circuit court where Judge Evola served. But, under the dubious theory that a high-profile case of this sort required "judicial continuity," Evola had conspired to have himself preside over the Miles Dane matter from beginning to end. Everything from the first appearance to sentencing—if it got that far—would happen in front of him.

Which was bad news for Miles because there was nothing in life that Mark Evola would like better than to see than Charley Sloan getting thrashed to a bleeding pulp on a high-profile case.

Evola is a boyish forty-one years old and goes about six-six. He is handsome as a movie star, his blond hair tinged at the temples with just enough gray to keep him from looking like a child. Back when he had been the prosecuting attorney of the county, I had beaten him badly on a major case, derailing his vast political ambitions.

Judging from the camera in the back of the room, I guessed he was figuring if he played his cards right, maybe this trial would raise his profile enough to get him back in the political game. Our current congressman was rumored to be suffering from end-stage colon cancer, and the job seemed likely to be opening up soon. A good performance here in front of the TV camera . . . who knows, maybe Washington might yet beckon. So the hearing began with a gratuitous civics lesson by the judge designed to impress the many journalists present—and presumably the voters of our district—with Evola's presidential qualities.

"A probable cause hearing," Evola said grandly, addressing himself toward the television camera in the back of the room, "is a sort of proving ground, in which the state presents the evidence against a person charged with a crime and attempts to prove that there is indeed probable cause to try the accused on those charges."

He went on at some length about the impartiality of this court, then pointed to the bronze statue he kept on his bench—the blindfolded goddess with her scales of justice held high—discoursing at length about what it represented and what a marvelous system we Americans had that forced the state to bring out its evidence in the cold, clear, unflinching light of public view. It sounded very pretty and it was all total hooey, every single syllable of it aimed at that live TV feed. Everybody in the room knew that any prosecuting attorney worth ten cents can make probable cause on a ham sandwich. I tried to keep my groans below the level of audibility.

Finally, Evola shut up and let Stash Olesky, our prosecuting attorney, get to work. Stash, like Evola, is blond. But there the resemblance ends. Where Evola exudes a bland, vapid charm, Stash, with his broad cheekbones and almost Asiatic eyes, looks like a Polish aristocrat, preparing to make a doomed charge against some invading army. There's a note of both courage and sadness in him, as though it pains him slightly as he lops you to pieces with his saber.

Stash's first move was to put Chantall Denkerberg on the stand. She walked to the stand calmly, wearing the same blue wool suit—half a step away from a nun's habit—that she had worn when she arrived at the crime scene. Or maybe all her suits looked exactly the same. Her shoulders were squared, jaw firm; she looked ready to do spiritual battle for the cause of right, truth, and justice. I suspected she would be an effective witness, and I was right.

Stash led her through a general explanation of her findings, eventually arriving at the meat of the case.

"Detective, at what point did you begin to form an opinion about the case?"

"Well, you're always making a mental list of suspects. But what I do is try to evaluate the totality of the evidence and just start matching things up. Basically when I walked into the room to interview Mr. Dane in his home on the morning of the murder, there were a couple of things that seemed peculiar about the crime scene. And what I hoped my interview would do was clarify or explain those peculiarities.

"Specifically, at that time, I had two concerns. My first concern had to do with the broken window I had observed on the second floor of Mr. Dane's house. I had been advised by Mr. Sloan, Mr. Dane's attorney, that he understood an assailant had jumped out that window. There was glass scattered in the yard beneath the window indicating it had been struck from the inside and broken outward. That was consistent with someone escaping the house there. Naturally I examined the ground underneath the window with a great deal of care. It was moist soil from the rain the previous day, with only patchy grass thanks to the fact, I guess, that there's not a lot of sunlight there. At any rate, given the condition of the soil, I would have expected to find footprints under the window. I didn't find any. I mean not so much as a dent in the soil. So that raised a serious concern in my mind.

"Second, I examined the body of the deceased. Normally when a person is attacked, they will defend themselves. The result of this is that the person sustains injuries on their hands and arms as they attempt to ward off the initial blows. Diana Dane's body showed no evidence of that sort of injury, which indicated either that she was asleep when she was attacked or that she knew her attacker and was therefore unprepared for the assault.

"So, these two things concerned me a great deal as I went into my interview with Mr. Dane. I was hoping his story would explain these two facts to my satisfaction."

Stash Olesky nodded. "And did it?"

Chantall Denkerberg glanced briefly at Miles Dane. "No, it did not."

"Why not?"

"There are two areas that you evaluate when you're an investigator. One area is the factual circumstances of the case. That's the old Jack Webb just-the-facts-ma'am side of the case. The other thing you evaluate is the demeanor and actions of the witnesses and parties involved in a crime. And as a trained and experienced investigator it's my job to take both of those things into consideration. In my view, Mr. Dane came up short on both counts."

Stash Olesky interrupted. "Let's stick with the Jack Webb issues first."

Detective Denkerberg nodded. "Given the facts I had gleaned up to that point, his story just flat-out didn't make sense. In a nutshell, this is what he said: He told me that he was working in his office; he said he heard a noise that concerned him; he was a little vague and evasive in describing the noise, but he said it made him nervous. That's a direct quote. 'It made me nervous.' So he went upstairs to see what it was. I have to mention at this point, by the way, that his office contains a huge weapons collection. Guns, knives, coshes, swords, you name it, all of them hanging on the wall.

"Now I don't know about you, but if I'm sitting in a room full of weapons and I hear a spooky noise inside my house, I'm going to grab something. A stick, a gun, a butter knife, *something*. But Mr. Dane said he didn't do that. He just went up the stairs unarmed. Okay, fair enough. So, according to his story, when Mr. Dane reached the top of the stairs, he saw a man in the hallway. The man fled into a bedroom at the end of the hall. Mr. Dane heard breaking glass, he gave chase, he arrived in the bedroom, the window was broken, he looked out, he saw the man fleeing across the lawn toward Riverside Boulevard.

"I should note here that my investigation of the top floor of Mr. Dane's home demonstrated clearly that if somebody had exited from the second floor without going down the stairs, then he would have had to jump out a window. There were no dumbwaiters, no back stairs, no doors, no fire escape." Chantall Denkerberg shrugged. "Had to be the window. But if somebody jumped, where were the footprints? It didn't add up.

"That was probably the most important thing. But also the crime itself. Why would a burglar beat somebody to death? There was a missing weapon on the wall of Mr. Dane's office. A martial arts type object called a bokken. A wooden training sword used by Japanese swordsmen. Mr. Dane suggested a scenario in which a burglar might have snuck it off the wall while Mr. Dane was using the bathroom that was attached to his office, crept upstairs, then at some point surprised Mrs. Dane . . . or she surprised him. Whichever case it was, the intruder got scared—this is still Mr. Dane's hypothesis—and in order to silence Diana Dane, he beat her to death.

"Again, this just seemed implausible on several levels. Why? Let me run through the reasons.

"First, there are all these expensive weapons on the wall. Fancy shotguns, nice old cowboy pistols, samurai swords, bowie knives. If, indeed, a burglar were going to steal something—well, the bokken seemed to me to be an unlikely weapon to grab. This is a weapon which Mr. Dane himself described as 'basically a black stick'—again, I'm quoting him. It was neither the most valuable nor the most dangerous weapon on the wall. It wasn't even especially eye-catching.

"Second, the victim, Diana Dane, was beaten horribly. Both experience and common sense tell me that a felon who's committing violence in order to escape detection isn't going to stay around and beat somebody beyond the point of death. What's the point? You want to escape? Give them a good smack and then scoot.

"Third, the lack of defensive wounds made the 'surprised burglar' scenario seem unlikely. He could only be surprised by somebody who was conscious. A conscious person, attacked by a stranger with a stick, will invariably hold their hands up to ward off the blows. That's an extremely predictable feature of human nature." Detective Denkerberg shook her head. "Nope. Mr. Dane's whole story seemed nonsensical to me. It didn't match the facts."

"Okay," the prosecuting attorney said, "you mentioned the Jack Webb side of the case. What about the human side? Did something bother you there?"

"It sure did. Look, this is a probable cause hearing, not a trial, so this is probably something I can say here that I might not be able to say in front of a jury. When an innocent person finds their spouse beaten to death, they call 911." She looked at Miles with naked disgust. "That man right there? He called his *lawyer*."

"You're saying," Stash said, "that based on your many years of experience as an investigator, that's not the normal behavior of an innocent person."

"Any fool knows it's not." Her eyes flashed. "And once I got there, all I got from Mr. Dane and from his lawyer, Mr. Sloan, was a bunch of evasiveness and ducking and weaving. Again, this is something that's only suitable for a probable cause hearing I guess, but Mr. Sloan kept interrupting the interview on one silly pretext or other. Pretending he was choking, things that wouldn't fool a four-year-old child." I flushed. "It was obvious he used the opportunity to coach Mr. Dane."

I stood up. "Objection. Coaching has a narrow legal definition. If I did interrupt the interview—and I'm not saying I did—but if I did, it would have been to apprise Mr. Dane of his rights, as per my duty as an attorney. Not to *coach* him."

"Sustained," Judge Evola said after a pregnant pause. "Choose another word, Detective."

"Call it what you want. It was obvious Mr. Sloan was not happy with how the interview was going. He could see as well as I could what a pathetic story his client was telling. I wasn't in the room with him, so I can't testify as to exactly what he told his client. All I'm saying was that the conduct of Mr. Sloan and Mr. Dane, taken as a whole again, and in the context of my experience as a trained investigator, blah blah blah, all the legal verbiage you need to qualify why I'm making this judgment—what I'm saying is, I smelled a rat."

"I object, Your Honor," I said. "This is not testimony as to probable cause, it's an attempt to tar my client with—"

"Stow it, Mr. Sloan, before you get rolling on one of your fourteen-minute objections. I get the drift of your objection, and I'm ruling against it. You know as well as I do that this is not a trial. Hearsay and hunches and so on are perfectly admissible in this venue."

Stash moved on quickly. "Did you arrest Mr. Dane at that time, Detective?"

"Certainly not. I don't arrest on hunches. I waited until we got hard evidence."

"Tell us about that."

"Well, first, I got the initial autopsy findings from the medical examiner. Dr. Rey's report confirmed the results of my initial examination of the body. There were no defensive wounds."

"And that was enough for an arrest?"

"No it was not. At that point I still didn't have any sort of motive."

"Did you come to find any sort of motive?"

"Yes, I obtained Mr. Dane's financial records. At that time I found that Mr. Dane was in very poor financial shape, with a large amount of debt and dwindling income. He held a fifty-thousand-dollar life insurance policy on his wife. In addition his wife apparently had a small trust fund that Mr. Dane appears to have stood to benefit from on her death. In my view these provided a financial motive."

Stash Olesky nodded, then reached into a large canvas gym bag and came out with a long black object with the slight but unmistakable curve of a Japanese sword. "Did this play into your decision to arrest Mr. Dane?"

"Yes it did. I'll identify that object, by the way, as a stick made of ebony wood, carved in the shape of a sword. As I mentioned earlier, martial artists apparently refer to such an item as a bokken. On our first examination of the property we were unable to locate the murder weapon. So we expanded the scope of our search last week, examining a location near the victim's home—specifically a boat owned by a neighbor of Mr. Dane's, which was docked a few hundred feet upriver from Mr. Dane's house. With permission of the owner, I opened a locker on that boat and found the bokken. The bokken was covered with a substance resembling blood.

"I secured the item, placed it in a paper bag, and using customary chain-of-custody procedures I personally transported it to the state crime lab. The state crime lab ran tests on the bokken. The results of those tests were as follows. First, the bokken was indeed covered with blood, and that blood was a DNA match with the blood taken from Diana Dane at her autopsy. Second, several hairs were found on the bokken. Again, DNA tests on the follicles of one of those hairs showed a match to Diana Dane. Third, several latent fingerprints were revealed by cyanoacrylate fuming. According to the state crime lab fingerprint specialist, those fingerprints were a match with those of Mr. Dane."

Stash Olesky took out another paper bag, set it on his table.

"Last line of questioning, Detective. During your conversation with Mr. Dane in his home on the morning of his wife's murder, what was he wearing?"

"A robe. A white robe. With white pajamas underneath."

"And did you see any visible evidence of blood on those clothes?"

"Not a speck."

"Did you ask him if he had touched his wife after he found her?"

"He indicated he had not."

"Did he say whether or not he had changed clothes between the time he discovered her and the time you arrived?"

"He indicated he had not."

"Can you tell us if you found anything besides the bokken in the location where you found what you believe to be the murder weapon."

"Yes I can. I found a pair of black wool trousers, a pair of black silk socks, a black Turnbull & Asser shirt, and a pair of black boots. They were covered with a substance that appeared to be dried blood. I might add that it's generally known that Mr. Dane wears black clothes almost exclusively."

Stash Olesky opened his paper bag, dumped the contents out on the witness stand. "Are these the clothes you found?"

"Yes, they are."

"So what happened then?"

"I sent the clothes to the state crime lab. DNA tests showed that they were indeed covered with blood and that the blood was Diana Dane's. At that point in time, I believed that I had probable cause to arrest Mr. Dane. I obtained a warrant and after a bit of a . . . fracas . . . I placed him under arrest."

Stash Olesky nodded. "Thank you, Detective. I believe that's all I have for you."

Judge Evola looked down at me. "Mr. Sloan?"

"Briefly, Detective. These fingerprints, you mentioned that they were latent prints, correct?"

"Yes."

"There are two types of fingerprints, are there not?"

"I'm not sure I follow."

"A latent fingerprint is left by the grease and amino acids on your fingers. An impression print, on the other hand, is one left in some soft or liquid substance. Blood for instance."

"That's correct."

"Were there any fingerprint *impressions* on the bokken? Bloody fingerprints, specifically."

Brief pause. "No. Only latents."

"Thank you. Let's turn to these bloody clothes. Any reason to think they might belong to Mr. Dane?"

"Yes."

"Other than the fact that Mr. Dane's favorite color is black?"

I waited, but Denkerberg just looked at me with an amused expression on her face. "Pray, Detective, let us in on that reason. Our breath is bated."

Chantall Denkerberg picked up the pair of black cowboy boots and turned the lip down. "It's this label. You want me to read it?"

"Sure, why not."

" 'Handmade by Royce Daniels, bootmaker of Harlingen, Texas, for Mr. Miles Dane.' "

In theory a defense attorney's goal in a preliminary hearing is to get his client kicked free for lack of probable cause. But realistically that almost never happens. As a result my real goal at the hearing was to force Stash to reveal as much of his case as possible. The old saw about never asking a question to which you don't know the answer doesn't apply to probable cause hearings. From a strictly technical standpoint, I had gained something of value. But the courtroom is about perception as much as it is about legal technique. So when you walk into a setup like that—valuable as it may be tactically—you feel a little silly. Stash Olesky was no Mark Evola, but he was not insensitive to the camera in the back of the room either: He'd set me up and tagged me with a nice combination right there on national TV just to let me know he could do it.

"Mr. Sloan?" It was Judge Evola. "Any more questions?"

I grinned. "I believe I've asked more than enough." There was some laughter from the courtroom. Judge Evola scowled theatrically, and the laughter died.

"Mr. Olesky, call your next witness."

To my surprise Stash Olesky stood, and said, "The state has no further witnesses."

It was an intensely ballsy move. Stash tends to be a belt-and-suspenders guy. I'd expected to see a nice little parade of witnesses—the ME, some state crime lab people, a couple more cops . . . But that was it: One witness, and he sat down.

Truth was, he probably had all he needed. With the right judge on the right day with the stars in the right configuration, I probably could have gotten the case dismissed. Problem was, I was the wrong lawyer with the wrong judge. No way in a million years Judge Mark Evola would give me this one. No trial meant no Court TV. No Court TV meant no chance at getting elected to Congress. It was an easy call.

Stash made his usual closely reasoned, methodical wrap-up. He focused on lies, evasions, inconsistencies, fingerprints, the apparent financial motive—and of course the bloody boots and clothes. Then I made my spiel. I focused on the murder weapon. No bloody fingerprints on the bokken meant no proof that Miles Dane had committed the murder. I suggested that the clothes could have been stolen by the intruder. Perhaps, I hinted darkly, they were even planted. It was a pretty good speech, and an utter waste of breath.

Judge Evola ruled from the bench without even bothering to take a recess. He was hoping, clearly, that the armchair quarterbacks at Court TV would label him as a Bold and Decisive Jurist. I noticed that he didn't address the room generally, but looked straight into the TV camera in the back of the room. "This court finds probable cause to bind Miles Dane over pending trial for the murder of Diana Dane. Trial in this matter is hereby set for January 2 of next year."

Then he stood up and swept out the door.

Fifteen

L isa and i sat down for dinner at my cramped little house. I live on a road that dead-ends into the railroad tracks, most of my neighbors being drawn from the upper echelons of the working class. It's a fine little house, nondescript, clapboard-sided, with a small front porch that suits a man of plain tastes. I've been thinking for some years that I'll get a nicer place soon, and so I haven't hung any art on the walls, and my bedroom windows are still covered with bedsheets. There are stacks of books everywhere that I keep meaning to organize or shelve or sell, but never get around to. At the rate I'm going, I may be here forever. But it still has an air of the temporary about it.

Lisa seemed eager to put on a domestic show, so I lounged around watching the *News Hour* on public TV and nursing a Diet Coke—which substituted for the triple scotch I would have been working on back in the old days—while she chattered about little things and cooked spaghetti.

I thought a change of mood might be nice, so when it looked like she was about ready to serve up the food, I rummaged around for some candles in the distant hope that I might have acquired some while sleepwalking. After coming up dry on the candles, I drew from my extensive collection of two classical CDs and put some Bach on the stereo. Lisa had set the table with linen napkins and my finest Corning Ware.

After putting the spaghetti on the table, she took out a bottle of nonalcoholic sparkling grape juice, popped the cork, and poured it into my two wineglasses. I own about as much crystal as I do classical music.

Raising a glass, she said, "I appreciate your helping me out. I really just . . . I didn't know where else to go."

"Well, you seem to be doing well. I'm glad you're here."

She made an attempt at a smile and took a sip of her grape juice. It struck me that there was something a little pathetic about drunks trying to stage a celebration with fake alcoholic beverages. But maybe it was just the feeling I kept having of all those years I'd wasted that colored my thinking on smaller things.

"I don't know why, Dad, but right now I'm feeling better than I have in years." She reached across the table and grabbed my arm. "I feel secure with you. Safe."

Something warm moved inside my chest.

"Back in New York, I always felt like . . ." She frowned. "You know in those cartoons how Wile E. Coyote always goes off the edge of the cliff and then stands there for a minute in mid-air? Then as soon as he looks down and realizes there's nothing underneath him, he starts to fall? That's how I felt in New York, as though if I ever looked down at my feet, even for a fraction of a second, I'd start to fall."

"Well, if you can't plant your feet on the ground in Pickeral Point, Michigan," I said, "then you can't do it anywhere."

She smiled wanly.

"So you want to tell me about New York, Lisa? About what happened there?"

She looked thoughtful. "No. Not yet." Suddenly her face changed, and her voice went enthusiastic. "Look, let's stay away from depressing things. Let's talk about the case."

"That's *not* depressing?"

She grinned. "You know it's not."

I grinned back. She was right. There was something bracing about being behind the eight ball. It was where I did my best work.

Her grin faded. "So look, you think he's guilty?"

I went into sage mode: "When I first started practicing law, Lisa, I made a big sport out of guessing who was innocent and who was guilty. But at a certain point, I realized that it was messing with my head to do that. You can torture yourself to death trying to figure out whether the people you represent really deserve to be zealously defended or not, but the truth is, you never really know. So eventually I figured out that the best thing I could do was to put that question in a little box, lock it away in some dark corner of my brain, and just do my job as vigorously as possible."

Lisa studied my face with her large, intelligent brown eyes. Finally, she tilted her head to the side, her lips curling up slightly at the corners, and said, "Bull. Shit."

I laughed a little. "Well, it sounds good, doesn't it?"

She kept looking at me with the half smile on her face. "You want to know what I think?"

"I'd love to know what you think."

"I think he's innocent."

I twirled my spaghetti around my fork, put it in my mouth. It was spectacularly awful. "Mm," I said. "Terrific!"

She watched my face as I chewed. "That bad, huh?"

"No, seriously." I forced down another mouthful of what was by any measure the saltiest dish I'd ever eaten in my life.

Lisa took a bite, spit it out on the plate. "Oh! God!"

"For a small Michigan town," I said, "Pickeral Point has some very nice restaurants. Might I offer to take you out to one of them?"

"Well, the good news, Dad, you can see I didn't fritter away all the tuition money you sent me on *foie gras* and cooking lessons from famous French guys."

WE ENDED UP eating at the Pickeral Point Inn, Pickeral Point's intermittently best restaurant. The Inn was Pickeral Point's one tourist attraction, a relatively well known hotel built around a quaint old river house. It had a nice bar where some of our more affluent rummies repaired at the end of the day, and a restaurant that not only had real china and real linen, but food that was well worth the money—provided, of course, that the cook, Jimmy, was sober. Which he was, mostly.

"Okay, back to this innocence-versus-guilt thing," Lisa said, after we took our seats by the window. Across the dark river, jets of flame spouted from one of the cracking towers at the Sunoco refinery, reflecting in muted blues and yellows on the river.

"Let me play devil's advocate," I said. "His story sounds ridiculous. The forensic evidence is pretty damning. He apparently has a history of violence. He's in desperate financial shape and derives a financial benefit from her death. Tell me where you see the light of innocence shining down on this man."

Lisa looked thoughtful. "Gut instinct."

"That's it?" I laughed. "Woman's intuition, something like that?"

Lisa poked listlessly at her fish. She didn't seem hungry. "I watched his face. He just didn't seem to be acting. I think he's really suffering. If it were a crime of passion . . ." She shrugged. "Look, some guy who routinely beats his wife goes one step too far, then out come the rain clouds and he's boo-hooing like a baby because he killed the love of his life. That happens all the time, I know. But there's no indication here that he ever beat her. From what you tell me, there are no police reports, no rumors, nothing. And the way he talks about her? No, I think he worshiped her. This would have had to come totally out of the blue."

"There's financial motive."

"A fifty-grand life insurance policy? Give me a break. That's peanuts for a guy like him. Financial trouble or no, fifty thousand will barely tide him over for another year."

"Okay, look, my gut says the same thing. But sometimes my gut is wrong. And in this case, I think I have no alternative but to put my gut in that little box I was talking about. Otherwise, I'll drive myself crazy. Same applies to you." I looked at her for a long moment. "And I don't have to tell you what happens when people like you and I start letting our emotions get out of control."

Lisa shook her head. "That's not what I'm talking about. What I'm saying is this: If you really believe your client is innocent, you're going to pursue a different strategy."

"With the evidence in front of us, we've only got two real choices. We try to hire some experts to shoot enough holes in their forensic evidence so they'll give us a manslaughter plea. Which seems unlikely right now. Or we fight this thing yard by yard by yard and hope we squeak by on reasonable doubt."

"I think you're missing one alternative."

I let out a long, slow breath. "Look," I said sympathetically, "I know where you're heading. What if somebody else did it? Right? All we have to do is uncover the malefactor and, *voilà*, free man, the trumpets shall sound, blah blah blah."

Lisa's eyes flashed. "Why is that so dumb?"

"It's not dumb. But speaking as an experienced lawyer I have to tell you that it's the great fool's gold of the novice criminal lawyer. It just never happens. Defense attorneys never, ever, ever pull that off. Why not? Because the police have already ruled out all the obvious suspects. Law enforcement has vast investigative resources. They can put street cops up and down every single street in Pickeral Point asking every single citizen of the town if they saw such-and-such on a certain night. They can serve search warrants, they can raid houses, they have criminalists and detectives and medical examiners and laboratories."

"And?"

"Okay. For the sake of argument. Just supposing that somebody else actually did it . . . do you have any idea how expensive it will be to hire a full-time team of investigators?"

"Let's just brainstorm," Lisa said. Suddenly, I can't say why, but I got the impression she'd been leading me by the nose all night. I just wasn't sure quite where she was taking me.

"Brainstorm away."

"If he's innocent, then why did he cook up such a bogus explanation?"

"You tell me. I can see you've given this more thought than I have."

"He's protecting someone."

I smiled in what I hoped wouldn't appear to be a condescending way. "Sort of like in Perry Mason?"

"Hey, Dad, we're brainstorming."

"Okay, okay. Keep talking."

"I think that dimwit Leon Prouty is telling the truth. I think he *did* see somebody coming out of Miles's house. And I think Miles knows that person, knows why he was there, and knows he killed his wife. But for some reason he feels he owes loyalty to that person."

It was an appealing thought. Of course, the American landscape is littered with bankrupt defense attorneys who have bought in to similar stories. I didn't want to disappoint Lisa. But at the same time, I couldn't afford to let myself believe in a fairy story—no matter how appealing it seemed.

"Okay," I said. "Just for the sake of argument. You're me. What do I send my investigators off to look for?"

"Start with his background. There's somebody out there that Miles owes. A friend, a business partner, a relative, somebody from his past. I'd talk to his family, his friends, his editors, whoever. Even talk to *her* family. It's back there somewhere. The killer's back there somewhere in his past."

I didn't want to let Lisa down. But there was reality to consider. I held up my hands, palms out. "Lisa, I don't mean to rain on your parade. I really don't. But here's *my* reality. I have to fund this trial on the price I can get for a fancy shotgun. Every dime we spend running down fruitless leads is a dime we can't spend on an expert witness. And if we're going to win this case, it's going to be with expert witnesses."

Lisa's eyes glittered as she stared straight at me.

"Expert witnesses, Lisa. For a price, they testify that DNA testing is unreliable, that blood spatter analysis is voodoo, that photographs can be faked, that white is black and black is white. And then, *maybe* the jury buys reasonable doubt."

Lisa's brown eyes just kept digging into me.

"What?" I said.

"You've got *me*," she said. "*I'll* be your investigator."

"I have a lot of other things that I could more fruitfully employ your talents on. If we can put together some compelling motions to exclude evidence, we might be able to get some real traction here."

"Come on, Dad. Just give me two weeks. What's the harm? Then I'll write as many briefs as you want. Look, two weeks ago you didn't even have me working for you at all!"

I chewed my fish for a while.

"Dad!" She took on that pained, adolescent, wheedling tone that turns fathers into spineless, acquiescent wretches.

I sighed. "A week," I said. "But that's it."

Lisa leaned across the table and kissed me on the cheek. "You're the best father in the world!"

For the pleasure—however unearned—that rushed through me during that brief moment, I would gladly have let Miles Dane rot forever in the lowest, hottest dungeon of hell.

"First thing tomorrow," I said, "let's talk to Miles. That will help give you some focus."

Sixteen

Because kerry county is not exactly a hotbed of crime, the entire prison population of the county is housed in a wing of the sheriff's department. The jail itself amounts to a small block of cells, a cafeteria, a tiny exercise yard surrounded by a high, barbed-wire-topped fence, and a dank, windowless room lawyers use to interview their clients. At ten o'clock the next morning we were sitting across the table from Miles in the interview room at the jail.

"Miles," I began, "as we start to put this case together, we're going to need to develop a sort of profile of you. A sort of history or time line of your life. Can you fill us in?"

"Where do you want me to start?"

"Birth."

Miles shrugged. "I was born here in Pickeral Point. My parents were, I guess you say, poor working stiffs. Daddy worked the docks, swept floors at the salt factory, that kind of thing. Mama was a cleaning lady. I spent my whole childhood with my nose in a book. Couldn't wait to get out of this crummy little town.

"Dropped out of school at sixteen. Traveled around the country. Washed cars, bussed tables, plucked chickens, drove trucks. Just general low-wage labor. And all the time I was writing. I'd roll up in some little burg, get work, pile up a little cash, quit, write a couple short stories or half a novel or whatever, send it off to a publisher, run out of dough, move on to another town about the time the rejection notices started showing up. That lasted three, four years. Ended up in New York in '68, finally sold my first book. Met Diana. Got married."

"Okay, let's hold it right there," I said. "Exactly when did these last things occur?"

"My first book? I sold that about a year after I got to New York. Sixty-nine, I guess."

"And you married Diana when?"

"Same year. Sixty-nine."

"How did her family react to your marriage?"

He shrugged. "Let's just say they weren't overjoyed."

"Practically speaking, how did that play out?"

He nodded, face expressionless. "Shunning, that's the old-fashioned word for it. They just cut her off. Just like that . . ." He snapped his fingers. ". . . she's a nonperson."

"All these years she's been cut off? No tearful reconciliation, nothing like that?"

Miles looked annoyed. "Why all these questions about her family? They're a bunch of rich, self-involved jerks. End of story. Anyway, they're all dead now. Except Roger."

"Roger?"

"Her brother. Real first-class creep. Groton, Harvard, Cambridge, Mr. Culture, Mr. World Traveler. Never worked a lick in his life, never did anything of note, but he still thinks he's God's gift to planet earth." He stared thoughtfully into the distance.

"What?" I said.

"I don't know. Families are strange, aren't they? He treated her like crap, but she always had a soft spot for him. Always." A crease formed between his eyebrows. "No, that's not quite right. It was more of a love-hate thing. There was some kind of real close connection, but also some anger."

"How about after he, what, shunned her?"

He nodded. "She didn't talk about him that much afterward. But anytime she did, she got this funny look in her eye." He shrugged. "Blood's thicker than water, huh?"

"Was there any financial impact when they cut her off? Did they disown her?"

"She had a modest trust fund that they couldn't touch, but otherwise, yeah, she walked away from their money. Can we move on to something else? The subject of her family puts me in a bad mood."

"Okay. So you're married, living in New York. What then?"

He smiled fondly. "Happiest time of my life. I was working, getting published. This was my big dream, you know? The books weren't exactly selling like hotcakes. But that was okay with me. I never expected to be . . ." He smiled ironically, waved a manacled hand around the jail room. "Never expected to end up some lucky, successful bastard like I am now, showered with blessings."

"Why'd you guys move back here?"

"Just got fed up with New York. This was back in the early seventies, when the city had declared bankruptcy and all that. Stop on the street for thirty seconds, some punk would steal your wallet and spray paint his gang tag on your nuts. When I finally sold *The Bust* for big money, I sort of figured, let's get while the getting's good."

"Why Pickeral Point?"

"Why not?" He smiled ruefully. "Come back a big success, lord it over all these little assholes who'd given me grief when I was a kid. All these guys who were big men on campus, hot dates, star of the football team, now they're bagging groceries. And me? I was on the damn *Tonight Show*."

"How long did the pleasure in that last?"

"About thirty seconds."

I laughed. "So what next?"

"The funny thing is, there's no next. By the midseventies I was making money hand over fist. I bought that big old house on Riverside. We traveled a lot. India, Africa, Japan. Europe, of course. I wrote, and Diana just came along for the ride."

"That sounds almost anticlimactic."

Miles closed his eyes and turned his face to the ceiling, a fond expression on his face. "Every marriage is different, I guess, but I really believe that what we had was unusual. We were just a matched pair. I worked, and Diana—oh, she gardened, she read, she cooked, she painted watercolors." He smiled gently. "But mostly we just . . . lived.

It was a really full life. Every day felt like a gift to me while we were together."

His brow furrowed for a moment.

"I can't begin to express to you the way I was brought up. I was raised by people who were absolutely devoid of worldly expectations. Partly it was a religious thing. My folks were both religious cranks. But it was partly just a lack of imagination. My mama and daddy, they came from the poorest, most miserable background, and they were so afraid of the world that they never raised their eyes from the dirt six inches in front of their feet. They didn't like each other. They didn't like me or my sisters. They didn't like their work. They didn't like anything. *Oh, Jesus is gonna take me home someday!*" He spat the last sentence out like an epithet. "That was their out, see—their excuse for never doing anything to improve their lot.

"I guess there's a side of me that's still angry at them. I used that rage to become Miles Dane, Famous Writer. I built a persona with it, a mask to hide behind." He squinted at the locked door behind me. "But sitting around being pissed off is for the birds. What finally dawned on me, what I learned from Diana, is that you can just live right now, right here, and that it can be perfect. Every moment can be a small jewel. That's what made Diana such a marvelous person, and why I feel so privileged to have had thirty years in her company.

"You're looking for a narrative of my life?" He laughed a little. "All the colorful episodes? Shooting holes in walls, getting in fistfights with movie stars, all that crap—it was just theater, public relations. My real life, the one I had with Diana, was just one small moment after another. Diana was the most marvelous cook. She could spend half an hour making a piece of toast. And she'd bring it out and it would be the best piece of toast you ever ate."

Lisa wiped one eye with the back of her wrist. "That is so *sweet.*"

"The prosecuting attorney is obviously looking at money as a motive," I said. "Tell me about the insurance policy."

Miles looked scornful. "What a joke. I bought that policy on her twenty years ago. It's a fifty-grand payout. I know there are people living in trailer parks all over America who are stupid enough to kill somebody for chump change like that, but I'm not one of them. If I were going to kill her for money, I'd have at least bumped the policy up to a million."

"You mentioned earlier that she had a trust fund," I said. "That came up in Denkerberg's testimony, too. What can you tell us about that?"

Miles shook his head. "This is going to sound strange, but I genuinely don't know much about it. Maybe it's a rich girl thing, but Diana had an aversion to talking about money. That's partly why we ended up in the financial hole we're in. I mean, aside from the fact that we've been living like rich people without having rich people's *income*. Anyway, all I know is that she got income from the fund. But it wasn't big money. Maybe thirty, forty grand a year? Back when we were flush, she used it for her hobbies, clothes, gas money, Christmas presents, the occasional vacation, that kind of thing. The last few years we've been living on it. But what happens when she dies—whether I inherit the principal or whatever—I honestly don't even know. Sounds strange, but like I say, I never even discussed it with her."

"Does she have a will?"

"Yes. I'm her sole heir. But the trust was set up by her father or her grandfather or something. Long, long time ago. So for all I know it may have provisions that prevent me from inheriting the money. Hell, it might revert to the family."

"If it looks like you could profit in any way from her death, we need to find out."

"She had a lawyer in New York. Somebody at a firm called Shearman & Something? You'll have to talk to them."

"Shearman & Pound maybe?" Lisa said, naming a well-known white shoe law firm from New York.

"Yeah. That's it."

After a moment I said, "Miles, Lisa and I had a long discussion last night. I told her that this job is best performed if you don't worry about whether your client is guilty or innocent. She disagreed. And now that I've heard your story, I think she was right."

"Oh?" Suddenly he looked resentful and annoyed again.

"My instincts say you're innocent. And if that's the case, then we need to know who really did this and why."

I let the silence eat at him for a while. I could see in his odd gray eyes that there was something he was holding back. It was a terribly frustrating. There's nothing worse than fighting your own client.

"I told you what I know," he said finally, his voice flat, uninflected.

"You told us what you *saw*," Lisa said. "That's not the same thing."

Miles looked over at my daughter, then back at me. He grinned. "She's a sharp one, isn't she?"

"You're not answering the question," Lisa said. "Let's just assume you told us exactly what you saw. Now tell us what you *know*."

Miles didn't answer.

"There was somebody at your house that night," Lisa said. "A man driving an old black Lincoln."

Miles's face went blank and unreadable, but still he didn't speak.

"Who was the man in the black Lincoln, Miles?"

Suddenly Miles stood, started banging on the heavy steel door with the flat of his hand. His face had gone hard—the same face he showed to Chantall Denkerberg, the same face I'd seen him wear on the TV shows back when his career was still hot. "Guard? Hey, bud. We're about done in here."

"Who was it, Miles?" I demanded.

As the guard's key rattled in the lock, Miles said, "You might fish around, see if the prosecutor would be willing to go for a plea. Manslaughter? Five, six years, something in that range? Hell, I might just take it."

Seventeen

AFTER THE TROUBLING meeting with Miles, I went next door to the courthouse to take care of a few minor matters, but the whole time I was thinking about what Lisa and I had discussed. Suppose Miles was innocent; then why would he be behaving the way he was? Why, after protesting his innocence, would he suddenly be saying he was interested in a plea? And what about the clothes and the murder weapon that Detective Denkerberg had found in the boat? How could you explain those away?

Either he'd fooled us both, and he did it. Or he was protecting someone. Someone who drove an old black Lincoln with the suicide doors.

I stopped by Stash Olesky's office on the pretense of asking him about Leon Prouty and some other small cases I was handling. As our conversation appeared ready to wind down I said, "You really plan to go all the way with Miles Dane, huh?"

"As opposed to what?"

I made a face to indicate that I hadn't given the issue much thought. "Oh, I don't know. You haven't offered him a plea yet."

"I've got his clothes. Covered in blood. Why would I offer a plea?"

"That reminds me," I said. "How in the world did you find those clothes? I looked at a map. That neighbor whose boat you found those clothes in is ten houses up the street. Don't tell me you searched every house, every yard, every boat, every dock on the entire street. Somebody tipped you."

Stash's face suddenly took on a cagey expression. "So? What's that got to do with a plea? Does he want to plead or not?"

I shrugged, languid as a sunbather on a beach in Tahiti. "I haven't really discussed it with him. He'd probably laugh in my face if I did. He maintains he's a hundred percent innocent, never say die, the whole nine. And you know what? I believe him. But I'm a big boy, Stash. Looking at what's out there right now, frankly, I wouldn't be doing my job if I didn't ask."

Stash met my gaze with his skeptical blue eyes. "One of my general rules in life is that anytime anybody says 'frankly' to me, they're being less than entirely frank."

I put a look of comic horror on my face. "Are you, sir, accusing me of prevarication? Meet me at sundown, my good man, and I shall challenge you to pistols at two paces."

"Only *two?*"

"Anything more than that, I'd be just as likely to shoot myself as to hit you."

Stash laughed.

"Seriously, though . . ." I said. "Any thoughts on a plea?"

Stash laughed again.

I stood and stretched. "I take it your derisive tone means you have no interest in offering a plea?"

Stash continued to laugh. "Get out of here before I think of something else to charge him with."

"You're a terrible, heartless man, Stash," I said. "And a discredit to your profession." This had become my standard farewell to the prosecuting attorney lately.

Stash, however, preferred to improvise a new insult every time. "The only thief worse than your clients is you, Charley."

And off I went. So there would be no plea.

AFTER THAT I paged Leon Prouty. He called me back on my cell about ten minutes later. "What," he demanded.

"It's Charley Sloan. You got a minute to talk?"

"I'm kinda busy."

"So am I."

Leon hawked up some phlegm. I'm sure that was his way of showing how much he liked me. "Yeah, okay. I'm at a job site."

"Not stealing anything, I presume."

"Nah, this is more or less legit."

I didn't care to ask what "more or less" meant; I just got directions and drove over.

I FOUND LEON and a crew of Mexicans planting bushes in the parking lot of an aging strip mall over on the bypass. The bushes looked half-dead, and the strip mall was by no means prosperous: a down-at-the-heels Bible store, a martial arts academy, a nail salon with a sign written in Vietnamese, and two empty spaces, their windows covered with plywood.

Leon was leaning on a shovel.

"Whassup," he said sleepily.

"Yeah, same to you, too," I said. "The reason I'm here is I wanted to talk to you a little more about this guy you claim to have seen coming out of Miles Dane's house."

"I *claim* to have seen?"

"You're practically a professional thief. I'm supposed to take your word for it?"

Leon Prouty shouted something in Spanish to one of the Mexicans.

"You speak Spanish?" I said.

"It's what I call Spandscapelish." He tossed his shovel on the ground, looked at me with a hard expression. "You got a lot riding on this case, Mr. Sloan. I seen what I seen. You want me to help you, then you got to help me. It's that simple."

"I told you the other day I can't pay you for testimony. That's unethical."

"Hey, then nothing personal, Mr. Sloan, but screw you and screw Miles Dane. Why should I give a damn about him?"

"I don't know. Common decency?"

"That don't pay my rent." He yelled something at another crew member. "Anyway, I don't like Miles that much."

I raised my eyebrows. "You *know* him?"

"Sure."

"How?"

"From church."

"Neither of you seem like the churchgoing type."

"I don't go much anymore. But we're both old snakeheads."

Snakeheads. I remembered that Regina, the receptionist at the police station, had referred to Leon as *that snakehead boy.*

"Snakeheads?" I said.

Leon looked at me curiously. "How long you been living in this town?"

"Somewhere in the neighborhood of a decade."

Leon nodded. "Surprised you don't know what a snakehead is by now."

"Why don't you just explain it."

"Tell you a little story, might interest you. Back around the Depression, they was a sharecropper by the name of Ralph Lee Dinwoodie from aroundabouts Philadelphia, Mississippi. Down on the delta. Ralph Lee, he come up this way intending to get a job at Ford. Overshot somehow, ended up working on the docks here. Within a couple years fifteen, twenty families, white sharecroppers, poorer than dirt, they all moved up to Pickeral Point. I don't know why, but all them families stuck together. The people in Pickeral Point never could seem to tolerate us. Never did mix. That little neighborhood over by the boat factory—you ever heard it called Snaketown?"

"Yeah. I never knew why, though."

"Well that's where us snakeheads live at."

"What's this have to do with Miles Dane?"

"Ralph Lee Dinwoodie? He's my great-great-uncle or something like that. And he's Miles's grandfather. That makes us some kind of shirttail kin."

"No kidding. So what about this snakehead thing?"

"All them rednecks—my people, *Miles's people*—when they come up here, they built 'em a little old frame church on the edge of town. Still there. Church of the Living Water? You ever seen it? And Ralph Lee Dinwoodie, he was the pastor. When he kicked, his son-in-law, Miles's daddy, took over preaching. Wasn't a full-time job or nothing, he was just a lay preacher. It's a charismatic church. Speaking in tongues, whooping, rolling on the floor, spirit-filled witnessing . . ."

"Where's the snakehead part?"

"That's what I was getting at. Miles's daddy one time he had him a vision. That passage in the Bible about drinking poison and taking up serpents? You familiar with that?"

"You're talking about snake handling."

Leon Prouty nodded. "Miles's daddy, man, he got him a bunch of rattlesnakes, started using them in the service. Hollering and preaching and waving these goddamn snakes around, jack, it must of been some crazy shit. This would of been when Miles was ten, twelve years old. So anyway, one day his daddy's going at it, fire and brimstone, kissing them snakes on the lips and everything, and that snake just— SHOOMP!" Leon mimicked a striking snake with his hand. "Sumbitch bit him right on the goddamn nose. The way I heard it told, he kept preaching and everybody's beating tambourines and singing and holler- ing. Big old test of faith, see? Because the faithful, according to the scripture, they can take up snakes and drink poison and it won't do nothing to them.

"Well pretty soon his face goes to swelling up. He's still waving them snakes around, preaching the Word, lo, though I walk through valley of the shadow of death, blahdy blahdy blah, and everybody's sing- ing and hollering. And old Miles, man, he's sitting right there on the front row watching it. Watching when his daddy falls down on the floor, all them snakes crawlin' around on his ass and everything?

"And do they take him to the hospital? Shit no! This bunch of crackers—*my* people!—they just keep slapping the tambourines and singing: Oh, *hell* yeah, they're mighty in the faith, ain't they? Miles's daddy, his head's blowed up like a balloon. Lips start turning black, ears swoled up, tongue sticking out. Oh, but he's mighty, mighty in his faith!" Leon Prouty pantomimed clapping and rocking, waving his hands in the air, his tongue sticking out and his eyes rolled back in his head.

He kept up this horrible eye-rolling performance until finally I said, "So what happened?"

The performance abruptly stopped. "What you think, Mr. Sloan? He died."

My eyes widened a little. "Right there in front of Miles?"

"Sure."

"My God. No wonder the guy writes such gruesome stories."

"So that's why they call us snakeheads. Church is still there, still the center of Snaketown. Ain't nobody taking up by-God serpents in there, though."

"Miles must feel terrible guilt about that. Terrible shame."

"Shame!" Leon Prouty looked at me quizzically. "Man, his daddy's a hero over in Snaketown. Took his faith right to the grave."

"You still go to church?"

"*Hell*, no. I don't believe none of that propaganda no more. But when I was a kid, old Miles use to show up every now and then. He'd only come to church when he was drunk." Leon laughed. "All us kids loved it. He'd get to confessing what a sinner he was, some terrible thing he'd did back in the day, bawling and crying like a baby. He'd come up for the altar call, lay there on the floor howling like a sick dog, 'Oh, I'm coming home to Jesus.' Then he'd head out the door, and you wouldn't see him again for like a year."

"What terrible thing had he done?"

"How should I remember? It was a long time ago." Leon shrugged. "Anyway, I got to get back to work."

"Doing what? Holding up your shovel?"

Leon raised his head back so he could look down at me in a vaguely threatening manner. "I don't *have* to tell you nothing."

"Did you see that guy or not? The one with the black car?"

"It was a black Lincoln Continental, early-sixties model, the type with the suicide doors. I told you that already."

"What else? What else did you see?"

"Asked and answered, Counselor." Leon smirked at me. "Come back when you willing to get serious about my situation."

Eighteen

I DROVE BACK to the office feeling irritated. Was Leon for real or not? I just couldn't tell. But my irritation deepened into a distinct sense of unease as I saw the TV trucks: There were five of them parked in the street outside my office, aerials sticking up in the sky, three from local stations, plus one from Court TV and another from CNN. When you're a defense attorney, five TV trucks is never a good sign.

I hopped out of my Chrysler and here they came, heading across the parking lot like an onrushing thunderstorm, microphones extended.

"What about the book?"

"Do you know about the book?"

"What are your comments about the book?"

"Which book would that be?" I said.

They got a little quieter. The CNN reporter said, "You haven't heard? They just reissued a book that Miles published back in the seventies. They drop-shipped six hundred thousand copies of it today. Nationwide."

I smiled blandly. "And?"

"It's called, *How I Killed My Wife and Got Away with It.*"

I blinked and stood there for a moment, looking, I'm sure, like everybody's picture of somebody caught flat-footed. Things were just getting better and better.

"Oh *that* book," I said finally, giving them my best attempt at a smile. "You may recall it says on the cover that it's a work of fiction. It has nothing to do with this case." Then I turned and walked up the stairs to my office, trying my best not to look like someone had kicked me in the stomach.

I had never heard of the book before.

Nineteen

I MET WITH Miles in the jail. He was sitting at the grimy table, hands flat on the Masonite surface, fingers splayed. He didn't speak when I entered the room, or when I asked him how he was doing.

"Okay, two things," I said. "First, Stash Olesky laughed at me when I brought up the possibility of a plea."

Miles continued to stare at the back of his hands.

"Did you hear me, Miles?"

He shrugged almost imperceptibly. "It was probably a bad idea anyway."

"Any interest in telling me why the sudden suggestion that you'd take a plea?"

"I just want this whole thing over with." His voice was soft, weary.

"I know," I said. "But you're just going to have to keep it together. There's no other choice."

He nodded.

I tapped my fingers on the table a couple of times. "You might have warned me about that book," I said finally.

"Book?"

"*How I Killed My Wife And Got Away with It.* Apparently they're getting all cranked up to sell it by the boatload."

Miles looked up for the first time. "Charley, I've written forty-seven novels in my life, of which thirty-three have been published. Every one of them involves murder. Honestly? They all start to run together after a while. That particular book just didn't spring to mind."

"So tell me about it."

"I wrote it as a paperback original for Elgin Press back in the early seventies. That was when Dan Rourke, my editor, was still at Elgin. He moved over to Padgett Press soon after that, and I followed him." He blew out his breath disconsolately. "I have to tell you, I don't even remember the book all that well. It's pretty much like the title says: It's about this guy who kills his wife."

"Why does he kill her?" I said.

He hesitated. "Basically? For the money."

I rolled my eyes. "Great."

"What can I say?" Miles said. "I invent murders for a living. There's just no way to make that convenient in a situation like this." He leaned forward. "I assume they can't admit it into evidence?"

"That's not the issue," I said.

"Then what is?"

"You're a smart guy," I said. "You tell me."

He studied me with his sad gray eyes, then leaned slowly back in his chair again, a humorless smile appearing on his lips. "Public opinion."

"You get the gold star," I said.

They talk about the court of public opinion. There's no getting away from it these days: A high-profile case gets on TV, and it's contaminated forever. You can change venue, you can excuse nine-tenths of the jury pool, you can make the jury suffer under a draconian sequestration regime. But the truth is that if a case turns into a media feeding frenzy, you're just going to be stuck with a certain number of jurors whose judgment will be affected by things they read in the papers or hear on the radio or see on the idiot box. Any lawyer who says it ain't so is kidding himself.

How I Killed My Wife and Got Away with It. I'm no humorist, but given about fifteen minutes, I could have written enough jokes for every talk-show monologue on TV that night. "Did you hear about that famous writer in Michigan who killed his wife?" Jay Leno raises his eyebrows, looks at the camera. "*Allegedly . . .*" And then the crowd dies laughing.

How I Killed My Wife and Got Away with It. Ten words. Ten words, and everybody in America would know the guilty bastard did it. Didn't matter that the book would probably never be admitted as evidence at trial, didn't matter that it was a work of fiction, didn't matter that the crime in the book would most likely have no resemblance to the real crime at hand. Those ten words would infect the air, and there'd be no getting rid of the stink.

A S IT HAPPENED, my meeting with Miles preceded an appointment for Lisa and me to go to the prosecutor's office, where we would cull through their documents and examine their proposed exhibit list.

Stash Olesky was waiting for me in his conference room, a grim look on his face, the list of documents in his hand.

"Let me see it," I said.

He handed me the list. At the top, Proposed Exhibit 1, there it was: *"How I Killed My Wife and Got Away with It, a novel by Miles Dane."*

"You knew about this already didn't you?"

Stash looked away.

"All this time, I knew you guys had something else hiding back there, but I couldn't figure out what it was."

"I'm disclosing it in a timely fashion," Stash said, his face taut. "That's all I'm obliged to do."

"Well, you're dreaming if you think it's going to be admitted at trial," I said. "Not even a judge as biased and prosecution-friendly as Evola is dumb enough to think he can let a work of fiction into a court of law and not get dinged on appeal."

"You haven't read the book yet," Stash said.

I figured that was just gamesmanship on his part. But still, there was something in his voice, a note of calm self-assurance, that made me nervous.

Twenty

THAT AFTERNOON I had to go down to Detroit to handle a case in Recorder's Court. When I got back into the office late that evening, Lisa was standing next to Mrs. Fenton's desk. In her hand she held a shiny new paperback. "I stood in line at Borders for an hour and a half." Lisa looked like she had just been force-fed a piece of three-day-old fish. "I've been reading it all afternoon."

I studied her face. "Don't tell me it's *that* bad."

"Worse."

"It's a work of fiction, Lisa. They can't admit it into evidence."

"Listen." Lisa opened the book and said, "Page one." Then she began to read.

"*Last night I decided to kill my wife.*

"*I had been considering the matter for a long time, of course, but now I am finally resolved. If this sounds heartless, do not abandon me yet. She is a vile, heartless creature—a monster, in truth—and deserves what I am about to give her. Oh, naturally I tell people how marvelous our love is, how deep the river, how wide the sea, how strong the current. And she plays her part in public. People, after all, are fools. They will believe anything. But the truth is, I fear and hate her, and she despises me. But as I say, please do not abandon me yet. Once you know her as I do, you shall cheer for me as I beat her to death.*"

I sat down heavily. "Ouch."

"It gets worse."

"Evola can't allow it to be admitted. He just can't."

"Oh, yes he can. And he will."

I studied her face. Lisa looked pretty sure of herself. "Why?"

Lisa pulled out a volume of Michigan's criminal statutes, opened it, tossed it on the desk in front of me. "It's all right there," she said.

I glanced at the book. "I've read the statute. What's in there that I'm not seeing?"

"Michigan law says there are five conditions you have to meet in order to convict on first-degree murder, right? Condition three is the trickiest one." She picked up the book and read from it. " 'Third, that this intent to kill was premeditated, that is, thought out beforehand.' "

"Which has what to do with this?"

She tossed me the book. "I've stuck bookmarks in there in a few places, underlined various passages. Check it out."

I opened the book and began to read the parts she had marked. When I was done, I set the book delicately on my desk, much like you might treat a bomb, and then I looked up at the ceiling. A numb, cold feeling had settled on the base of my neck.

"Oh my God," I said. "Oh. My. God."

"I better go to New York," Lisa said. "Don't you think?"

I breathed out heavily. "Yeah," I said. "Get on the phone to Shearman & Pound."

Twenty-one

ON THE WAY to take Lisa to the airport down in Detroit, I stopped off at the jail and requested a meeting with Miles. He had asked me to bring him a battery-operated radio, a couple of books, some wool socks, a few other odds and ends.

Lisa and I went in and sat down with him in the interview room.

"How about some music?" Miles said. "Every kid in here has a radio, and they're all playing this goddamn rap music from dawn till dusk."

Lisa turned on the radio. There was something wrong with it and after a good deal of fiddling it became clear that it only picked up one signal—a Canadian station with a French-speaking announcer, as it happened.

"This book," I said, after Lisa finally gave up on the radio. "It's very bad news."

Miles blew some air out of his mouth, puffing out his cheeks. "Yeah," he said. "I got to thinking about it. About what's in that book, I mean. I haven't read it probably in twenty-five years. But once I started going over the story in my mind . . . Well, there's an awful lot of coincidence there, isn't there?"

"Maybe more than coincidence," Lisa said.

"That's what I mean," Miles said. "Coincidence in the sense of not really being coincidence at all."

"Can you think of anybody who would have read this book?" I said.

"Somebody who might have tried to manipulate the death of your wife to make it look like . . . well . . ."

"You're talking about somebody framing me," Miles said.

I was silent for a moment. "I've been a criminal defense attorney for over twenty years, Miles. I've never even *heard* of a successful frame-up. Or even an unsuccessful one for that matter. Frame-ups are for the movies. Too complicated for real life. But I am thinking maybe somebody nudged the facts around a little, knowing that there were some parallels with this book."

"Will the judge admit it?"

I cleared my throat. "I hope not. We'll go to the mat on this one."

Miles stared across the room for a while. The woman jabbering away in French on the radio finally shut up and started playing some music, an old French waltz with a sweet and wonderfully maudlin fiddle part.

"No," he said. "I'm at a total loss here. That book's probably been out of print since we left New York. I just, I just . . ." He sighed a long, racking sigh.

We sat silently for a while, Lisa and I looking at Miles, and Miles staring gloomily at the floor.

After a minute or so of this dismal scene Lisa stood, took Miles by one manacled hand and pulled him to his feet. She slid herself inside the circle of his arms and rested her head against his shoulder, then led him into an awkward dance around the room to the sound of the plaintive fiddle. His ankle chains clinked softly in waltz time as they dragged on the floor.

As their dance continued, Miles slowly relaxed, as though all the tension and horror of the past weeks had begun slowly to drain away. The initial awkwardness of their movements disappeared, and soon they were dancing smoothly, despite the chains, as though both their bodies were under the control of a single mind. By the end of the song, Miles was beaming as he danced, eyes closed, seemingly lost in some other place.

After the song ended and the French announcer began talking again, we packed up and left without saying another word, leaving Miles standing in the middle of the room, eyes still shut, lips upturned slightly at the corners, rocking gently back and forth to the music in his head.

Twenty-two

How do I hate expert witnesses? Let me count the ways.

In a case like this one, you need experts. It's a given. Somebody to undermine the blood evidence, the hair, the fiber, the blood spatter, whatever. Maybe a psychologist to say that Miles Dane was incapable of doing what the prosecuting attorney says he did. A defense attorney can't live without them. But boy oh boy do I hate them.

The first call I made was to James D. Meriwether, MD, from Chicago, the retired medical examiner of Cook County and a legendary expert witness forensic pathologist. His expertise was in finding fault with autopsies. He combined all the traits you want in an expert: a bulletproof résumé, first-rate knowledge of the field, brass balls, the instincts of an actor, a firm jaw, and a lovely head of hair.

Here's how the phone call went.

"Charles, marvelous to hear from you." He had a big, radio announcer's voice, well modulated, oozing charm. "I've been following your case with a great deal of interest."

"Wonderful, Dr. Meriwether. I go by Charley. I've heard great things about you."

"All true." Ha ha ha. Big laugh, a man not afraid to enjoy his own sparkling wit. "I'm due at the skeet range in a few minutes. Shall we cut to the chase?"

"I'd be interested in using you for the Miles Dane case."

"Marvelous. Based on what I've read, I think I could be of great value to you. FedEx me a copy of the ME's report, the police file, all pleadings in the matter, and a retainer in the amount of $20,000, and I'll get started on it tomorrow. My rate is $750 an hour and my total bill including prep, expenses, and testimony will likely run between forty and sixty K. I bill by the month, and if payments aren't up-to-date as of trial, I don't testify."

Like I said, let me count the ways. Reason one: greed.

"I'll be honest with you, Doctor," I said, "I just don't have that kind of budget. Of course I can offer a great deal of exposure and—"

"Exposure doesn't heat my pool, Charley." The big self-congratulatory laugh again. "Were I you, I'd instruct your client to dig around in the sofa for a few more nickels. Call me again when Mr. Dane can afford the best."

So much for phone call number one. Phone call number two went to the Right Reverend Doctor Bobby Ray Armitage III, MD, JD, MDiv, a professor who taught at Emory University in Atlanta in the schools of law, medicine, *and* divinity. Given all the time he'd spent earning degrees, I figured he'd spent a good fifteen minutes in the actual practice of law, medicine, or the ministry. But that was alright. He had a hugely impressive résumé, and I thought the divinity part would play well on the stand. Plus, I'd heard his rates were reasonable.

"Mr. Sloan I can't tell you what a *pleasure* it is to talk to you. Really. I've been following your case and it *really* looks like a travesty, a *terrible* injustice."

"Well, I certainly think so."

"What can I do for you, sir?" He had the accent of a rich Southerner of the old school, but dripping with the sort of exaggerated concern that I associate with pointy-headed liberals of the Eastern university genus.

I gave him an outline of the case, buttering him up about his qualifications and his good judgment. Then he told me about several cases involving poor, downtrodden innocents whom he'd represented after getting out of Yale Law back in '71.

Finally—reluctantly—he broached the subject of fees. I told him that I could spare $7,500 plus T&E, cash on the barrelhead, take it or leave it.

After thinking about it for a minute, Bobby Ray Armitage said. "Okay. What do you want me to say?"

My heart sank. Reason two: dishonesty. I hate guys like Meriwether for their arrogance and greed. But at least Meriwether is honest. It's the whores who really bother me.

I floated a trial balloon: "I want you to testify that the autopsy is flawed, that the ME is a scoundrel and an incompetent, and that my client could not possibly have committed the crime."

"Make it ten grand even, I'll testify the pope's a Southern Baptist," the Right Reverend Dr. Armitage said. Apparently his pool cost a good deal less to heat than Dr. Meriwether's.

People like Armitage make my skin crawl. I told him I'd be in touch if and when I needed him.

After that it was more of the same and more of the same and more of the same. It took almost thirty calls to assemble a team of experts whom Miles Dane could afford and who didn't make me feel like taking a shower when I was done speaking with them. Thirty phone calls and I'd already blown well over half my budget for the trial.

I ONCE DREW a grid onto the back of a napkin to describe the qualities you might find in an expert. Here's how the thing came out:

| Attractive | Actor | Ethical | Cheap | Strong Credentials/Knowledge |
| Ugly | Poor performer | Whore | Expensive | Weak Credentials/Knowledge |

The perfect witness is an honest brilliant good-looking person, well educated and with a masterly command of the field, who has the acting instincts and skills of a Jack Nicholson and who is willing to testify, not for money, but for the sheer love of doing good. Such a person, for all practical purposes, doesn't exist. So you make do.

For my blood spatter expert I had to settle for a cheap, honest woman of modest credentials. She was also gorgeous—which is more important in the courtroom than we'd like to admit. For my autopsy expert I found a forensic pathologist with middling credentials, who seemed reasonably ethical in his approach. I had never met him so I wasn't sure how he'd be on the stand . . . but he sounded okay on the phone. There's no such thing as a cheap doctor, but under the circumstances, his fees were pretty darn fair. My psychiatrist—in case I ended up needing one—was a close friend, Bob Williams, who came cheap as a personal favor to me. And last of all, since it seemed like a long shot that I'd need a tool mark expert, I broke down and went with the expert witness version of a truckstop whore.

By the time I was done, my twenty-grand budget for experts had roughly doubled. The one thing that was entirely plain to me after I'd finally gotten all my experts corralled: This trial would eat me alive financially.

Particularly if I lost. State prison, after all, is not much of a place to raise money so you can pay your lawyer.

Twenty-three

"DAD? DAD? HELLO? Are you there?" As soon as I heard Lisa's voice on the answering machine, I knew something was wrong. And ten to one I knew what it was. "Dad can you call me? I, um . . . look, just please call. It's important. Kind of a good news, bad news thing." She left the name and number of the hotel where she was staying.

People, places, and things: That's the slogan of AA. The central tenet of the high church of addiction recovery is that alcoholics run into trouble when they find themselves amongst the people, places, and things where they used to drink. Stay away from the old crowd, you've got a chance of staying clean. Hang out with your old running buddies, you fall off the wagon.

I'd just sent my own daughter back to the place and the people and the things where she'd run into trouble in the first place. Stupid, stupid, stupid.

I felt like I'd had a pretty good year. After paying my rent, my mortgage, Mrs. Fenton's salary, my car payment, alimony payments to my third wife (who has stubbornly refused to remarry and who even more stubbornly believes that she should continue to live on the same grand scale she did when we were married and I made a great deal more money than I do), and the eye-popping sticker price of another year at an Ivy League law school, I had about three grand left in the bank. I hadn't made arrangements to sell the shotgun yet, so the fifty-grand retainer that I was due from Miles Dane still only existed in virtual reality. A couple more flights to New York and I'd be running on fumes. I did some back-of-the-envelope calculations, then called my travel agent and told her to book me on a red-eye to New York.

After that I stowed a beautiful wooden box in the trunk of my Chrysler, got in the car, and drove to the airport. I kept hitting redial on my cell, trying Lisa's room at the hotel, but nobody answered.

M Y FLIGHT REACHED La Guardia at a little before two in the morning. I called Lisa at her hotel again, but nobody answered. I took a cab to the same Midtown hotel, checked in, then went to Lisa's room and knocked on the door. It was past three by then. Still no answer. My heart sank.

"Lisa! Lisa! Are you there?" I banged on the door with my fist. "Lisa!"

A door down the hall opened and a sleepy-looking young guy glared at me. He wore a gold ring through his upper lip, and black geometrical tattoos ran from his right shoulder to his wrist.

"Sorry," I said. When you start waking up the tattoo-and-lip-ring people, it's time to pack it in for the night.

T HE NEXT MORNING I called Lisa's ex-roommate and a variety of her law school acquaintances and professors who I hoped would know where Lisa was. But none of them had seen her.

Since wandering the streets aimlessly in hopes of bumping into her seemed like a fruitless plan, I decided to get some work done and wait for her to call. First, I called Sotheby's and asked to speak to whoever was in charge of selling shotguns. Eventually I reached a man named Elliot Fosterthwaite III. He sounded very busy and preoccupied until I explained that I was looking to sell a near-flawless boxlock Purdey double gun with Damascus barrels and extensive engraving. He allowed as how he might be able to spare a moment or two that morning.

I took a cab down to Sotheby's, where I was treated to tea on Spode china and a great deal of fussing.

Elliot Fosterthwaite, a tall man with a fake British accent and a double-vented English suit with the seams pulled just a hair too tight, praised the gun to the heavens. Some unusual details in the lock mechanism, the marvelous condition of the barrels, the intricacy and condition of the gold inlay on the brightwork—well, it was a terribly, terribly exciting gun. Possibly verging on *important*. Pity there was some unfortunate wear on the brightwork. Elliot shouldered the weapon and pretended he was blasting a brace of pheasants.

"How soon can you sell it?" I said.

"Lucky for you, we have our major firearms sale coming up very, very soon."

"How soon is very very?"

"May 11." Elliot smiled.

"That's six months!"

Elliot Fosterthwaite blinked. "I suppose we could put it in with the antique arms in February." A sad smile. "But I'm afraid the catalogue's already been printed. And if you really want the sort of hammer price this gun deserves, you'll need to wait for the firearms collection anyway."

I put the gun back in its walnut case and headed for the door.

I CALLED LISA's hotel room again. No answer. Then I visited the gun maven at Christies. The outlook for quick cash turned out to be as dismal there as it had been at Sotheby's. Finally, I checked the yellow pages. Which led me to take a cab to a store on the Upper East Side—R. Phelan & Son, on Lexington Avenue—which billed itself as "Purveyor of the World's Finest Arms."

I was greeted at the door by a man in his late seventies who introduced himself, not especially warmly, as Seamus Phelan. Like Elliot Fosterthwaite, he was done to the nines in handmade English togs. His accent, however, was pure New York.

I opened the walnut case, revealing the disassembled shotgun.

"Hm." Phelan peered at it apathetically, then sighed loudly. "Well. Let's have a look in the back."

I followed him through a door into a tiny, dark, Dickensian workshop, where he put on a worn leather apron. He fitted the barrel on the stock, hefted the weapon, then screwed a jeweler's loupe in his eye, using it to scrutinize the engraving, then the barrels. Next he used a very expensive-looking ebony-and-brass-handled screwdriver to disassemble the gun, taking out the lock and examining every scrap of the mechanism in minute detail. During the entire inspection he never spoke a word, only grunting dubiously now and then. When he was done, a litter of parts lay on his workbench.

"I hope you know how to put it back together," I said, aiming for a little humor.

"Well, the good news," he growled, "it's not a fake."

"I'm aware of that," I said. "The provenance is entirely in order." So as to avoid my seeming like a sucker, Miles had given me detailed instructions about the lingo used by shotgun aficionados.

"Provenance!" The old man snorted. "Had a fellow come in here the other day with bills of sale going all the way back to Lord Acton for a supposed Cogswell & Harrison hammer gun. Cogswell & Harrison? Hah! It was a second-rate W&C Scott that somebody had tarted up a little, fooled around with the lock, added some cheap Spanish engraving, so on, so forth. It wouldn't have fooled a four-year-old child. Every one of those bills of sale was a forgery. You'd be amazed."

"Be that as it may, we both agree this one's real. Are you interested?"

He shrugged, made a face. "Got too much inventory now."

"I didn't see a Purdy with Damascus barrels and gold inlay out there," I said. Not that I'd have known a Purdy from a water-cooled machine gun.

Another broad shrug, another face. "Let me see the papers."

I showed him what I'd brought. He narrowed his eyes when he saw the bill of sale to Miles Dane. "Miles Dane? He's that guy. That writer. The one that killed his wife."

"Allegedly. I'm his attorney."

There was a sudden glimmer of interest. "He's raising cash to pay the shysters, huh?"

"Not really," I said. "He's just shuffling some assets around. Rich people do that from time to time. Makes them feel frisky."

Phelan didn't crack a smile. He looked down at the disassembled shotgun, then said, in the most skeptical New York tones, "Well. I suppose I could ask the old man, see what he says." He turned and hobbled up a dark staircase in the corner of the room, moving slowly and quietly, as though he were trying to sneak up on somebody. The old man? If Phelan *père* actually existed, he must have been a hundred and ninety years old.

I waited for a long time. Eventually Phelan the Younger hobbled back down.

"He's not sure," Seamus Phelan said.

"Not *sure*? Look, spare me the good cop, bad cop," I said. "Just give me a number."

Phelan smiled for the first time, very briefly. "There's no good cop," he said. "Me and the old man, we're both the bad cop."

"How much?"

"We could go forty."

"Put it back together," I said. "I'm going back to Sotheby's."

"Time you pay the commission, insurance, catalogue fees, handling, cartage, whatever other nonsense they can nickel-and-dime you with, Sotheby's ends up a terrible deal."

"Put the gun back together."

Phelan didn't move. "Plus you've got to wait till the firearms sale comes up in May. You try selling it at the antique arms sale, you won't get what you want for it."

I crossed my arms and gave him a hard stare.

"Okay," Phelan said. "The old man says I can go forty-six."

I just stood there, didn't move a muscle.

After what seemed a very long time, Phelan said, "Hold on." As he went creeping up the stairs again, I wiped a little sweat off my brow. Eventually he came back down with a check in his hand.

"Final offer," he said, and tried to hand me the check.

I looked at the check and laughed. Despite my bravado, however, I had a sinking feeling that I wouldn't do a lot better in any sort of reasonable time frame.

Phelan curled his lip. "We both know the score here, Mr. Sloan," he said. "Your client has his keister in a crack and needs cash. You're over a barrel. You can go to any gun dealer in the city, they'll sniff it out as quickly as me. You don't stay in this business for long without knowing what's what. Difference between me and the others—most of them, they can't raise this kind of money in five minutes."

To tell the truth, this was about what I'd expected. But still, cold hard reality puts a knot in your gut. I took the check, folded it in half, put it in my coat. So that was it. Now I was going to have to make this entire case fly, not on eighty thousand, but on fifty-two five. Which would barely cover expenses.

This whole case was feeling more and more like a train wreck.

Twenty-four

To my infinite relief, Lisa answered the door of her hotel room when I knocked. She looked terrible—her skin pale and greenish.

"Where's your meeting?" I said.

"I haven't been in almost a year."

"That's not what I asked. Where is it?"

"A YWCA up near Columbia."

"Does it meet tonight?"

She looked at her watch nervously. She was clutching a large leather portfolio under her arm, as though afraid it might run away if she put it down. "This afternoon actually."

"Let's go," I said.

The AA meeting began at four-thirty. Lisa and I sat next to each other in the back row of folding chairs. She was still carrying the leather portfolio.

"My name is Charley," I said as the meeting began, "and I'm an alcoholic."

"My name is Lisa," my daughter said. "I'm an alcoholic."

If there were things she needed to say, I didn't want my presence keeping her from saying them. I leaned over and whispered to her as the other members introduced themselves. "This one is yours, not mine. I'll be waiting outside."

Twenty-five

Aᴼᴿᴛᴇʀ ʟɪsᴀ ᴄᴀᴍᴇ back outside, I said, "You slipped. It happens. It was thoughtless of me to send you here. Let's head on out to the airport and fly back to Michigan."

"I can't," she said. Her mascara had run and was now all over her cheeks. I took out my handkerchief, wiped her face.

"Am I wasting my time being here?" I said.

She looked up and down the street, as though expecting someone to come up and grab the leather portfolio she was still clutching in her arms.

"Lisa?"

"I don't *know*, Dad!" she said.

"Let's at least go back to the hotel."

She looked at her watch. "Can't."

"What do you mean?"

"Look, on the phone I said I had good news and bad news. The bad news is that I called Shearman & Pound's trust department. I couldn't squeeze anything out of the woman I talked to. You know how it is; at first she wouldn't even confirm that Diana Dane was a client. I said the prosecuting attorney would get the trust documents sooner or later, so she might as well give them to me now. She said, 'Mr. Olesky has already requested them. We're currently litigating the matter.' "

"So what's the good news?"

"I'm having a drink with Diana Dane's brother."

"Really?"

"I got him on a pretext," Lisa said. "We're getting together at the Oak Bar down at the Plaza Hotel. I'll see if I can work things around to Diana and Miles, pump him for information."

"Drinks?" I said dubiously.

"I'll be fine." She put something resembling a smile on her face and hugged the portfolio to her chest.

"No you won't."

Lisa looked up and down the street again. Suddenly it was as if something had melted in her eyes. "I'm sorry, Dad. I'm being a jerk. We'll go together. When we get there, you can get a table next to us and sort of keep an eye on us. If you're watching me, I know I won't have a problem sticking to soda water."

We began walking.

"So what's in the portfolio?" I said after we'd gone three or four blocks.

She gave me a sidelong mysterious look. "You'll see."

THE OAK ROOM at the Plaza is an old, famous bar where people smoke cigars and show off how rich they are by swilling drinks that cost ten dollars a pop. It has a twenty-foot-high ceiling, marble floors, big chairs, good service, and just about the right amount of noise—enough to make you feel like you're being fun and witty in the company of other fun and witty people but not loud enough to drown out your conversation. In short, back in my days of drink and megalomania I would have loved the place. Now, however, it made me feel like an aging hick lawyer. My suit wasn't as nice or as well pressed or as well fitting as most of the men's in the room; I was alone at my table; and the smell of expensive cigars and single malt whiskey reminded me of the many things gone forever from my life.

Lisa sat down at a small round table about eight feet away from me, setting the portfolio next to her chair. She had just gotten her coat off when a very tall man wearing a bow tie and a Brooks Brothers suit approached her table. He was probably six-foot-three, broad-shouldered but somewhat stooped, with a head of soft white hair that floated over his face like airborne lint. He looked like a university professor who'd played lacrosse or football in college, then let himself go. His lower lip protruded slightly, and his face was asymmetrical so that one side looked quite pleasant and the other somewhat predatory, as though two different instincts were warring inside him.

"Lisa?" he said.

"Good afternoon, Mr. van Blaricum." Lisa showed her even teeth and suddenly looked very much like a grown-up.

"Please. Call me Roger." Somehow he didn't strike me as the call-me-Roger type. His manner was slightly pedantic, and his accent was Old New York: Mr. Howell from *Gilligan's Island* with a little bit of Brooklyn in the vowels. He pulled out her chair ceremoniously, signaled to the waiter. "Two scotches, neat."

"Ah . . ."

"Something wrong?" Van Blaricum blinked, mildly surprised.

Lisa hesitated. "No. No, scotch is fine." The knot in my stomach tightened.

They settled in and exchanged a few pleasantries, then van Blaricum said, "I have to tell you I was terribly intrigued by your note." He favored her with a smile that seemed to mean something different on each side of his face. "But of course I'm wondering how you found me."

"Oh, people know people in this business. You understand."

She had not yet told me the nature of the pretext she had used to entice Diana Dane's brother to this meeting, so I was intensely curious.

"The business. Yes." He smiled musingly. "Oddly, I've never even heard your name before."

"I'm primarily based out of Milan," Lisa said breezily. "The bulk of our clients are Italians and Swiss."

"You're quite young to be running your own shop."

"Oh, I hope I didn't give you that impression. I'm an associate of Aldo Pozzoni—though in this case I'm acting on my own account. You're familiar with him, I'm sure?"

"We've spoken. Twice, I think." Roger van Blaricum said it as though that were two times too many. "You know, my dear, I'd love to chitchat of course. But you intimated on the phone that you have something of unusual interest to show me."

Lisa picked up the worn leather portfolio, set it square in the middle of the table, the buckles toward her chest. "Put your drink on the floor, please, Mr. van Blaricum," she said, placing her own scotch next to her foot.

Van Blaricum eyed her briefly, as though not accustomed to being told what to do. But then he did as he was told, placing the drink next to the leg of his chair. Lisa took a large white cloth out of her purse and carefully wiped the tabletop. Van Blaricum's eyes were fixed on the portfolio.

Lisa opened the straps on the portfolio and pulled out a white folder, which she opened and passed to van Blaricum. His right eye widened when he opened it, but his left seemed to narrow slightly.

"Good God!" he said. "Where did you get it?"

I was trying not to be too conspicuous about watching the pair, but I had to let my glance linger. Inside the folder was a large piece of heavy paper with a scene printed on it in bold colors—reds, blues, greens. I'm no art expert, but it appeared to be a Japanese woodblock print. And it certainly took no expert to make out the subject matter: The print showed a man having anal intercourse with a woman wearing a mask that looked like a demonic Buddhist temple guard.

"The last of the famous thirty-nine erotic scenes of Hayakawa. Executed circa 1825 in an edition of six. Of those only one full set exists *in toto*. I understand that a second set—*almost* complete—exists in . . ." Lisa smiled knowingly. ". . . private hands, shall we say? Sadly, however, I understand that the owner of the second set is missing this particular print."

Van Blaricum stared at the print for a long time. Finally, he looked up at my daughter with a curious mixture of emotions in his eyes. Greed on the right side of his face, puzzlement on the left. "How, my dear, did you obtain this?"

Lisa smiled with merry superciliousness. "Now you know that's considered a somewhat tasteless question in this business," she scolded.

Half of van Blaricum's face frowned. He flipped the print over, jabbed his finger at a small red circle. "I know this print. That's the Metropolitan Museum's stamp. This is the Met's copy."

Lisa continued to smile. "Was. It's been deaccessioned."

"No it hasn't. I would have heard."

"The Met is unloading some of their more, ah, frankly sexual material. Rather quietly, so as not to create some sort of stupid media feeding frenzy. Being the conservative, mainstream shop they are . . . well, fellatio and rim jobs and so forth, they don't play well in front of the elementary school tour groups, do they? So they figure they might as well dump things of that nature on the quiet and buy something they can actually show."

Van Blaricum's jaw clenched and unclenched. He flipped the print over, stared at it. "This is stolen," he said softly. "You're putting me in a public place with a stolen print. I can't take terribly kindly to that."

Lisa shrugged. "Fine. That's your opinion. Give it back, and I'll be on my way."

Van Blaricum couldn't seem let the print out of his hands. He looked around furtively. To my horror, our eyes met. I smiled blandly and looked away. Fortunately, he didn't seem to recognize me. At a minimum, he must have seen my face on the news; but I suppose he just didn't make the connection.

"Mr. van Blaricum?" Lisa's voice grew soft and insinuating. "Would you, by any off chance, be the private collector who's missing the thirty-ninth in the series?"

The pleasant side of his face smiled. "Obviously you already know the answer to that question."

"There are merchants and there are collectors, Roger. Yes? The true collector is driven by a passion for their chosen field, not by the need to turn a profit. You're a collector. I can see it in your eyes. And given that for you it's about possession rather than profit, I suspect that the question of whether this was deaccessioned or whether it fell off the back of a truck is not, ultimately, of great interest to you. So. My question to you is, are you interested or not?"

Van Blaricum didn't speak.

Lisa reached across the table, pulled the print out of his hands, and stowed it back in her bag.

There was a long pause. Finally, van Blaricum reached down and picked his drink up off the floor. His soft white hair floated dreamily in the cigar-laden air. As he was lifting the glass, it slipped out of his hand. He made a grab for it but was too late. It had smashed into bits.

Van Blaricum jerked his hand back. "Ow! Damn it." His hand was suddenly dripping blood. He yanked a white handkerchief out of his pocket, awkwardly trying to tie it around his bleeding thumb.

"Here. Let me." Lisa carefully tied the handkerchief around his hand, pulling it tight.

"How much?" he said hoarsely.

Lisa took out a ballpoint pen and wrote a figure on her cocktail napkin.

Van Blaricum looked at the number, smiled, then looked carefully around the room, as though searching for police operatives or cameras. "Well, I'm terribly sorry, but under the circumstances I really couldn't offer you anything for the Haykawa anyway. Too many uncertainties about where it came from." He scribbled something on the napkin, pushed it back to her. "Here's my private line if you have anything more, ah, sanitary to offer me."

My eyes are not what they once were, so I couldn't make out exactly what was written on the napkin, but it looked like he'd written his name and a number. Not a phone number. It was number followed by quite a few zeros. A counteroffer.

"That's a shame," Lisa said. "I guess I'll have to go elsewhere. Here's my cell in case you reconsider." She crossed out the earlier number, scribbled another figure below it. Again, it wasn't a phone number.

Van Blaricum eyed the napkin. His protuberant lower lip went in and out once.

"That's my only number," Lisa said. "It won't change."

Van Blaricum reached out and touched the napkin thoughtfully with the tip of his finger. It trembled as though the napkin had been wired to a light socket. He took a deep breath. Finally, his head dipped slightly, and he said, "Alright."

Lisa leaned forward in a confidential, flirtatious manner. I felt uneasy watching her: It seemed she was doing her best to let van Blaricum look down her blouse. I had to admire her work, but it made my skin crawl at the same time.

"I'll tell you a secret if you'll tell me a secret," she said with a mysterious smile.

Van Blaricum seemed more interested in the number on the napkin than in her cleavage. "Secret?" he said finally.

"We all have our little perversions, hm?" Lisa said, showing her teeth. "Peculiarities, I meant to say."

Van Blaricum's eyes had a moist, hungry sheen, but he didn't say anything.

"Me, I'm an absolute fool for celebrity gossip."

Van Blaricum's malignant eye studied her for a while. "And?"

"Tell me about her."

Van Blaricum didn't speak. "Who?"

"You know who. Tell me about her and Miles. Something about their past."

Still van Blaricum sat silently, the wheels obviously turning in his head.

"Have you found me to be a disappointing person so far?" Lisa said. "Unsurprising? Uninteresting? Incapable, so far, of delivering the fascinating, the titillating, the rare, the unusual? Tit for tat, what do you say?"

Van Blaricum's eyes had narrowed slightly. He looked nervously around the room. Our eyes met a second time. Suddenly I saw a dawn of recognition.

Van Blaricum's face went white as he realized what was going on.

For a moment it seemed as though he was frozen, unable to move. Suddenly he rose slowly to his feet, shaking his head. "You disgusting, vile, cheap, terrible, ugly little people. Have you *no* shame?" He unwrapped the handkerchief from his cut hand, waving the large red splotch in front of Lisa's face.

"What's the problem?" Lisa said, still trying to bluff her way past his suspicions.

"You've been talking to MacDairmid, haven't you?" van Blaricum said. "Well, if Miles gets off, my sister's blood is on *your* hands!" he shouted. Then he threw the bloody handkerchief in her face.

As the red-stained piece of cloth fell onto the table, leaving a smear of blood on Lisa's face, he turned to me and said, in a slow malevolent voice, "You want to know the funny thing, Sloan? It doesn't matter if he gets off or not. He wants her money. But that's the one thing he'll never get." He smiled slightly. "Never, ever. Or didn't MacDairmid tell you that?"

"He never had any interest in her money," I said.

"Oh? Well, watch his face when the bastard shows up to take her fortune," van Blaricum said. "Then you'll know the truth."

"Is there a problem here?" The maître d' had appeared suddenly at my elbow, looking uneasily at the bloody handkerchief on the table.

"No problem," I said, scooping up the handkerchief and stuffing it in my pocket. "In fact, we were just leaving."

Twenty-six

ELL, THAT COULD have gone better," Lisa said. We were sitting in the overpriced restaurant in the lobby of our hotel. She was looking at me with a brittle smile on her face.

"You tried," I said. "It was a pretty good effort if you ask me."

She kept looking at me like she was waiting for the hammer to fall, for me to say something nasty about what she'd done. We ordered our meal, then I said, "Okay, so I have to ask. Where did that print come from?"

"I did some research on the Internet, trying to find out about the van Blaricum family. Turns out Roger is all that's left of them. So I figured he might help me figure out what Miles has been trying to hide. If anything.

"What I found out after doing some research was that Roger was a big collector of Japanese erotica. So I have this . . . well . . . there's this guy I know. He's an Asian art specialist for the Metropolitan Museum. I called him up trying to find out about van Blaricum. It turns out my friend knew a great deal about Roger. Not a big fan of Roger's, either. Anyway, we talked, and eventually my friend told me that the Met has a print that van Blaricum had been pining over for years.

"So I . . ." Another big sigh. "You know how one of the big things about recovery is you're supposed to stay away from your old drinking partners, your old haunts, all that stuff? Well, this guy was kind of a . . ." She sighed loudly.

"A drunk," I said.

"Right. Anyway, I got together with him hoping I could get my hands on that print. A loan or something. Naturally he said no. So we went out to some trendy little hot spot, I plied him with Glenfiddich, showed a little leg, eventually we got all silly and he . . ." She put her face in her hands. "I know it was stupid. It was stupid and manipulative and awful . . ."

She stared out the window for a while.

"The bottom line," she continued, "is that once he was fairly well plastered, he took me over to the Met, and he snuck the print out the back door, saying he'd let me use it—twenty-four-hour temporary deep-cover extremely unofficial loan kind of thing."

"And while you're doing this," I said, "you joined in the fun, had a nip or three yourself?"

"One thing led to another, yeah." She looked at the floor, her brown eyes looking bleak and hopeless. "You know, it's weird, I keep feeling like half of me is proud of being such a slick operator and half of me is disgusted with myself."

"That's the story of the first thirty-odd years of my life," I said. "I pulled off several grubby, sneaky little legal coups that I'd never have even tried if I'd been sober. Trust me, it's not worth it."

We sat in silence until the food arrived. I tucked into my chicken, but Lisa just picked at the salad she had ordered.

"While you're examining your salad leaf by leaf," I said, "you want to tell me what happened to you this year? Why you left school?"

Lisa shook her head. "Not yet." For a moment she looked glum. Suddenly she glanced up, full of enthusiasm. "So, what do you think he meant when he said—what was it exactly?—watch the bastard's face when he shows up and takes her money?"

"I assume he meant that Miles's greed will be evident on his face whenever he gets her inheritance."

Lisa frowned. "Yes, but he had just said that Miles will never ever get her money."

"It doesn't make sense, does it? But maybe more importantly, who is MacDairmid? You asked him to talk about Diana's past, and more or less the next thing he said was, 'You've been talking to MacDairmid.'

As though whoever MacDairmid is, he would know something about some kind of dark secret in her past."

"Oh, I'm glad you mentioned that," Lisa said. "I went by Roger's co-op yesterday, slipped the doorman a small gratuity, as they say. It was obvious he was no great fan of Roger van Blaricum. Didn't know anything about Diana, but he said that there was this old guy who had been some sort of butler/driver/general factotum for the family for a million years and who Roger had fired a couple years back. The doorman said this old guy wasn't happy about it, and that if anybody would have some juicy information on the van Blaricums, it would be this old guy. His name's Ian MacDairmid."

"I guess we better track him down, huh?" I said.

"Only problem, this guy MacDairmid was apparently pretty long in the tooth when he was fired. The doorman figured he could be dead by now."

Twenty-seven

ACCORDING TO THE phone books, there was only one Ian MacDairmid in the entire city of New York, and he lived out in the far reaches of Brooklyn.

No one answered the phone when I called, so the next morning we took the subway out to where he lived—a five-story walk-up in a neighborhood populated by one of those odd New York ethnic mixes, Koreans and Latvians. We pressed the buzzer, but no one answered. Lisa kept pushing the button.

"We can wait," I said. "He'll probably show up after a while."

Lisa started pressing all the other buzzer buttons at once with the ham of her hand. "This is what they do on *NYPD Blue*," she said. Eventually a tinny, unintelligible voice answered in what, for all I could make out of it, could have been English, Latvian, or Korean.

"We're trying to find Ian MacDairmid," I said.

"Go away!"

That phrase, though, came through loud and clear.

Lisa kept pressing buttons. A certain amount of abuse in a variety of languages came out of the little speaker.

Just as I was about to suggest she stop pressing buttons, a very thin man threw open the glass door to the meager vestibule. He wore a turban over dyed blond hair, and a silk bathrobe hung open, exposing his hairless chest. "What in blue blazes do you people want?" he said. His accent sounded like pure Alabama.

"We're looking for Ian MacDairmid," I said.

"Do I look like a hundred-year-old Scottish man?" the man in the turban said.

"No, but do you know where we can find him?"

"He's usually in the park feeding the flying rats." The man in the turban waved his index finger at Lisa. His nails were long and French-manicured. "And if you mash that dadgum button again, girly-girl, I will scratch your eyes out, no matter what the cost to my fabulous Lee Press-ons."

Then he slammed the door shut.

W E WALKED DOWN to the small park at the end of the street. There were a few bums and some elderly Korean women, but we didn't see an old man. As we were leaving, Lisa pointed at a small green bench tucked behind a weeping bronze memorial to veterans of the Spanish American War. Sitting on the bench was an ancient man wearing a tweed cap, a pipe clamped in his teeth. He was reading a newspaper printed on pink paper, the *Financial Times*.

"Ian MacDairmid?" I said.

He looked up from the newspaper, studied my face for a while, then folded the newspaper in a very precise manner and set it on the bench next to him. His eyes were bright blue and very clear.

"Ah, Mr. Sloan." He spoke with a soft Scottish accent. "It crossed my mind that you might look for me."

I raised my eyebrows. "Oh?"

"And who is the lovely young lady with you?" Ian MacDairmid's thick hair was barely tinged with gray, but his face bore the deep wrinkles of someone well into his eighties.

"My daughter Lisa," I said.

The old man patted the bench. "By all means, rest yourself, my dear," he said.

Lisa sat beside him. The old man exuded the scent of pipe tobacco.

"You'd be wanting to know something about Diana," he said. "Something about her past, something that might assist your defense of her husband."

"You're making this awfully easy," I said.

"People change, I suppose," he said. "But I don't see Miles Dane doing this wretched thing. He never seemed that kind of lad. Beyond that rather tepid assertion, however, I sincerely doubt I have anything to say that would be of value to you."

"You'd be surprised. Sometimes little things have a lot of significance."

The old man shrugged. "I've got all day. Ask anything you like."

I asked a number of questions about how Miles and Diana had met, but learned nothing new. Eventually I ran out of questions.

"This is a little ticklish," I said finally, "but we suspect that perhaps there's something our client isn't telling us."

"Such as?"

"It's possible—we really don't know—but it's possible he's protecting someone, someone from fairly deep in his past. Can you think of someone he might have known, someone he might be protecting?"

The old man sucked on his empty pipe again. "No, sir, I can't," he said finally.

"We met with Roger van Blaricum yesterday. He seemed to think you might know something."

"Did he?" One eyebrow rose slightly. "I'm surprised he was willing to talk to you."

"He wasn't exactly forthcoming. But he mentioned your name. Then he said something strange. During our conversation he expressed the opinion that Miles had killed Diana for her money. But then he said, 'That's the one thing he'll never get.' Can you shed any light on what he meant?"

MacDairmid grunted softly, then slowly filled his pipe, pulling the leaf out of a soft leather bag. When he was done tamping down the tobacco, however, he didn't light the pipe, but just held it in his hand. Finally, he spoke. "First a few ground rules."

I glanced quickly at Lisa, who raised her eyebrows in surprise. I turned back to MacDairmid and spread my hands. "Such as?"

"I won't testify. I'm eighty-three years old, and I'm not in your jurisdiction. You can't touch me if I ignore a subpoena, so I shouldn't try if I were you. Second, I'd rather my name not be mentioned to other witnesses, should the occasion arise. I'm being hypocritical, no doubt, but discretion was always treasured in my profession."

I thought for a moment. He was right. Even if his testimony was of value, the likelihood of my being able to drag him into a courtroom across state lines was approaching nil. "Fair enough," I said finally.

He drew on the unlit pipe, making a soft whistling noise. "The crux of the state's case, from the standpoint of motive, is that Miles was in it for the money, am I not correct?"

"We won't really know until the trial, but I presume that's right."

"Let me tell you a story then." The old man's eyes went thoughtful. "It is frequently the custom of British servants to take on the worldview of their masters. That never really happened to me, but it might, nevertheless, aid your understanding of the story if I told it from the perspective of the family and reserved my own judgments on the matter until later."

"Okay."

"Diana van Blaricum met Miles Dane in 1968 as I recall. He was a *busboy*." MacDairmid said this in a slightly ironic tone. "In the view of Diana's mother—and of Roger, too, who had become the man of the family after his father's death a few years earlier—he was a calculating little nobody from nowhere. But nevertheless Miles caught her eye. And once he had it, he was relentless. In the family's view, he calculated that through her, he could gain the world. First publication and afterward, fortune, fame, etc., etc. Her money and connections, of course, would open all the doors for him."

I nodded.

"Diana was something of a naif. Her family generally thought her a fool. Being young and romantic, all this skulking around, the flowers and candy, the cheap saloons that Miles took her to down in the Village and so on—well, no doubt it was terribly attractive to her. So she allowed him to do what he wanted with her."

"Which was what?" Lisa said.

The old man laughed. "He got her pregnant, of course."

Lisa leaned back slightly, raised one eyebrow.

"Miles was a clever enough boy—again, I'm giving you the family view, as I said, not my own—Miles was a clever enough boy to see that

Diana was the sort of girl to whom abortion was unthinkable. According to the family, he calculated that if he got her pregnant, she would be forced to marry him. And then he'd have access to her money."

"I don't mean to ask a stupid question," I said, "but you know all of this how?"

MacDairmid smiled thinly. "Servants are like furniture. A cliché, but it's nonetheless true. Things may be said around people like me that would never be discussed in front of one's peers. Masters have no secrets among their servants."

I nodded.

"At any rate, Miles succeeded in what the family believed was his intermediate goal. Not terribly long after they met, Diana was with child." MacDairmid sucked on the pipe. "But in his long-term goal he was not immediately successful."

"So at that point she wasn't willing to marry him?"

"It's not that simple. The late Mrs. van Blaricum gave her daughter the following choice: She told Diana that if she didn't give up the child and spurn Miles, the family would take her trust fund away and leave her to her own devices. Diana was young and unsophisticated, and she had no understanding of just how difficult it is to tamper with an existing trust. At any rate, Diana naturally didn't find the notion of being penniless quite as attractive as she found the notion of drinking in the occasional bar down on Bleecker, so she promised to do what her mother asked. She signed the documents terminating her parental rights. The child was born, and sadly there were terrible complications that left Diana infertile thereafter. At any rate, after she awoke from the anesthetic, she was informed that in the course of these complications, the child had died."

"So why did they end up getting married anyway?"

"They didn't at first. Miles continued to secretly pursue Diana. And she defied her mother's wishes to the extent that she allowed him to continue to court her. As a servant I was privy to some of these comings and goings. Diana knew I was not entirely unsympathetic to Miles, so she relied occasionally on me to cover for her. This secret courtship went on for another year or so. Eventually the ambitious young Miles consulted with a rather good lawyer who informed Diana that since her money was held in a well-constructed trust, there was really nothing the family could do to cut her off. Whereupon she immediately married Miles, and we—the family I'm speaking of—cut all ties to her, and the rest, as they say . . ." He spread his hands wordlessly.

Ian MacDairmid sat for a while looking at Lisa with a crafty smile on his face.

"What?" Lisa said.

"Are you a lawyer, too, young lady?"

"A law student."

"Do you know anything about trusts then?"

"Just what I learned in corporate law. Which is to say, not much."

"Then I must back up a little. Roger van Blaricum and his mother were awful people. But Diana and her father were quite the opposite. Deeply, intractably decent. The old Mr. van Blaricum was trained in the law. He didn't practice, but he taught a course at Columbia and wrote the occasional monograph. Unlike many men of his station, he concerned himself with the well-being of his servants, and because he perceived that I was interested in things generally, he would often lecture me on subjects that caught his interest. As a result I received, over the course of many years, a rather broad legal education—simply by standing in the same room as Mr. van Blaricum.

"Which brings me back to the issue of trusts. When one is the beneficiary of a trust, as I'm sure you know, one doesn't control the money in the trust. One can't simply will the money when one dies, because, strictly speaking, it's not your money at all."

"The point being?" I said.

"All of Diana's money—her family money, I mean—was held in trust. Her father discussed the matter with me at some length when his father was having the trust drawn up, so I know about the matter in rather great detail. At any rate, here's how Diana Dane's trust was drawn up. When she died, the trust specified that one of two things was to happen. If she had what the lawyers call 'issue'—"

"Meaning children by blood," Lisa said. "Not adopted children."

"Precisely. If she had children by blood, those children would automatically become beneficiaries of the trust upon her death. If, on the other hand, she had no issue, no children of her own blood, then the trust was to liquidate, and the proceeds would pass, unencumbered, to her heirs in whatever manner she might specify in her will. She could will them to the Barnard College endowment, to the Fund for the Protection of Beanie Babies, whatever she chose. Or, of course, to her husband."

"Now hold on," I said. "I'm prepared to believe that you got a pretty extensive lecture on this subject from Diana's father. But you're saying you remember *all of this* from a few conversations held decades ago?"

"Not precisely. As you may have found out in the course of locating me, I was fired some while back by Roger van Blaricum. I'm old, and he had been looking for an excuse for some while—but the proximate cause of my sudden retirement was that he found me snooping into his affairs."

"In what way?"

"As the chief servant, I took it upon myself to be familiar with every aspect of the van Blaricum family's business. During the days of the old Mr. van Blaricum I had been in the habit of keeping copies of family documents. As I said, Mr. van Blaricum lectured to me often on the law. I think he found his life quite dull, and my education became a sort of hobby of his. I think nothing would have pleased him more than if I had quit working for him and gone off to university." He looked wistfully off at a knot of old Korean women on the other side of the small park. "But that was not who I was. Nevertheless, he would take copies of a great many family documents—wills, trusts, deeds, etc.— and underline important passages and make marginal notes and then give them to me. After his death, I continued to, well, make a study of the family's legal matters. His hobby had become mine. I justified it to myself on the rather specious grounds that it helped me perform my duties more thoroughly." He winked at Lisa. Or perhaps it was only a twitch in his eyelid.

"At any rate, after his father's death, I knew that Roger van Blaricum wouldn't have approved of my little hobby. But I continued to do it because it pleased me. At one point just a few years ago, Roger— who has rather expensive tastes—attempted to gain access to the assets of his own trust by means of a lawsuit. His trust, I might add, is a virtual duplicate of Diana's. As chief domestic in his household, I had absolute access to all of his correspondence with his lawyers in the matter. I made a certain amount of study of all the rather complex ins and outs of that case. As it happened, one day last year Roger caught me in his office photocopying several briefs, and that was the end of my sixty-year employ with the van Blaricum family."

"So what's all of this got to do with Miles?" I said. "My understanding is that the trust fund was not terribly substantial in the first place."

The old man raised one eyebrow. "Where did you get that impression?"

"That's what Miles told us."

"Well Miles is wrong. The income from the trust is exceedingly modest, this is true. And perhaps he therefore assumed that the underlying principal was equally modest. In case you've missed the financial news lately, the stock market has done rather well over the past forty years. This has rather profound implications for any sort of trust."

"So you're saying that if she dies and the trust liquidates, he, as her sole heir, gets . . ."

"Let us say that the principal underlying the trust amounts to a not insubstantial amount of money."

"My, my," I said. My stomach did a flip-flop.

"My, my indeed." The old man pursed his lips, then took out a Zippo and lit his pipe, studying me all the while with a look of amusement on his face.

"From the sly look on your face," I said, "I assume there's something you're not telling me."

"You said that if she dies he inherits the principal. And then I gave you the sly look."

"Is there some hidden clause you didn't tell me about?"

"To the contrary, I already told you."

I frowned. "Assuming they have no children by blood, he inherits. It's that simple. And they *don't* have children, Mr. MacDairmid."

MacDairmid's blue eyes continued to stare unblinkingly into mine. The twinkle, however, had taken on a slightly rueful quality.

"I believe what I said earlier was that Diana was *informed* that the child she bore in 1969 had died." MacDairmid exhaled a cloud of smoke. "The poor child, in fact, survived and was healthy as a horse. A boy. The family placed him in foster care. Some years later Mr. van Blaricum let slip in my presence that he had intentionally initiated some sort of bureaucratic impediment that prevented the child from being qualified for adoption while he was an infant. That gives you a sense of the sort of man Roger van Blaricum is. Vindictive. As a result the child spent several years in a miserable orphanage in Utica. According to Mr. van Blaricum, when the orphanage was closed down in the early 1970s, the boy was then shuffled through ten or fifteen different foster families before finally being adopted by a rather brutal disciplinarian on a farm upstate."

Lisa was staring at him. "Why hasn't Roger revealed this publicly?" she said finally. "This could change the entire complexion of the case."

MacDairmid smiled. "Surely you jest. First, the bastard—and I mean that in the ancient sense of the term—is an ugly little family secret. And Roger is not the sort to air his dirty linen in public."

"But that way, if Miles should happen to win the case, he'll probably get Diana's money. Surely Roger wouldn't want that."

MacDairmid's left eyebrow rose slightly. "I wouldn't be at all surprised if he's waiting to see what happens."

"Meaning what?"

"Think about it. If he revealed that Miles and Diana's child is alive before the trial, then Miles could claim he'd known about the child all along. Which would remove his apparent motive for killing Diana. No, Roger would doubtless rather see him convicted first." He drew on the pipe. "If, on the other hand, Miles wins the case, however, Mr. van Blaricum still has the opportunity to prevent him from receiving his inheritance."

"That son of a bitch!" Lisa said.

"Mm," said the old man. "No one would ever accuse him of being short on guile, however."

"You said you were reserving your own judgment about Miles until later," I said. "Do *you* think he's after her money?"

"The rich are frequently color-blind when it comes to other people's views of money. Any fool could see that Miles was never after Diana's money. In my view, he was a simple creature who only wanted two things out of life. He wanted to write and be rewarded for it; and he wanted to spend his life with Diana. He absolutely worshiped her." MacDairmid tapped the embers of his pipe in his palm, tossed them on the ground. A pigeon came up and pecked at them, then ruffled its feathers in annoyance and strutted away.

"Now I won't say that he was oblivious to her money. Miles was no fool, no child. He knew that money and connections could help his career. But that was never his goal."

"Was Miles ever told that his son had survived?"

"I believe not. At the time the child was born, his paternity was neither documented nor acknowledged, so he would have had no say-so in the child's disposition."

"So this child of Miles and Diana's," I said. "Do you know his name?"

"No. Mr. van Blaricum never told me that." MacDairmid shook his head sadly. "Poor little bastard. Poor, poor little bastard."

Twenty-eight

Lisa and I took a cab straight to the airport. Four or five raindrops hit our windshield on the way through Queens, with the result that when we got to the airport, we got the usual pack of lies from the airlines about weather delays. The rain delays turned into missing engine parts, then into canceled flights, and suddenly it was nightfall. Our reserved seats on the one-fifteen direct flight to Detroit had now turned into standby tickets on a ten-thirty-five flight with a layover in Minneapolis—so we adjourned to one of the overpriced restaurants for dinner.

Since our options did not include a couple of fingers of scotch as a tonic for the irritation of spending most of our day wrangling with the airlines, Lisa and I used shop talk as our next best distraction.

"Let's assume for the sake of argument that Miles *didn't* kill his wife," Lisa said. "Why would he say one time that he can only work in absolute silence, and the next minute he says he's blasting Beethoven while Diana was killed? Why would he make up this improbable story about some strange home invader killing Diana for no good reason? Why the lies? The only logical answer—*if* he is in fact innocent—is that he's protecting someone."

"We're agreed on that."

"So it's got to be the son, don't you think? He's protecting his son."

"Possibly. But according to MacDairmid, he was never told that the boy had survived."

"What if he found out somehow? Maybe the kid contacted them recently. Maybe he's blackmailing Miles. It could be a lot of things. If so, all we have to do is find him and put him on the stand, right? Plus, it's like MacDairmid said, if Miles knows about him and knows that the son will inherit Diana's trust fund, his very existence blows away the state's whole theory of motive."

I sawed off a piece of tough, overcooked steak, but didn't answer.

"What?" Lisa said.

"One of the most frustrating things about being a lawyer, Lisa," I said after I'd finally masticated my steak into submission, "is that it's hard to practice law without clients. There is no bigger pain in the ass than a client. Clients lie, they obfuscate, they withhold information, and then when you do your job and save the day for them, they refuse to pay the bill.

"That said, consider this delicate issue: What do you do when a client's stated wishes are clearly counter to his legal interests?" I took a sip of my Diet Coke and wished, for about the fifth time during the meal, that I was drinking something stronger.

"Take Miles Dane for instance. Say you're right, Lisa. Say he knows about his son's existence. Say his son killed Diana. And let's say Miles knows it. Say that out of guilt or shame or God only knows what motive, Miles is protecting his kid. Given all that, what's my next move?"

Lisa looked confused.

"Here's the obvious law school ethics class choice. I march cheerfully into the jail wrapped in the Grand Ole Flag of legal ethics, and I tell Miles: 'Okay, we believe you have a living son and we believe you know of his existence. We believe you know that under the terms of Diana's trust, your supposed pecuniary motive is out the window. Now, Miles, did your son kill your wife?' Miles may then admit he's covering for his long-lost son and thereby give me the tools to crack him out of the slammer.

"But. Here's what I *think* he'll say. He'll say, 'As far as I know, Charley, my son's dead; a mysterious stranger killed my wife while I was blasting Beethoven; and I don't want you pursuing some ridiculous line of inquiry about some alleged son who, to the best of my knowledge, died thirty years ago.' At which point I'm ethically obliged to hew to his instructions. With the likely result that I'll lose the case and Miles will spend the rest of his life writing his memoirs with a nice soft crayon over in the state pen at Jackson. Miles may believe that my reputation as a legal brilliantisimo will save his bacon. I, however, am not suffering under that delusion." I did battle with my steak again, finally surrendering after a long fight. "Like I say, a dilemma."

"But you're ethically obliged to tell him," Lisa said. "I mean . . . aren't you?"

"I'm convinced, Lisa," I continued, "that the law school ethics class answer is the wrong one. So being the good lawyer that I am, I have concluded it's time to do what we lawyers do best: to wit, split hairs. As long as Miles is unaware that we know his son is alive, then he can't instruct us to ignore that avenue of investigation. I can then—in clear conscience and marching forward beneath the banner of the ethical guidelines of the State Bar of Michigan—send you out to pursue the investigation into this alleged long-lost son, and see where it leads you.

"This approach is ethically defensible because at this time the only evidence we have for this man's existence is the word of an old man who may or may not be in a position to know what he's talking about. So right now, we're just conducting a simple factual investigation of moderate pertinence to the case. At such time as you get some results— *if* you get them at all—I will inform my client of his options. Because heaven forfend that I leave my client in the dark!" I smiled and lifted my Diet Coke in toast. "Ah, The Law. Consider its majesty."

Lisa peered at me with an odd look on her face. "You look awfully pleased with yourself, Dad."

I grinned. "You want to know something funny? I am, kind of." My grin went away. "But that means you'd better get real busy as soon as we get back home."

Twenty-nine

FOR TWO DAYS after we got back to Pickeral Point, Lisa acted mysterious. She had installed herself in the spare office—the one I store old files in—and set up a phone and a desk in the corner, hiding herself behind piles of old bankers boxes. She didn't talk, just stayed in there with the door closed. I just hoped this reclusiveness had nothing to do with drugs or alcohol.

Late in the afternoon of the second day she walked into my office, and said, "Got him!"

"Got who?"

"Miles and Diana's son."

I smiled broadly. "How'd you pull it off?"

"Lots and lots of phone calls. Eventually, I called the New York Department of Vital Records and told them I was an ER doc and that I needed to find the birth parents of a John Doe who'd been adopted. I said that if he didn't get a transfusion of some obscure amino acid from a blood relative within eighteen hours, he'd die. Of course they didn't want to tell me without a court order, so I was all '*Right now, dammit, he's gonna die and it's all on your head!*' Blah blah blah. That didn't work, so I said his wife was threatening to sue for wrongful death if we didn't get this amino acid, and she would name this bureaucrat personally in the lawsuit if he died. Boom, the waters parted. It wasn't until after she gave me the name that she goes, 'Wait a minute, if this guy's a John Doe, how do you know who his wife is?'"

I laughed.

"Turned out his birth name was Unnamed Child van Blaricum."

"Unnamed Child? Boy, the van Blaricums really went all gah-gah over him, didn't they?"

"Apparently so. So then I walked downtown and called the New York Department of Social Services on my cell phone and told them I was a cop in the Pickeral Point Police department and if they didn't believe me they could call information for the number and then call me back at the station. Then I went over to the police station and chatted up the girl at the front desk—you know the one I'm talking about? Regina, the one that's sweet on you?"

"No she's not," I said.

"She *is*." Lisa sounded indignant. "Anyway, while I was talking to her, I said, 'Oh, by the way, a client's probably going to call me while I'm here at the station.' Next thing I know, the phone rings. 'Oh, great, honey, she's right here.' *Voilà*, I'm an officer of the law. So based on my urgent need as a police investigator, this DSS caseworker gives me the history of Unnamed Child van Blaricum. According to her records, first he gets renamed David van Blaricum, then it's changed to David Reid by a family who was thinking about adopting him but backed out some-where between the name change and the adoption finalization, then when he was twelve years old he was finally adopted, and his adoptive parents inflicted the name Otto Gerd Heusenfelter on him."

"That could come in handy," I said, "if he ever decides to become a Nazi."

Lisa laughed. "*Then* I called his adoptive parents, the Heusenfelters of Clinton County, New York. Farm country, up near Vermont. And the Heusenfelters said they haven't talked to him in five years. Not since, get this, *he got out of prison last time*."

I raised my eyebrows. "No kidding. How interesting. Where did he do time?"

"It's more like, where *didn't* he go to prison. He was lodged at the Clinton County Jail for battery, then at Rikers Island, where he did a time-served bit for a burglary in the city, then he was a guest for six months at the Nassau County Diversion Center on Long Island. As-sault, that time. Then the Volusia County Jail in Florida, for simple possession. Then CCI in Columbia, South Carolina, for aggravated assault. That was in 1992. But then I hit a wall. No records since then that I was able to find. Not just criminal, I mean no records, period. No credit bureau, no nothing.

"So I call his adoptive parents in New York again. I go: 'What's the deal, you said he got out of prison five years ago, but I can't find a record of it.' Direct quote from this Heusenfelter guy: 'That son of a bitch hated us so much, he went and changed his name.' I ask him, 'To what?' 'Why the hell should I care? Biggest mistake we ever made, getting involved with that ingrate.' So I checked around to see if there'd been an order entered to change his name. New York, no. Florida, no. South Carolina, bingo. I go back and check again under his new name. Lo and behold ... tah-dah! ... he's back in New York in the midnineties, this time at Sing Sing for aggravated assault again. So I call the police department in the little town where the offense occurred, guess what he did?"

I shook my head.

"Beat a guy almost to death with a tree limb. The victim's been in a wheelchair ever since."

"A tree limb?"

"Gets better." Lisa raised her eyebrows suggestively. "There's one more conviction. Assaulting an officer. Guess where he served time?"

"Got me."

"Yes, friends. Jackson State Penitentiary. Right here in the good old state of Michigan. Committed the crime over in Grand Rapids. Weapon of choice? Here's the beauty part ... he beat his victim with the handle of a posthole digger."

My eyes widened. "He really likes to swing a stick, doesn't he?"

"Yup. And guess when he got out?"

"Tell me."

"Three months before the murder of Diana Dane."

I leaned back in my chair. I wouldn't be surprised if my mouth was hanging open. "What did he change his name to?" I said finally.

She tossed her legal pad on my desk. In the middle, scrawled in Lisa's large, messy hand, was the name of Miles and Diana Dane's son. *Blair Dane.*

"Dane, huh?" I looked up and said, "So if we painted him as the real killer in trial, I guess he'd be hard-pressed to go with the Gee-I've-never-heard-of-Miles-and-Diana-Dane defense."

Lisa smiled broadly.

"Well this is great work, kid," I said. "This is terrific. Now all we need to do is find him."

Lisa's face fell a little. "Yeah. Well, see, that's where I'm hitting a snag."

Thirty

IT TOOK HER three more days, but eventually Lisa walked into my office with a grin on her face. "Success!"

AS WE DROVE out to the place where Lisa believed we'd find Blair Dane, I was comforted by the presence of my little Smith & Wesson.

It was an hour northwest of Pickeral Point, deep into farm country. We crested a low rise, and there in front of us, in the middle of a vast field, was a large, unpainted cinder-block building that looked something like a warehouse. From our view, it looked as though the building had no windows, and only one door.

"So this is, what, a cult kind of thing?" I said.

"Hard to say," Lisa said. "They call themselves the Brothers of Christ, Reborn."

In the field in front of the building a long row of men wearing shapeless brown clothes were bent over in a line, hoeing the hard, dark soil. If the men hadn't all been white, it could have been mistaken for South Carolina circa 1850, a gang of slaves chopping cotton.

I drove down the straight gravel road that bisected the field and rolled down my window when I came abreast of the line of men. "Excuse me," I called. "Where can I find Blair Dane?"

The men kept breaking dirt clods with the hoes, ignoring me, not even looking up. There was something trancelike about their movements.

I called out again. One man looked up furtively, made a quick gesture toward the ugly concrete box of a building, then went back to his hoeing. "Nice folks," I said to Lisa. "Very cheerful and welcoming. How much do you know about them?"

"Precious little. They're all men. Except the chief honcho. Her name is Sister Beatrice. She used to be a Catholic nun, but left the order after some kind of scandal that nobody seemed interested in talking about."

I parked the car, and we got out and knocked on the door. Eventually it opened, and a young man wearing the same shapeless tan clothes as the men in the field looked out at us. On closer inspection, the clothes looked homemade—right down to the coarse homespun cloth. The young man had a very large necklace hanging on his chest—a cross made of welded horseshoe nails—and his feet were bare. He looked at us, but didn't speak.

"Good morning," I said cheerfully. "My name is Charley Sloan, and this is my daughter Lisa. We're looking for Blair Dane."

The young man still had the flat gaze of an inmate, the pale prison skin, the jailhouse muscles. "Wait here." He closed the door.

We waited for about five minutes, then the door opened again. This time it was a different man. The second man wore the same necklace, the same homespun clothes—but on him they seemed to fit better, almost like a military uniform. He was about my age, late forties, with piercing blue eyes, gray hair, and a short gray beard. "My name is Jack. We've been expecting you," he said, smiling pleasantly. His voice was gentle, but somehow commanding. He motioned us into an entry room lined with unpainted Sheetrock.

"If you'd both take your shoes off, please, Sister Beatrice can spare ten minutes with you."

"We're here to see Blair Dane," I said.

"Yes. That's what Sister will talk to you about."

"I want to talk to *Blair*."

"Take your shoes off, please," he said again. Friendly but firm.

When in Rome. We did as we were told, sliding our shoes into a large wooden rack full of identical work boots.

"This way," he said, turning toward a staircase made of bare concrete block stairs that ran up the inside of the front wall. I can't say what it was, but there was something ominous about the place, as though we were entering a prison or a fortress. At the top of the stairs we turned and found ourselves in an open, barrackslike room with no ceiling, just open joists holding up a corrugated steel roof.

Along one wall was a long row of bunk beds, while along the other wall stood a row of crudely built plywood cubicles, each with a desk and a chair inside. The windowless room was very dimly lit by two rows of bare incandescent bulbs hanging from the joists. The bulk of the floor was covered by a large straw mat of the sort seen in Japanese houses. At the far end of the mat a small white-haired woman sat cross-legged, reading a book. We approached and she looked up.

"Thank you, Jack," she said.

Jack walked back downstairs without another word.

"Please. Sit." She gestured at the floor in front of her. She was a wrinkled, brown-skinned woman of somewhere between sixty-five and eighty. Either she had a lot of wrinkles for a sixty-five-year-old, or she exuded an awful lot of physical energy for an eighty-year-old. I couldn't quite tell which was the case. Her eyes were green and canny. She wore her glossy white hair in a bowl cut, and she was clothed in the same drab homespun as the others.

I grunted a little as I lowered myself to the floor.

"I find sitting on the floor to be excellent for the posture," the old woman said, her tone chiding but jocular. "It keeps the joints limber, too. Even when you're an old crone like me." She smiled almost imperceptibly. "So you're here about Miles Dane's son."

My eyebrows went up.

"We may look like flaky religious nuts to you, Mr. Sloan, but that doesn't mean we don't read the newspaper."

"I was surprised you knew that he was Miles Dane's son. How did you find out?"

"That's what he told me when he first came to live here."

"Ah. Well, I appreciate your taking time away from your studies, but I won't take up another minute of your time if you could just point us to Blair. As I'm sure you heard, we're here to talk to him, not you."

The sprightly little woman nodded. "Sure. Unfortunately, that won't be possible."

"With all due respect, Sister," I said, "that's not your decision to make."

"True enough. I'm simply conveying Blair's wishes to you."

"Where is he?" I said sharply.

"I'm afraid I'm one of these crazy old bags who doesn't intimidate easily." Sister Beatrice laughed. "Let me tell you a little about this community. Back when I was still in the Church, I was involved in prison ministry. What I saw was lacking in the lives of most of the boys I met in prison was discipline. Oh, prison offers discipline, but it's a discipline based upon threat and punishment. What I recognized was that once these boys left prison, they needed a regime with the sort of austerity and lack of choice that is found in prison. But it had to be motivated by other means. Lacking the lash and steel bar here, we find our discipline in the teachings of Jesus Christ." She held up her bible. "The Gospels are a rather stringent and radical set of teachings, if one bothers to really read them. Here we *do* read them. And we act upon them."

"That's fascinating."

"Sarcasm will not help your cause here, Mr. Sloan. Please listen. You might learn something." The little woman's smile faded for the first time. Her bright green eyes seemed quite cold once her teeth stopped showing. "To participate in this community is to renounce things. I understand you're an alcoholic, Mr. Sloan."

"How did you find that out?"

"Pay attention please, Mr. Sloan. I already told you I read the newspapers. As a recovering alcoholic, you have made a choice to renounce certain temptations the world has to offer. I gather that you have the sort of personality which allows you to pull that off successfully. Most of these boys"—she waved at the long row of empty bunk beds—"do not. Their renunciation of the world requires a shepherd. I am that shepherd. I don't make choices for them, I simply provide a herd in which they can live, protected, in essence, from themselves."

"You've protected Blair from himself?"

"Blair is not a fool. He has been a career criminal, but he was rather a good one. He has recognized these flaws in himself, and he's here to fix them. If he can't fix them, he'll stay here until he dies. If he does fix them, marvelous, then he will return to the world."

"This is all laudable," I said, "but I'm attempting to save an innocent man from false imprisonment. I believe Blair can help me achieve that."

"No, Mr. Sloan. Let's not be naive. What you want is a sacrificial goat. You want to hand the jury a plausible alternative suspect. You want to drag him down. And I won't let you do that."

"Ah. So now it's your choice, not his."

"That's ultimately immaterial. If he goes back to the world, he'll lose his soul again, as sure as I'm sitting here."

"I can subpoena him."

The cool green eyes locked onto mine. "And I can hide him."

"You'll go to prison if you do."

This got me a big smile. "Look around you, Mr. Sloan. I live in a house made of bare cinder block. No windows, no doors, no TV, no family, no privacy, and precious little ventilation. I've lived here for thirteen years. Do you honestly think the idea of a few weeks in the poky frightens me?"

I had to admit, it probably didn't.

"That may be. But do you want to destroy all of this, Sister? All the good works you're doing here?" I made a wide sweep with my hand. "I *can* make that happen. If I have to."

"I'm sure you're a good lawyer, but no you can't. This endeavor is bigger than me."

Seeing I was making no progress, I decided to shift gears. "I'm sorry, Sister. I don't mean to be overbearing. I've got a lot of weight on my shoulders right now. If I'm barking up the wrong tree here, I'd like to know so I can move on to something else. Can you at least tell me your impressions of Blair?" I said. "What kind of guy is he?"

"He's like a lot of men here. Troubled. His upbringing was wretched and loveless. He doesn't trust easily. Like most criminals, he's overly impulsive. He's easy to anger. That's the bad part. But he's also very bright and very articulate. More self-aware than your run-of-the-mill thug. That's why he's here: He recognized, during his latest sojourn in the penal system, that the reason he had such a tough time was not that the world was unfair, but that he had a problem dealing with the world. He is determined to fix that problem. He has come to understand that only through work, discipline, renunciation of desire, and faith in Christ can he hope to become a happy and productive person."

For the first time, Lisa spoke. "Let's put it out in the open then, Sister. Do you think he killed his mother?"

She shook her head. "Absolutely not."

"We have very compelling evidence to indicate he was in the house the night of the murder." This was a bit of a stretch, but I figured I'd see how she responded. "If he didn't do it, why not go to the police, explain his presence there, and tell what he saw?"

Sister Beatrice studied my daughter for a moment. "Let me put this in simple English: That's not going to happen."

"Can I ask you one question?" Lisa said.

"What's that?"

"Does he own a black Lincoln, midsixties model?"

Sister Beatrice studied her for a while. "*I* drive an old Continental. I've loaned it to him on occasion."

"The kind with the rear doors that open backward?"

"I think we've about clarified our positions here, hm?" Sister Beatrice looked back down at the book she'd been reading when we walked in, and her lips began to move.

"Sister . . ."

She didn't look up from the book.

I raised my voice. "Sister."

She was still looking at the book as she said, "I know I'm being a pain-in-the-neck old religious crank, but if I look up again and you're still sitting there, I'm going to have some of my boys hustle you out. They don't get treats like that very often, and I'm afraid they're liable to make the most of it."

We made fairly good time back to the car.

Thirty-one

THERE IS PROBABLY nothing grimmer or sadder than a jail on Christmas Eve. Every peeling gray-painted steel door, every rusting steel bar, every slipshod weld and deteriorating caulk joint, every crumbling slab of concrete amplifies the message of hopelessness and shame, the life-stops-here quality so central to what jail is all about. It is not just that a jail is a hard place to escape from, but that even barriers erected with such apparent disinterest and negligence are nevertheless so easily capable of hemming in a life. Jail says this: The wild freedom of the individual is nothing in the face of even the most careless and inefficient bureaucracy. In this place, you are a nullity: Get used to it.

It was Christmas Eve, and the time had come when I couldn't avoid talking to Miles about his son any longer.

The warden said I could bring him dinner—plastic utensils only. Presumably so he couldn't tunnel out of the jail with a spoon. So while we talked in the depressing little interview room, reeking of industrial disinfectant, he ate with a plastic fork out of a plastic box I'd bought at a franchised cafeteria: turkey and dressing, mashed potatoes, cranberry salad. It wasn't the most appetizing thing in the world . . . but it was the same thing Lisa and I planned to eat a couple of hours later.

After some halfhearted pleasantries, I said, "Look, here's the thing. We know about Blair."

Miles set down his plastic fork and looked up from his cheerless meal. His face wasn't showing anything.

"Did he do it, Miles? Are you protecting your son?"

Miles looked up at the gray concrete ceiling. "I don't want him involved, okay?"

"Miles. Let's get real here. Without Blair, you're toast. You understand how your wife's trust works, right? The money goes to blood children, not to you. Stash is going to argue in trial that you killed Diana for her money. If we can ambush him and argue that you knew about Blair's existence, then motive goes out the window."

Miles chewed on his turkey.

"Furthermore, Miles, I believe Blair was at your home the night of the murder."

Miles scowled. "See, this is what I wanted to avoid. You want to use him for reasonable doubt. You want to say, 'Hey, lookee here, folks, here's this violent dirtbag in the house the night of the murder, *he's* the one, *he's* the real killer.' "

He was right, of course. "Reasonable doubt, Miles. Unless you want to spend the rest of your life in the penitentiary, then you've got to give me the tools to reach reasonable doubt."

"And who pays the price for that reasonable doubt?" Miles picked up his plastic fork, stabbed a piece of turkey, stuffed it in his mouth, chewed, swallowed. When he was done, he said, "Nope. I won't let you do that to him."

I drummed my fingers. "How long have you known about Blair?"

Miles's eyes brimmed suddenly with tears. "I always knew," he said. "That jerk, Diana's brother, Roger—he told me a few weeks after the birth that the child hadn't actually died. He had that snotty Harvard accent: 'Marvelous thing, having connections. We've pulled a few strings, made sure your little baaahstard goes to the grimmest, foulest orphanage in the state. And I'll make certain he stays there forever.' I could have tried to get custody, but I knew that if I did, I'd never have had a chance with Diana. See, I felt sure that if I kept after her, I could win her over eventually. But not if that child was part of the equation. She was only nineteen. It would have been too much for her then; the idea of walking away from her family, her money, her life, shackling herself to a screaming baby and a husband who didn't have two cents to rub together—it just would have been impossible for a nineteen-year-old socialite to make a decision that radical. I traded that child for Diana." Miles wiped one eye with the back of his hand, smearing some gravy across his forehead. "I couldn't ever bring myself to tell Diana."

"Did he do this thing, Miles? Did he kill Diana?"

"I felt so responsible. For how that poor kid turned out."

"I'm asking you a question. Did Blair Dane kill your wife?"

Miles kept eating, tears running down the sides of his nose. Finally, he said, "Do what you have to do, Charley. But if you accuse my son of anything in court, I'll fire you on the spot."

I sat there looking at him.

"Can you just go away?" He prodded his mashed potatoes. "I'm trying to enjoy my Christmas Eve dinner."

Thirty-two

THE HOLIDAYS HAD flashed past in a nerve-racking blur. Everywhere you looked, there was Miles's face. On the TV, in the papers, in the magazines. It was impossible to relax, impossible to shop or eat or even walk across the street without being accosted by journalists or kooks, impossible to escape from the pressure, the cameras, the incessant phone calls.

And it didn't help that when the journalists got tired of slicing at Miles's character, they turned their knives on me. Everyone from the *New York Times* down to *Hard Copy* had something unflattering to say about Charles Sloan, Attorney at Law. They talked about my alcoholism, they talked about the year I'd been suspended from the practice of law for a variety of shady things done while under the influence of eighteen-year-old scotch, they'd interviewed two of my ex-wives (neither of whom, needless to say, had anything good to say about me), and of course they never failed to show the same blurry Polaroid snapped by the insurance investigator, a photo of the car I'd crashed through the door of an emergency room down in Detroit while plastered on Courvoisier. I tried to stay away from the television and the newspapers, but it was hard to do. Until you've lived through something like that, you have no idea how it chafes the spirit. You try to leave the person you were behind, and he just keeps sneaking up behind you, tapping you on the shoulder and leering at you.

For two solid weeks the temperature never rose above four

degrees below zero, and the sun never came out from behind the clouds. A week before Christmas, one of the cracking towers over in Sarnia blew out a pipe and caught on fire. For days the wind whistling steadily out of Canada dropped a film of black, stinking ash over the thin snow until by Christmas Eve all of Pickeral Point looked like a black-and-white photo of some grim nineteenth-century English industrial town. It was a miserable, miserable month.

L ISA AND I sat down on Christmas morning and looked at the meager pile of presents we'd managed to pick up for each other. By the time we'd opened the first present, we were talking about the impending trial. Finally, I said, "Why don't we put these things away and open them after it's over."

I didn't have to specify what *it* was.

I took Miles's pronouncement to "Do what you need to do" as license to keep the Blair-Did-It strategy alive as an option: I placed him on the witness list, buried among a number of character reference witnesses, and hoped that Stash would figure him for a distant cousin.

I had filed two motions to exclude. First, I moved to exclude the book *How I Killed My Wife and Got Away with It*. Having read the book, I was doubtful that he would grant the motion, but it was not unreasonable possibility.

In the second motion, I moved to exclude the bloody clothes and the bokken as fruits of an illegal search. It was a ridiculously long shot, but I felt obliged to do it just to cover all my bases. So I was surprised—even a little shocked—when I got a call the day after Christmas from Judge Evola's secretary saying that the judge wanted briefs from me on both of the exclusion issues. Not just for the book, but for the clothes and the bokken as well. Evola's secretary said that he would hear oral arguments on both issues on the day before trial.

As a result, Lisa spent the entire week between Christmas and New Year's working on the briefs and doing research on the subject. Truth was, I hated to take her away from the other work she was doing. I had experts to prep, documents to organize, witnesses to run down . . . We were dreadfully undermanned for a task as daunting as this trial.

But I couldn't afford to blow the opportunity: If we excluded the book, that would help our case significantly. But if we managed to exclude the clothes *and* the bokken, Stash Olesky had no case. No clothes, no bokken—Miles goes free. It was that simple.

Thirty-three

JUDGE EVOLA HELD the two motions up in front of his nose, closed his eyes, and sniffed deeply. Then he opened his eyes and put a wide smile on his face. "You know what I smell here?" he said.

It was New Year's Eve, six o'clock in the evening, and we were sitting in Mark Evola's expansive chambers on the third floor of the county courthouse. There was a lot of memorabilia hanging on the walls from back in Evola's glory days as a basketball player at Michigan State. During daylight there was a nice view of the river over his left shoulder, but right now all I could see were the reflected lights of Canada, leaving twinkling, wavering smears of white on the dark river. Stash Olesky sat beside me in a red leather chair.

I was surprised Judge Evola had even been willing to hear arguments on my motion to exclude the clothes and the bokken. Normally it would have been dismissed out of hand. But since he had, I figured maybe I had a fighting chance. Until I saw his face, anyway. Mark Evola is a hail-fellow-well-met type of the worst kind and usually acts excruciatingly cordial to me despite how deeply he hates me. But today his smile had gone thin and hostile. His true feelings were sneaking out.

"What I smell here, Charley," he said, "is desperation. But, please, let's hear your argument."

I began to launch into a summary of the position Lisa and I had worked out for the motion to exclude the clothes and the bokken. Evola leaned back and sat there with his arms crossed, looking at me with an amused expression on his face while I monologued. I must have gone on for half an hour before he said, "Thank you so much. That was quite educational."

"Your Honor, if I could respond," Stash said.

"Oh, save the wear and tear on your throat, Stash." Mark Evola reached into his pocket, took out a fat gold pen, then slid a sheet of paper out in front of him. It was obviously an order. He signed it with a flourish. "Motion for exclusion of evidence *dee*-nied!"

I stared at him. "Just like that?"

Evola leaned forward. "Charley. I—and this entire jurisdiction—have gotten sick to death of your cheap tricks and your sly little maneuverings. You and I both know what this is." He held the two motions to exclude up in the air, pinched between two fingers for a moment, then let them go. They drifted down in a heap on his desk. "These are BS. Total BS."

"Your Honor . . ."

"You don't have to Your-Honor me in chambers. It's just Mark, Stash, and Charley, and we're just having a little chitchat on a subject of mutual interest." The smile grew broader. "And here's my view on the matter. The police acted on a legitimate tip. They gained consent. They made the search. It's perfectly admissible."

"Then do you mind my asking why you made me shag all this . . ." I pointed to the stack of papers, the seventy-five-page briefs—all of which represented hours and hours of frantic research on the subject— ". . . why you made me shag this stuff up here from my office—on a holiday evening, no less—why you made me and my clerk spend countless hours preparing for this brief, why you encouraged me to squander vast amounts of our extremely precious time on this motion, when you obviously had made up your mind long ago?"

"Because, Charley—my dear, close and personal friend—I just wanted to see the look on your face." Mark Evola grinned broadly, then pulled out another order and signed it. I could see without even reading it that he was denying my second motion, the motion to exclude the novel *How I Killed My Wife and Got Away with It*.

"Now wait a minute," I said angrily. "You want to rule the seizure is legal, fine, I'll buy it. But that book is another matter! It's a work of fiction, and it has no place in a murder trial."

"Let me try this again, Charley. Dee. Nied. That clear enough for you?" He pushed both orders across the desk toward me. "See you in court, old buddy."

STASH AND I walked down the stairs of the dark empty courthouse together in silence.

He let us out the front door with a key. "Sorry," Stash said. "I didn't know that would happen."

I shrugged. The winter wind was bitter coming off the river from Canada. The air temperature had already made pretty good progress down toward a predicted low for the night of ten below.

"Look," Stash said. "You and me, we're friends. But I know how you are in court. If you come in cleats high, I'm gonna take it right back at you."

"I know that."

He looked out at the dark river. "You want to come over to my place, catch the Michigan State game? Might take our minds off things."

"Nah. Thanks. I wouldn't be able to enjoy it." I put out my hand and we shook.

"You're a miserable excuse for a lawyer and a discredit to the bar," he said.

I smiled, but my heart wasn't in it. In the cold, it felt as though my face might crack. I had a suspicion this trial might get ugly, and that prospect made me feel a little down, like maybe our friendship might not be quite the same after this. "Yeah. You, too, buddy."

We turned and walked away from each other, the wind clawing at our coats.

TRIAL

Thirty-four

WE ALL KNOW who Charley Sloan is." Stash Olesky waved a couple of fingers airily in my direction. Jury selection was complete, the courtroom was crammed to capacity with reporters spilling out into the halls. And in the back of the room was the all-seeing eye, the camera from Court TV, running a live feed into umpteen million households nationwide.

"Charley Sloan," the prosecuting attorney of Kerry County continued, "he's far and away the best-known defense attorney in our little county. A man of . . ." He smiled wickedly, first to the jury, then to the reporters in the back of the courtroom. "He's a man of some, ah, reputation? Shall we say? Back a few years we all saw him on *Hard Copy* and those other trashy shows when he was involved in another case that made the national headlines. Now, I know Charley personally, and I like him. And goodness knows he's a heck of a fine lawyer. But some people in the press, on the TV, homespun pundits down at the barbershop, wherever, have tried to say that this trial is all about Mr. Sloan. Well, folks, I'm here to tell you right now, this trial is *not* about Charley Sloan, and I refuse to make an issue out of his reputation. Or his tactics. Or the class of people he's represented in the past. And certainly not of his unfortunate and well-documented personal problems."

Yeah, right, I thought. That, of course, was precisely what he was doing. My friend Stash was coming in cleats high right out of the box. I knew it, the judge knew it, Stash knew it, every single person in the jury box knew it. Even the folks out there watching the live feed on Court TV knew it. But there was no point jumping up in front of the jury and complaining about it, not just yet. Opening statement was no place to be getting on the jury's bad side. As the prosecutor had alluded, my reputation was cloudy enough as it was. The best thing I could do was sit there looking like a harmless country lawyer, slightly puzzled at all the fuss.

"No, folks," the prosecuting attorney said. "The only reason I even bring up Charley Sloan at all is because I'm setting the scene of this awful crime. All I'm doing is acquainting you with the undisputed facts of what the Pickeral Point police observed when they arrived at 221 Riverside Boulevard on the night of October 21 of last year. The evidence will show that the first thing Officer Jerry Ingram saw when he responded to the scene of Diana Dane's murder was Charley Sloan, who stepped out the front door of Miles Dane's home, and said, 'Officer, my name is Charley Sloan, and I'm representing the interests of Miles Dane. You have questions for Mr. Sloan, you ask me before you ask him. Now, if you'll step inside, I'll show you the corpse.' "

That wasn't exactly what I'd said. But it was close enough. The prosecuting attorney paused and looked significantly over at me, then turned his gaze toward Miles Dane, who looked straight ahead with his haunted gray eyes.

"And, for that matter, it's not about Mr. Dane's reputation either. Mr. Dane's a famous man in his own right, and some of you folks may have heard whispers here and there about him."

Finally, I felt compelled to stand up. "Your Honor." I smiled a wounded smile, spread my hands in supplication. "I know, I know. Opening statement, latitude and so on. Fair enough. But at some point, gosh, I really must insist that the prosecuting attorney actually address the issue of what this trial *is* about. I'm growing intensely curious to know if he intends to present a case here or not."

There was some laughter from the reporters in the gallery. Judge Mark Evola scowled down at me from his full six-foot-six-inch height.

The prosecuting attorney jumped in. "By all means, Your Honor, Mr. Sloan is exactly right. As it happens, I was just getting there."

"Proceed then," the judge said.

"By all means." Stash Olesky frowned at his notes, like I'd made him lose his place. I knew for a fact that he memorized his opening statement, that his "notes"—like his put-on ruralisms—were actually a device to increase his folksy appeal, to make him seem less like the courtroom shark that he really was. "What the state of Michigan *will* prove in the trial, and what the evidence *will* demonstrate, my friends, is chillingly simple. You peel back all the hype, all the publicity, all the cameras and newspaper reporters, all the jokes on late-night television— you look past all that ephemeral noise, and, folks, this evidence is real, real simple. Real, real stark.

"What the state will prove and what the evidence will clearly show is that on the night of October 21 of last year, someone took a weapon off the wall of the locked room where Miles Dane stores his vast collection of dirks and daggers and samurai swords and guns and ninja throwing stars and halberds and all manner of other nasty-looking weapons, and that person walked up the stairs of his lovely home over there by the river, and that same person beat Miles Dane's wife Diana to death. Didn't just hit her a lick or two that killed her by mistake. No, the evidence will show Diana Dane was beaten relentlessly, for approximately ten to fifteen minutes. Possibly more. Furthermore, the evidence will indicate that she was killed either by someone she knew or that she was killed while she slept. Then the killer stood there and watched her while she died. The forensic evidence and the testimony of witnesses will show all of this clearly.

"Statements made by Miles Dane himself will show that Mr. Dane was in the house while the murder was committed. The evidence will also show that the defendant, after discovering his wife, waited for a significant period of time before calling anyone. And when Mr. Dane finally got around to making a phone call—one phone call, I might add . . ." Here, just in case no one had understood, Stash Olesky held up his index finger and stared at it accusingly.

"He made *one* phone call. And who did Mr. Dane call? The ambulance? Nope. The police? Nope. Nine-one-one? No, sir. Sheriff, fire department, priest, funeral home? No, ma'am. No, my friends, the evidence will show that when he finally got around to picking up the phone, he called Charley Sloan. His lawyer. These are the plain facts, people. Plain facts, undisputed by Mr. Dane."

The prosecuting attorney shrugged theatrically, put his hands in his pockets, strolled toward the jury. "I guess I could run on for a while, take up your time telling you all about the mountain of incriminating evidence that the state of Michigan has managed to pile up against this cold-blooded killer. But I won't. I could tell about all the lies and inconsistencies in the story Mr. Dane told the Pickeral Point police. But I won't. I could tell you about how the state police lab found the defendant's fingerprints on the murder weapon. But I won't. I could tell you about the defendant's bloodstained clothes." Stash Olesky took his time, studied the face of each juror in turn. "But, folks, your time is valuable, and this case is dead simple, and the evidence will be clear. You don't need to hear me give some long tedious speech. So let's just forge right on. I'm just going to *step out of the way*, my friends, and let the evidence speak."

Stash Olesky stepped to his left and made a big, sweeping motion with his arm, like a toreador avoiding the unstoppable rush of a huge oncoming bull.

"And when you're done hearing and seeing that evidence, you will be as outraged and saddened and horrified as I am. And, I predict—notwithstanding all of Charley Sloan's well-known theatrics and razzle-dazzle—that you will not require a great deal of deliberation before you find Miles Dane guilty of murder."

He stood in the middle of the courtroom one hand still shoved deep in his pocket, and surveyed the jury again for what seemed a very long time.

"Murder?" he said finally. "Wait. No, not just murder. First-degree murder. *Premeditated* murder. That's the how the criminal code of Michigan characterizes the worst crime a human being can commit. Premeditation. Maliciously planning the crime in advance. I have prosecuted hundreds of cases in my life, but never have I prosecuted a case where the premeditation of the act was so coldly and clearly and shamelessly and unambiguously laid out in advance. After you see the evidence, I think you'll agree with me. And when you do, you'll have to find Miles Dane guilty of the premeditated murder of his own wife. It's that simple."

"Again, folks, I'm not asking you to believe me. All you have to do is believe the words of the defendant. Because we will introduce a written plan, a veritable confession, a virtual road map of this crime." Stash Olesky held up a shiny paperback book with a bright red cover, waved it in the air. "It's all right here. We will admit into evidence the very words of the defendant, and when you hear them read out in open court, believe me, your blood will run cold."

He tossed the stack of paper on the table next to him, then finally pulled out the inevitable last stop. Sad-faced and shaking his head, Stash Olesky slid his hand out of his pocket, trotted out the trusty index finger again, pointed it directly at Miles Dane.

"Premeditation, folks. Murder in the first degree. The plain facts will show this. Mr. Dane is guilty, guilty, guilty."

Then he sat down.

B RAVO!" I SAID enthusiastically, clapping my hands three times in slow succession. "What a courageous and self-effacing fellow we have in our prosecuting attorney."

I smiled broadly and approached the box. "Isn't that brave of Mr. Olesky? He's not even going to make a case against my client. He's just going to . . ." I did a quick little shuffle step to the side, felt my left knee creak. Stash Olesky is half a dozen years younger and a great deal more graceful than I. "He's just going to *step aside*. He's going to *let the evidence speak*!"

I aimed my most aggrieved smile at the prosecuting attorney.

"Well, folks, I want you to do something before I tell you what *our* evidence will show. Ladies? Gentlemen? If you would, just turn your heads and look to the back of the courtroom." I pointed at the Court TV camera that was aiming directly back at me. The jury members turned and looked. As did everybody in the courtroom, craning their heads, trying see where I was about to take them. "Right back there you will see the biggest liar in this courtroom. The TV camera. During my statement, during this trial, during every moment you weigh the evidence in front of you I want to you to remember one thing. Re-member that camera."

I let a few moments pass. "Now, let's get back to the evidence. You notice Mr. Olesky, in his rather brief statement, didn't tell you a whale of a lot about that evidence, did he? Oh, he talked about *me*. Said a great deal about me. Threw in a few nasty asides about my client, too. Told you how horrible this crime was. But, my gracious, when it came down to brass tacks, to the *facts* of the case, he just said there was— what was the word? A *mountain* of evidence? When he got to the part where he had to draw a line connecting my client and the actual com-mission of the crime, well, he just stood mute didn't he? What arro-gance! As though it might bore you to actually hear the nature of the case he plans to present against my client." I gave him a hard stare.

"I give Mr. Olesky credit for one thing, though. He and his vast array of state-employed minions have indeed assembled a mountain. A mountain of distortions. A mountain of half-truths. A mountain of in-sinuations. A mountain of hype. A mountain of . . . well, decorum doesn't permit me to use the term that springs immediately to mind." I winked at the hatchet-faced old farmer in overalls, Dahlgren, who sat on the front row of the jury box. He grinned back. Every defense lawyer needs an ally, an emissary into the jury room—and I planned to make Dahlgren mine.

"No, I take that back. In fact, there is a word. There is a single, simple, clear word that encompasses Mr. Olesky's entire case against Miles Dane." I stalked across the room and snatched a paperback book off the defense table, then brandished it in the air, showing off the lurid picture of a man holding a curved black stick over a bosomy, cowering woman.

"Fiction!" I slammed the book on the table. "What Mr. Olesky— in *fact*—has assembled is a vast mountain of fiction." I stalked toward the jury. "Fiction."

"So when you hear and consider this vast mountain of so-called evidence, keep asking yourself this: Fact or fiction? Fact or fiction?

"So let's talk about the plain facts that Mr. Olesky is so proud of. What is a fact anyway? I'll tell you what a fact is. In the context of this case, a *fact* would be the direct, sworn testimony of somebody who saw this man coldly bludgeon his wife to death. You will hear no such fact in this trial. A *fact* would be a sworn confession by the defendant that he did what Mr. Olesky says he did. You will hear no such fact in this trial. A *fact* would be the existence of a videotape showing Mr. Dane walking into his wife's room and killing her. You will neither hear, nor see, nor smell, nor taste any such factual evidence in this trial.

"Why not? The reason is simple. You see, since the courageous Mr. Olesky lacks any such facts, any such direct and unimpeachable evidence that Mr. Dane *in fact* killed his wife, he will rely on a huge number of small, trivial, arcane, technical details which, like a child's wooden blocks, may be assembled in a thousand million different ways. Moreover . . . as he piles up this mountain of blocks, he will attempt to blur the line between fact and fiction. He'll show you a fact, then he'll show you some fiction, he'll show you a fact again, then more fiction again, fact, fiction, fact, fiction. And then, finally, he'll wave his wand and try to hypnotize you into thinking they're the same thing.

"So every time he tells you he's stepping aside to let the facts speak, *Watch out!* Because he's probably trying to pull a fast one on you. Every time he shows you a 'fact' ask yourself: Is this really a fact or not? Is it a fact or is it the opinion of some supposed expert in the field, who, because of their position in the law enforcement bureaucracy, is predisposed to believing in Mr. Dane's guilt? Ask yourself: At what point does a fact shade over into fiction? At what point does fiction become fact?

"Oh, yes, there will be a great number of little pieces of information here that the prosecuting attorney will refer to as facts. But when piled into a mountain, they will rapidly turn to fiction. A pile of blocks may be as big as a mountain, but that doesn't make it a mountain. It's still just a pile of blocks. And when this trial is over we will show you just how that same pile of blocks can be assembled to tell an entirely different story than the one Mr. Olesky is about to tell."

I walked back to the defense table and stood by my client. He stared straight ahead as I placed my hands on his shoulders.

"There will be one small difference between Mr. Olesky's story and our story. The difference will be that our story will not be fiction. Our story will be true.

"So. Let me address the evidence. Let me tell you what *we* will show."

I walked over to the jury box, turned my back to them and pointed at my client. "Exhibit A. The man you see right here is Miles Dane. Famous writer. Chiseled features. Strong jaw. You've seem him on TV wearing the black cowboy boots and the black turtleneck and the black jeans and what the TV reporters always refer to as his 'omnipresent shoulder holster.' " I lowered my arm and strolled across the courtroom. "Maybe you've heard on TV about how he gets in fights with movie stars at Hollywood extravaganzas and how he shoots holes in the walls of New York office buildings. Oh yes, my friends, you've got the *evidence* of your own eyes!"

My laugh came out full of scorn. "But there's something rotten about all that supposed evidence showing Mr. Dane as some kind of brawling tough guy. What we will show you in this trial is that all that supposed evidence comes straight out of the boob tube. In this trial you won't hear testimony from a single soul in Pickeral Point, Michigan, who'll show Mr. Dane to be a violent man. The evidence will show that he never got in a fistfight with anybody over at Freddie's Fish Barn. Never wore his gun into Klein's Five-and-Dime down on Main. Never pistol-whipped anybody over in the produce section at Kroger's. Why will the evidence fail to show anything like that? Because there are no TV cameras in Pickeral Point, Michigan!

"No TV cameras in Pickeral Point, you say? What's that got to do with the price of tea in China? What's that got to do with Miles Dane being charged with murder?" I spread my hands. "Sadly—a lot.

"Let me tell you a story." I walked over to the jury box, with my hands clasped earnestly together, Father O'Reilly about to make a solemn moral point to his boys at the orphanage. "The evidence will show that when Miles Dane was sixteen years old, he dropped out of high school and hit the road. He left the town of Pickeral Point as a short, skinny, dreamy, pimply, despised kid from the crummiest house on the crummiest street in the crummiest neighborhood in Pickeral Point, Michigan. But he left with a dream. And when he came back, he was the man you see before you. A man seemingly transformed. Tough guy, famous writer, barroom brawler, shoulder holster, black cowboy boots.

"But who *is* Miles Dane? Who is he *really*? Is he the man that the prosecuting attorney is about to parade before you, the brawler that this supposed mountain of evidence will portray? Or is he still, when you get down to it, the sweet boy who left this town with the wild, secret, unlikely, ambitious dream of turning himself into a writer? Which one is fact, folks? Which one is fiction?"

"You talk about a mountain of evidence, Mr. Olesky? Well I may not have the whole state of Michigan standing behind me. I may not have an army of police investigators and assistant prosecuting attorneys and paralegals and forensic technicians from the state police. I may not have a troop of bureaucrats at my beck and call. Over at that table it's just me and my loyal daughter sitting there next to Mr. Dane. But we've got our own little mountain of evidence. And what we will show you is that the *real* Miles Dane, the one who lives at 221 Riverside Boulevard, is not the same fellow that the world sees through that lens back there—he's not a brawler, not an abusive person, not a crazy man, not a gun-toting, knife-wielding maniac. He is a gentle, loving family man, a man who has suffered the cruelest and most ironic tragedy of all: Not only has his beloved wife, his very soul mate, been snatched away from him—but *he* has been accused of committing the awful crime which removed her from his life.

"Oh, we'll bring out experts with fancy degrees and diplomas and high-sounding titles who will paint a very different picture of the supposed evidence, the *circumstantial* evidence, in this case. But, folks, that will not be the mountain on which this case will ultimately rest.

"*Our* mountain will not be circumstantial, folks. *Our* mountain sits right there in that seat—a man of uncommon decency and devotion and loyalty. But to see him, you must look skeptically at all of the fiction and *circumstantial* detail with which Mr. Olesky is about to bombard you. You must try to see it as it is. It is all an illusion. It is Court TV. It is CNN. It is the airy magic of bright lights and camera lenses, of fancy charts and graphs, of complicated scientific words.

"Did Mr. Dane contribute to this fiction? Indeed, he did. The evidence will show that he invented a mask, a fictional version of himself. The evidence will show that as an ambitious and driven young man, Miles Dane invented, quite frankly, a scary mask. Armed brawler in black. Gun-carrying loudmouth. Testy, hot-tempered little tough guy. All that was missing was an eye patch and a hook. And he wore that mask with great discipline for a long time, showing nothing of his real self to the world. That mask is the invention of an ambitious young man, come back to haunt him. But that mask, folks, like the prosecuting attorney's case, is utterly fiction.

I pointed to the back of the courtroom. "The mask is the camera's lie."

I looked sadly at my client and then walked across the courtroom, my back to the jury. When I finally turned toward them, I said, "So I ask you to examine the evidence as adults, not as credulous children. I ask you to pierce through all the Hollywood magic, all the New York folderol. Because if you look hard enough, you will not only see through this illusory mountain of *circumstantial* evidence, but you will also see through the somewhat unappealing mask that an ambitious, callow Miles Dane created many, many years ago as a means to keep food on his table while he pursued his craft, his calling, his passion. Look hard, and you will see through to this man's warm and decent heart."

I walked slowly across the courtroom again, savoring the sound of my footsteps on the hard old marble floor. I'd been keyed up for weeks about this trial, fearing it. But now that I was here, now that I was finally working, I felt like a man who'd been allowed to breathe after being held for a long time underwater. I'd been talking about masks, about reality, about being the person you really are, and it struck me in that moment that whoever Charley Sloan is, I guess I am most him when I'm standing up there trying to save a client's bacon. When I reached Miles Dane, I put my hands on his shoulders and squeezed him hard enough to make him wince.

"Inside this man," I said, "you will not find the heart of a killer. You simply will not.

"So as you examine the evidence, don't let that camera back there sell you the same lie it has sold to Mr. Olesky and his bureaucratic minions. Just look at the facts.

"Fact." Another squeeze of the shoulders. "If *your* hearts are clear, then your eyes will see the truth. I beg you. Open your hearts to this man, and the *fact* of who he really is will blossom before you like a flower." Okay, a little cornpone, maybe. But Hallmark Cards doesn't stay in business because the American public is afraid of a little schmaltz. I looked scornfully toward the electronic eye in the back of the room, then let my face soften as I looked back down at Miles Dane. "*This* man."

I gave him a last hard squeeze. And damned if a tear didn't appear at the corner of one of his eyes and run down the side of his face. It was a moment of transcendent courtroom beauty, a moment I will never repeat, not if I stand before the bar for another thousand years. I could have jumped up in the air and shouted hallelujah.

Instead, however, I inclined my own face a few degrees toward the jury and put two fingers up to one eye as though stanching a few tears of my own. Then I sat and buried my face in my hands. I know, I'm a shameless ham. But this is my job. And let the record reflect that, like his client, Charley Sloan loves his work.

Perhaps, beyond all reason.

Thirty-five

STASH OLESKY'S FIRST witness was the responding officer, a young kid named Jerry Ingram. He wore his dress uniform, and although the linen was crisp and the leather spit-shined, there was something vaguely bedraggled about him. He was fair, blond-haired, with the last vestiges of adolescent acne still clinging to his pale cheeks. After the clerk swore him in, Officer Ingram set his hat next to the microphone, then sat down nervously.

After asking Ingram a few questions about his training and his work assignment, Stash Olesky said, "Now Officer Ingram, directing your attention to October 21 of last year, during your shift did you receive a radio call from 911 dispatch?"

"Yes sir." The kid's voice was nervous and squeaky.

"Could you tell us about that?"

"Well, I got one about a cat stuck in a tree . . ." Ingram looked puzzled when some of the reporters tittered in the back of courtroom.

"Okay," Olesky said patiently. "So maybe you got several 911 calls. But is there one that sticks out in your memory? A particularly important one."

Ingram blushed. "Oh. I see. I'm sorry." He cleared his throat, then spoke as though he'd memorized the next line with great struggle and effort. "Yes sir. At approximately 4:11 A.M. in the morning, this officer responded to a Code 3 at 221 Riverside Drive."

"Just tell it in your own words, son," Olesky said. "You don't have to say it like it was written down in your report or anything. Just tell me what happened like you were telling your girlfriend."

Ingram swallowed. "Um. I don't, currently, right now I'm not seeing nobody."

Olesky nodded patiently. "I know you swore to tell the whole truth. And I appreciate your honesty on the subject. You have a mother?"

"Yes sir."

"Terrific. Tell the folks in the jury what happened just like you'd tell your mother."

"Okay." Ingram blinked. "Well. What happened is I had gotten the Code 3. That's the radio code for an emergency deceased person call. So I rolled up at 221 Riverside. I knew it was Mr. Miles Dane's home because he's like the most famous guy in town. So I got out of my cruiser and I went up and I knocked on the door with my baton. That's how they tell us to do it in training. With the stick? So if anybody inside is deaf or asleep or whatever . . ." He cleared his throat uncertainly. "So anyway the door opens and there's a gentleman standing there. He tells me his name's Charley Sloan."

"Did you recognize Mr. Sloan?"

"Yes sir. He's pretty well known in law enforcement for getting criminals off around here."

I hoisted myself out of the seat. "Your Honor!" I did my best to sound grimly aggrieved. "I have to protest that spurious characterization."

Judge Evola scowled. "Officer Ingram, I'd ask you to limit your testimony to your direct observations." He turned to the jury. "Mr. Sloan is a criminal defense attorney. He has represented a variety of individuals, some of whom have been found guilty, some not. His extensive track record on that score is of no concern to this trial, and you should disregard anything suggesting otherwise."

"Thank you, Your Honor."

Olesky smiled at the officer. "I know you're fairly new to the courtroom, Officer Ingram, but you're doing fine. Continue with your story if you would."

"So Mr. Sloan tells me that he's representing the owner of the house, Mr. Dane. And then he says for me to follow him upstairs and he'd show me the, um, the decedent."

"When you say 'decedent,' Officer, you mean a dead person."

"Yes sir."

"So he indicated at that time that he was aware there was a dead person up there."

"Yes sir."

"He didn't say, Officer Ingram, there's a woman upstairs in need of medical attention, somebody's hurt upstairs, anything of that nature?"

"No sir."

"Did he say anything else?"

"He asked me if I had ever been involved in securing the scene of a murder before. I told him no, and he said that he'd help me out."

Olesky raised his eyebrows slightly. "Well, wasn't that kind of him."

"He seemed pretty friendly, yes sir."

"I bet he did. What happened then?"

I stood and said, "Your Honor, could I have a brief word with you and Mr. Olesky?"

Judge Evola squinted malevolently at me. "Mr. Sloan, are you currently engaged in examining a witness?"

"Why, no, Your Honor," I said, all innocence and confusion.

"Well, just because you have the urge to butt in and start making demands doesn't mean this court will allow you to do so. If you have something to say in this courtroom while Mr. Olesky is engaged in this examination, it had best be in the form of an objection."

I tried to look hurt. My main goal in objecting was to show the jury that Judge Evola despised me. It was all part of my general plan to paint Miles as the innocent dupe, steamrolled by callous functionaries and factotums of a careless and heartless judicial machine. "Okay, then, I must object to the hearsay portion of this witness's testimony as regards my role at the scene of the crime. Naturally his observations relating directly to the crime are relevant—"

"Good. Thank you," Evola interrupted me. "Mr. Olesky, do you wish to address that issue in any way?"

"Officer Ingram's testimony as to anything Mr. Sloan may have said goes to the officer's investigatory observations, which, as Mr. Sloan is well aware, are bright and clear exceptions to the hearsay rule."

"What this goes to," I bellowed, waving my finger, "is a general and transparent attempt by Mr. Olesky to smear my client based upon strange and bizarre allegations and insinuations as to *my* conduct."

"Denied. Sit down, Mr. Sloan."

I sat down slowly, slumping a little and looking terribly dejected. Poor ol' Charley, taking an unfair beating from The Man.

"Continue, Officer Ingram," Olesky said.

"Well, Mr. Sloan, he said that there had been a break-in and that somebody had been killed by a burglar. Then we went upstairs, and he showed me the decedent. I asked him if there was anybody else in the house and he said that the only other person there was the decedent's husband and that he was pretty distraught, so he told me that while I was securing the scene he would take care of Mr. Dane, and that I didn't need to talk to him. He said a detective would take care of that later."

"At that time did Mr. Sloan identify who the victim was?"

"Yes sir. He said her name was Diana Dane, that she was Mr. Dane's wife."

"So what happened next?"

"Mr. Sloan said that I ought not to go in the room with the victim, that I was liable to disturb important evidence. He said that if I wanted to look like a professional to my superiors, I should go outside and put up crime scene tape, leave the examination of the body and the scene to the detectives. He pointed out some trees and stuff that I could wrap my tape around."

"So what did you do then?"

"I went out and started stringing tape around the property."

"Just out of curiosity, did Mr. Sloan's advice turn out to be popular with your superiors?"

Ingram blushed again. "Well, Sergeant Borden, my supervisor, he got a little hot about me leaving Mr. Sloan and Mr. Dane in there alone with the body."

"Thank you, Officer."

Judge Evola leaned forward. "Mr. Sloan, do you have any questions for this witness."

I stood without leaving the spot where I'd been sitting. "Officer, did you observe me doctoring evidence?"

"No, sir."

"Sneaking out of the house with weapons under my coat, anything along those lines?"

"No sir."

"Moving furniture? Hiding secret decoder rings?"

"No sir."

"Good. You're a fine young man, and if in my zeal to protect the scene of the crime from contamination so that evidence leading to the capture and conviction of the *real* killer could be preserved, I may have gotten you in dutch with your boss, well, I sincerely apologize."

Thirty-six

A FTER LUNCH STASH put Detective Chantall Denkerberg on the stand. She looked even more Catholic-girl's-school than ever as she walked to the front of the courtroom. Spine straight, hair cut short and neat, blue suit, starched white cotton blouse, sensible blue shoes.

"Detective Denkerberg," the prosecuting attorney began, "could you tell us about the morning of October 21 of last year?"

"I received a page from Dispatch at 4:07 A.M.," the detective said in her firm, big voice, "indicating that a violent death had occurred at 221 Riverside Drive. I was instructed to investigate. At that time I proceeded to the scene. I was greeted at my car by Sergeant Dale Borden, the senior uniformed officer at the scene. He and his officers had just arrived and were in the process of securing the scene. At that time he informed me that the victim was named Diana Dane, a white female, age fifty-seven. His observation at the time was that it appeared to be a homicide by beating."

"And who was the next person you spoke to?"

"As I approached the front door of the residence, a man came out and identified himself as Charley Sloan. Mr. Sloan indicated that he was an attorney and that he represented the victim's husband, Mr. Miles Dane."

"Did Mr. Sloan say anything else?"

"He said that Mr. Dane had told him that the murderer had apparently been a burglar who had jumped out a window after committing the crime. Then he added that Mr. Dane was very distraught and that he would not be capable of making a statement until later that morning."

"You run into lawyers often at crime scenes?"

"Almost never. In my experience innocent people don't call their lawyers the minute a crime is committed."

I popped out of my seat. "Objection!" I said. "In twenty years of law practice that is the most inaccurate and prejudicial thing I've ever heard. The defense moves for a mistrial!"

Judge Evola looked down at me darkly. "First, Mr. Sloan, you can forget about a mistrial. Motion denied. However, I'm going to sustain the objection. Detective Denkerberg, keep your opinions to yourself if you would." He turned to the jury. "Ladies and gentlemen, Detective Denkerberg has implied that because someone calls a lawyer, one may infer that they are guilty of something. Not so. People call lawyers for all manner of reasons. I'm instructing you to put this statement out of your minds and give it absolutely no weight."

The old put-it-out-of-your-minds trick. Ladies and gentlemen, please pay no attention to the elephant sitting over there on your sofa. Evola was enjoying the moment, I could tell.

Stash continued. "Detective, typically what do you as an investigator prefer to do when you reach the scene of a crime?"

"I do two things. First, I want to tour the perimeter and make certain the crime scene is secure. While doing so I begin to identify potential avenues of investigation. Second, I want to speak at least briefly to any and all witnesses. In this case I was prevented from doing that by Mr. Sloan."

It was time for me to hop up again and look apoplectic. "Your Honor, not only is that factually inaccurate, it entirely misrepresents my intent at the time! What I was trying to do was *assist* her. Mr. Dane's wife had just been murdered. He was extremely distraught and I merely suggested to Miss Denkerberg that by giving Mr. Dane time to collect himself, he could most coherently explain what had transpired that night, and thereby best aid police in their finding the *actual* perpetrator of this heinous crime. Apparently I was unsuccessful in that because here we sit with Mr. Dane unjustly pilloried and—"

Judge Evola whacked his gavel lazily on the bench a few times. "Mr. Sloan, that'll do just fine. Save your windy speeches for closing arguments. And if you want to get up here on the stand and testify that Detective Denkerberg's recollection of events conflicts with yours, you may feel free to do so. Objection denied."

I sat.

"Detective Denkerberg, continue please," Stash said.

"At that point I circled the property. I noted that there was a window open on the second floor. I photographed and documented the fact that there was glass on the ground outside the window indicating that the window had been broken from the inside. I then carefully examined the ground under the window. It was at that point that I became somewhat puzzled."

Stash looked interested. "Oh?"

"At that time I had no reason to doubt the story Mr. Sloan had related—the burglar-kills-Mrs.-Dane-and-jumps-out-the-window scenario, if you will. So when I saw the broken window, I naturally assumed the perpetrator had jumped out that particular window. Well, it had rained the day before, and the ground was very soft beneath the window. Anyone jumping out that window would almost certainly have left footprints when they hit the ground. Very likely even indentations from hands and knees as they pitched over to regain balance. So I was quite puzzled when a very careful search revealed no footprints at all."

"Surely something? Scuff marks, dents, something?"

The detective shook her head. "Nothing. Just glass."

Stash Olesky proffered several of her crime scene photographs, which appeared to confirm the lack of footprints.

"What did you do then?"

She explained about her further examination of the grounds, then her investigation of the house as she circled in toward the body.

"Eventually I reached the body."

"Tell us about your first impression."

Chantall Denkerberg showed emotion for the first time. She looked at Miles Dane with fire in her eyes, and said, "Horrific violence. I've investigated hundreds of homicides and assaults in my career and this was by far the worst beating I'd ever seen. Diana Dane was barely recognizable as a woman."

"Did you make any immediate determination as to cause of death?"

"Obviously the final determination on that would be the medical examiner's purview. But it was clear she'd been beaten savagely." She went on to describe where Diana Dane lay, the condition of the room, the apparent lack of struggle, the blood on the walls and ceiling, then she explained how she and the state police crime scene technician had worked together to document everything.

"So did you ever get a chance to talk to Mr. Dane?"

"Yes. Eventually Mr. Sloan slithered in and said Mr. Dane was ready to talk."

Up I went, hands raised heavenward. "Your *Honor*! Please!"

Judge Evola raised his eyebrows at Detective Denkerberg. "You're an experienced witness, Detective," he said piously. "If you want to engage in sly character attacks, do them elsewhere. This is a court of law."

"I demand you sanction the witness," I said. "A night or two in jail might assist her in doing her job a little more conscientiously." *Slithered* in? I wasn't posturing now: I was mad.

Judge Evola gave me a big, cool smile. "Mr. Sloan, when you get to be a judge, you can do what you want. In my courtroom, however, you will not presume to instruct me in how to do my job."

I didn't apologize. I just stood there with my arms folded, giving Denkerberg the evil eye.

"That's your cue to sit, Mr. Sloan," Evola said, still smiling.

I went down slow, not hiding how I felt.

Stash Olesky jumped in quickly, not wanting to let me disturb the flow of his examination. "All slithering aside, Detective, what happened next?"

"Mr. Sloan led me to Mr. Dane's office in the back of the house and introduced me to him. I then questioned Mr. Dane about the events of that night. He explained to me that he had been in his office most of the night and into the morning. Frankly, it took a while to get the story out because Mr. Sloan kept interrupting on some pretext or other."

"Objection!" I said. I didn't even stand up this time.

Stash held up his hand. "Now, Your Honor, let's get real here. This is a highly trained and experienced investigator. In the course of conducting an investigation she's drawing on years and years of experience to draw conclusions as to the *totality* of the scene she's investigating. Mr. Sloan—and his conduct—are part of that scene. It's part of her evaluation of what's what. The state contends that she is not merely entitled but *obliged* to testify as to *all* the facts and impressions on which she drew to make her conclusions in this case. To steer around Mr. Sloan as though he were some untouchable, unseeable black hole in the middle of the room is to mislead the jury and to render a disservice to the cause of justice."

"Your Honor," I said. "Once again I must protest that this case is not about me. It's about Mr. Dane's guilt or innocence."

Evola frowned as though this were a grudging decision. "Alright, Mr. Olesky, as long as your witness sticks very carefully to how Mr. Sloan's conduct impacted her evaluation of the crime scene and her immediate impressions of the case, I'll allow it. But tread lightly. Mr. Sloan is not on trial here."

"Thank you, Your Honor," I said, "for coaching the witness on how to hide prejudicial testimony behind the rules of evidence."

"Don't test me, Mr. Sloan," Evola snapped.

I sat quickly.

Stash smiled. "Very good, Detective. Did Mr. Sloan's conduct in some manner change or contribute to the totality of your evaluation of the case as it presented itself at that place and time?"

I rolled my eyes. This was leading the witness at its finest.

"It did."

"Good. Let's get to the whys and wherefores later. You were about to discuss your conversation with Mr. Dane."

"Yes. Mr. Dane indicated that he customarily worked from midnight until four in the morning. He then explained to me that on or around three-fifteen or three-thirty that morning, he'd heard a noise, a suspicious sound that had made him leave his office. He indicated he'd gone upstairs and seen a man fleeing down the hallway adjoining his wife's bedroom. He added that he was unable to give a description of the man, saying that the lighting was bad. I asked if he saw the man carrying a weapon. He said he wasn't sure. Mr. Dane then said he chased the man down to the guest bedroom. As he was approaching the room, Mr. Dane said he heard a loud crash, like breaking glass. Upon entering the room, Mr. Dane indicated he had found the room empty and a window had been smashed out. He had then looked out the window whereupon he saw, I believe the exact words he used were 'a shadowy figure' fleeing across the lawn toward the road."

"That was the entire substance of his story?"

"Basically, yes."

"Let me shift gears a little. How was Mr. Dane dressed?"

"He was wearing a white robe, white pajamas."

"Did he indicate that he'd been wearing them when he discovered his wife's body?"

"That was what he claimed."

"So he hadn't changed clothes."

"Like I say, that was his story."

"Anything to indicate he had had physical contact with his wife after she was beaten? Were there bloodstains on the clothes?"

"No. None whatsoever."

"Okay, let's turn to his behavior. Was there anything you noted about Mr. Dane's demeanor that you found worthy of note?"

"He seemed combative, uncooperative."

"As a trained investigator, what did you make of that?"

"It seemed, on the face of it, inconsistent with a grieving man. Different people react differently to stress, of course. I won't say it's an absolute rule . . . but in my experience as an investigator, the family members of a victim generally view police as allies, not enemies."

"You mentioned Mr. Sloan's behavior. Again, we're not interested in whether you like Mr. Sloan or for that matter whether his presence there seemed to imply anything. I'm asking whether Mr. Sloan acted in a way that seemed significant to you as a trained investigator."

I sighed loudly enough for the jury to hear me.

"Yes," Detective Denkerberg said. "As I mentioned before, he interrupted the interview in a way that seemed clearly, to my ear as a trained investigator, to be a bogus pretext. He pretended he was choking, so I went to get him a glass of water. When I got back from the kitchen, I found the door closed and locked. I couldn't hear what they were saying, but I could tell that Mr. Sloan had a lengthy conversation with his client while I was standing out in the hall."

I tried my best. "Your Honor, I have to make a continuing objection to this whole outrageous line of inquiry!"

"Duly noted."

Stash moved quickly forward. "What was your conclusion as an investigator regarding this lengthy conversation?"

Denkerberg's answer was pretty well framed under the circumstances. She didn't want this case tanked on appeal any more than Olesky did. "Again, taken by itself, the conversation wasn't noteworthy. I'm as much a supporter of the right of every citizen to receive legal counsel whenever and wherever they feel that need or want it. But taking the entire situation in its totality, given the lack of footprints outside the broken window, given the fact that Mr. Dane had not bothered to call the police or an ambulance—well, all of that put my radar up, you might say. And so Mr. Sloan's presence and behavior . . . well I felt like if you added all that up, a picture was emerging of a witness who was not being entirely forthcoming."

Stash seemed to like the answer. And I didn't blame him. Chantall Denkerberg obviously knew her way around a courtroom. "While you conducted your interview, was there anything in Mr. Dane's office that seemed noteworthy."

"Yes, the office contained a large collection of weapons."

"What sort of weapons?"

"You name it. Various pistols, shotguns, rifles. Various bladed weapons. I later counted and found sixty-seven items in his collection. Everything from a fairly expensive-looking Japanese sword to a crude knife, which was apparently a homemade shiv confiscated from an inmate at a federal penitentiary."

"Did anything in particular take your notice?"

"Well, the collection was obviously carefully maintained. All the objects were hung on the wall from, I don't know if you'd call them pegs or hooks, but they were made from the same wood as the paneling on the wall. The weapons had been recently dusted, the guns were oiled, and so on. Under each and every weapon in the collection I observed a small brass tag that gave some information about the item— what it was, when it was manufactured, etc.

"During our conversation we had some general chitchat about the weapons. Mr. Dane seemed proud of the collection and he stated that it was worth over a hundred thousand dollars. At that time he said that as a result of the collection's value, he kept his study locked at all times."

"Did you observe anything else of particular note about the collection?"

"Yes, I did. There were two empty hooks about eighteen inches apart, with a small brass plate attached to the wall below them."

He set another photograph on the edge of the witness stand. "And this photograph, which I've just had the clerk mark as State's 31, is it a true and accurate depiction of that empty rack?"

"Yes it is. At that time I made some comments about the collection, then I asked Mr. Dane what normally resided in that particular rack. He replied that it was an item called a bokken, that it was a wooden object used by Japanese swordsmen for practice purposes. More specifically, he said that this particular item was made of ebony. He said there are three or four species of ebony and that this particular bokken was made from Gabon ebony, which is the most expensive and rare kind."

Stash nodded. "And, Detective, did you inquire what had happened to this bokken?"

"Yes. At first he indicated that it had been missing from the collection for some while. When I asked what had happened to it, he said he didn't know; so I called attention to his earlier statement that he kept the door to his office locked at all times due to the value of the collection and asked how this weapon could have gone missing from a locked room. At that point he changed his story and indicated that maybe it had only gone missing that night.

"So I asked if it was possible that it might have been stolen by this supposed burglar who had allegedly killed his wife. Well, maybe so. How could that have happened with the door locked? He indicated that, well, actually he kept the door unlocked while he was working. So he surmised that he had gone to the bathroom that night, and while he was in the rest room, this alleged burglar had snuck into the room and stolen the stick. So I said, 'With a wall full of weapons, including several valuable-looking guns and swords, why steal a stick?' Mr. Dane then indicated that it was possible the burglar had been surprised by hearing the toilet flush in the adjoining bathroom and that he had grabbed the stick—not because he wanted to steal it, but because it was the closest weapon at hand—and that the burglar had then fled from the room to avoid detection. He further surmised that the burglar, fearing that he might be discovered and possibly even attacked by Mr. Dane, had fled upstairs, where he must have then been surprised by or confronted by Mrs. Dane. In order to silence her—again this was Mr. Dane's speculation at the time—the alleged burglar had probably attacked her with the bokken."

"Detective Denkerberg, in your experience as an investigator are there any sort of rules of thumb about how people behave when in fear of a potential attack?"

"Yes. Psychology says if you feel threatened, you flee to safety. Generally, people flee inward and upward when in their own homes because they perceive their home to be a safe haven. Burglars or other trespassers, on the other hand, when surprised during an invasion of a home, tend to flee down and out. For them, safety lies in mobility and escape."

"So let me be clear," Stash said. "Mr. Dane said he surmised that the burglar heard the toilet flush in his office, realized somebody in the house was awake, then got scared, and as a result fled upstairs?"

"Right. Which seemed entirely inconsistent with normal human behavior. If a burglar felt threatened, he would likely head for the nearest door. The front door of the house actually lay between Mr. Dane's study and the stairs. So a burglar would have had to actually flee *past* a natural route of escape to go upstairs. All of this seemed logically inconsistent."

"So taken in totality, using your judgment and experience as a trained investigator . . ."

"I smelled a rat."

Stash Olesky strolled over to the defense table and laid his hand on the defense table in front of Miles Dane. "You smelled a rat." He let the phrase reverberate in our minds for a while then turned to the witness again. "What else did you discuss during this interview, Detective?"

"Nothing of substance. Mr. Sloan more or less brought the interview to a close, saying that Mr. Dane was tired and distraught, etc. etc., and that he could be interviewed further at a later time."

"Did such an interview ever take place?"

"No."

Stash then held up a red-covered paperback book. "Detective, have you ever read this book?"

"Your Honor!" I said in my most wounded tone. "I must object to the admission of this work of fiction as both irrelevant and entirely prejudicial. Fiction has no place in a court of law."

Evola looked at me coldly. "Mr. Sloan, you made a motion on this subject in pretrial, and I ruled quite unambiguously. Your objection is noted. I do not wish to hear from you any further on the subject."

I sat—to all appearances, grudgingly. Once again, this was performance art: Evola had ruled. The objection was purely a play for the jury.

"Detective?" Stash said.

"Yes. This is a book called *How I Killed My Wife and Got Away with It.*"

There was a soft rumble from the back of the courtroom.

"How did this book first come to your attention?"

"An old copy of the original book was dropped off anonymously at the station right after Mrs. Dane was killed. I read through the book at that time."

"Did you feel it was germane to your investigation?"

"In certain respects, yes."

"Tell us about that."

"Well, the book is about a man who murders his wife in order to get her money."

I stood. "Objection. Once again, Your Honor, this is precisely the problem I'm talking about. This is a nuanced work of fiction in which the main character's motives are never entirely clear, and here comes Detective Denkerberg, a person with no literary training or expertise, who's trying not only to characterize the entire novel in one sentence, but then to suggest that the motives of this made-up character are the same as those of my very real client."

Evola didn't even look at me. "Overruled."

I scowled, gave the jury a look, then shook my head in disgust.

"Detective. You were saying?"

"At the time I was focusing my efforts in the case on trying to gather evidence. In particular, we had not yet found the murder weapon. So I was particularly struck by something in the novel *How I Killed My Wife and Got Away with It*. The character in the book kills his wife with a bokken. And then he frames another character, a close friend, for the murder. He does this by planting the murder weapon in his friend's boat. I saw this and sort of went, 'Ah-hah.' "

"Why did you go ah-hah, Detective?"

"Because Mr. Dane lives on the river. He had four or five neighbors within a quarter mile who had boats docked behind their houses. So I went up and down Riverside asking Mr. Dane's neighbors if I could examine their boats. They all gave consent. On the morning of October 23, I searched a boat owned by a Dr. and Mrs. Roy Beverly who lived at 233 Riverside Boulevard. In the forward life preserver locker, I found a set of black clothes and a curved stick made of black wood."

Stash proffered the black clothes. "Are these items the ones you found in Dr. Beverly's boat?"

"Yes, they are. One pair of black boots. One black shirt. One pair of black pants. Upon examination, I noted that all of these items were covered with copious amounts of what appeared to be dried blood."

"Could you take that pair of boots out of the evidence bag for me?"

Denkerberg pulled the boots out of the plastic bag.

"Is there anything written or printed on them?"

"Yes, inside the left boot, right here, is an inscription printed in ink. It says, 'Handmade by Royce Daniels, bootmaker of Harlingen, Texas, for Mr. Miles Dane.' "

Stash then took the ominous black weapon out of a paper bag and held it up in the air. "And this?"

"That's the other item I found on the boat."

"What is it?

"It's what martial artists call a bokken. A wooden sword."

"What did you do once you'd found these items?"

"I took them into custody, logged them in, sealed them. Then I transported them personally to the state crime lab in Lansing. They never left my person between the time I found them and the time I delivered them to the lab."

"What sort of tests were performed there?"

"The items were tested for the presence of blood. As I had anticipated, they were covered with blood. The crime lab was under instructions to perform a DNA comparison on that blood."

"Let me now give you something that's been marked as exhibit 46. Can you identify this?"

"Yes, it's the DNA report. According to the report, the blood found on the clothes was a DNA match with that of Diana Dane."

"Any other tests performed on that ebony stick by the state crime lab?"

"A wood identification test was performed. According to the report the wood found in the bokken was Gabon ebony."

"Any other tests?"

Chantall Denkerberg nodded. "Yes. They fumed the bokken with cyanoacrylate ester and were able to lift two latent prints from the wooden surface."

"Can you explain the difference between a latent print and an impression print?"

"A latent print is a fingerprint left by the natural oils and amino acids in your body. An impression print is a print left with some other substance not naturally found on the skin. Ink, paint, blood, that sort of thing."

"I'm going to proffer to you what our fine clerk, Mrs. Wilson, is marking as exhibit number 58. Thank you, Mrs. Wilson. Can you identify this?"

"Yes. It's the fingerprint report from the state police. It identifies the prints found on the bokken as being of the latent type."

"And according to this report, was the crime lab able to match the prints to any known person?"

"Yes they were."

"And whose fingerprints were they?"

"Miles Dane's."

"What happened then?"

"I had a murder weapon, I had a suspect, I had prints, I had the suspect's clothes with the victim's blood on them. As such I believed I had probable cause for an arrest. So a warrant was drawn up by your office, and I placed Mr. Dane under arrest for the murder of his wife."

Thirty-seven

MY CROSS-EXAMINATION OF Detective Denkerberg had to wait until the next day.

Most lawyers get a fresh haircut and wear their best suit for important days in court. Not me. Back in my heyday as a hotshot lawyer in Detroit, I was a silk-suit-and-Gucci man, not afraid to pay eighty dollars for a pair of socks or eight hundred for a pair of shoes. But that man has, in a sense, died; and so instead of wearing the mask of courthouse big shot, I try to go the opposite route and play the underdog. My opponents like to portray me as a calculating and manipulative shyster, but it's a charge that's hard to make stick against a pleasant-looking, rumpled, slightly dumpy fellow who seems—at first glance, anyway—barely competent to get his tie on straight.

For the cross-examination of Chantall Denkerberg, I'd worn my worst, most rumpled blue suit, a polyester tie that had never looked even vaguely fashionable, and a pair of twenty-year-old Johnston & Murphy wing tips that, to put it mildly, were a little down at the heel.

I began by saying, "Detective Denkerberg, I was glancing over the transcript. When you told us about your qualifications, did you forget to mention that you were the president of my fan club?"

The courtroom was briefly filled with laughter.

Denkerberg looked at the judge. "This is a joke. Do I have to answer that?"

"I'll rephrase the question," I said. "Because, believe me, a man's life and reputation and freedom are at stake right now, and I don't find that to be at all humorous. Here's my question. Do you dislike me?"

"I guess you could say that."

Stash Olesky stood. "Your Honor, come on. I object to this line of questioning as entirely irrelevant. Mr. Sloan complained in his opening harangue that I was making this trial about him—which is, of course, not the case—and now he's about to launch right into the very issue I have tried very diligently to steer around."

"Your Honor," I said, "I wouldn't question Mr. Olesky's diligence in a million years. However, it's my contention that Miss Denkerberg's dislike of me colored this investigation from the very beginning, blinded her to other suspects, and led her up the path toward a gross miscarriage of justice. The state has opened the door to this issue on numerous occasions, and my client, therefore, has a right to cross-examine this witness on the subject."

Judge Evola scowled. "I'll give you a few questions. But if you start playing games, I'll cut you right off."

"Thank you," I said. "Miss Denkerberg. Detective, I mean. When you reached the scene of the crime, you spoke to me almost as soon as you got out of the car, correct?"

"I've testified to that, yes."

"Did you know who I was prior to meeting me?"

"I'd heard of you."

"What's my reputation in the law enforcement community?"

"You're tricky."

"That's all? Just . . . tricky?"

"I heard you were a drunk."

"Guilty as charged, officer. Just got my seven-year chip, seven years of sobriety down at AA. Ever heard the word 'shyster' used to refer to me?"

A long pause. "I couldn't say. Maybe."

"Ever heard of Angel Harwell?"

"Of course. She was accused of murdering her father several years ago. You got her off."

"Oh, now you're being coy. What else did you hear about that case?"

"Based on some things that came out after the trial, it's generally believed that she was in fact guilty of the crime."

"So when you saw good old Charley Sloan standing out there in front of Miles Dane's house, it's fair to say you thought something to the effect of 'Oh, there's that shyster who gets all the guilty guys off'? Am I right?"

The detective pursed her lips for a moment. "Every case is an individual case. I looked at this as—"

"I didn't ask you about every case. I asked you about what you thought when you saw me that morning. Charley Sloan is the guy who slithers in and gets guilty slimeballs off the hook. Isn't that what you thought?"

"That seems unlikely."

"I'm not making book here, Miss Denkerberg. I'm asking a yes-no question." I made my voice as sarcastic and insulting as I could. "Let me make this simple: What was your impression of me when you drove up there that morning?"

The gasket finally blew: "What do you want me to say, that I think you're an unethical shyster and that you represent guilty scumbags." Her jaw was clenched, her skin slightly pale, and small red spots had appeared on each cheekbone. "Okay, that's what I think. So what?"

Perfect. I looked at the jury and shook my head sadly. Then I counted silently to ten, giving them plenty of time to let her admission sink in.

"Isn't it true, Detective, that the minute you drove up to 221 Riverside Boulevard and saw my smiling face, this is what you thought to yourself? You thought: *Okay, I get the picture. If Charley the scumbag-loving shyster is standing there, then Miles Dane killed his wife. Right? Hm? There's Charley. Miles Dane did it. Case closed.*"

Denkerberg's pallor deepened, and the red spots on her cheeks got brighter. "That's absurd. I did what I always do: I examined the evidence."

"Mrs. Rathrock," I said to the court reporter, "could you read back Miss Denkerberg's earlier testimony? I believe I pointed out a particular passage before court went into session."

The court reporter flipped through the steno tape to a section she'd marked with red pen. "Detective Denkerberg: Quote. 'Taking the entire situation in its totality, the lack of footprints outside the room, some inconsistencies in the story, and Mr. Sloan's presence and behavior . . . well I felt like if you added all that up, a picture was emerging of a witness who was not being entirely forthcoming.' Unquote."

"Mr. Sloan's *presence*," I said. "In your testimony earlier, you said that not just my behavior but my very presence was significant. Now you deny this. Were you lying then, or are you lying now?"

Stash objected.

"Question withdrawn." I walked closer to the witness stand. "Miss Denkerberg, what was your initial impression of Mr. Dane? Was he likable?"

"I didn't think so, no."

"From the get-go, you didn't like him?"

"That's fair to say. But that didn't influence my judgment as an investigator."

"Of *course* not." I laughed sarcastically. "However, let me ask you this. As a trained investigator, who, in your experience, is the most likely suspect when a married woman gets murdered?"

Detective Denkerberg grew somewhat more composed. "When a married woman is found to have been murdered, statistically speaking, the husband is the most likely person to have killed her."

"The husband is the most likely suspect."

"Statistically speaking."

"This was an intensely brutal crime, was it not?"

Denkerberg nodded. "Yes."

"How did you feel when you saw the shattered body of Diana Dane lying on the floor that morning?"

Denkerberg thought for a moment. "I wanted to do my duty and find the perpetrator."

I let my eyes widen in disbelief. "Come on! Are you some kind of robot? *I* saw that poor woman, too. I'll tell you how I felt. I felt sick. I felt outraged. I felt angry. Are you telling me you didn't feel that, too?"

"Of course but—"

"You felt angry."

Denkerberg flushed slightly. "Certainly I felt angry."

"Drawing on your experience as a trained investigator, isn't it true that anger has a way of diminishing rational thought, of driving people to take precipitous, sometimes thoughtless action?"

"Spare me the dime store psychology. I—"

I could feel her starting to turn my way. I interrupted: "Excuse me, Miss Denkerberg, but your job here is not to offer up commentary on my questions. I asked you a simple question. Doesn't anger make people stupid?"

"This case was a lay-down," Denkerberg snapped. "It was obvious from the minute I walked in there. But that doesn't mean I'm stupid. I—"

"How many times do you intend to weasel out of my question, Detective?" I was pressing in, pressing in, not letting her finish a thought. "Does anger make people do stupid things or not?"

"It can, but—"

"And you *were* angry."

"Yes, I was angry."

"Thank you," I said sardonically.

"I carefully and methodically built a case. And I made no final conclusions until I gathered the evidence. And every shred of evidence I found pointed unambiguously at one man. Him." She pointed a long finger at Miles Dane. It shook with anger. "He did it. He killed Diana Dane. I had evidence."

I strolled slowly to the bench, eyeballed her finger, then looked at the jury. "Months later and she's still so angry she's shaking."

Before Stash could object to my commentary to the jury I turned back to Denkerberg. "You just mentioned evidence," I said. "Let's turn to some actual evidence for a moment."

"By all means," she said, lowering her shaking finger.

"When you found these bloody clothes, who was with you?"

"I was alone."

"*Were* you?" I smiled knowingly at the jury.

"Yes."

"That was three days after you examined the crime scene, correct?"

"Yes."

"And during your search of Mr. Dane's home, looking for a weapon, you would have had access to Mr. Dane's closets, wouldn't you?"

"Yes, but—"

"Thank you. Were you at any time alone in Mr. Dane's home?"

"Of course. But it's ridiculous to imply that—"

I cut her off again. "And were you ever alone with the bloody corpse of Mrs. Dane?"

After a long pause. "I suppose."

"How far was Mr. Dane's closet from Mrs. Dane's body?"

"This is ridiculous."

"Answer my question!" I shouted. "How far were Mr. Dane's clothes from his wife's dead, bleeding corpse?"

Denkerberg glared at me. "Ten feet," she whispered finally. "Maybe fifteen."

"So an unethical officer of the law, someone in an angered and agitated state of mind, could easily have picked out some clothes from Mr. Dane's closet, smeared them with blood, and taken them away for further use—just in case, at a later date, the evidence against Mr. Dane seemed a little light. Yes or no?"

She glared at me.

"Let the record reflect the witness's refusal to answer that question," I said.

"I did not smear blood on Mr. Dane's clothes."

"Thank you for your honesty. And were you alone when you conducted the initial examination of the soft ground under the window that Mr. Dane said the burglar smashed out and jumped through."

"Initially. But then the crime scene technician arrived."

I sighed like I was schooling a recalcitrant child. "Once again you're weaseling out of my question, Miss Denkerberg. Were you by yourself when you examined the area beneath the broken window at 221 Riverside Boulevard?"

"Yes."

I handed her a photograph. "Could you identify this photograph, which has been previously marked as State's Exhibit 11?"

"It shows the area underneath the broken window."

"Could you tell me what this is?" I pointed at what looked like a couple of indentations in the ground.

"Those are, ah, those are depressions in the soil."

I looked confused. "Wait, wait, wait. Earlier you testified that you found absolutely nothing in the soil under that window."

"Well, naturally in order to thoroughly examine the area, I had to get close. And in doing so, I left two depressions in the soil."

"*Depressions?* Come on! You're being coy again. These are footprints aren't they?"

"That's what I just told you."

"No, it's not. You said depressions. I said footprints. Miss Denkerberg, what size shoes do you wear?"

She looked at me for a long time. "Size twelve."

I looked surprised. "Size twelve! My goodness. No offense, but those are some pretty big feet you have."

She glared at me. I suspected I'd hit a nerve, that she was embarrassed about the size of her feet. "I'm a tall woman," she said primly. "My feet are proportionately large."

"Big enough to step on the impressions left by a man's foot?" I said. "Big enough to cover them?"

"That's ridiculous."

"I didn't ask for an editorial, Detective. My question is quite simple, are your feet big enough to cover the impressions left by those of a normal man? Yes or no?"

"There were no impressions. There were no footprints. If someone had jumped from that height, he almost certainly would have pitched forward and left hand—"

"What are you afraid of?" I snapped. "Just answer my question."

She sighed loudly. "Okay. Yes. I suppose my feet are about the same size as a man of normal stature. So yes, if I were crooked and a liar, I could have stepped on a shoe print and obscured it. But I'm not, and I didn't."

I smiled. "That's your testimony. Would you not agree that from a forensic perspective, putting aside all vague and nebulous theories and smelling of rats and feminine intuitions and so on, that there were only three pieces of evidence in this case that matter?"

"No, I wouldn't agree with that."

"I'm going to object to that question," Stash said.

"I'll rephrase: If you hadn't found that bokken with my client's fingerprints and the blood on them, if you hadn't found my client's clothes with the blood on them, and if you hadn't determined that there were no shoe prints under that window, would Mr. Dane be on trial today?"

"That's irrelevant. We *did* find them."

"Not *we*, Miss Denkerberg. *You*. *You* found the bokken. *You* found the clothes. *You* examined the ground. *You* left your own footprints."

"Your Honor, is Mr. Sloan intending to ask a question sometime today?" Stash Olesky said.

"I'll move right along, Your Honor," I said. "I just have a few more questions. Isn't it true that you were so angry about this murder that you were willing to do anything to make a case? Even manufacture fake evidence?"

"I would never, ever, ever manufacture evidence."

"Well, you've done it before, haven't you?"

"No."

I gave her a look of surprise. "Wait, are you telling me that in January of 1993, while serving as a robbery squad detective on the Detroit police force, that you *weren't* accused of having planted evidence? I've got the records right here if you'd like me to refresh your memory."

Denkerberg's face was blank for a moment. "I was accused by a drug-dealing, lying pimp with a record as long as his arm, yes. And the accusation proved to be one hundred percent false."

I handed her the record from the Detroit police files. "So this record of accusation I'm showing you, documented by the Detroit Police Department, it's complete fiction."

"Correct."

"Manufactured."

"Correct."

"You were accused . . . yet not guilty!"

"Correct."

"Sort of like Mr. Dane, wouldn't you say?" I wheeled, walked back to the table, and slapped the piece of paper down with a loud bang. "I'm done with this woman."

I RAN INTO Stash in the hallway at lunch. He was carrying a bag of food from Edna's Café over on Farm Credit Street. "That was a pretty nice cross," he said. He had a deep-fried chicken finger trailing out of his mouth like a cigar. "I'm curious how it feels trying to make a decent cop look like an asshole?"

"That's my job," I said. "I don't mind doing it when my client's innocent."

Stash snorted, the chicken finger bobbing up and down from the corner of his mouth.

"Anyway, Stash, just because she's a good cop doesn't mean she isn't an asshole."

"True. But this isn't Detroit, Charley. I'm not sure a Kerry County jury will go for all that police conspiracy baloney."

"You knit the scarf from one side while I unravel it from the other," I said. "As long as I pull off enough yarn by the time we get to Miles's witnesses, then you're sunk."

He pretended surprise. "Oh, you have witnesses?"

"Ha ha."

Stash pulled the chicken finger out of his mouth and waggled it between his fingers like Groucho Marx. "Wanna buy a duck?" he said.

"Laugh all you want," I said. "Reasonable doubt. That's all it takes."

I walked away with a confident smile on my face. But Stash knew as well as I did that every jury had its own definition of reasonable. And you never knew what it was until the foreman read the verdict. With Blair Dane on the stand, I felt confident I could get there. But without him? Well, we'd just have to see.

Thirty-eight

"THE STATE CALLS Dr. Ernesto Rey."

The medical examiner of the county, Dr. Rey, was a very small, almost delicate man, whose dapper dress was tempered by a slightly gloomy air, as though every one of those dead people he'd cut up had left a smudge on his karma.

Dr. Rey eyed me warily as he walked to the witness stand. The last time we'd been in the same courtroom together, I'd made him look quite foolish. As far as I know, he's a reasonably competent medical examiner, but I'd caught him with his pants down in court one time, and I'm sure he's never forgotten it.

"I don't know if I can take this," Miles whispered to me.

I put my hand on his arm. "Do your best," I said. We both knew this was where the "graphic testimony" was going to happen. I couldn't even imagine how awful it would be to sit there in his seat as they showed pictures of his murdered wife.

As Stash Olesky stood and prepared to wade through Dr. Rey's tedious list of qualifications, I stood, and said, "Your Honor, the defense is prepared to stipulate to Dr. Rey's qualifications. Dr. Rey is well-known to me for his breadth of knowledge and his impressive résumé, as well as his many years of excellent service to this community." I smiled and sat down. Dr. Rey blinked. He'd probably been awake nights for a week, expecting to get a world-class smack-down of a cross-examination from me. And here I was giving him a free pass. He couldn't believe it.

Even Stash Olesky looked a little surprised.

"I thank you for that uncharacteristic generosity, Mr. Sloan," the prosecuting attorney said. "Now, Dr. Rey, I'm going to show you a document which I'm identifying as State's Exhibit Number 53. Could you identify that, sir?"

Dr. Rey examined the small stack of stapled pages Stash had handed him. "This is the Report of Examination I prepared after performing an autopsy on Diana van Blaricum Dane."

"Very good, Doctor. See that paper clip there? On page seven of Exhibit 53? Right. Could you read the paragraph that begins with the heading 'Conclusions.' "

"Yes. 'Based upon this examination, I find the cause of death for Diana van Blaricum Dane to be blunt force trauma with attendant exsanguination and shock.' "

"Could you put that in laymen's terms?"

"Simple. Diana Dane was beaten to death. Maybe more accurately, she was beaten so badly that she bled to death and her heart finally stopped."

Olesky nodded sadly. "Doctor, let's turn to page three of your report. Could you just take your time and work through that page, telling us what you did and what you found?"

"Sure. Basically this section outlines the results of a careful examination of the wounds on Diana Dane's body."

I looked over at Miles. His skin was pale, his face taut, but essentially expressionless. He stared straight at Dr. Rey. It's a peculiarly distasteful thing to be forced to mix professional judgment with normal human emotion: At that moment I believed that Miles was doing his best to maintain his composure in the face of a nearly indescribable horror. But the lawyer in me was thinking it would sure look better to the jury if he wept or groaned a little. *Anything* to show he actually felt some emotion.

Stash Olesky cut in. "Dr. Rey. I've got a large blowup of a chart you made in your report. If it would help your testimony, I'd be happy to put that on the easel next to you."

"That would be very helpful, thank you."

Stash's paralegal, a very attractive young lady wearing a skirt that was just this side of immodest, put up the easel. There seemed to be a pleasantly unnecessary amount of bending over involved in the process. Stash used that distraction to accomplish the dull work of admitting the chart into evidence and marking it as State's Exhibit 54.

"Please, Doctor, continue."

The doctor took out the biggest red magic marker I'd ever seen, with a point about an inch wide. I took a deep breath. Here we go.

"As I said earlier, Diana Dane's person presented in the form of someone who had obviously suffered severe trauma. 'Trauma' is a medical term that essentially refers to what happens to the human body when it's struck by objects with sufficient force to damage tissues and/or bones. I examined the body carefully. With the court's permission, I'm going use this chart to lay out my findings."

Dr. Rey stood next to the chart. On the chart were line drawings of two female figures, front and rear, and two side views of female heads. The chart was full of small black marks that had obviously been drawn on the preprinted chart with a pen of some kind. "When you write a medical report, you're supposed to use very precise medical terminology. Anterior, posterior, so on so forth. That's all there on pages three through five of the report, but for the sake of clarity, I'm going to spell out what I found in plain old everyday language."

Dr. Rey took his red pen and held it over the chart. "Based on the pattern of the wound, it is my belief that the first blow Diana Dane received was right here on the right temple. WHAM!" Rey slashed the red pen over a black mark across the temple.

"There's a depression fracture, bruising, and massive damage to the brain tissue and blood vessels underneath. Based on the long, shallow depression, I would judge this blow to have been made by a long, thin item. Such as a stick."

Olesky said, "You went WHAM when you drew the line. What are you suggesting about how hard this blow was?"

"Extremely hard. The cranium, the skull, is a very very tough structure. To break a hole in it with a stick requires a blow of great strength."

"Wait, wait, wait," Stash said. "Back up here. I can see Mr. Sloan over there chafing at the bit to object that we don't know if this was a stick or a poker or a steel I-beam."

"Well, yes and no. If you'll flip back to page two, you'll see that I recovered what I characterize in the report as a 'glossy black fragment' from Diana Dane's head. At the very location where this blow was made. I recovered several similar fragments from other locations on the body. At the time I was puzzled. To my eye, they looked like plastic. But if you'll turn to page fourteen, the appendix consisting of a supplemental report from the state crime lab? You'll see that all three of those objects were identified as being splinters of wood. Gabon ebony."

Stash held up three plastic bags, each with a tiny dark splinter in it, took them over to the clerk, and had them marked as evidence. "I'll call your attention, Dr. Rey, to what's just been marked as State's 55, 56, and 57. Are you familiar with these items?"

The doctor pretended to examine them with great skepticism. Finally, he looked up, and said, "Why, yes. Those are the three fragments I recovered from Mrs. Dane's body." He reached over and made some more red slashes on the body. "They were found here, here, here."

"And did you find the presence of these fragments of ebony to be meaningful in any way?"

"Yes I did. As I noted in the addendum to the reports, page eight, signed and dated by me on November 1 of last year, the pattern of the wounds and the presence of the ebony fragments strongly indicate that Diana Dane was beaten with some sort of stick made from ebony."

"Very good. Please continue."

"Generally speaking, Diana Dane's body was heavily bruised, and many of her bones were fractured. I've been a forensic pathologist for twenty-three years if you include my residency at the University of South Dakota, and—outside of a few car accidents—I can't recall seeing a body more heavily bruised than hers. Which makes re-creating the exact order and location of the blows a bit difficult.

"But basically here's what I think happened. The first blow, as I said, struck her here. On the temple. Based on the particularly lethal location of this first wound, and based on the lack of defensive wounds, fingernail scrapings, etc., I don't believe Diana Dane defended herself. In fact, I suspect she was sleeping.

"Whether or not she was not sleeping to begin with, the first blow would likely have rendered her unconscious. It very likely would have proved to be a fatal wound over time even if she had not been struck again—though the fact that the killer then continued to strike Mrs. Dane renders the point moot. First he hit her several more times in the head and face." More dramatic red slashes across the face of the line drawing. "Here, here, here, here, here, here, possibly here, possibly here. Broken jaw, broken nose, broken left orbit, crushed eyeball, left upper incisor and bicuspids knocked out, more potentially fatal trauma to the brain, here and here." Suddenly Dr. Rey looked angry. "This was a savage, unnecessary beating. It just went on and on and on."

Miles Dane stared at the chart, jaw clenched, face pale. But no expression. No expression. If I could have punched him to make him cry, I swear I would have done it. But, no, he looked cold as yesterday's fish.

"Here! Here! There! Here! Again, again, again." Dr. Rey's face had gone slightly red. "Now the attacker began beating her in the torso. Broken ribs, punctured lung, ruptured spleen, bruised liver. Ah! Now . . . torn femoral artery!" He slashed red on the groin of the figure. "I'd like to make particular note of this wound to the femoral artery, the artery which runs from the torso down the groin into the leg. Why? Two reasons. First, it just requires a huge amount of force to tear that artery. And more important, because there is no hematoma accompanying that rupture."

"Is that significant?" Olesky serving up another soft lob.

Rey's eyebrows shot up. "Yes, it is. Very. Normally when an artery is torn inside the body, the heart drives blood out through the tear into the surrounding tissue. But in this case, it didn't. What that means is that by the time this blow was administered, Diana Dane's heart had stopped. She was already dead, and the attacker was still hitting her."

"How long, Doctor, would it have taken her to die?"

"Hard to say. I would think a minimum of ten minutes. Maybe as much as half an hour."

Olesky stood there staring at the doctor. He blinked once, then said, incredulously, "You're saying that whoever killed Diana Dane, stayed in that room for at least ten minutes and maybe as long as half an hour . . . and continued hitting her all that time?"

"Not continuously, no. But, intermittently, yes, she was struck over a period of at least ten minutes. Probably a good deal longer. The killer stayed there and kept pummeling a dead body."

"My God," Stash Olesky said softly.

Next to me, Miles Dane didn't even blink.

"How many blows, would you estimate?"

"Difficult to say with such extensive tissue damage. Probably between thirty and forty."

Stash Olesky gathered up his notes and began walking back to his chair.

"Oh, one last thing," Stash said. "I almost forgot . . . Were you able to make any estimate of the time of Mrs. Dane's death?"

"Yes, I was. Our technician arrived at the scene to process the remains at four-fifty. He took a core temperature at that time, which was recorded as eighty-nine degrees Fahrenheit. He also recorded the temperature on the thermostat of Mr. Dane's home at sixty-eight degrees. Using standard TOD—time-of-death—calculations for core body temperature decline versus ambient temperature, I concluded that Diana Dane had been dead for three to five hours at that time." He paused significantly. "Meaning she was killed somewhere between midnight and 2:00 A.M."

"Let me direct you to Mr. Dane's witness statement, which has been marked as State's 23. Could you read . . . yes, right there, the underlined portion."

"It says, 'Mr. Dane indicated that he had called Mr. Sloan within ten minutes of discovering his wife had been murdered, i.e. at approximately 3:30 A.M.' "

"And, Doctor, how does that jibe with your medical findings?"

"It doesn't."

"You're saying he misspoke?"

"Or he lied."

Stash Olesky stood silently, letting that one soak in for a while. Finally, he said, "Thank you, Doctor. I believe that will be all."

Judge Evola eyed my client, then me, with a look of naked disgust. "Mr. Sloan?"

"The good doctor has done his usual thorough job, for which I thank him. Just a couple quick questions." I didn't stand, just leafed through a folder. "Ah, here we are. Time of death calculations. These are estimates, correct? Not accurate to the minute, right?"

"Not accurate to the minute, no."

"And their calculation is based on a predictable rate of cooling based on ambient temperature, correct?"

"Correct."

"So if it's zero degrees in the house, the body's going to cool faster than if it's, oh, sixty-eight degrees, correct?"

"Right."

"The colder it is, the quicker the body cools."

"Exactly."

"So if thirty-degree air pouring into the house from the broken window just down the hall had lowered the temperature in the room, that would throw off the calculations."

"Slightly. But I gather that—"

"One other question." I cut off his answer. "In the movies we're always seeing medical examiners take out this little saw, you know with the rotating blade? Looks like something out of wood shop? And they use it to cut the top of the person's skull off, and everybody winces? You ever see that in the movies?"

"Sure."

"Did you do that? Did you cut open Diana Dane's head?"

"No."

"So you didn't remove and examine her brain?"

"No."

I raised my eyebrows, looking slightly puzzled. "Isn't that pretty standard?" I said. "Examining the brain?"

Rey shifted backward in his seat, and his voice dropped slightly. "It's a judgment call. It causes a rather gross disfigurement of the features and so out of respect for the survivors—"

"Into the microphone, please," I said mildly.

"I'm sorry. So, yes, out of respect for the victim's family, if there's a fairly obvious call, we try not to open the cranium."

I hefted a big book, dumped it on the table in front of him. "Recognize this book, Doctor?"

"Yes. It's *Krantz & Krantz,* the standard textbook on autopsy technique."

"There's a paper clip there on page 276. Could you take a gander at the part that I've highlighted?"

Dr. Rey opened the book gingerly. "It says that opening of the cranium is a standard part of an autopsy, particularly in cases involving head trauma. But then it lists a number of exceptions which—"

"Opening the cranium is a standard part of the autopsy, particularly in the case of head trauma. But you didn't do it."

"As I said before, no."

"Dr. Rey, can you tell us what the temporal artery is?"

The medical examiner tapped his laser pointer on the side of his head. "It's a major vessel here under the temple."

"And if that vessel ruptures, how quickly will it result in death?"

Rey swallowed. "Well, that really is quite a rare thing when . . ."

"Please. Simple question. How quickly will the rupture of the temporal artery cause death?"

"I couldn't say exactly. But fairly quickly."

"Meaning what? Five seconds? Ten? Thirty?"

"More likely it would be slower than that."

"But it's *possible* that a blow to the temporal area could cause someone's heart to stop in well under a minute."

Rey's eyes cut from one side to the other. "Distantly. But as I say, it's a very rare thing that the artery would rupture that way in the first place."

"You yourself testified that the first blow was to her temple."

"Yes."

"Shattered the cranium, releasing needle-sharp fragments into the brain?"

"Yes."

"But since you didn't bother to examine her wound except in a purely superficial way, you can't say for certain how long it took for her to die, can you?"

"My judgment is that . . ."

I wasn't interested in his judgment, so I cut him off. "Dr. Rey, you just admitted you have no basis for that judgment, didn't you? You didn't bother to check. She could very well have died in seconds as a result of a ruptured temporal artery, couldn't she?"

Rey sighed. "Possible. Distantly."

"Could have died in seconds. Thank you."

Thirty-nine

"YOU ALRIGHT, MILES?" I said, after the jury had filed out. His face was bloodless, his lips almost blue.

"I'm okay," Miles said. "I think maybe I need to walk around a little."

I signaled to the bailiff. Walking around, for its own sake, was a luxury not afforded to criminal defendants who weren't free on bond. "Could you take Mr. Dane to the rest room?"

The bailiff nodded. Miles stood slowly, walked three or four steps, paused as though considering something weighty and important, and collapsed.

The bailiff caught him on the way down, and we laid him out on the hard floor. Miles came to in a few seconds, but seemed content to lie there, looking up at the ceiling and saying, "I'm fine, I'm great, I'm okay," until a doctor arrived five minutes later.

After the doctor had pronounced that his heart was fine and that he had probably fainted because of anxiety, I accompanied Miles to the secure bathroom in the basement of the courthouse.

He stood in front of the stainless-steel sink, shaking his head and looking at the fun house image of his face reflected in the warped steel mirror. "How is it possible?" he said finally. "A thing like that? What unleashes it?"

"I don't know, Miles," I said.

He closed his eyes for a moment. "I envy you," he said finally.

"Oh?"

"I wish I had somebody like you do."

"What do you mean?"

"You and Lisa. I know you've been through some things, you have a tough history, whatever. But it's obvious that you two have really hit it off, that you lean on each other."

"Really?"

"Really."

I smiled sadly. "That's nice to hear." I wanted to say something reassuring, but what could you say in a situation like that? He had lost his wife, and his only son was a thug—a thug who might well have killed Diana—and there was nobody else at all. Nobody but me anyway. And however nice a guy I may be, a lawyer is a damn poor substitute for a friend.

Miles leaned over the steel sink, splashed some water on his face, then looked around for a towel. There were none, towels being another of those luxuries of which the accused are undeserving.

"Here," I said. I blotted his face with the lining of my jacket.

"Hell, man, you didn't have to do that." Miles suddenly looked like he was going to cry.

"Part of the job." I slapped him on the back. "Can't have my client go back in there looking like he sat too close to the pool at Seaworld."

He seemed as though he was about to turn toward the door, but then stopped and looked me in the eye. "Don't screw things up with your girl, Charley. Promise me that."

"Does it seem like I might?"

He shrugged. "I'm just saying. Human relationships are fragile," he said. "Don't let them get away from you."

I cleared my throat. "You ready to go back?"

He straightened, and his face changed. "Hell, no," he said in the gruff combative voice he usually reserved for talk-show hosts. "Change of plan. It's jailbreak time. I'll be the first accused felon in history to escape by flushing his own ass down the crapper."

It wasn't a funny joke, but we both laughed anyway, with the mildly frantic laughter you drag out when things are looking really grim.

Forty

"THE STATE CALLS Robert Gough."

Robert Gough was a slight, vigorous-looking blond man, probably in his late twenties. He wore a beige, four-button suit that looked like something a pro basketball player would wear to a nightclub, and a long goatee sprouted from his lip. His hair had been tinted or highlighted to look slightly more blond than it was naturally, and it stuck up in a way that made him appear as though he'd just gotten out of bed . . . though I suspected the look had actually required a great deal of effort and hair gel. His shoes were two-tone, beige on cream.

He sat in the witness box as though he owned it, unintimidated at the prospect of appearing live on national television.

Stash Olesky said, "Mr. Gough, welcome to Michigan."

"I'm sorry I have to be here under these circumstances." He didn't look especially sorry.

"I wonder if you could tell us your occupation."

"My title is senior editor with Elgin Press in New York City."

"What is your educational background?"

"I have a B.A. in English Literature from Harvard College, and I worked for several years toward my Ph.D. in English at Columbia University—though I never completed my degree. I've been in the publishing industry for seven years, first as an assistant, then as an editor. My current job title is senior editor."

"So it's fair to say you're well versed in the interpretation of literature."

"I think that's fair, yes." He smiled, aw shucks—but there was something just a shade condescending about his manner.

"What sort of publisher is Elgin?

"We're the second largest publisher in the United States, a subsidiary of the German publisher Hauer-Stern Verlag. We publish everything from children's books to mass-market fiction to biography to religious books."

"Are you familiar with the defendant in this case?"

"Yes I am. Mr. Dane published six novels at Elgin Press. The first was published in 1968, the last in 1973. I believe all of his subsequent books were published by Padgett Books. At any rate, over the years we have retained the United States paperback publishing rights to all six of those novels."

I stood slowly and said in my most weighty and wounded tones, "Your Honor, I'm sure Mr. Gough is an interesting fellow, and I'm sure the jury is just as fascinated by the subject of how the publishing industry works as I am. But I'm really going to have to object. I think everybody is well aware of where this testimony is heading. We are about to head into deeply irrelevant and obscure—not to mention fictional—territory, which, if allowed, would be terribly prejudicial to my client's case." Again, I was preaching to the jury, with not a prayer of getting anywhere with the judge.

Mark Evola favored me with a bright smile. "Mr. Sloan. Next time feel free to say, 'Objection, relevance. Or objection, prejudicial,' before launching into another lengthy oration. Particularly regarding a matter on which I've already made a very clear ruling. Your objection, if that's what that speech was, is denied."

"Your Honor! Surely you won't deny me the opportunity to argue my client's case?" Again, this was strictly a show for the jury.

"Surely I will. You've had that opportunity, and I have ruled. Mr. Olesky, please continue your examination of this young man."

Stash smiled. "Mr. Gough, you said earlier that Elgin Press owned the rights to publish six books written by Mr. Dane. Have they remained in print all these years?"

"No, they haven't. There's a legal process by which Mr. Dane could have regained his rights to these books, but he never exercised that option, and so we continued to own the rights through a great many years."

"So did you bring any of those six books back into print?"

"Yes, we did. We brought one of them back in a fresh new edition. New cover art and so on."

"Why the sudden interest in a new edition?"

Bob Gough smiled a little. "When Mr. Dane was charged with the crime that is at issue in this trial, I perceived that there would be an increase in demand for Mr. Dane's work. It came to my attention that we still owned the rights to these six titles, so I moved ahead forcefully to meet that demand."

"So you're basically in it for the money."

Bob Gough didn't appear at all nonplussed by the question. "Of course. Elgin Press is a business. We published three books on the O.J. Simpson trial, Monica Lewinsky's unauthorized biography, a book about the tragic deaths on Mount Everest. It's just a reality that tragedy and titillation sell. In this case we felt that there would be significant demand for some of his old titles."

"Any book that's been particularly successful in this regard?"

"Yes. I don't think it would surprise anyone in this room that Mr. Dane's third novel has sold quite a few copies recently."

Stash took a new paperback book with a bright red cover off his table. "Let me get this marked as Exhibit 59. Thank you Mrs. Wilson." He handed the book to Bob Gough. "Is this the novel you're talking about, Mr. Gough?"

Bob Gough ran his fingers though his long goatee, studied the book, then said, "Yes it is."

"Can you read me the title?"

"It's called *How I Killed My Wife And Got Away with It.*"

The courtroom had been silent all morning, but suddenly there was a rustling in the back of the room. Somebody yelled, "You murdering bastard!"

Judge Evola leveled his gavel at the back of the room. "Bailiff, remove that woman. Any more of that, and I clear this courtroom."

The rustling and hubbub slowly subsided.

Judge Evola turned to the jury, and said, "At a later time, ladies and gentlemen, this court will give you some very clear, written, formal instructions with regard to how and why you are to consider the contents of this book as regards Mr. Dane's guilt or innocence on the charges at issue in this case. But I think it's imperative that I point out to you right from the get-go that the testimony you are about to hear is going to involve a work of fiction. That means that what happened in this book is just a story dreamed up to entertain people. Just because the character in this book says, 'I did so-and-so,' doesn't mean that Mr. Dane did so-and-so. Continue, Mr. Olesky."

"Thank you, Your Honor. Mr. Gough, is it your understanding that every word of this book was written by Miles Dane?"

"Yes."

"Could you turn to the first page I've marked there, yes, with the paper clip, right there—I guess that would be the title page? And would you read the highlighted passage."

"Sure. It says, 'This book contains the unexpurgated text of the original novel, *How I Killed My Wife and Got Away with It*, copyright 1971, Miles Dane.' "

"Unexpurgated, meaning . . ."

"Nothing has been removed. This used to be standard boilerplate language in paperback reprints, but it's hardly ever used today. We just threw it in to reinforce that this is the exact same book he wrote back in '71."

"And to your knowledge this is a true and accurate statement? Nothing has been changed?"

Gough shrugged. "Hey, there could be a couple of typos or something. Point is, we didn't change a bunch of clues to fit the charges against him, we didn't alter the story line, or anything like that. We took the old edition, sent it to the typesetters; they typed it up; we proofed it and printed it. That was pretty much it."

"You proofread it yourself?"

There was the briefest of pauses. "My assistant did. She's a very competent editor in her own right."

Stash Olesky nodded. "Couple of questions about the details of this novel. First, would you read the cover?"

"Be glad to." Bob Gough took out a pair of odd-looking tortoise-shell glasses and perched them on his nose. "At the top in, oh, I'd say this is about fourteen-point type, it says, 'The astonishing best-seller that reveals . . .' There's an ellipsis after that." He went *bip bip bip* in the air with his index finger. Then, sounding more than a little pedantic, he turned to the jury, and said: "You know, three little dots?"

"Go on, Mr. Gough."

Gough cleared his throat. " 'The astonishing best-seller that reveals . . .' " *Bip, bip, bip.* "Great big letters: 'How I Killed My Wife and Got Away with It.' Then underneath that it says, little letters, 'the controversial story by,' huge letters, 'Miles Dane.' Then under that it says, 'Find out why! Find out how! The terrible truth!' "

"Okay, let me stop you for a moment. First thing, this is a work of fiction, is it not?"

"Oh, absolutely. It's a novel. It's made-up, just like a fairy tale."

"And yet, there's nothing on the cover to indicate that it's a novel."

"Strictly speaking, that's absolutely correct."

"Isn't that misleading?"

"It's what we in the industry call sizzle."

"Mr. Gough, I don't mean to be rough on you, but it sounds like sizzle is a code word for misdirection."

Gough chuckled noiselessly. "Sell the sizzle, not the steak. That's how it's done. Look, at Elgin we market certain books to people with sophisticated literary sensibilities. We market other books to people who are trying to better themselves. We market books to people who want to learn about science or philosophy or history or religion. When we sell a book like that, we try to be sophisticated in our sales approach. But this is not one of those books. We marketed this book to appeal to a segment of the American population who are looking for crass sensationalism. And I think we did a darn good job of that."

"Okay, fair enough. Mr. Gough, could you give me an outline of the plot?"

"Sure. The narrator is a young man named Lowell Wink, who is married to this shrill, demanding, just really awful woman named Vanessa. Now Lowell, he grew up poor in some jerkwater little town in Michigan." A quick grin to the jury. "No offense. Anyway, his wife is rich. She's an heiress whose family are New York social register types. The circumstances of their marriage are left somewhat obscure, so we don't really know why this oddly matched pair actually married. But basically the book is about how this guy Lowell plans and executes the murder of his wife, then walks away with her trust fund while more or less thumbing his nose at all of her obnoxious rich relatives."

"I'm going to ask you to read a section on page twenty-one," Stash said. "There, where it's been highlighted in yellow? Good."

Bob Gough flipped through the book. "Okay, here we go. It says, 'Oh, yes, on the outside, my wife is all sugar and cream. When we go out together, she's the picture of loving devotion, of grace, of sweetness, of attentiveness. If I sweat, she wipes my brow. If I thirst, she serves me water. But it is all an act. In the confines of our home, the real Vanessa arises like a creature from hell. Bitter, foul, evil, manipulating. But tomorrow that will all be over. I have endured her taunts, her pettiness, her little jealousies, her peevishness, her selfishness, her domineering for long enough. Tomorrow her blood shall be spilled on the altar of my suffering.' " Bob Gough paused. " 'Oh, yes, and tomorrow I shall have her family's millions.' "

"So is he just after her money?"

"Well, at the beginning of the book, he seems like this sad sack who's being pushed around and controlled by this vicious woman, and so at first it's like he's just trying to get out from under her thumb. The way the murder unfolds initially, it seems kind of defensible. But after he kills her, he has to do a bunch of scrambling around to get himself off the hook. Including framing his best friend. And in the course of doing that, we begin to see that he really is a lot more manipulative and resourceful and sleazy than we first thought. That's part of the charm of the book. Lowell is what we call an unreliable narrator. Basically he lies to the reader. At the beginning he tells you all about what a horrible person his wife is, and so, like I said earlier, at that point he seems quite sympathetic. But then as you get further into the book, you begin to see that everything she said and did in the first few pages of the book, stuff that looked really nasty and mean . . . well, there's a second way of interpreting it—one that, let's just say, makes good old Lowell not look like the poor, oppressed loser that he had made himself out to be. And one that makes her out to be a lot more decent than she was. See, the way the book works and what makes it so ingenious is that Mr. Dane kind of sucks you into sympathizing with this guy, and then as time goes on, you start to see that this character is really a monster."

Stash Olesky looked like he intended to let this sentence linger in the air for a while, so I took the opportunity to rise and say, "Your Honor, I want the record to reflect my continuing objection to this outrageous line of questioning. This book is fiction, fiction, fiction and it appalls me that the jury is being subjected to this blatant attempt to slander and slur and smear Mr. Dane with—"

I intended to run on in this vein until Judge Evola stopped me. Which he did very quickly by slamming his gavel down several times. "Sit, Mr. Sloan. The record already reflects your objection. You seem to have gotten the idea that you can just pop up at will and slow these proceedings down with pointless, groundless interruptions. Would an evening in jail do anything to disabuse you of that notion?"

I looked sorrowfully at the jury and shook my head, hamming it up a little—underdog Charley trying to hold his own while the foot of a tyrannical bureaucrat was pressing down on his neck. "I apologize, Your Honor."

"Good. Mr. Olesky? Pray continue."

Olesky said, "Turn, if you would, Mr. Gough, to page forty-six. Just start there on the highlighted paragraph."

Gough began reading, " 'I have had an interest in Oriental weaponry for some years. On occasion Vanessa would grudgingly allow a *centime* or two to slip through her fingers so that I could add to my collection. I owned gleaming and ancient Japanese swords, ivory cudgels of peculiar and insidious design, razor-sharp bits of iron that could be coated with poison and hurled secretly at an assassin's target, Chinese poleaxes, knurled sticks attached together with lengths of chain, dirks with handles carved deeply with coital dragons . . . ' " Gough looked up and grinned. "It has a wonderfully purple quality, doesn't it? Nobody writes this way anymore."

Stash smiled back, but not with a great deal of warmth. "Just keep reading if you would."

"Sorry." The young editor looked back down at the book. " 'I lingered with my collection for a few moments, letting my gaze trail across the lovely, savage curves of wood and steel. When finally I chose my weapon, I reached for simplicity. It was a peculiar curved black stick, pure ebony, which I am told is used by Japanese swordsman to practice their killing techniques. Its black, impenetrable surface mirrored my own dark mood.' " Gough looked up. "You want me to keep going?"

"Please."

" 'I stealthily crept up the stairs, careful not to wake my slumbering wife. As I eased open the door of her chamber, I froze. Her breath had caught for a moment and she stirred uneasily in her bed. The silk sheets sighed beneath her lovely form. Oh, the ugliness her beauty concealed!

" 'Suddenly the rage rose in me as all the accumulated slights she had hurled at me over the years frothed to the surface of my fevered brain. I leapt forward and swung the black stick, striking her as she lay. The ebon instrument . . .' " Gough grinned and shook his head. "I'm sorry, but, God, *the ebon instrument*? Please, that is *too* classic. It sounds like Anne Rice porno, doesn't it? Anyway, let's see . . . 'The ebon instrument fell perfectly as I'd aimed it, the air splitting with a sharp crack as it crashed into her right temple.

" 'I had expected her to simply die, but she did not. She let out a groan, as if in the throes of passion and one arm spasmed, ripping open the pure white silk dressing gown to reveal her soft, full bosom. How many times had she toyed with me, allowing me a glimpse of those perfect breasts, then laughing at my desire and sending me away? How many times she teased me with the power of her beauty before banishing me to the wilderness of my cold, lonely bed?

" 'I felt an almost carnal pleasure. I had intended simply to kill her. But instead I mounted her and had my pleasure as she lay gasping and inchoate, mouthing garbled syllables of pain. When I was done with her, I rose and took the black stick in my hand and began to beat the life from her. First, I beat the beauty from her face, the beauty which, alone, had given her the power to control me. Then I beat the rest of her body, reducing that temple of magnificence to a broken shell. And still she would not die, but lay instead, moaning on the bed.

" 'But the end, I knew, must come soon. So I sat and watched as her red lifeblood seeped away, as the moaning faded, gaining strength with every moment of her suffering, recovering some sense of the man I'd once been—not the weak, cringing tool she'd made of me, but something simple, proud, and strong. I don't know how long I stared at her, but finally the urge overcame me again, and I struck her lifeless body several more times, purging myself of the last of her bitter poison.' "

I looked over at Miles. His face was white, his lip trembling slightly. He covered one eye with a pale hand.

Stash Olesky jumped in, and said, "Thank you. Now, if you'd turn to page fifty-one."

Gough flipped a couple of pages and began reading. " 'I busied myself making it appear as though a break-in had occurred. I upset the lamp and took a handful of my wife's jewelry from her bedside table, hurling it out the window into the river. Then I removed my clothes and walked naked to the basement. I placed the clothes in a paper bag, which I secreted behind the furnace. After that I showered, shaved, pomaded my hair, put on a white silk robe, and lit a cigarette.

" 'I felt as though a great weight had been lifted from my shoulders. There was a slight question as to what I should do next. A phone call of course. But who should I call first? Better safe than sorry. I dialed the number of Joseph Dancer, Esq., the finest criminal lawyer in the city.

" ' "Yes," I said, when he answered. I put a quaver in my voice. "Mr. Dancer! Something terrible has happened!" ' "

Stash interrupted. "That's fine, Mr. Gough. Now if you'd skip over to the following page where the . . . yes, that's it."

Gough turned the page. "Here. Okay. 'The stick! The bloody clothes! It had been my intention to dispose of them at my leisure. But I realized that I could not hide them in my house. They would have to be stored somewhere—somewhere near our home, but not on our property. I looked desperately out the back window. Up the river I saw my salvation: a twenty-one-foot cabin cruiser owned by my neighbor and best friend, Horace Bellows, was moored at his dock not five hundred feet away. It was winter, frigid. The likelihood of anyone using the boat in this terrible weather was minuscule. I ran out the back door, up the shoreline, clambered aboard the cabin cruiser, and hid the bloody clothes and the ebony sword behind a cluster of life preservers. I was home just seconds before my lawyer, Dancer, arrived.' "

"Alright, Mr. Gough, I apologize for all the reading I'm making you do, but we're almost done." Stash consulted his notes. "Here we are. Turn to the last page of the novel, if you would, and read the final paragraph."

Gough did as he was told. He seemed to be stifling an urge to smirk as he read: " 'And so it was over. This verdant suburb, I knew, was not for me. I would return to the town where I had grown up, poor and despised. At first they would laugh behind my back and make jokes about me. But I would drive a Cadillac and live in a grand house by the river and keep a gardener and a maid and I would leave sizable tips on restaurant tables. In time they would forget the boy I had been. In time I would become someone new, someone greater, someone who could not be despised or hated or sneered at. Because in the end people don't care about the past, not in Pickeral Point, Michigan.' "

Stash sat down, and I popped right up.

"Mr. Gough," I said, "it seems like you have a great deal of contempt for the American reading public."

Gough smiled, apparently somewhat amused at the fussy Midwestern lawyer. "Not at all. I have contempt for a certain slice of the American reading public. There's a difference."

"Ah!" I said. "So you're suggesting that this book is appealing, what, to stupid people?"

"Hey, I really like the book," Gough said after a moment of consideration. "I think it's a terrific read, a nice fun creepy clever ingenious book. But, yes, I'd admit our marketing campaign was aimed more toward the down-market reader than toward the connoisseur of sophisticated crime fiction."

" 'Down-market reader.' That sounds like a code word for idiot."

Gough's mouth turned up slightly at the corners. "That's not entirely inaccurate."

"So are you implying that only an idiot would believe that this book incriminates my client?"

"Hm." Gough looked thoughtful. "I guess here's what it comes down to. I don't honestly know in any detail what the facts show about Mr. Dane's guilt or innocence, or how much similarity there is between the crime in the book and the actual crime that took place here last year. And frankly? The only people who matter when it comes down to what incriminates or doesn't incriminate Mr. Dane are the people over there in the jury box. I imagine they're bright enough to make that call."

"So it's fine and dandy to smear Mr. Dane's reputation, to poison his life in front of the entire world . . . as long as he walks away a free man?"

"For whatever it's worth, I anticipate that Elgin Press will be sending him quite a sizable royalty check before this is all over with."

"That doesn't answer my question. Do you feel comfortable poisoning this man's reputation by trying to confuse the difference between reality and fiction?"

Bob Gough, looked at me unblinkingly. "He wrote the book, not me."

I returned his gaze for a long moment, then said, "I hope that assuages your conscience. No more questions."

Stash Olesky stood. "Brief redirect, Your Honor. Mr. Gough, let's amplify an issue that Mr. Sloan has just raised. You're not just being callous here, are you, when you imply that you don't feel responsible for poisoning Mr. Dane's reputation? No, let me rephrase that. Do you feel that you've done anything of your own volition to harm Mr. Dane's reputation?"

"I don't, no."

"Why not?"

"Look, in my earlier testimony I said something to the effect that 'it was brought to my attention' that Elgin owned the paperback rights to this book. It had been out of print so long, nobody at Elgin even knew we still had the rights to it."

"I'm sorry, Mr. Gough, but that doesn't answer my question."

"What I'm saying is, *he* called me and suggested we put out a new edition of the novel."

"Who called you?" Stash said.

As Bob Gough smiled, his long blond goatee jutted out from his chin. "Who do you think? *Him.*" His finger was pointing right at Miles Dane.

Forty-one

GOOD GOD, MILES! What were you thinking?"

We were sitting in the conference room next to the courtroom, Miles with his left ankle chained to the floor.

Miles looked away. "You were the one saying I couldn't afford a decent defense. I just, I was thrashing around trying to think of a way to bring in some money, and I made the call on the spur of the moment. I didn't even think about the titles of the books, or what they were about. Hell, Charley, I wrote that stupid thing thirty years ago."

I studied his face. "I asked you about this book the day I heard about it. Remember what you said? 'Gee, I've written forty-seven books and I barely remember it.' You lied straight to my face."

"I guess . . . I guess I was just afraid you'd tell me I was an idiot for putting the book out again."

"Which, frankly, you were."

"Well, what difference does it make? It's done now." Miles looked hangdog. "Anyway, the good news is you'll get paid for your work," he said quietly. "Which was kind of in doubt for a while there."

"That's not the issue. At the very least, if I'd known you were responsible for the book coming out, I'd have steered around that particular line of questions."

"Surely you don't think I'd do this intentionally? Sabotage my own case?"

"I don't know what I think," I said finally.

Forty-two

AFTER THE MIDMORNING break Stash Olesky looked at the next witness, and said, "Agent Pierce, could you state your full name and occupation."

"My name, sir, is Orvell John Pierce, Junior. I am an agent with the Michigan State Police. My area of specialization is crime scene investigation. As such, I offer the resources of the state police to jurisdictions such as the city of Pickeral Point, which don't have their own crime scene specialist."

Orvell Pierce was an angular black man with a pencil-thin mustache and protuberant black eyes. He was dressed in a brown suit that looked about half a size too large. His speech and manner seemed excessively formal. Though he was undoubtedly experienced at testimony, he looked stiff and ill at ease. Maybe it was that camera in the back of the room. Then again, maybe he was just a nervous man.

"Agent Pierce, did you receive a request for assistance from the Pickeral Point Police Department early on the morning of October 21 of last year?"

"Yes sir, I did. I was paged at my home at approximately four-twenty-seven in the morning, and I responded to the scene of an apparent homicide at five-oh-eight in the morning."

"Could you tell me what you did at the scene?"

Agent Pierce explained how he had met Detective Denkerberg at the scene, how—at Detective Denkerberg's direction—he had videotaped the area surrounding the house, then had gone inside and assisted her in the processing of the crime scene.

"Did you have occasion to make any analysis of the blood spatter evidence in the room?" Stash prompted.

"Yes I did."

"Could you tell us what blood spatter analysis is?"

"It will not be news to the jury that when the skin of a live human being is broken, the individual bleeds. Or that when a human body is struck or cut or shot, it also bleeds. Blood spatter analysis is the study of how drops of blood are disseminated through space in the course of violent assaults.

"Using the principles of physics, it is possible to reconstruct—based upon the size, shape, and location of blood drops found at a crime scene—exactly where that blood came from and how fast it was moving, thus assisting in reconstructing the nature of the crime. In this case there was a copious amount of blood in the room, so a considerable amount of my time was invested in documenting and analyzing that blood spatter evidence."

Stash Olesky had a thick report marked as evidence, then presented it to the witness. "Agent Pierce, can you identify this document?"

Agent Pierce narrowed his eyes, studied the document. "Yes sir. That would be my report based upon the blood spatter evidence present at 221 Riverside Boulevard."

"And is that your signature on page six?"

"Yes sir, it is."

"Good. I'd like to direct you to the first paragraph on the first page. Could you read that?"

"It begins, 'Executive Summary.' Then it reads, 'It is the opinion of the undersigned agent that blood spatter evidence on and around the body of victim Diana van Blaricum Dane at 221 Riverside Boulevard is consistent with the following conclusions:

"One. The victim was struck while she lay in the bed.

"Two. The victim did not move appreciably during the course of the assault.

"Three. The victim was struck by a person of normal stature using an overhand (i.e. baseball bat) type grip.

"Four. The attacker used a grip consistent with that of a right-handed person.

"Five. The victim was repeatedly struck with an object approximately one and a half to three feet in length.

"Six. As the assault proceeded, the attacker circled the bed on which the victim lay, attacking her first from the direction of the door, and moving toward the window as the attack continued."

"Seven. The assailant struck the victim approximately thirty-seven times."

When Agent Pierce had finished reading, Stash Olesky said, "Now come on. You expect us to believe you can really figure all of that out just based on a few little drops of blood on the wall?"

"On the wall. On the floor. On the bed. On the door. On the ceiling." Pierce might have been stiff. But that didn't make him a poor witness. He knew exactly what he was doing up there. "As you may have noted, Mr. Olesky, the phraseology I used in my report is that the evidence presents in a manner, quote, *consistent with the following conclusions*, unquote."

Olesky nodded earnestly. "Tell me a little about how blood spatter analysis works. The physics of it, I mean."

Agent Pierce launched into a mind-numbingly dry discourse on the physics of blood spatter. First he explained about his training on the subject in various FBI seminars and university courses, then he cited a host of journal articles that confirmed the substance of the blood spatter field's analytical tools. Then he wrote various formulas on the board that meant nothing to me, or, I suspect, to anyone else in the courtroom.

The upshot, though, according to his testimony, was that it was possible to measure the direction and size of blood drops, to punch in some numbers on an HP calculator and determine within about a ten to twenty percent range of accuracy which direction the blood came from, and what angle it had fallen from, and, by inference, how hard it had been slung.

"Okay, fair enough," the prosecutor said. "But who's to say you didn't push the wrong button on your calculator?"

"Personally, my standard operating practice is that I perform each and every calculation three times to ensure that doesn't happen."

Stash nodded with theatrical impatience. "Yeah, yeah, yeah. But still, I mean some smart professor over at some big university has a theory about this, and maybe some ivory tower types wrote up an article or three about this thing in a university journal somewhere. That's all real nice. But I'm still skeptical. How do you *prove* this stuff works in the real world?"

"Yes sir, I understand your concern. To alleviate the possibility that the theory is not in accord with reality, what I do is I make a reconstruction of each and every constellation of spatters. As I said earlier, each time there is contact with the body or the blood-covered weapon is slung, you get what we call a constellation, a set of related blood spatters from that particular motion or blow. What I do is I map each of those, diagram them, photograph them, make my calculations. Then I go back to the lab, where I have a special room set up in which I can personally reconstruct each and every constellation and/or drop of blood spatter on the wall, ceiling, and floor.

"In this case, we had a suspicion as to the nature of the actual weapon used to kill Mrs. Dane. It was believed to be a Japanese wooden martial arts practice sword, an object called a bokken. So I went to a martial arts store in Detroit and purchased a bokken of the approximate physical dimensions of the object we believed to be the actual murder weapon. Then I took it back to my blood spatter test room at the lab and I reconstructed each constellation. The way I did that is I tacked large sheets of white paper to the ceiling and to the wall, and then I dipped the bokken in pig's blood, which I obtained from a slaughterhouse. Then I slung blood off the bokken based on what my calculations and my observations had predicted. I then compared the length, breadth, diameter, and pattern of the spatters I made on these pieces of paper with those found at the crime scene.

"You'll find the actual reconstructed spatter patterns appended to my report. I found that each reconstructed constellation was materially similar to that found at the scene. Which is to say I have an extremely high degree of certainty that my report represents an accurate reconstruction of the physical dimensions of the assault against Mrs. Dane."

Stash Olesky looked at Agent Pierce for a long time. "Whew!" he said finally. "That must have taken an awful lot of time."

"It did. But some things, sir, cry out to be done right."

Stash Olesky thanked the crime scene investigator for his testimony, then I stood.

"Agent Pierce," I said, "I, too, want to commend you on the fine and thorough job you did with the blood spatter evidence. That's very impressive indeed."

"Thank you, sir." He looked at me coolly, as though he was the sort of man who was well-bred enough to turn the other cheek despite the fact I'd spit on his shoes.

"Would you direct your attention to page one of the report? Conclusion number five. Could you read that?"

"It says the victim was struck by an object approximately one and a half to three feet in length."

"One and a half to three feet." I handed him the ebony bokken. "Agent Pierce, how long is the bokken that has been marked as exhibit 37?"

"Approximately forty inches."

"I think forty-one inches would be the right number, wouldn't it, Agent Pierce? That's practically *four* feet."

"Yes. But when I say it was one and a half to three feet in length, I meant that portion of the weapon which extended beyond the hands. So . . . If the bokken was held in a two-handed grip, like a baseball bat, there would be about three feet of the stick extending beyond his hand. Possibly even less if he choked up on it a little."

"But you didn't say that in the report, did you? You didn't say one and a half to three feet *beyond the hand*. Sounds to me like you were talking about the whole weapon!"

"You may note the word approximate, Mr. Sloan. Regardless of where his hands were, there is a certain margin of error here. Forty-one inches is well within the margin of error."

"Oh! Margin of error!" I slapped the report down on the defense table. "That's a fancy phrase to cover up the fact that she could have been hit with anything between a toothpick and a full-grown oak tree, am I right?"

Stash Olesky objected.

"Withdraw the question," I said. I picked up the report and flipped through it thoughtfully. "You know, I glanced through your report a couple of times, and I kept hunting around for the place where you demonstrated that *Mr. Dane* was the person holding the murder weapon. I'm sure I didn't look hard enough, but, gosh, I just couldn't seem to find it."

Agent Pierce sat solemnly, but didn't speak. He just kept looking at me with that turn-the-other-cheek expression.

Finally I said, "Agent Pierce?"

"I'm sorry, Mr. Sloan, I was waiting for you to ask a question. I was rather under the impression you had just made a speech."

That got a nice little titter from the jury. I smiled genially, a nice guy who doesn't mind a few yucks at his own expense.

"Let me try phrasing it in the form of a question then, Agent. Does your report in any way, shape, or form indicate the identity of the person who wielded the murder weapon?"

"Other than that it was a right-handed person of normal stature, no."

"Ah. A right-handed person of normal stature. That narrows it down. So in that sense, it could have been you?"

"No sir, I'm left-handed."

"Oh, thank goodness!" I said. "You're off the hook then."

I got my own little titter out of that one. But it was small consolation.

"Right-handed." I intoned the words ominously.

"Yes sir."

I went up to Agent Pierce, reclaimed the bokken, and walked back toward the defense table. Then, without warning, I tossed it to Miles Dane. Startled, he caught it one-handed.

"Agent Pierce, would you identify which hand Mr. Dane caught that stick with?"

Stash Olesky jumped out of his seat. "Objection!"

"I withdraw the question," I said.

But the jury could see. Miles Dane was holding the bokken in his left hand.

Forty-three

"THAT WAS AMONG the cheapest tricks I have ever seen in my life," Stash said over lunch, looking fairly annoyed. We were seated across the rickety table from each other down at Rae's Diner, near the wharf. "You and I both know your client isn't left-handed. You coached him."

"Nope," I said.

Stash was eating the cube steak and creamed spinach. "Then how . . ."

"As you know, he's secured to his chair every day by the bailiffs. Usually they cuff him by the ankle. But today I told them his ankle was getting chafed raw." I smiled. "So I had them cuff his hand to the chair. His *right* hand. I left my coat on the table so nobody could see the handcuff."

Stash sighed loudly, then began laughing. "If I didn't have that son of a bitch buried already, I'd be pissed."

"Keep whistling, pal. The graveyard's coming up on the left."

Stash Olesky didn't even look up from his creamed spinach.

Forty-four

THE STATE CALLS Regina Mills."

A tall thin woman walked slowly to the front of the courtroom. She had the appearance of somebody who was used to being looked at. She must have been seventy, but her face had been recently stretched into a wrinkle-free zone, so now her skin had the taut look of Saran Wrap. She had obviously once been quite beautiful and now looked immensely frightening.

She sat and was sworn in.

"Mrs. Mills," Stash said, "could you tell us where you live?"

"Well, normally we winter in Sarasota," she said. Her voice was pitched high, her diction pretentious. "But Douglas, my husband, Mr. Mills, he's been ill this year, so we stayed in Michigan for the operation. Our home here in Pickeral Point is at 223 Riverside Boulevard."

"And where is that in relation to Miles and Diana Dane's house."

She raised her chin slightly, as though not wanting to admit the fact that she lived in the vicinity of lesser personages than herself—though whether it was writers or accused murderers she found so distasteful was not clear. "Next door."

"How close are your homes?"

"I should say two hundred feet at most."

"Close enough to hear anything from their home? Television, stereo, conversation, anything like that?"

"It's not my custom to listen in on the affairs of neighbors. But ordinarily we are far enough that one can't hear much of anything from the Danes."

"On the night of October 21, did you have occasion to hear anything unusual?"

"As I say, it's not my custom to pay attention to other people's private matters. Unfortunately, my husband was in some discomfort due to his, ah, condition. And he couldn't sleep. It was our nurse's day off, so I was forced to help him with his . . ." She flushed slightly. "Well, there are some medical matters, personal hygiene matters I suppose you could say, that required my assistance. He wanted water, this and that. Suffice it to say, I got not a whit of rest that night."

Stash tried to look pleasant. "Right. But did you, while you were up tending to your husband, hear anything out of the ordinary?"

The chin tipped upward a little, but she didn't answer.

"I think we've established that your neighborhood is a quiet one and that you're not the eavesdropping type. Nevertheless."

"Yes. Well. I did hear something."

Stash, I'm sure, was ready to strangle the woman. He smiled genially. "And that was . . ."

"Yelling. I had exerted myself somewhat in the course of moving Douglas from one place to the next and had gotten rather warm. So I stepped outside very briefly, just to feel the air on my face. That was when I heard it."

"Heard what?"

"The yelling."

Stash nodded. "The yelling. Tell us more."

"There was someone yelling. I heard a man and a woman yelling. Some sort of altercation or disagreement. The sound was coming from the direction of the Danes' house."

"An altercation or disagreement. How far away were you?"

"As I said. At most, two hundred feet. It must have been quite loud, too, because there are any number of bushes and trees between our homes that would have deadened the sound."

"And what time was this?"

"Just after midnight."

"You sure it wasn't later? Couldn't have been around, say, three o'clock?"

"No. I had just started watching a movie on the television. *Spartacus*."

"The old Charlton Heston picture?"

"Kirk *Douglas*," Mrs. Mills said disdainfully.

"Oh, right, right. I always get them confused." Stash grinned at the jury. "I'm going to proffer—thank you Mrs. Wilson—I'm going to show you what has just been marked as Exhibit 64. Could you identify this?"

"It's the *TV Guide* for the week dated October 18 through 23 of last year."

"And if you could tell us when *Spartacus* was playing that night?"

"Here it is. It's on Turner Classic Movies eleven until two in the morning."

"Thank you, Mrs. Mills."

Stash sat down, and I stood up.

"Just a few brief questions, Mrs. Mills. How long have you and the Danes lived next to each other."

"Since 1975 or thereabouts. Whenever they moved in."

"And in that time have you ever heard yelling coming from their house?"

She looked up at the ceiling, took a long time to think. Finally she spoke in her high, firm voice: "Never."

"Let me be clear. Arguments, disagreements, screaming, *anything* of that nature?"

"Never."

"Anything to indicate the Danes were at each other's throats on a regular basis?"

"Never."

"Never ever?"

"I said *never*. Never ever, I believe, is what they call redundant, Mr. Sloan."

"You're absolutely right. Never is quite clear enough. You never heard an argument out of the Danes in the whole twenty-five years you lived next to them. Thank you so much for your valuable testimony."

Forty-five

We've got to find this guy," I said. Lisa and I were sitting around the office that night eating pizza. The mood was glum. "We've got to find Blair Dane, and we've got to put him on the stand."

"How?" Lisa said.

"Well, we know where he is, right?"

"We know where he *was*."

"We've got no choice. We subpoena him, we send a couple of burly deputies out there, and we bring him back under court order."

"And if he's at the store buying milk or hiding in a storm drain?"

I sighed. "Then we're out of luck."

"So there must be a better way."

"Name it."

We sat in silence for ten minutes.

"Here's what I want you to do," I said. "Draw up a material witness subpoena. That will give the sheriff the authority to hold a witness in custody. It's usually used by law enforcement, but there's nothing in the statute that says we can't use it ourselves. I'll call Evola and see if he'll sign it tonight. Then we'll see what happens."

Evola grudgingly signed the document that night, standing out in the foyer of his house in slippers and a bathrobe covered with Michigan State logos. He didn't speak to me, just signed the document and walked back down the hall, his slippers slapping against the floor, leaving his exceptionally pretty wife to close the door behind me.

A T JUST BEFORE six in the morning, accompanied by two sheriff's deputies, we arrived at the Brothers of Christ compound and knocked on the door.

The man named Jack answered the door, his hair wet from the shower, looking a great deal more chipper than I felt. "Well, hello, Mr. Sloan. Back again?"

The senior deputy said, "Is there a Blair Dane here?"

"You have a warrant, I assume?"

"A subpoena."

"Ah. May I?" He held out his hand. The sheriff's deputy handed it to him. Jack read it with great care.

"You know guys, this is a subpoena, not a search warrant. Without a warrant, I don't believe you have the right to actually enter this building." He paused a beat. "But because we're friendly and cooperative citizens with nothing to hide, I'd be happy to invite you in. Conveniently all of the brothers here are seated at the breakfast table as we speak. Then have a look through the house. Take your time. Feel free to ask for identification from anybody. They'll be perfectly happy to oblige. Unfortunately you'll find that there's nobody by the name of Blair Dane living here."

He then opened the door, and we went in.

Our search uncovered nothing. Blair Dane was gone.

Jack stood at the door and waved pleasantly as we drove off toward the rising sun.

I T HAD BEEN a thin, thin thread, and a distant hope. But at this point, distant hopes were about all we had.

Forty-six

FIRST THING NEXT morning, Stash put a local lawyer, Tony Merritt, on the stand.

"Mr. Merritt," he said after the usual preliminaries, "have you ever performed any work for Diana Dane?"

"Yes, I have."

"And what did that work consist of?"

"I prepared a will for her."

Stash handed him a small stack of paper, recently marked by the clerk. "I'd call your attention to Exhibit 38. Can you identify this?"

"This is the will I prepared for Ms. Dane."

"Could you read that line, yes, right there, that my lovely assistant Miss Genovese has marked with the yellow Hi-Liter?"

"It says, 'I hereby leave my entire estate to my husband, Miles Dane.'"

"My entire estate. That would include the proceeds of her trust if it were liquidated?"

"I wasn't involved in the trust. So I can't really speak to that except to say that from her verbal representations to me, she said there was a trust and that it would be liquidated when she died, and that if she predeceased her husband, then the proceeds were to go to Mr. Dane."

"Did she indicate the size of that trust?"

"No, she did not."

"But as long as she died before him . . ."

"Right. He got the whole shooting match."

THE NEXT WITNESS was a tall attractive woman of about forty, who wore the sort of clothes that managed to look both casual and terribly expensive at the same time. I know all about that kind of wardrobe: My second wife, whose tastes ran toward the same sort of garb, left me with a credit card bill of seventy-one thousand dollars and change when we split up, virtually all of it spent on clothes.

"Would you state your name and occupation for the record," Stash Olesky said after she was sworn in.

"My name is Sharon Molina, and I'm an attorney at the law firm of Shearman & Pound in New York City." She looked almost frighteningly at ease in the witness box, a hint of smile on her face, black hair glossy, tasteful bits of gold at the ear and throat.

"What is your legal specialty?"

"I'm in the firm's trust department. Trust work involves managing the legal and business affairs of trusts."

"And if you could explain what a trust is, Ms. Molina?"

"Technical mumbo jumbo aside—" A flash of bright, white, straight teeth to the jury. "—a trust is a legal arrangement, a contract basically, by which one person's assets are controlled by another person to accomplish a specific end laid out by whoever established the trust. My practice primarily involves trusts established by high-wealth individuals who wish to preserve their wealth for future generations, to minimize taxes, or to accomplish various charitable purposes. There are quite a few complexities involved—legal, financial, and tax-related—and so a good deal of thought and experience are required to construct and maintain trusts so that, in fact, they do what they are intended to do."

"I see. And was Diana Dane a client of yours?"

"Strictly speaking, no. The other thing I failed to mention is that once a trust is established, it must be maintained. The assets of the trust must be managed and the wishes of the founder of the trust—as set down in the written trust—must be executed. The reason I bring this up is that, again, strictly speaking, Shearman & Pound is a trustee—

meaning that we actually hold title to the assets which are held in trust as per the instructions by the late Diana Dane's grandfather under testamentary trust."

"Let me get this straight . . ." Stash biting his lip in mild puzzlement, playing country lawyer to the hilt. "So you don't actually work for a living person?"

"Correct."

"No boss, no nothing? Must be nice."

A brief, not entirely warm smile. "Legally speaking, our boss is the language of the trust itself. Naturally we are required to account for our actions to the beneficiaries."

Stash handed her a document. "Could you identify this?"

"This is the deed of trust that establishes an entity known as the Testamentary Trust of Albert Goodwin van Blaricum. It's dated 1961 and is signed by Albert van Blaricum, Diana's grandfather, as well as by a predecessor of mine at the firm."

"You say every trust has a purpose. What is the purpose of this trust?

"To provide the late Mrs. Dane with income throughout her life."

"So when people talk about somebody having a trust fund, that's what this is."

"Exactly."

"How much money did this trust provide for her?"

"Well, it's rather unusual actually. It's typical to structure a trust in the following manner: You put a big pot of money into trust. That pot of money is known in the law as your *res*. In layman's terms, that's what you might call your principal. The trustees invest the principal. Some reasonable proportion of that income goes to the beneficiary of the trust, and the rest is plowed back into the principal. That way the principal grows, income grows, and, one hopes, over time the beneficiary will continue to maintain an income that keeps par with inflation or perhaps even outpaces it."

"Okay."

"But as I mentioned, Diana Dane's trust was unusual. It provided a fixed income. An annual check in the amount of thirty thousand dollars was to be written, irrespective of the size of the principal. Every decade, that amount was to be increased by three thousand dollars."

"Why was it structured this way?"

"Bear in mind that in the early 1960s when the trust was established, thirty thousand dollars was a fairly significant income. But, that said . . . This is, of course, not written into the deed of trust—but my understanding from the previous trustee at Shearman & Pound is that Diana's grandfather didn't wish his granddaughter to live a life of complete ease. He was a sort of old school Puritan type who believed that an excess of spending led to bad character."

"So the current income that Ms. Dane was getting from the trust?"

"Thirty-nine thousand dollars, payable each year on the first of January."

"So what happens to all that money—the *res*, the principal, whatever you want to call it—when she dies?"

"According to the original trust instrument, the *res* or principal was at that time to pass to any natural issue of Ms. Dane."

"Natural issue. That means children. Children she bore from her own body."

"Exactly."

"So if she died without having children?"

"The trust assets were to be liquidated and the proceeds would flow to her estate. As such, she could then dispose of it in her will in any way she chose."

"And to your knowledge, Ms. Molina, does Mrs. Dane have any children, natural or otherwise?"

"I'm not aware of any."

"Okay. So how big a trust is this? How much principal is there?"

"I don't have the exact figure in front of me . . ."

"Let me hand you a document that the clerk is marking as State's Exhibit 67." Stash waited on the clerk, then handed a two-page photocopy to the trust lawyer. "Are you familiar with this document?"

Sharon Molina favored him with a large smile. "Yes I am." Behind the smile was a certain amount of tension. I gather there had been a fair amount of legal wrangling on Stash's part in order to compel Ms. Molina to reveal the size of the trust. She, of course, knew what the ultimate outcome would be, but fighting Stash had given her firm the opportunity to bill the trust for a great many hours at four hundred bucks a pop. "This is an asset report as of September 29 of last year for the Testamentary Trust of Albert Goodwin van Blaricum, deceased, Diana Dane, beneficiary."

"And referring to page two of this document, could you tell me the size of the trust?"

"As of September 29 of last year, the trust contained assets with a total value of twenty-eight million, four hundred and twelve thousand, two hundred and eleven dollars and ninety-one cents."

There was a loud stirring in the courtroom as the size of the number sank in.

Stash stood there as though thunderstruck. "Twenty-eight *million*?"

A smile of amusement bordering on condescension. "Twenty-eight, as they say, and change."

"Wow! All Mr. Dane has to do is murder his wife and he gets twenty-eight million bucks?"

Up I came from the chair. "Objection, Your Honor!"

"I'd like to answer that question, Judge," Sharon Molina said. "I believe it bears on the matter at hand."

"That's outrageous!" I said.

"No, I think I'd like to hear the answer," Evola said.

"Murdering his wife would not be enough to secure him the money." She showed us her fine teeth. "He'd have to get away with it."

"NO WITHERING CROSS-EXAMINATION?" Stash said to me after Sharon Molina's testimony. We had planned on lunching at Edna's Café, so we were coming down the stairs together.

If I'd asked too many questions about how the existence of "issue" would affect the trust, it might have tipped my hand about Blair Dane. Dane was on my witness list, but so far as Stash knew at this point, he was just some distant relative of Miles's—a character witness, maybe.

"No profit in it," I said. "The harder I go at the trust, the worse it looks for Miles."

Stash frowned and studied my face. I had a hunch he was getting a funny read from my expression, so I said, "Oh, about lunch . . . Something came up with another client that I need to tend to. I'm going to have to beg off on lunch. See you in court."

I clapped him on the shoulder and headed toward my car.

Forty-seven

IT'S TRADITIONAL FOR prosecutors to wrap up their case by putting a
member of the victim's family on the stand who can be safely predicted to bawl their heads off, leaving the jury with a sense of outrage
and a thirst for vengeance. At the end of the afternoon, after a number
of minor witnesses, I had noted that Diana's brother, Roger van Blaricum, was the only witness left on Stash's list, so I expected him to be
called in the thirst-for-vengeance slot. This pleased me. He was such
an irritating fellow, I felt he would do as much good for Miles's case as
for the state's.

But apparently Stash, on meeting him in the flesh, came to the same
conclusion that I did. After a brief, whispered conversation with his
chief assistant, Stash stood, and said, "Your Honor, the state of Michigan rests."

IT WAS GETTING late, so Judge Evola recessed for the day. I walked
across the street, fending off a dozen or so reporters, grabbed a sandwich at Kramer's Deli, then drove back to my office. Mrs. Fenton, as
usual, had gone home at the stroke of five, so the entire office was dark.
There was plenty of moonlight coming off the river to see where I was
going, so I walked through the dim room and into my office.

I was fumbling for the light switch when a soft voice said, "Don't."

That was when I saw him. Seated in a chair beside my desk was a man, his back to the river, face cloaked in darkness.

My heart was racing at top speed. "Who the hell are you?" I said, trying not to sound as petrified as I actually was.

"You know who I am."

It only took me a moment. "Blair Dane," I said softly.

"Yup."

"Is all this darkness entirely necessary?"

"I don't see any need of you knowing what I look like." His voice was high and clear, and there was a strangely unemotional quality, almost as though he'd been drugged. The most violent client I'd ever had, an enforcer for a Detroit drug gang back in the good old days, had the same tuneless sound to his speech. It was hard to put a finger on the precise reason, but the general effect of his speech was enormously frightening.

I shrugged, then walked around to my desk, hoping he wouldn't see how my hands were shaking. I tried to convince myself that this was an opportunity, that if he was intending to hurt me, he'd have already done it. "I need a cigarette," I said, reaching into the drawer of my desk where I keep my .32. My heart kicked up another notch as I felt around. Plenty of rubber bands and pencil stubs. But the gun was gone.

"Save yourself the trouble, Mr. Dane." I saw a silver gleam in Blair Dane's hand. "Smith & Wesson's my brand of smokes, too."

"Look . . ." I said.

"No, *you* look." Still in that same sleepy, drugged voice. "I am not a nice person. I want you to understand that nice and clear. I am a not nice person who is real, real tired of being in jail. With me so far?"

"Sure."

"You are a guy who would like to drag me into your case somehow and accuse me of murder and try to send me back to Jackson. So let me say this just once. I did not kill my mother. And I will not go back to the Jackson State Penitentiary under any circumstances whatsoever. I just will not allow that to happen."

"If you didn't do it, then what are you afraid of?"

No answer.

"I'm not out to frame you or blame you. All I want is to know what happened that night. I promise."

I sensed that Blair Dane was amused—though he didn't make any sound, and his face was as dark and invisible as ever. "You tell me you need a pack of cancer sticks, and then you reach for a gun. If you were in my shoes, would you trust the promises of Charles Sloan, Esquire? Hm?"

The fear was starting to wear off, and now I was getting annoyed. "Hey. Give me a break. You broke into *my* office. What am I supposed to do, sit here and say, *Do you mind if I grab my pistol?*"

"That's exactly my point, Mr. Sloan. Miles Dane has a gun to his head, and your job is to do whatever it takes to get that gun away before the state of Michigan pulls the trigger."

"Okay," I said. "What are you here for?"

He seemed to be thinking. "You've seen my rap sheet. Sheets, plural, I guess I should say. You think: Sure, violent guy, liar, career criminal, scumbag . . . why *wouldn't* he kill his mother? That's who he is, right?"

I didn't answer.

"All I'm saying is this: Comes a time when a guy like me has to face up to who he is. I'm not unlucky. I'm not put upon. I'm not conspired against. I'm not downtrodden. I've never been sent to jail for crimes I didn't commit. I made my life. I did what I did. I have been an unworthy piece of toilet scum for a very very long time. And during my last incarceration, I faced up to all of that for the first time. With the help of Jesus Christ, I will build a new Blair Dane. But if I go back to Jackson for something I didn't do, the new Blair Dane goes right down the crapper."

"I can't defend your father if—"

"We're not talking about you. Or Miles Dane either. We're talking about me. What I'm telling you is, you have a nice daughter. Very attractive young girl. Full of promise and all that shit, I'm sure. It would be a tragedy for her, and for you, and for me, if you made any further efforts to have me snatched up by a bunch of redneck deputies and brought into the courtroom under duress to serve as your sacrificial lamb. Do you understand what I'm saying?"

"You're threatening my daughter."

"Good. So we understand each other."

"If you're really trying to build a new Blair Dane, Blair Dane the nice guy, the harmless citizen," I said, "does this really take you in the right direction? Morally? Spiritually? Whatever?"

"I have prayed on that matter. My Savior, quite honestly, has not given me very firm or clear guidance. It's one of those deals where desperate times demand desperate measures, you know what I'm saying?"

"Maybe you ought to pray some more."

"This isn't debate club," Blair Dane said.

"No it isn't." With that, I flipped the switch on my desk lamp.

In a way, I wished I'd left the light off. He was a scary guy. Even seated I could tell he was probably close to six-foot-four, and his shoulders were broad and thickly muscled—the benefits of the prison yard gym, no doubt. Though he was only a little more than thirty-one years old, his long hair had already gone very gray. His teeth were crooked and tobacco-stained. Across the back of one hand was a muddy green jailhouse tattoo that read GO DOWN SHOOTING, with a crude picture of a revolver inked beneath it. But what was most striking about him was a certain dead quality in his pale blue eyes, an unnatural stillness.

"I deserve a chance," he said, standing. He looked down at me with his emotionless blue eyes. "Give me that chance."

"All you have to do is sit there and answer a few questions," I said.

"If that's your plan, then you better keep a good watch on that girl of yours. Lot of crazy, ruthless people out there." He studied me with his dead eyes for a moment, then he slid out the door into the darkness.

"There's still time," I yelled. "You still have time to do the right thing!"

Outside there was only darkness and a bone-chilling cold.

Forty-eight

THERE WERE A couple of items I wanted to talk with Miles about, but by the time I had gotten finished taking care of some matters with Stash, I found out that Miles was about to be loaded into the transport on the way back to the county jail. I had been hoping to avoid a time-consuming trip to the jail, so I ran down the hallway to the secure garage where the transport van was located. Miles was being ushered in the back door just as I broke out into the cold air of the garage. He had been changed out of his jacket and tie, put back into an orange jumpsuit, manacled at the wrists and feet.

"Mind if I have a moment with my client, Deputy . . . ah . . ." I squinted at the plastic tag on the deputy's chest, my eyes not being what they once were. ". . . Deputy Dehaven?"

"It's pronounced DEE-Haven." He looked irritably at his watch. "We're running late already. Sheriff's got me on a schedule, make sure everything goes smooth."

"It'll just take a moment."

Deputy Dehaven, the driver of the transport van, was a short guy with a red face who obviously spent all his spare time lifting weights. He had massive shoulders and short, bowed legs. Most cops are good folks, but there's a sizable minority of people who end up in law enforcement because it gives them a chance to push people around. This deputy was one of those guys. I had run into him a few times and didn't like him. "Nope. Can't do it, Mr. Sloan."

"Can I ride along then?" I said.

"Nope."

I got out my cell phone, "I think I'll call Sheriff Rice myself, see what he thinks."

Dehaven gave me a long, dubious look, then said, "Gimme your bag."

I let the deputy examine my battered briefcase, then climbed into the back of the van. He slammed the door behind me, closed it with a padlock. It was a standard-sized Ford van, with a heavy cage of steel mesh surrounding the passenger compartment. Two steel benches, amateurishly spray-painted a bright red, ran along each side of the van. There were no seat belts, so when the deputy floored the accelerator and headed off into the night, I nearly slid off onto the steel floor.

I spoke softly so that the deputy couldn't hear me. "Okay, we've got some choices to make," I said. "Basically we can either start with your character witnesses, try and build you up as a good guy, and then move on to forensics, or we can go the other way around—start by trying to undermine the forensic evidence and wrap up with character."

Miles frowned. I could barely make out his face in the dark. "You know what I think? I think if we start with forensics, then move to character, they're going to want to see me on the stand. That's the logical conclusion of the he's-a-nice-guy defense, wouldn't you say? But right now we aren't sure whether it's wise to put me on the stand, correct?"

I nodded. The van hit a bump, and my head nearly hit the ceiling. "Does this guy always drive like this?" I said, as the deputy tore around a corner, tires screeching.

Miles nodded. He was holding on to the bench with both manacled hands. "I think he's a frustrated NASCAR driver." He smiled a little. "Anyway, what I was going to say was, let's get the character thing out of the way, try to get a warm fuzzy feeling about me, then see how the forensics goes. If we feel good at the end of forensics, we won't need to put me on the stand. On the other hand, if forensics goes badly, we can save me as our Hail Mary at the end."

We screeched around another turn, nearly fishtailing, then accelerated on the straightaway. I banged on the mesh between us and the deputy. "You think you could keep it under a hundred?" I said.

Deputy Dehaven didn't even look at me. "When I get to tell you how to do your job, Counselor, then you can start telling me how to do mine."

Miles rolled his eyes. "I tried the same thing, but he won't listen."

I slid back down the long steel bench, out of the deputy's earshot. "I think you're right. I'll put Dan Rourke on the stand first thing tomorrow, then move on to forensics later."

"Dan Rourke's a good—"

I didn't find out what Dan Rourke was because the next sound I heard was a screech of tires and violent bang. I know it was just my imagination, but after that it seemed as though I heard the screaming of birds, and it was as though I was being borne through the air by a vast, black cloud of angry crows, their wings buffeting my face and body.

THEN THE CROWS were gone, and I was lying on the ceiling of the van. There was a pain in my back, and the world had gone silent. I don't think I had been knocked out exactly, just momentarily stunned. It was obvious that we had been hit by something, and that the van had flipped over. I sat up and looked around the dark steel cage.

The van had been smashed so hard that the rear door had been wrenched open, frigid air coming in through the gap. For a moment I thought it was the dark that kept me from seeing him. But then I realized it wasn't my eyes at all: Miles Dane was gone.

I threw my briefcase through the gap in the doors then crawled out and stood up. The van lay at the corner of a stand of brushy acreage. There were no cars in either direction, no lights.

Then I heard an engine cranking up, and a large truck with the name of a local furniture company stenciled on the side came backing out of the scrubby trees. The left front fender of the truck was a mess of buckled steel; obviously it had hit us, causing us to flip over. I expected the truck to stop, but it didn't. It simply swung around, did a Y-turn in the road, and began driving away, heading back toward town.

"Hey!" I yelled. "Hey!"

The next thing I knew, the furniture truck was gone. I heard something behind me, a sizzling or popping of fluid hitting hot metal. Then I smelled smoke.

"Miles!" I yelled. "Miles?"

There was no reply.

Suddenly I had a terrible feeling. What if this was a jailbreak? What if Miles had hired somebody to hit the van? A dozen nightmarish scenarios ran through my brain. Maybe Blair Dane had been driving the truck. Maybe he hit us intentionally. Maybe he had kidnapped Miles or . . .

The popping and sizzling continued, then suddenly it was no longer dark. A small flame was licking off the top of the upside-down vehicle, off the area around the engine. A small flame that was rapidly growing higher.

And then in the flickering light of the flame I saw the face of the deputy. He was hanging upside down, his shoulder belt pinning him to the seat. There was blood on his face, and he wasn't moving.

As I was about to move toward the upended van, a car pulled up, slammed on its brakes, its headlights pinned to the flaming wreck.

"Little help!" I yelled.

There was a loud sucking sound, a sickening *whoooomp* from the van. I turned back to see a large fireball erupting from the engine compartment. I also saw Miles Dane.

He was shielding his face with his cuffed hands, while kicking out the window on the other side of the van with his prison-issue sandals. It was obvious that he was trying to help get the unconscious deputy out of the van. I ran around to the other side of the van to try and help, but the fire was so intense that I couldn't get closer than about ten feet.

Miles reversed his position on the ground, began trying to crawl into the smashed-out window.

"Miles, don't!" I yelled.

But by then all I could see were Miles's orange sandals. Fortunately, the fire was still confined primarily to the engine compartment and the top of the vehicle. But it was clear that the gas tank would go up soon— and when that happened, the whole thing would blow.

It struck me then that the reason Miles could approach the van and

I couldn't was that it was cooler near the ground. I fell to my belly and wriggled forward across the weedy ground. I had no plan to be a hero; I guess I just wanted to protect my client, figuring the faster we got the deputy free, the more likely Miles would get out before the gas tank went up.

When my head reached Miles's sandals I saw that he was struggling with the seat belt. With his manacled hands, he appeared to be having trouble getting the buckle unfastened.

"Let me do it," I shouted.

"You got a knife?" Miles shouted back.

"Get out! I've got free hands."

"I'm in already. Give me a damn knife!"

I reached in my pocket, pulled out the small locking liner knife that I carry with me everywhere I go, flipped it open, handed it through the shattered window. Miles had to contort his body to get at it, but he managed. Then he began sawing at the belt. It seemed painfully slow. I could hear people screaming outside the van now, cars pulling off the road, but my mind was focused on how to get the deputy out of the car.

I crawled around to the other side of the van. I could feel the heat on my back now, pressing down. The window by the Deputy Dehaven's head was already broken.

"Hurry, Miles."

He was still sawing awkwardly at the belt with his cuffed hands, his face grim and set. Suddenly the belt gave way and the big-shouldered deputy fell on his head in heap. I grabbed his epaulets and yanked, but they just tore free.

"Get out! Get out!" Somebody was screaming from the road.

The fire was roaring above us now.

Miles buried his hands in one of the deputy's armpits and, with surprising strength, forced the big man's head and torso out the broken window. I was able to lock my hands around his chest and heave him another foot or two out of the window.

"Get the hell out, Miles!" I said.

Then I was on my feet and dragging the heavy man away from the fire. I had not gotten more than twenty feet when the gas tank caught fire and a huge ball of flame erupted from the top of the van, illuminating the entire area. There must have been eight or ten cars on the side of the road now. But I couldn't see Miles. I dropped Dehaven and tried to run back toward the van to get Miles, but the heat was so strong I couldn't get close.

As the first explosion of the gas tank died down, the wind shifted, and the van disappeared in a cloud of heavy black smoke.

"Miles!" I screamed. "Miles!"

There was no answer.

The headlights of the various cars cut eerie swaths through the black smoke that surrounded us.

And then, suddenly, there he was, staggering out of the smoke, his orange jumpsuit blackened, his face smudged, one orange sandal missing. He tripped on something and fell to the ground.

"Call 911!" I shouted.

But there was no need. I could hear the sirens already, howling toward us.

A S IT TURNED out, other than some cuts on his foot from kicking out the window, Miles was completely unscathed. The deputy, however, had a concussion and was hauled straight off to the hospital. He had regained consciousness before the ambulance had arrived, and seemed like he would be alright.

Miles and I stood on the side of the road watching the ambulance disappear down the road.

"Thought you'd skipped out on me for a minute there, Miles," I said.

Miles looked wistfully off into the dark trees. "Don't think it didn't cross my mind," he said.

Then a sheriff's deputy came up behind us. "Let's go, Mr. Dane," he said. His voice sounded, not precisely gentle, but somehow respectful.

The crowd of gawkers on the side of the road watched silently as the deputy led Miles to the car. But as they slid him in the backseat, everyone began to cheer. Miles gave them a brief, rueful smile through the window, then the cruiser pulled onto the road and headed off toward the county jail.

Forty-nine

IT WAS BRIGHT and early Monday morning when I petitioned to have an additional character witness added to my list. I argued that the reason for amending my list was that this person had only recently become acquainted with my client, and that the nature of their relationship made it only fair that he be added. Stash fought me hard, but I won.

At eleven o'clock the jury was ushered in.

When they had settled themselves in their seats, I stood. "The defense calls Deputy Clarence Dehaven."

Clarence Dehaven wore his uniform, hat under his arm, gun on his hip as he climbed onto the stand. Every crease was knife sharp, every inch of his shoes was shiny, every button was in place. The only thing that wasn't regulation was the large white bandage on his forehead.

"Good morning, Deputy Dehaven," I said. "Are you acquainted with my client?"

"Yes, I am."

"How so?"

Dehaven was not the kind of man to give a defendant a lot of slack. But there was a look of genuine gratitude in his eyes as he looked at Miles. "Mr. Dane there," he said, pointing, "he saved my life."

I led him through the whole story as he knew it. When I had finished with the facts, I said, "Deputy Dehaven, does it seem like my client is the kind of man who would kill his wife?"

Dehaven looked at him a long time, then looked at the jury. "I don't know, folks. I don't know what's in that man's heart. All I know is my four-year-old daughter still has a father because Miles Dane put his life on the line for a man he didn't know . . . or probably even like. That must be worth something."

Two of the female jury members were wiping tears from their eyes. Even the old farmer, Dahlgren, looked a little choked up.

"Thank you, Deputy," I said.

Sometimes in a case you can feel the wind shift, like everything is about to change—and after that your whole case is smooth sailing. For a moment I imagined that I was feeling that change in the air. Of course sometimes you think the wind has shifted, but it's just an illusion. And the thing is, you never really know, not until that verdict comes in.

M Y NEXT WITNESS was Daniel Rourke, Miles's editor at Padgett Books.

He approached the stand with a painful gait. Dan Rourke must have been a large, vigorous man once, but now his body was sagging and swollen, his motions slow and tentative. His white hair was still enviably thick, though, and his blue eyes were bright.

When he sat, his face was sweaty and slightly flushed, despite the cool weather. It made me nervous. I suspected that he'd had a drink before getting on the stand.

"Mr. Rourke, what sort of work do you do?" I said.

"I'm an editor." I was encouraged that his voice was firm, and his eyes seemed focused and clear. "My title is executive editor emeritus with Padgett Books in New York City."

"Tell us about Padgett."

"We're the largest publisher in America. We publish everything from how-to to tell-all, bodice rippers to Nobel prize winners."

"And do you know Miles Dane?"

"I do. I've been his editor since 1969, back when I worked for Elgin Press. I edited his first novel, which came out that same year. I've known both him and his wife Diana since that time, and have counted them as my friends for over thirty years."

"Were you in a position to observe Miles and Diana's relationship?"

Daniel Rourke smiled with a fondness touched by sadness. "They were one of the world's great couples," he said expansively.

"So you know them intimately?"

"I believe I do. Back when they were living in New York, I saw them all the time. It wasn't just a business relationship we had. Miles was—and is—a close friend of mine. These days we see each other at least two or three times a year."

"What about Diana?"

Daniel Rourke seemed to fade for a moment. "I'm sorry. The question was . . . wait, yes. Diana. Well. Diana was a shy woman. Reserved but very warm. She had what they used to call grace. It used to be that grace was the best thing a woman aspired to." His eyes crinkled. "Now women aspire to have tattooed asses and pierced nipples."

That got a good laugh from the audience.

Judge Evola leaned toward him. "Keep it between the lines here, if you'd be so kind, Mr. Rourke," he said gently. "We're in a court of law."

Rourke smiled wickedly. "My profoundest apologies, Your Honor."

"Mr. Rourke," I said, "you were more than just fond of her, weren't you?"

Rourke looked at me for a moment. "Yes," he said softly.

"In love with her? Would that be fair?"

"Long ago, yes."

"So as the other man in this troika, if there's anybody who'd be predisposed to looking at their marriage with a critical eye, I'd think it would be you."

"I suppose that's fair to say." He smiled sadly. "For five years Miles and I had a relationship that was almost as close as a father to a son. We saw each other constantly, and in the twenty-odd years since, I've continued to socialize with them regularly. In their home. In mine. At my place on Martha's Vineyard. And in all that time, I never saw them raise their voices at each other. I never saw them pick at each other, or fight over little things, I never saw anything but respect and tenderness."

I picked up the copy of *How I Killed My Wife* that had been marked as an exhibit and flipped it open. "Would you do me the favor of reading this aloud?"

Rourke patted vaguely at his jacket, suddenly looking apprehensive. For a moment he seemed almost panicked. "I seem . . . it looks . . . I think I forgot my glasses," he said. I had specifically instructed him to bring them.

I smiled. "No problem. If there's no objection from counsel, would the court indulge me?"

"Fine," Evola said.

"This is from page forty-nine of the book Mr. Sloan wrote in 1970 entitled *How I Killed My Wife and Got Away with It*: 'In public my wife and I are the picture of marital bliss. But it's only a pose. We hold hands, we fondle, we gaze at each other. But it is an act sustained by spite, a sort of playing out of our hatred. Everyone is fooled. But it is all a lie.' " I closed the book. "What's to say this wasn't the case with Miles and Diana."

Rourke laughed. "Look, this is fiction. Fiction always distorts reality in some way. Sure, it's an amusing book because it plays on this fear we all have that we never really know people. But the truth is, we *do* know people. *How I Killed My Wife* is simply not psychologically accurate. This book is about two people who despised each other. People who despise each other just reek of hatred. Anybody with fifteen minutes of experience in real life knows this. People like the characters in this book, they make your skin crawl. That was never the case with Miles and Diana."

"Okay, what about a different theory? Suppose Miles and Diana didn't hate each other. Maybe he was controlling her. Maybe she was so beaten down by some sort of secret mental abuse that she just acquiesced to whatever he wanted. Plausible?"

"Hah!" Rourke raised his bushy eyebrows. "That's a hoot. Diana came off as soft and graceful. But once you got to know her, you realized her spine was made of steel. If anything, she was the stronger one of the pair."

"If I could follow that up . . ."

"Wait. Let me finish. Miles has always affected a tough-guy image. But the truth is . . ." He smiled at Miles. "Truth is, Miles is a sweetheart. The poor little guy wouldn't hurt a flea."

"But look at his books, Mr. Rourke! All this violence and gore. Manipulative people, liars, religious fanatics, killers. That stuff had to come out of his head."

"Sure. But so what?"

"Well isn't this kind of fascination with violence and evil a little . . . strange?"

Rourke looked at me with amusement. "Strange? Let's be adults. Look at this spectacle." He swept the room with his finger. "Why are all these people here? Hm? It's the smell of blood. Why are two million people out there glued to their TV sets right now? It's the smell of blood. You and I, Mr. Sloan, are standing in the very center of the modern equivalent of the Circus Maximus. The human animal loves the scent of blood, of mayhem, of anger and violence. Every man, woman, and child on this planet has a manipulator and a liar and a destroyer inside. But that doesn't mean we act on them. Miles simply made a profession out of giving voice to the demons that live in all of us.

"But at the core, he remained a sweet romantic. Yes, his books are about liars and cheats and killers. But if you read them to the end, the wicked always get their just deserts. That's where the real Miles shows through. What really motivates him is a deep and profound hatred of wickedness. And since there was no wickedness in Diana Dane, I must tell you that the idea that he could kill her is so ludicrous as to beggar the imagination."

"Wait, wait. You say everybody gets punished in his books. Not in *How I Killed My Wife and Got Away with It.*"

"Not so. In his original draft, the narrator tells the story from jail as he awaits his trip to the electric chair. His title for the book was *Just Deserts*. I told him it would be more fun if the character got away with it. He resisted that suggestion. So I told him if he didn't rewrite it, I wouldn't pay him for the book." Rourke smiled mischievously. "It may shock you to find out that at that point he came around to my way of thinking fairly quickly." Rourke laughed. "The title was mine, too, by the way."

Rustles and coughs from the back of the courtroom.

"What did you think when you heard Miles had been charged with killing Diana?"

Rourke shook his head sadly. "The truth? I laughed. I couldn't believe it. His love for Diana was at the very core and center of his being. She was the pillar that held up his entire life. It's an impossibility that Miles Dane killed Diana."

"Thank you, Mr. Rourke," I said.

"Impossible!" he said again.

Stash Olesky stood quickly. "That's a lovely sentiment, and would that it were so. Are you saying that Mr. Dane is incapable of violence?"

"*Serious* violence, yes."

"Is it not true that on December 9, 1991, the *New York Times* reported that Mr. Dane fired a gun at you?"

"True."

"Is it not true that on January 1, 1979, it was reported in the *Los Angeles Times* that Mr. Dane physically assaulted Charles Bronson at a bash thrown at the Playboy Mansion?"

"True."

"Is it not true that on the fourth of June 1983, Mr. Rourke, the UPI wire picked up a story that Mr. Dane had struck an unnamed actress with a rattan stick in the lobby of the Beverly Hills Hilton?"

"Absolutely."

"Then, how, precisely, Mr. Rourke, would you define *unserious* violence?" Stash Olesky whirled and stalked back to his chair. "Strike that. I have no further questions."

I stood, smiling. I had bushwhacked him beautifully, if I don't mind saying so. "Redirect, Your Honor. Mr. Rourke, I'd like you simply to answer the prosecuting attorney's last question."

"Gladly. As it happens, Mr. Olesky, I would define those incidents as unserious violence precisely because they were not violence at all. They were entirely staged for the purposes of gaining publicity. Charles Bronson is—or at least was—a friend of Miles's. Their 'fight' was a publicity stunt to get attention for *Fisticuff*, which was Mr. Bronson's latest movie at that time. Not so incidently, *Fisticuff* happened to have been adapted from Miles's book of the same title."

"A fictional fight?"

"One hundred percent pure fiction. All of them."

D URING THE BREAK I ran into Stash in the hallway. "I know, I know," he said. "Never ask a question you don't know the answer to."

I smirked. "I wasn't even going to say it."

"Too bad he couldn't erase the blood from those clothes, Charley. Or his fingerprints from the bokken."

"Oh, don't worry," I said. "I've got somebody else for that."

Fifty

I DEALLY YOU WANT to start strong, then trot out your middling witnesses, then finish with your strongest witness. Unfortunately, I was short on truly strong testimony, so it was time to move on to the middling witnesses. Middling, actually, was probably a charitable way of describing Leon Prouty. But I figured he couldn't hurt us. So we might as well get him on the stand, chum the waters for the somebody-else-did-it theory, and then get rid of him as quickly as possible.

Leon strutted up to the podium wearing a cheap blue suit I'd bought him the day before, white socks, cheap black shoes, and a clip-on tie. I'd bought him a real tie, but he refused to wear it, claiming it choked him.

After swearing him in, I said, "Leon, brass tacks here. You're no choirboy."

"Nope."

"You've served time for a variety of offenses."

"Yup." He grinned, showing off his rotten teeth.

"You were arrested a while back for stealing all of the sod and bushes off of a recently landscaped property, true?"

Another dumb-ass grin. "They call it midnight landscaping."

"And I'm defending you in that case, correct?"

"Uh-huh."

"You came to me and said you knew something about this case and that if I would defend you for free, you'd testify about what you knew, correct?"

He squinted at me. "Man, you making me out like some kind of liar! What kind of lawyer are you anyway?"

"Well, that goes right to the issue here, doesn't it? Why should these people believe you?"

He looked insulted. "Man, I'm a *thief* not a liar!"

I gave the jury a look like, *Folks, your guess is as good as mine.* Then I forged on. "Leon, where were you on the night of October 20 and the early hours of October 21 of last year?"

"Uh . . ." He wrinkled his nose. "Let's say I was in the vicinity of Miles's house."

"Doing what?"

Leon cleared his throat, ran his tongue around the inside of his mouth, put a comical look of calculation on his face. "See, I believe the constitution gives me the Fifth Amendment situation on that."

I scowled. "Leon, you have to do better than that."

Leon showed his awful teeth. "Put it like this. There was some midnight landscaping going on across the street from Miles's house. I'm not saying I was involved in it. But I was, let's say I was present in the neighborhood."

"Okay. So you were there. Did you see anything interesting going on at Mr. Dane's house?"

"Interesting? No. But I seen *something.*"

"What did you see?"

"Seen somebody drive up."

"Tell us about this person you saw."

"He was driving a old Lincoln, mid sixties, a real classic. Black. Suicide doors, whitewalls, I mean this ride was flat-ass *cherry.*"

"Mr. Prouty," the judge said. "Next word of profanity, you go across the street to county, no bail, no parole. You with me?"

Leon looked at the judge sullenly. "Sorry, man. Your Honor, I mean."

"So what did this man you saw look like?"

Leon shrugged, grunted.

"Speak English, Leon," I said.

"It was dark."

"You saw that the car well enough to identify the year and model, but you didn't see what this man looked like?"

"I was a ways away. He had his back to me. What I seen, he wore a black leather jacket."

"And when did he arrive?"

"I don't know. Maybe ten, eleven."

"And when did he leave?"

A big shrug. "Before midnight."

"Why do you remember that?"

"Cause he wasn't there when the old guy showed up."

Suddenly I felt a little ill. There is no feeling worse than putting a dubious witness on the stand, and then watching him start to lie. This was the first time he had ever mentioned a second person arriving at the house. But I was stuck. I couldn't ignore the statement. "Old guy?" I said

"Yeah, this old dude. See me and these Meskins I was working with, we had to meet up with this boy down in Detroit at like one o'clock. So to get there more or less on time, we had to leave at like twelve-thirty. So this old guy rolls up just as we was leaving. Which would have meant he was there at like midnight. Maybe a little later. And the guy in the Lincoln had done took off by then."

"How could you tell this second man was old?"

"I don't know. Couldn't really see him good. I guess he had white hair and stuff."

"So two men came to the house the same night that Diana died, and both of them were there sometime in the vicinity of midnight."

"Yup."

"Thank you, Leon. That's all I have for you."

Stash hopped up eagerly. "Well, Mr. Prouty, great to see you again. What's this, about the tenth time we've met?"

Leon shrugged, muttered something surly but unintelligible.

"Let me show you something, Mr. Prouty." Stash dropped a small stack of paper on the table. "You recognize this?"

Leon shrugged.

Stash's voice was at its most sarcastic. "I trust you can read?"

"Yeah."

"Then tell me what this is. No mumbling, no shrugging."

"It's like a statement type deal."

"A statement type deal. You spoke with Detective Denkerberg, and she typed up a report which you had to read. And after you read it over, you signed it. Right there where it says: 'I testify that the above statement is true and accurate, sworn this day,' bang, signed by you, Leon Prouty. Huh? Right? Speak up!"

"I guess, yeah."

"You *guess* that's your name. Okay. Now show me the part in your statement where you mention this second man—this alleged white-haired old man that you just testified about."

Leon looked around the room uncomfortably.

"Show me, Mr. Prouty. Time's a-wasting."

"I guess, uh . . . I forgot to mention him."

"You forgot to mention him! Mr. Prouty, please, who are you kidding? You've known from the beginning what's at stake. Miles Dane is on trial for murder. You sat down for a solid hour with a detective, you swore to tell the entirety of the truth about what you observed that night, and then you just kind of . . . *forgot?*"

"Well . . ." Leon rubbed his face in his hands, as though hoping the entire courtroom might just up and disappear.

"You didn't see an old man there that night, did you?"

"I seen what I seen," he muttered.

"You didn't see this alleged man in the black Lincoln, either, did you?"

"Yeah, I did."

The prosecuting attorney's voice slashed the air like a fencer's sword. "You lied then, you lied now, everything you've said was nothing but a pack of lies, wasn't it?"

Leon shrugged, and he looked away from Stash's cold blue eyes.

"There was no one there that night was there, Leon? No one at all."

Leon Prouty didn't say a word.

"I'm done with this fraud." Stash stalked back to his chair.

I WOULD GLADLY have strangled Leon, but he fled out of the courthouse the moment that recess was called.

Fifty-one

I HAD DECIDED to lead off the forensic testimony with my autopsy expert. Ira Dimmock had good qualifications, but when I had finally met him in person, just days before trial, I immediately regretted my decision to retain him. There was something, I hate to say it, creepy-looking about him.

His testimony, as it turned out, was uneventful. He testified that, yes, it was possible that Diana Dane's temporal artery had been burst by the first blow to her head and that it was possible her heart had shut down in less than a minute. While he was unwilling to argue that Dr. Rey's failure to open Diana Dane's cranium was out-and-out bad practice, the fact that Rey had neglected this aspect of the autopsy gave Dimmock the room he need to cling to his *it's-possible-she-died-in-seconds* line with a doglike ferocity, and Stash was unable to shake him from it.

After we were done with Dr. Dimmock, I turned to my tool mark expert.

HELEN RAYNES, PH.D., was a member of Mensa, had scored the highest on the SAT of anybody in her high school class, and was Phi Beta Kappa and *summa cum laude* in college. I knew these things because she told me. Several times. When she wasn't telling me how smart she was, and how well trained, and how well qualified and how insightful, she was telling me about all the men who had unsuccessfully made passes at her in various restaurants, bars, and hotels while she was on the road testifying. She not-so-subtly implied that a pass from me, however, would not be looked upon with disfavor.

There was, in fact, nothing about Helen Raynes that could be described as subtle. Her dresses were bright shades of red or green, with extravagant peplums, large lapels, and tiny waists—all of them so tightly fitted that her large bosoms and ample hips threatened to pop right out into public view. Her fingernails were long and painted bright red, and her lips gleamed with opalescent lipstick. Her hair—a toxic-looking shade of auburn that could only have come out of a bottle—radiated out from her head in a mute testimony to the extraordinary powers of modern hairspray.

But she was a seasoned witness. A seasoned whore, you might say. In a weak moment—and lacking anybody else suitable—I had decided to use her supposed expertise in the field of tool mark identification.

Her rep in the legal community was that she would testify to pretty much anything—provided your check didn't bounce. She had developed a theory of the case which bordered on outlandish, so I had originally decided not to use her. But since reasonable doubt was still a vague— if distant—possibility, and since the likelihood of Blair Dane showing up to testify seemed ever more remote, I decided I had no choice but to use her. Even outlandish theories have, on occasion, provided a jury with reasonable doubt.

So off I went: "Dr. Raynes, could you begin by telling us about the science of tool mark identification."

"Certainly." Helen Raynes looked me in the eye. She wore a red suit with a raw silk blouse cut so as to reveal just exactly enough cleavage to catch your attention, but not enough to look entirely unprofessional.

"Tool mark identification, Mr. Sloan, is the forensic science which deals with the identification of marks left by tools. This all might seem a bit obscure." She smiled broadly at the jury, showing off some flawless cosmetic dental work. "But in fact, tool mark identification has proved extremely valuable in criminal investigation. When a firing pin of a pistol hits the casing of a bullet cartridge, it leaves a little dent. To the naked eye, it looks like nothing. But to the trained tool mark specialist, that little dent is as unique to that particular pistol as a fingerprint is to an individual person. Tool marks left in metal, wood, plastic, and other materials can be used to identify all manner of tools. Knives, screwdrivers, hammers, beer can tabs . . . Any metal tool leaves a unique imprint on anything it strikes or touches. You'd be amazed at how many cases have been solved this way."

"Good," I said. "Now just to get everything out on the table, you're not testifying for free are you?"

"No, I'm not. I'm being paid."

"Fair enough. But let me ask you this: What's to keep you from just making up some kind of complicated-sounding theory in return for a fat paycheck?"

Helen Raynes straightened in her chair and leaned forward, which served the dual function of making her look earnest and of revealing just a fraction more cleavage. She could have won an academy award for the look of sincerity on her face. "Mr. Sloan, my reputation *is* my livelihood."

I nodded back, just as sincerely. "Very good. I'd like to show you what has been marked as State's Exhibit 55. Could you identify this for me?"

She took the small plastic bag I gave to her, put on a pair of reading glasses, scrutinized it briefly. "That is a splinter of wood which was recovered from the head of Diana Dane during her autopsy."

"And have you conducted any sort of examination of this splinter?"

"I have. I examined it with a scanning electron microscope at both one hundred and five hundred powers of magnification."

I had several images marked as exhibits, then handed them to Dr. Raynes. "Could you identify these, Doctor?"

"Yes. These are images produced by the scanning electron microscope of the largest of the three fragments or splinters. That's exhibit— what was it? State's 55?"

"Fifty-five, yes. And did any of these images bear on your analysis?"

"Yes. This picture here, Defense Exhibit 9, is of particular interest."

Lisa quickly placed a three-foot-high blowup of the same image onto an easel next to the stand. It looked like a grainy photograph of Mount Vesuvius, turned sideways.

"Is this the same image?"

"Yes."

I scratched my head. "Okay. You've got me, Doctor. What is it?"

"In fancy technical language? It's what we call the fat end of the splinter." She smiled at the old farmer, Dahlgren, on the front row of the jury box. He smiled back. "You see, Mr. Sloan, when a splinter of wood is torn from a larger piece, we normally expect to see a ragged edge where the individual fibers bend and then finally break."

"Well this looks fairly smooth," I said. In fact, it didn't look like much of anything to me, smooth or otherwise. I was just parroting what Raynes had told me.

"Exactly. Based upon my analysis, this surface is consistent with having been sliced with a very sharp object such as a knife."

"Okay, next," I said, "can you identify this?" I handed her the bokken.

"This is the bokken that the state has argued was used to beat Diana Dane to death with."

"Did you examine it?"

"Yes. As with the splinter, I conducted a visual examination. Because of the way my electron microscope operates, I was unable to examine it under the electron microscope without cutting it apart. I did, however, examine it under a conventional optical microscope."

I handed her several photographs. "And are these photographs that you made though that microscope?"

"Yes. What these photographs show is the place where this splinter was split off the bokken." Lisa put another photograph on the easel. If the earlier image had looked like a mountain, this one looked like a fogbank in a swamp on a dim morning. "This photo is of higher magnification and shows the lip of the tear that matches with the splinter."

"Anything noteworthy?"

"Two things. First, based on a comparative analysis of the fibers, this is definitely the exact location from which the splinter, State's Exhibit 55, was torn."

"And second?"

"You'll note here, here, and here . . ." She used a laser pointer to outline three minute and indeterminate-looking lines that ran perpendicular to the scar on the surface of the dark wood. "Three small lines. These are tool marks."

"What do they indicate to you?"

"A thin metal tool was inserted under the splinter and twisted in a counterclockwise direction."

I played dumb again. "Okay, now it's the contention of several very well-trained folks in this case that somebody whacked Mrs. Dane with this bokken, and that in so doing, this little piece of wood sort of chipped off the bokken and lodged in her flesh. But you seem to be saying something different happened."

Dr. Raynes nodded. "You bet your sweet bippy, I am." This got a laugh from a couple members of the jury.

"Spell it out," I said. "Tell me what you're saying."

"Somebody pried this splinter off the bokken, then sliced the end off with a thin-bladed knife. A penknife, a scalpel, something of that nature. They then placed the splinter on or in the wound on Mrs. Dane's skull, where it was found by Dr. Rey."

I frowned. "Huh? Why would somebody do that?"

Stash Olesky stood. "Objection. I'm perfectly willing to listen to this witness's wild speculations on technical matters, but she's in no position to enter Mr. Dane's mind. Or anyone else's for that matter."

"Your Honor," I said. "Dr. Rey, Agent Pierce, Detective Denker-berg—all of these so-called experts were allowed to speculate ad nauseam about what they think Mr. Dane did and why they think Mr. Dane did it. Our witness is helping us provide a reconstruction of the crime based upon her expertise. She should—in fact, she *must*—be allowed to continue."

Judge Evola sighed heavily. He didn't want to give it to me, but he had to. The one advantage I had in this trial was that Evola didn't want some armchair quarterback lawyer with a nice haircut spouting off on Court TV that afternoon about how the judge had just opened the door to an appeal. He gravely intoned: "Keep it close to the wind."

Whatever that meant.

"I shall," I said, with equal gravity. "Go on, Doctor. Why would somebody cut a splinter off this bokken and place it on Diana Dane's body?"

"Pretty simple, Mr. Sloan. Miles Dane is being framed."

There was a soft mutter from the audience.

"Do you really believe that?" I said.

"It's quite clear, Mr. Sloan. Once you examine the evidence and see that this splinter was very purposefully cut from the bokken, you realize that somebody is monkeying with the evidence. Fudging the facts. Was it someone in law enforcement? Possibly. But I doubt it. So if it's not somebody in law enforcement, who does that leave? It leaves the real murderer. And why would the real murderer plant evidence on the body? For one reason, and one reason only: to frame Miles Dane."

"Explain," I said.

"Look. The state's case here presumes that Miles Dane used an old novel he wrote as a sort of script for murdering his own wife. The assumption is that because the character he created in the book got away with the crime, Mr. Dane thought he could get away with the real crime by doing everything exactly the same as it was done in the book. But come on! Only a ninny would be dumb enough to think that. Obviously somebody killed Diana Dane. With what, I don't know. But it wasn't this." She brandished the bokken. "No, whoever did it, they set the whole scene so that it would look as though it could only have been Mr. Dane. Planted the fragment, wiped blood and hairs on the bokken and on Mr. Dane's clothes, then placed the bokken and the incriminating clothes in the same sort of location as they had appeared in the book. But let's not be children here. Simple logic says that if Mr. Dane wanted to kill his wife, the absolute *last* thing he'd want to do was plagiarize an idea from a book that the police could find in any library—a book, moreover, that had his own name printed in two-inch-high letters on the cover!"

"Thank you, Doctor," I said. "That makes such good sense that I'm going to sit down and let Mr. Olesky try to prove you wrong."

Stash Olesky stood, looking angry. He knew Helen Raynes's reputation as well as I did. "Doctor, shattered bones are pretty sharp, are't they?"

"I suppose they can be."

"Is bone harder than wood?"

"Ebony is a very hard wood."

"That's not what I asked. Is bone harder than wood?"

Helen Raynes looked a little sour. "Generally, yes. I suppose."

"Thank you for that bold admission. Now, was Mrs. Dane's skull fractured?"

"Yes."

"So, given that by your own admission bone is harder than wood, what's to stop a fragment of bone from shearing off this splinter just as cleanly as a knife?"

Helen Raynes smiled derisively. "It might seem that way to a layman. But when you've studied these things as long as I have, you realize it wouldn't work that way. It couldn't."

"Why not?"

"The three marks that I pointed out earlier? The direction of the grooves demonstrates that they were made by twisting, not by a lateral shearing force."

Stash squinted at the large blowup of the gouge in the bokken. "You can tell all of that from this blurry little streak?" He pointed at a vague ridge in the wood.

"Yes, I can."

Stash raised his eyebrows, then gave the significant look to the jury. "Earlier I believe you testified that the ridges were here, here, and here. The one I just pointed at?" He shrugged. "It's just a random squiggle."

I breathed out slowly. Why had I put this woman on the stand?

Dr. Raynes cleared her throat and stared at the chart for a moment. "I'm sorry I wasn't really paying attention where you were pointing." She squinted at the huge poster. "You're right, I was mistaken."

"You were mistaken. What else were you mistaken about?"

"Nothing," she said firmly.

"Ah. Then perhaps you did it intentionally?"

"Did what?"

"Fudged the facts—as you so nicely put it just minutes ago."

"I would *never* tamper with evidence."

"Notwithstanding all the money you're being paid to help the defense, you'd never fudge the facts."

"Absolutely not."

"You've never fudged the facts on anything in your life?"

Dr. Raynes blinked. It wasn't much, but it scared me a little.

"I know, I know!" Stash moved along breezily. "You've got your reputation to think of. But what exactly *is* your reputation?"

The courtroom was silent.

"You were a tenured professor at the University of Montana, were you not?"

"Yes," she said softly.

"For what reasons can a tenured professor be forced from her position?"

"A variety, I suppose."

"Do you suppose that fudging the facts in your research might be one of those reasons?"

No answer. I knew something bad was coming, and I was powerless to stop it.

"Doctor? Hm? If a researcher falsifies data in their research in order to come to a predetermined conclusion, would that be grounds for dismissing a tenured faculty member?"

"Objection," I said. "This is totally irrelevant and speculative."

"Denied," Evola said. "I'll bet fifty cents Mr. Olesky is going somewhere with this."

"And you'll win that bet, Your Honor," the prosecuting attorney said. "Doctor, I'll ask you again: Is the falsification of research data considered to be sufficient grounds for the removal of a tenured professor at most universities?"

"Yes."

"And were you fired from U of M because you falsified data in your research?"

"I was not fired."

"Oh?"

"A jealous colleague made a variety of spurious accusations. They were never proven."

"Come on. That's a lie, isn't it? Wasn't a report submitted to the faculty senate recommending your dismissal as a result of your dishonesty?"

There was a long pause during which Helen Raynes's face went slowly pale. "Who told you that?"

"I'm asking the questions here." Stash's voice cracked like a whip. "Was or was not a report made to the faculty senate recommending your dismissal?"

"It was a sealed report. A preliminary report, nonbinding." Her voice had gone shrill. "The final recommendation of the committee was never made. I would most certainly have prevailed if . . . had all the . . . if the facts had been fully examined."

"But instead you resigned, didn't you?"

"My business was just taking off, so I decided it wasn't worth the agony of fighting the thing for another year."

"What about your precious reputation?"

"Excuse me?"

"In your earlier testimony you claimed that your reputation was the *one* thing that ensures your truthfulness on the stand."

Stony silence.

"If your reputation is so important to you, Doctor, then why didn't you stick around and beat the charges?"

Helen Raynes made an obvious effort to regain her composure, but her voice was still high and weak, and her skin was pale as death. Her career, her reputation, and her livelihood were going down the tubes right there on national TV. "As I said, my business was just taking off. I had just received a large contract. It seemed an opportune time to go."

"I bet it did." Stash shook his head in disgust and sat down.

Fifty-two

"S ON OF A *bitch*!" Lisa said, slapping the table. "That pompous, bogus, boobs-hanging-out woman knew there was a time bomb in her past, and she never told us."

"Let it go," Miles said.

We were on recess waiting for my final expert witness.

"Let it go," Miles said again. "We've got to focus on what's coming next." He paused briefly, smiled glumly at me. "What *is* coming next, by the way? I'm waiting for the part of this trial where ace attorney Charley Sloan goes on a honking big tear and saves my ass."

"Can I go strangle that woman, Dad?" Lisa said.

Anywhere but here, I was thinking. I turned around and looked around the courtroom, looking for inspiration. The first face I saw was that of Roger van Blaricum, Diana's brother. He was no more than eight feet away, half of his face looking back at me with the careworn, injured expression of a grieving brother.

And the other half of his face was smirking at me.

Fifty-three

"THE DEFENSE CALLS JoEllen Flynn."

JoEllen Flynn had no great reputation, no publications, wasn't an unusually forceful witness, and her experience in the field of crime scene investigation was unremarkable. But she was honest and diligent. And drop-dead gorgeous. Don't bother calling me a chauvinist: Sex sells in the courtroom just as well as it does on the breath-freshener commercials.

JoEllen Flynn was in her midthirties, black Irish—raven-haired, pale-skinned, high-cheekboned, tall. She'd been a crime scene investigator for the state police post in Lansing for a few years, then had quit her job to raise children. From what she told me, she testifies in a few cases a year to make gas money and pay for the annual family trip to Disney World.

"Ms. Flynn," I began, "have you had an opportunity to review the evidence in this case?"

"Yes sir. I reviewed the entire police file, including the autopsy report, toxicology, the witness statements, and the crime scene reports, plus state police Agent Orvell Pierce's blood spatter analysis report."

I began by using her to point out that the fingerprints found on the bokken were latent prints rather than impressions left in the blood. She made the point that the fingerprint evidence provided no clear evidence that Miles Dane had used the bokken as a murder weapon. I then moved on to the main reason I'd brought her to the stand.

"I'm going to show you what has been marked as State's Exhibit 60, Ms. Flynn," I said. "Can you identify this document?"

JoEllen Flynn examined the paper I handed her. "Yes sir. That's Agent Pierce's blood spatter analysis report."

"Let me direct your attention to page one of that report. There where it says 'Methodology.' Could you read that portion silently and then tell us whether you have any comments as to the soundness of his methods?"

JoEllen Flynn looked at the paper for a while, chewing her lower lip. She looked a little nervous. "Yes sir. Well, it all looks about right. These are standard and accepted methods in the field of blood spatter analysis."

"Good." I handed her more papers. These were covered with spatters of a dried red-brown liquid, the pig's blood Agent Pierce had used to re-create the blood spatter from the crime scene. "Can you identify these items?"

"Yes sir. These are the papers on which Agent Pierce splattered blood. In other words, those are his verification tests."

"And these? State's Exhibits 15 through 27?"

"These are photographs of the actual blood spatter from the room where Diana Dane was killed."

"Now, I know Agent Pierce has already testified on this subject, but could you just briefly recap the logical connection between the test sheets and the actual photographs?"

"Sure. Basically the way this process works is you measure the size and shape of the blood spatter. Using a standard formula that you can punch into any scientific calculator, you can predict roughly where the drops came from and how fast they were moving. Working back from that, you can reconstruct the location and direction of motion of the object from which the blood was spattered. So the point of these"—she held up one of the spattered pieces of paper—"is just to verify that the calculations worked, that they correctly predicted what would happen in actuality."

"So have you had an opportunity to compare Agent Pierce's blood spatter to those in photographs of the actual crime scene?"

"Yes sir."

"And what did your comparison reveal?"

"Basically, that the test spatters are slightly shorter than the actual ones in the room. Here, see, in the crime scene photograph you have a blood drop that's an inch and a quarter long, and here in the test, same size of drop, but it's an inch and an eighth. I compared twenty-nine tested spatters against similar test spatters and I found that twenty-three of the twenty-nine were slightly shorter."

"What does this indicate to you, Ms. Flynn?"

"Look, I can't question Agent Pierce's basic conclusion. There is a margin of error in these calculations. So when Agent Pierce here in conclusion number four on page one of his report states that the object used was approximately one and a half to three feet in length, I think he's got it about right."

"Now the bokken, state's exhibit one, it's forty-one inches, is it not?" I said triumphantly.

"That's right. But as Agent Pierce pointed out, I think he was naturally referring to the amount of the weapon extending beyond the hand. Not the total length of the weapon. That's the standard way of calculating this."

Thank you for that entirely unhelpful clarification, darling. Now would you like to shoot me in the head? Beautiful, she was. But not the most helpful witness I've ever had.

I tried to smile. "Okay, Ms. Flynn. Fair enough. But even assuming he was talking about the length extending beyond his hand—and I'm not sure he was—were his conclusions accurate?"

"Again, these are approximations. He estimated the weapon was one and a half to three feet in length. Hold the bokken with one hand, you've got more than three feet of weapon extending from the hand. Hold it like a baseball bat, you're looking at right around three feet. Which is at the extreme end of his approximation. In my experience, when you do a series of tests and the tests show that the midpoint of an approximate range is shorter than the object you're comparing with, there's a good chance you're dealing with the wrong object."

"Let me get this straight . . ."

"I'll try to say this in a simpler way, Mr. Sloan. If he'd done one test, and the spatters had been in the right range, but slightly low—

hey, no problem. But if you do twenty-nine comparisons, and the tests consistently indicate something that's slightly shorter, yeah, you're probably looking at a shorter weapon."

I held up the black bokken in its plastic sleeve. "Simple English. You think she was hit by something shorter than this."

"Yes sir. If I were to guess, it was probably something just under two feet long. Highly unlikely it was three."

"Thank you. Mr. Olesky, she's all yours."

Stash stood up. "Hi, Ms. Flynn, good to see you again."

"Hello, Mr. Olesky."

"You ever played softball, Ms. Flynn."

JoEllen Flynn smiled shyly. "Yes sir. My team was state champs in high school."

"If I may say so, you look as fit as a high school girl," Stash said. The soft soap was making me nervous. Usually Stash likes to stampede right for the jugular.

JoEllen Flynn blushed. "Thank you."

"You ever heard the expression 'choking up on the bat'?"

"Sure."

"What does it mean?"

"Well, some hitters grip their bats farther up on the handle than others. That's called choking up."

Stash handed the bokken to her. "Show me."

She took the bokken and held it in a batter's grip. "Normally, you'd hold it right down here on the end. But if you wanted to choke up, you'd just move your hands a few inches higher. Like this."

Stash pulled a neon green tape measure of his coat pocket, extended it from the tip of the bokken to JoEllen's thumb. "Could you read that off for me, Ms. Flynn?"

"Twenty-nine inches."

"That's just a hair over two feet, isn't it?"

JoEllen's gaze flicked toward me, then back to Stash's face. "More like two and a half," she said.

"But closer to two feet than three."

She shrugged. "As you say, by a hair."

Stash nodded, looking satisfied, then released the catch on the tape measure. It went zippppp back into the tape case.

"Last question, Ms. Flynn. Why do people choke up on a bat anyway?"

JoEllen Flynn looked at me helplessly. "It swings easier."

"It swings easier."

"Swings easier."

Stash took the bokken back, choked up on it about six inches, swatted once at the air. "You're right. Swings nice and easy."

Fifty-four

THAT NIGHT AFTER trial recessed for the evening, I told Lisa that we were going to have to put Miles on the stand. We were sitting around the office eating what must have been our two hundredth pizza of the past two months.

"Right now we barely have a theory for this case," I said. "It's all very well to stand up in front of a jury and say, 'Well, maybe it was a police conspiracy, maybe he was framed by somebody, maybe it was a burglar, gee, we just don't know.' But if you really want reasonable doubt, you want a bad guy, a genuinely plausible alternative suspect. And right now, we don't have one."

"So how does Miles on the stand help us with that?"

I breathed out heavily. "I've got to get him to talk about Blair. It's the only hope we have."

"He won't do it," she said. "You know he won't."

"It's all we've got."

"We've got Blair," she said. "If we can find him."

"Forget about Blair," I said sharply.

She looked at me strangely. "What?" she said. I hadn't told her about my little meeting in the office with Blair the other night. The way I looked at it, the less she had to worry about, the better.

"I've got to prepare for tomorrow," I said. "I don't have time to try finding him."

"I'll go," she said.

"Absolutely not. I need you here."

"I just need to lay a little of that famous Sloan charm on him," she said, picking up my car keys. "Don't worry, Dad, I can turn him around, I promise you."

Then she plunged a folded piece of pizza into her face, stood up, and headed for the door, sauce dripping down the side of her chin.

"Lisa, dammit!" I yelled. "Bring back those keys."

"UHMMmmmhuh-huh," she said. Then she was gone.

I jumped up to go after her, but tripped over the pizza box and went down on both knees into a large deep dish supreme. By the time I'd gotten to the door, the taillights of my Chrysler were already heading up the road.

I started shivering when I came back inside and couldn't stop for almost an hour. I turned the heat up, which made the room hotter but did nothing to get rid of my memory of Blair Dane's cold eyes, or the dead quality of his voice.

Fifty-five

I WOKE UP in my office the next morning at around six and looked outside. My car was not in its space. I called my home number, but nobody answered. I felt a nervous tickle again. *It would be fine,* I told myself. She wouldn't be able to find him, so she'd come home with her tail between her legs. Hell, she was probably driving over to the office right now.

I tried to think about what was in front of me for the day. Worst-case scenario, I had to be ready to close before lunch. I started going over the questions I'd need to ask Miles.

By seven o'clock I was getting antsy: I still hadn't heard from Lisa, still didn't know where my car was.

My house is only about six blocks from the office, so I hiked over, grabbing a bag of doughnuts from the bakery at the IGA on the way. When I got to the house, there was no car. Inside, no coffee made, no messages on the phone, no evidence that Lisa had slept in her bed. Now I really *was* getting nervous.

I looked at the clock. Seven-thirty-five. I was due in court at nine, so I called for a cab. I had to spell my name three times to the cab dispatcher. He was Indian or Pakistani, and I only understood about one word in three that he said. After I hung up the phone, I started pacing around the room, going over my closing in my mind. Problem was, I had to prepare two different arguments. One was the Blair-did-it speech. The other was the mushy reasonable doubt speech. I was feeling dreadfully, woefully underprepared.

I got so absorbed in my speech that when I looked at the clock again I was surprised to see that it was eight-seventeen. The cab still hadn't arrived. My house was about a ten-minute drive from the courthouse. Plus I had to drop by the office. Call it fifteen minutes.

I picked up the phone to dial the cab company, but the line seemed dead when I held it up to my ear.

"Hello?" a puzzled-sounding voice said after a moment.

"Lisa," I said. "Thank God. Where are you?"

"Outside Saginaw."

"Saginaw!" Saginaw was almost two hours away. "What are you doing there?"

"Long story. Anyway, I think I got Blair. He's been crashing with some jailhouse buddy."

"You *think*?"

"He's here, okay? I'm with him. I think I can get him to testify."

"Leave him be. It's too dangerous."

"I got to go before he skips on me." She sounded harried and strung out. I was worried that she had been drinking—though it may have just been the fatigue in her voice.

"I can't put him on the stand if you're in Saginaw."

"Then stall. Either we'll be there or . . . Oh shit!"

The phone went dead in my ear. I looked at the clock. Eight-twenty-one. My heart was beating like a trip-hammer. If the cab didn't get here soon, I'd be late.

I called the cab company. "Sloan," I said. "Charley Sloan. Where's my cab?"

"Who?"

Why oh why oh why had I not taken three hours out of my day at some point in the past two months to buy Lisa a car? We had talked about doing it every other day, but then something else always seemed to come up.

It took another five minutes to impress on the Indian cab dispatcher the urgency of my situation. Finally, he assured me that a cab would be there in three minutes. Or maybe five. "But eight minutes, tops, my friend! Or nine! Absolute tops, nine! Or twelve!"

I slammed the phone down before his numbers got any higher.

THE CAB ARRIVED fifteen minutes later, belching blue smoke. According to my calculations, if everything went perfectly, I'd be strolling into court at precisely one minute before nine.

About halfway to my office, the ancient cab's engine gave out and the cab settled on the side of the road. The driver began talking in excited Hindi or Bengali or Urdu on his radio.

"How long?" I said.

"Relax, my friend." He turned and gave me a big smile. "The cavalry is on the way."

"How long?"

He shrugged, easily. "Oh, certainly no more than an hour."

I dug my cell phone out of my briefcase. The battery, of course, was dead.

Fifty-six

How pleased I am that you have condescended to join us, Mr. Sloan."
Judge Evola's toothy smile was as cold as my fingers. The jury was
already seated, the Court TV camera running, everybody looking ready
for a hanging. I'd hitchhiked, grabbed a ride from a kid in a VW bug
with a broken window and no heat. It was almost ten o'clock, and I was
so cold I couldn't feel my fingers.

"My deepest apologies to the court," I said. "I had car trouble and
a broken cell phone, then the—"

Evola interrupted me with a wave of his big hand. "Well I hope the
cat didn't eat your next witness." Laughter from the jury box. I looked
over at the jury. They were glaring at me. It was written all over their
faces: I was the scumbag lawyer holding things up while his guilty client
sat there trying to look innocent. I got the feeling that unless I did
something awfully dramatic, Miles Dane was going down.

Other than Blair Dane there was only one more witness on my list.
The one witness I had prayed I wouldn't have to use.

"Your Honor, if I could beg the court's indulgence, I'd like just the
briefest of moments to confer with my client."

"No doubt you would. That privilege, however, is reserved for those
who arrive on time to this court. Call your next witness, Mr. Sloan."

Notwithstanding the judge's instructions, I leaned over and whispered to Miles, "It's your call. Are you willing to roll the dice on reasonable doubt?"

Miles knew what the score was. We'd discussed the pros and cons of his testimony several times. What I had said to him was that he would only testify if it seemed that the jury would really have to stretch to find reasonable doubt.

Miles stared bleakly in front of him. "I don't feel like rolling the dice on reasonable doubt right now," he said finally.

"I have to warn you," I whispered, "this won't be pretty."

"Meaning what?"

"Meaning, if you go up there, you're putting yourself in my hands. You just have to trust that I have your best interests at heart."

He stared straight ahead for a long time, his fingers gripping the table like someone was about to drag him away to his death. "Do it," he said finally.

"Whatever it takes?"

"Whatever it takes."

This wasn't a clear license to introduce Blair, but it gave me room to do what I needed to do. "Your Honor," I said in my courtroom voice, "the defense calls Miles Dane."

The journalists in the back of the room all stirred. This was it, the money shot, the part they'd all been waiting for.

Miles walked slowly to the stand. He looked small, tired, drawn, old. Not the romantic figure he used to cut. No black clothes, no cowboy boots, no shoulder holster. His white shirt was too big around the neck, and his blue suit hung a little low in the cuff. He looked like an accountant who was coming due for retirement. The only thing left was those haunted gray eyes.

I walked into the middle of the room, waited until every eye was on me. I could feel the Court TV camera focused on my back. I paused for a moment. My heart had been beating wildly, but now, suddenly I felt calm and strong, as though all the energy of those thousands and thousands of eyeballs had just been sucked into my chest, filling me with certainty and power.

"Mr. Dane," I said. My voice was loud, slow, grave, strong. "You are a liar. Aren't you?"

Miles's eyes widened. I don't know what he expected me to say, but it damn sure wasn't that.

His mouth opened and closed.

"I mean seriously," I said. I put my hand in my pocket, strolled toward him, eased my tone into a conversational gear. "Come on. 'Fess up. You're a big fat stinking liar, am I right?"

"What?" He had finally managed to find a voice.

"Your story. The mysterious and nefarious cat burglar sneaks into your office . . ." I widened my eyes comically and wiggled my fingers in the air. ". . . and he steals this stick and then silently creams your wife for fifteen minutes and then jumps nimbly out the second-floor window without leaving so much as dent in the ground? Give me a break. It's the most cockamamie bunch of baloney I've ever heard in my life. Wouldn't you agree?"

He stared at me. Judge Evola stared at me. The jury stared. Even Stash Olesky was surprised—and he knew I didn't mind throwing a curveball when I was behind in the count.

I strolled over to the clerk's seat, picked up State's Exhibit 37, that black piece of wood carved in the shape of a samurai sword, walked down the center aisle between the pews until I reached the back of the room. The camera panned as I walked, and everybody in the room turned their heads as I walked past them.

Everybody in the room except one: Sitting on a chair next to the door was a man who appeared to be asleep. He wore a green Starter jacket, jeans, and a Detroit Tigers baseball cap pulled down low over his face. "Hey!" I said. "Are we boring you?"

The man didn't stir.

"Wake up!" I poked him with the murder weapon.

No answer.

My face gave the impression that the sleeping man had really pissed me off. I rared back, then swung the murder weapon, smashing the man in the head with the stick. The stick made a resounding whack, and the man's hat flew through the air. People gasped.

It was a dummy, of course, leaned up against the wall by the kid who'd given me the ride in his VW. I'd given him twenty bucks for his trouble. But still, for a second there, it had looked pretty real.

I whacked the dummy savagely again. The sound resounded through the room. Then again, then again. The poor fellow slipped over sideways, fell on the floor. I kept whacking him until Judge Evola came out of his shock and began beating his gavel on the bench.

"Congratulations, Mr. Sloan," Judge Evola shouted, his voice barely audible above the sound of the stick. "You've just earned yourself a one-thousand-dollar fine for that performance."

I kept smashing away until Evola sicced the bailiff on me. The bailiff—a big corn-fed guy with a tricked out .45 auto on his hip and a look in his eye like he'd just love an excuse to knock a couple of my teeth out—didn't have much trouble restraining me. And honestly, I didn't fight all that hard. By then Evola was shouting something about jail time.

"Let's have a recess," Evola said, when things had finally quieted down.

He cleared the courtroom.

"I'm making a point, a permissible demonstration," I said.

"And I'm making you pay the treasurer of Kerry County a thousand dollars for making a joke out of this courtroom. A thousand dollars *and* a week in the county lockup. And if you think I'm letting you get a mistrial for this stunt, you're dreaming, Sloan." He put his hand over the microphone, and whispered, "Now step your ass back."

AFTER THE JURY had been reseated, I stood and walked back into the middle of the courtroom.

"When I hit that dummy, Mr. Dane," I said, "you'll confess, won't you, that it made a good deal of noise?"

He nodded.

"Speak up," I snapped. "This is a court of law."

"Yes," Miles said. His eyes were narrow. "It was loud."

"Now the story you told Detective Denkerberg was that fifteen minutes of that went on inside your very own house and you didn't hear a goddamn thing."

"That's another thousand dollars and another week in county for the profanity, Mr. Sloan. Next thing you do, I'm filing a petition to the state bar and see if we can't relieve you of your license to practice law."

I have no doubt Judge Evola looked terribly pleased with himself, but I ignored him entirely, my eyes riveted on Miles Dane's face.

"Well?" I said, opening my arms wide like I was inviting a punch in the face. "Tell me, Mr. Dane. Speak the truth."

"No . . . I . . . It was him. It was . . . I *saw* him."

I laughed derisively. "Oh, sure. Fifteen minutes up there, beating your wife to a pulp, and you heard, what, a funny noise? And then, great, this guy, what did he do, did he *parachute* out the window so he wouldn't leave footprints? And then carefully planted your fingerprints on the murder weapon using, maybe, secret methods known only to the CIA?"

"What do you want me to say?"

"*Speak the truth!*" I shouted. Then, I lowered my voice and laid the words out nice and slow. "Stop. Insulting. These. People." I pointed at the jury. "Just tell them what really happened."

They say a good lawyer never asks a question he doesn't know the answer to. But when the cards are stacked against you, sometimes you just have to take a leap, a calculated risk, and hope for the best. I was flying through the air again, the terror and exhilaration and power of the moment filling me like a drug.

Miles Dane blinked. Then slowly his face hardened. He leaned back and crossed his arms. In a loud voice, he said, "I refuse to answer that question on the grounds it may incriminate me."

My heart sank. So much for all that exhilaration. So much for all that energy getting sucked into my chest. Other than "I did it," Miles Dane had just chosen, from the hundreds of thousands of words in the English language, the worst possible response available.

But there I was. Standing in the middle of a room full of strangers, on live feed to a television audience of millions, nowhere to hide, nowhere to run, right in the middle of the most conspicuous and spectacular failure of my entire career. I wanted to run down the aisle and out the door crying for Mommy. But in for a penny, in for a pound. "Are you implying you killed your wife?"

"I think I'll invoke my Fifth Amendment protection again, Mr. Sloan." He then turned to Mark Evola. "Also, Judge, is it kosher to fire your lawyer while you're on the stand?"

Evola was looking pretty well shell-shocked by this point. "Ladies and gentlemen, we're going to take a few moments to sort this out. Bailiff, would you escort these fine people to the jury room." He stared around the room. "And clear the courtroom, while you're at it." His eyes narrowed as he pointed his gavel at the camera in the back of the room. "And you, young man, turn that bug-eyed thing off right this minute."

Say this about Charley Sloan. The guy keeps it interesting.

Fifty-seven

BEFORE WE CHAT, Your Honor," I said, "could I take a moment with my client? If, indeed, he is my client."

If Judge Evola's eyes had been laser beams, I'd have gone up in smoke on the spot. He glared for all he was worth, then finally said, "I guess you'd better."

I had the bailiff hustle Miles into the small conference room adjoining the courtroom. As soon as the door was closed, Miles said, "You happy now?"

I laughed in a way not intended to convey mirth. "What the *hell* do you think you were doing in there, Miles?"

"This is bullshit, Charley," he said, shaking his shackles at me. We faced each other like a couple of wrestlers.

"You know what you just did in there?" I said. "You just gave yourself a one-way ticket to Jackson Prison."

"Don't goddamn lecture me!" Miles said. "I told you not to drag this other issue into this courtroom."

"Just ten minutes ago, you told me to do whatever it took."

"Yeah, but I'd already made it clear to you that there was one issue you absolutely had to must steer clear of."

"Issue? *Issue?* What, are you afraid to give this *issue* a name? Your son! His name is Blair."

"Go screw yourself."

"Don't put this on me," I said. "After abandoning your son to the tender mercies of the state of New York, after letting him go through God knows what hell, it's a fine time to be protecting him from the consequences of his own actions."

"Don't talk to me about that boy!"

"Boy? He's a grown man."

"I don't care. He's my son, and I don't want you saying his name."

"Hey, I've met your son. I don't like him. He just killed your wife, and you're *protecting* him? What is wrong with you?"

"He deserves a chance, goddammit! I let him down once—*we* let him down, me and Diana both. We let that bastard Roger destroy his life. And now I'm giving him one last chance to make something better of himself."

"It's too late," I said softly. "It's too late for blame or shame or guilt or recrimination. The truth is, your son is a dangerous, conscienceless thug."

"No! No!"

And then Miles flung himself on me, battering helplessly at me with his shackled arms. He caught me by surprise, and I fell over backward, hit the ground with a thunk. There were stars in my head, and then we were rolling around on the floor like a couple of dumb kids.

I don't know how long it went on. Probably less than ten seconds. Then Miles started sobbing, pushing his face into my necktie and crying like a baby.

"What am I gonna do, Charley? I got nothing, man. What am I gonna do?" He kept saying it over and over. I hugged him and stroked his hair for a while. All the while he was crying, I thought about Lisa, about holding her when she was a baby. I had hadn't thought about that for years and years. Eventually Miles quit crying, and we just lay there like exhausted lovers on the dirty tile floor.

Miles rolled over on his back and stared up at the ceiling. "Shit. What have I done?"

I sat up, dusted myself off as best I could. When I'd fallen, I'd bashed my face on the floor. I could feel my eye swelling up.

"So am I fired or not?" I said.

"Nah."

"Are you going to testify about Blair? Are you willing to tell what really happened?"

Miles continued to stare at the ceiling. For the first time since I'd taken on the case, he looked at peace. "No," he said. "I've got nothing to live for now that Diana's gone. Maybe there's something in Blair that's worthwhile. Something that's worth salvaging. I want to give him the chance to find out."

"How did it happen?" I said.

"Back then? Back in '69? In my heart I wanted to keep the child. But Diana said that if she did, her family would cut her off. In my head . . . well, I knew how hard my writing career was going to be, and I knew if we got married and tried to raise that child after Diana got cut off from her inheritance, that my dreams would go down the tube. So I said, sure, let her give him up. Then when I was told he had died, it felt like such a relief to me." He put his manacled hands over his face. "Later we had a lawyer look into things and we found out that in all likelihood her family couldn't have cut her off from her trust. But by then it was too late."

"The murder," I said. "I meant how did the murder happen?"

"He contacted us a few months ago. Blair did. My son." He said the word wonderingly. "He told us who he was. Told us he was our son. I figured he was probably a scam artist, so I hired a detective from New York to check it out. But as it turns out, there was no doubt. He was definitely our son." He lay there for a while. "Of course along with finding out who he was, we found out he was a criminal."

"What did he want?" I said. "Money?"

Miles shook his head. "Nope."

"What then?"

Miles took a long time. "Blood."

"Like, revenge?"

"No. Just . . . blood. He wanted a vial of blood from each of us."

I frowned. "*Blood?* Why?"

"He told us he had some sort of genetic disorder. A shortage of some obscure blood factor that made him unusually susceptible to infection or something. He was a little vague about it, but the bottom line is he wanted blood for some kind of experimental therapy."

"That's it? He didn't want, I don't know, recognition or a relationship with you or anything like that? Just *blood*?"

"Just blood."

"And did you give it to him?"

Miles nodded. "Yeah, both of us did. That was about six weeks before the murder.

"And then what?"

"He called again later, said he wanted to talk. But not to me. Just to Diana. He said he had something very important to talk to her about. Very urgent. Had to be that night."

"How did you feel about that?"

"I didn't like it. But I feel so . . . responsible. For who he is, how he turned out. I didn't think we could say no."

"And then what?"

"He came over that night."

"When?"

"I'm not sure. I got back from the gym at about ten o'clock, and I found them together talking in the living room. When I walked in the door, they both looked up and seemed disappointed that it was me, as though they were expecting somebody else. Then Blair looked at his watch, and said, 'I guess he's not coming.' "

"Did you talk to him?"

"Only briefly. It was obvious to me that he wanted to talk to Diana privately."

"How did he seem?"

"Very sweet. Very polite. Sometimes doing research for my books I've interviewed criminals, real bad people, and a lot of times you have this creepy feeling, you know? Like they're manipulating you? And I didn't feel that way at all with him. He seemed very . . . genuine. It was strange, it was almost like he was being tender with me. Like he didn't want me to feel bad about who he was, what he'd been through."

"You said that when you walked in, he said, 'I guess he's not coming?' Who was he talking about?"

Miles shrugged. "Beats me. Whoever it was, apparently he never showed up. Anyway, after that, I went to my office and left them."

"Where?"

"In the living room. After a while I heard them arguing. Yelling. I went back to the living room to make sure they were okay. And again they looked up at me like I was intruding on something private. Diana told me everything was fine." He sat quietly for a while. "So I went back to my office. The shouting started again. So that's when I put on the Beethoven. Just like I told you the first time. I turned it up nice and loud and just lost myself in my writing. After that I didn't hear a thing." Tears began leaking out of his eyes. "About one o'clock I turned down the music. The house had gone totally silent by then. I worked until three. Then I went upstairs to go to bed. That's when I found her."

"Why'd you change the story?"

"I was damned if I did, damned if I didn't. Who'd believe me if I said I was lounging around the house while somebody beat my wife to death?"

I wanted to say that the story he'd made up had only made things worse. But there was no point in going there.

"What about the bokken?" I said. "What about the clothes?"

Miles shook his head. "I have no idea."

"And the window?"

Miles looked sheepish. "Yeah. That was me. Like I say, the thing I was afraid of was they'd decide it was impossible that I had sat through a murder. So I engineered an exit. Not very well, apparently. I didn't even think about the footprints." He sighed. "Jesus, how could I have been so stupid?"

Somebody knocked loudly on the door, then the bailiff's voice, muffled: "Judge wants you back in the courtroom."

I hoisted Miles back to his feet. "I'm just going to ask you one more time, Miles. Please. You've got to tell them what really happened."

He shook his head. "Do what you've got to do. But I'm not sending my son to jail."

"Even if it means—"

"How many times do I have to tell you? Diana's dead, my career is dead, I've had a good run. But now it's over."

"What if he shows up and testifies?"

Miles shrugged. "That's his decision. But I won't make it for him." He reached out and touched my face lightly with one manacled hand. "Sorry about the eye. It's bleeding a little there, bud."

I wiped it on my sleeve. I had bigger things to worry about than a little cut on my face.

Back in the courtroom, Judge Evola said, "Well, it sounded like you gentlemen were having a nice time in there. Mr. Dane? Are you still resolved to fire your attorney?"

"No, Your Honor. He's just trying to do his job."

"I'm not going to have this trial sabotaged with some kind of trumped up inadequate counsel claim."

"This is not a ploy to get a mistrial, Your Honor, I promise," Miles said.

Evola glowered at Miles.

"Alright. Back on the stand, Mr. Dane."

He walked up and sat down, then the jury filed in.

"Mr. Sloan, please continue with your examination of the witness."

I have, on occasion, felt at a loss in a court of law. But never has my mind been so entirely blank, so empty of stratagems or plans or theories or lines of attack, as it was at that moment. I stood and waited for the master plan to come flooding into my brain.

It didn't. Not a flood, a trickle, not even a drop.

"Mr. Sloan?" Judge Evola said.

The silence seemed to go on and on. It might have only been a few seconds, but it seemed interminable.

"Mr. Sloan?"

I turned to my witness. "Okay, Miles. Let me wrap this up. Did you lie to Detective Denkerberg about what happened?"

"Yes."

"Why?"

"Because the real story just seemed so implausible."

"So did you kill your wife?"

"I loved her so much. More than anything in my life." He looked down, and was silent for a while. Finally, he began to cry.

"Miles," I said softly. "Did you kill her?"

He shook his head, the tears streaming down his face. "No. No, never."

"Do you know who did?"

"I guess, yeah."

"And will you tell me who that person is?"

He shook his head, wipes his eyes. "I'm sorry, no. I have my reasons, but I just can't say."

"You're covering for someone aren't you? And you have been since the beginning."

"I can't answer that."

"That's why you told the ridiculous story you told to Detective Denkerberg, isn't it?"

"I can't answer that," he said again.

"That's why you lied."

"I just can't . . ." His voice broke off and he looked out the window of the courtroom. A long time seemed to pass. The room was completely silent.

"Your Honor," I said finally. "Mr. Dane and I seem to have gone about as far together as we can go."

Mark Evola turned to Stash. "Mr. Olesky?"

The prosecuting attorney didn't even stand up. "I believe we've all heard enough lies from this man. I'll refrain from compounding the problem."

"Please return to counsel table, Mr. Dane," the judge said. Miles wiped his eyes then, walked slowly back to the table, where he sat with a pacific, resolved expression on his face, a martyr calmly heading off to the face the lions.

"Next witness, Mr. Sloan."

I stood again, on the theory that altitude might put some ideas in my brain. I had no witnesses, no strategy, nothing left to do. Unless . . . I looked at my watch. It was barely eleven o'clock.

"Your Honor," I said. "It's practically lunchtime." It was, of course, no such thing. "My next witness will require extensive examination. If I may, I'd request we adjourn until lunch."

Evola didn't even blink. "It's not even eleven o'clock. Call your next witness or be ready to close."

I had, of course, no more witnesses. Other than Blair Dane, that is, and there was no sign of him. Evola had studied my witness list and knew this as well as I did. I needed to stall—but how?

There was only one possibility.

"One moment, Your Honor." I took out the witness list, ticked off everybody who had testified. There was nobody left on mine but Blair Dane. And only one name left on Stash's list.

I looked up and scanned the room. There he was, right on the front row.

"Your Honor, if I may, I'd like to call a witness from Mr. Olesky's list."

Evola raised his eyebrows questioningly at Stash.

Stash drummed his fingers for a moment, thinking. "Your Honor, I'm not sure I approve of that," he said finally.

"I'm entitled to call anybody who's on the list," I said. "My list *or* yours."

The judge took out his casebook and thumbed through it for a while. Finally, he looked up, and said, "Counsel's right, Mr. Olesky. Call your witness."

"Defense calls Roger van Blaricum."

Fifty-eight

I SAW THE look of surprise on van Blaricum's face. He frowned, then stood and walked stiffly to the witness box. I had forgotten how tall he was, six-three at least, but with somewhat stooped shoulders. He was dressed in tweeds, double-vented, double-breasted—an English squire dressed for the provinces. His white hair floated above his face like a cloud.

After he was sworn in I began by asking a long, drawn-out series of questions about his background, his hobbies, and his education. Maybe the jury didn't find it interesting, but I was quite fascinated to know that he had received a doctoral degree in Japanese literature from Cambridge, and that he was fluent in three Asian languages, and that he had studied some obscure Japanese martial art at a shrine outside Tokyo, that he collected Japanese art, and that he had never actually held a salaried job in his entire life. I had asked just about everything I could think of about his background, and it was still barely eleven-thirty.

"Mr. van Blaricum," I said. "In 1968, your sister got pregnant, did she not?"

Stash Olesky stood. "Objection. We've been treated to a rather impressive display of irrelevancies here, and I'd ask Your Honor to draw this to a close."

As it happened, this was the first relevant question I'd asked. "Your Honor," I said, "the relevance of this question will be made crystal clear in the fullness of time. It goes, in fact, to the very heart of Mr. Dane's defense."

"It better," the judge said. "Continue."

I repeated the question.

Van Blaricum gazed vaguely into the distance. "I don't believe I recall that, no."

I blinked, went back to my table, pulled out Blair Dane's birth certificate. "Does this refresh your memory, Mr. van Blaricum? The birth certificate of Unnamed Child van Blaricum, daughter of Diana van Blaricum?"

Roger Van Blaricum fussed with a pair of reading glasses, making a long show of studying the document. "I was in Cambridge at that point."

"I thought you got your Ph.D. in 1967."

He cleared his throat. When he spoke his voice had gone defensive. "Well, I was in and out of the country. Maybe I was in Japan. It's possible she did, yes, get pregnant at that point."

I looked disbelieving. "Your sister not only got pregnant, but gave birth and gave up her child to the state of New York . . . and you can't even say whether you were aware of it or not?"

Van Blaricum cleared his throat. "Alright, yes. It was an embarrassment to our family, and I, well, it's still a bit painful to speak about it."

"Embarrassment does not abrogate the oath you just swore, Mr. van Blaricum," I said.

"I'm well aware of that."

"Good. Isn't it true, Mr. van Blaricum, that you and your mother applied a great deal of pressure on your sister to have an abortion?"

Van Blaricum's gaze was cool. "No."

"Isn't it true that you and your mother threatened to disown your sister, to cut her off from her trust fund if she kept the child."

Van Blaricum cleared his throat again. "It was a typical family spat. Things get said in the heat of the moment. I can't imagine that anything quite so strong would have been said."

"Oh no? Isn't it true that you and your sister haven't spoken in over thirty years?"

"No."

"Oh?" My voice went frosty. "Mr. van Blaricum, when *was* the last time you spoke to your sister?"

Van Blaricum thought about it for a long moment. "About a week before she died, I suppose."

I raised my eyebrows. Miles had said they hadn't talked in almost thirty years. "By what means? Phone? Fax? In person?"

"Phone."

"Really?" I went to my pile of exhibits, pulled out Miles Dane's phone records, which had been entered into evidence during the prosecution's phase of trial, tossed it on the witness stand. "Does this refresh your memory? Show me the call."

Van Blaricum scanned the phone bill. "Right there. October 11. She called me. That's my telephone number."

I stared at the call he had pointed out. A 212 number, New York City. I read out the number dubiously. "There are quite a few reasons she might have called a 212 phone number. Can you verify your claim that this is your number?"

He took a slim wallet out of his breast pocket, slipped something out of it. "Let the record reflect," Van Blaricum said, "that I'm showing Mr. Sloan my business card. It has the same number on it as the one listed in my sister's phone records." I looked at the cream-colored card he had handed me. The number matched the one on the phone record.

I was unsure quite what to do. I decided to trust Miles, see where it took us. Van Blaricum really couldn't do us any harm, and, after all, I was mainly just trying to stall until lunch. "I was given to understand that you hadn't been in touch for thirty years."

Again, a long period of consideration. It looked like Van Blaricum was trying to figure out whether he should lie or not. "Well, there was an extended period during which we didn't speak terribly, ah, frequently . . ."

Suddenly I felt a twinge of something, the sort of odd sensation you feel when you're sure that somebody is watching you. But what the source of this feeling was, I couldn't quite identify. "Why all of a sudden, a week before her death?"

"You asked me the *last* time. We'd spoken quite a few times in the past month or so. I had decided that we had been out of touch for too long and that it was time for reconciliation."

"One moment." I walked back to the counsel table.

"He's full of shit," Miles whispered to me. "If he'd called trying to reconcile, she'd have told me."

"Did she tell you anything about this?"

Miles hesitated, finally shook his head slightly. "No."

I addressed van Blaricum again, "What did you talk about with your sister that night?"

Stash Olesky stood. "I'm sorry, Your Honor, but I'm going to object. I really see no relevance to the case here."

He was right. This line of questions had revealed something puzzling—interesting in a gossipy way—but I didn't see that it had any relevance to the case. "I'm happy to move on, Your Honor," I said. Then I turned back to the witness. "Mr. van Blaricum, let's go back to 1969. At that time, did you or did you not force Diana to give up her child for adoption?"

"We convinced her that it was in her best interest."

"And did you or did you not convince her to break up with the child's father, Miles Dane."

Van Blaricum looked at Miles through cold eyes. "Well, if we did, it didn't work terribly well, did it?"

"What happened to that child, Mr. van Blaricum?"

"I have no idea."

I walked back to the counsel table.

"Mr. van Blaricum, do you recall having a conversation with my assistant, Lisa, about a month ago?"

"Your daughter lied to me, misrepresented herself to me."

"So you *did* have a conversation with her."

"She posed as an art dealer so that she could dig up dirt about Diana."

"Answer the question. Did you speak to my daughter?"

"Yes. We spoke."

I scrabbled through my exhibit bag, picked up a pocket tape recorder, and pressed the button on the side. It seemed to take forever to cue up the portion of tape I wanted. But when I did, I pressed PLAY and held it up to the witness box microphone. Out came the conversation from the Oak Room.

Van Blaricum's voice came out of the tape recorder. *"You want to know the funny thing, Sloan? It doesn't matter if he gets off or not. He was after her money. But that's the one thing he'll never get. Never, ever. Or didn't MacDairmid tell you that?"*

Then my voice: *"He never had any interest in her money."*

Then van Blaricum again: *"Oh? Well, watch his face when the bastard shows up to take her fortune. Then you'll know the truth."*

"I was puzzled at the time, Mr. Van Blaricum, by what you meant. I thought you were calling my client a bastard. But you weren't, were you? You were saying, watch Miles's face when his illegitimate son, Blair Dane, shows up to inherit Diana's trust fund. Which, as her blood issue, he is entitled to do, correct?"

Stash threw up his hands. "I really have to object, Your Honor. This tape has no foundation. It may have been obtained illegally. And I have a continuing objection as to the relevance of this entire line of questioning to this proceeding."

"Can't you see what's going on, Judge?" van Blaricum added. "He's attempting to smear my sister, to paint her as immoral or detestable so that the jury won't feel sorry for her. This is loathsome."

"Could we have a sidebar please, Your Honor?" I said.

"Approach."

Stash and I walked to the front, and I said to the judge, "It's my contention that my client's son—who is on my witness list by the way—probably killed Diana Dane. I'm trying to establish motive. My client has every right to a defense."

"So far his defense seems to be limited to taking the Fifth," Stash growled.

"My client believes that his son Blair killed his wife. We already have testimony affirming that fact that Blair Dane, as her blood issue, would inherit the trust. But right now my client is unwilling to testify against his own son. He's between a rock and a hard place. That's the stone-cold truth here."

Evola leaned toward the court reporter. "Off the record for a moment." Then to me: "You wouldn't know the truth if it hit you in the head, Sloan," Judge Evola said, smiling broadly. "Okay, Mrs. Rathrock, back on the record."

"My client has a right to put on a defense. It's the jury's job to decide what the truth is, Your Honor. Not yours. You better believe that if I appeal on the grounds my client was denied the right to an affirmative defense, this conviction will be reversed in a heartbeat, and you'll be the goat on national TV."

Evola's face was hard, and I could see the wheels turning, weighing everything against that congressional seat. "Alright," he said finally. "Keep going. I'm ruling against Mr. Olesky's general objection. But on the narrow issue of the tape, Mr. Olesky is dead right. This tape lacks foundation. Further, I'm not convinced that it was obtained legally under either Michigan or New York law. Moreover, you never disclosed it to the state, as you are obliged to do under the rules of reciprocal disclosure. Therefore, no tape. And if I decide that you're just slinging mud, I'm shutting you down."

I was satisfied. The tape didn't need to be entered. It had already done its work. And the longer we blathered, the more the clock ticked toward a break.

Stash sat down, the judge instructed the jury to disregard the tape, and I began my examination again. I still had a lot of time to kill before lunch, and Lisa still wasn't here with Blair. I asked a number of additional questions about Blair Dane—details regarding his adoption, his history in foster care, and so on—but it seemed clear that van Blaricum simply didn't know the answers. I was reduced to asking questions, slightly rephrased, that he'd already given the answers to. I could feel the sweat on my brow, on my lip, soaking through my shirt. Eleven-forty, eleven-forty-one, eleven-forty-two. Time seemed to be standing almost still.

"Asked and answered. Asked and answered!" Stash was looking exasperated. "If Mr. Sloan has no more questions for this witness, let's move on."

"I'm inclined to agree," Judge Evola said, smiling brightly.

"Could I have a very brief break to explore a couple of issues with my client?" I said. "Just ten minutes."

"You should have explored them last night."

"Your Honor, this witness has raised a couple of issues which I simply have to discuss with my client."

Judge Evola kept flashing his broad smile at me. "Back when I played ball at Michigan State, Coach managed to break down a whole game plan during one commercial break. You have two minutes."

"Thank you." I walked over and sat next to Miles. "Thoughts?"

Miles shook his head. "It's just weird. Why would he have gotten back in contact with Diana? I don't get it."

"Forget about that," I said. "We need to keep the ball rolling with your son. How can we get him to cough up some more stuff about that?"

"Thirty seconds, Mr. Sloan," Judge Evola called cheerily.

We sat in glum silence. My eye had swollen so much where Miles had elbowed me that I could barely see out of it, and it was beginning to throb. When I was a kid I'd fought Golden Gloves for a while, and it brought back memories of how it felt to be beaten up, to sit there in the corner of the ring right after getting pounded in the face by some better, faster, stronger fighter, knowing you were just going to have to go out and get pounded some more.

"Let's go, Mr. Sloan!"

I stood and walked toward the witness stand. My eye was really hurting. I just wanted to go home, take an ice bag and a bottle of scotch, lie down in the corner and get crying drunk. I touched the cut over my eye, took a deep breath. When I pulled my fingers away, the tips of my fingers were red with blood.

Blood.

The word, or at least the idea of it, ran around in my brain for a while, like a gunshot echoing in a cave.

"Blood," I said.

The courtroom was very quiet.

"Excuse me?" van Blaricum said.

"Blood!"

"Is that a question, counselor?"

And suddenly, I realized, yes, it was.

"One moment," I said. I walked back over and picked up a photograph taken by Agent Pierce of Miles Dane's living room. On the coffee table was something that jogged my memory. A book of Japanese erotic woodblock prints. And something else. When Miles had talked about the night of the murder, he said Blair had indicated that somebody else was supposed to be visiting the house that night. *I guess he's not coming*, was the phrase Miles had reported. The tumblers in my mind were beginning to fall into place. And then there was Leon Prouty's testimony about a second man, an *old guy*.

I raised my gaze to the witness. "Blood, Mr. van Blaricum. When did Blair Dane approach you asking for blood?"

Van Blaricum blinked. "What?"

"You heard me. When did Blair Dane approach you asking for blood?"

"That's absurd."

"Blair Dane will testify that he approached everyone he could find who was related to him and asked for a blood sample. According to him, he had a genetic disorder and needed some kind of blood factor from a relative for therapeutic purposes. Are you testifying that he didn't approach you and ask for blood?"

Roger van Blaricum looked testy. "I know virtually nothing about this person. This must be the fiftieth question you've asked that I don't know anything about."

"That's not my question. You're a blood relative, through Diana. Blair Dane knew that. If he asked them for blood, he would have asked you, too. He asked you for some blood, too. Didn't he?"

There was a long pause. Something seemed to be creeping into his eyes. It was that odd thing I'd noticed the first time I'd seen him, the way half of his face seemed to look one way, and half the other. Half-angry, half . . . what? Frightened? Why would he be frightened? "No," he said finally.

"He asked, but you didn't give him the blood, did you?"

I felt something rising inside me then, a lightness, like I was being buoyed on a current, hurtled down a torrent toward something that I sensed but couldn't yet see.

"How could I give him something he didn't ask for?" A triumphant glint in his eyes.

And then, there it was in front of me, the answer.

I smiled a little. "When did your hair turn white, Mr. Van Blaricum?"

Up went Stash again. "Objection. This is ridiculous."

"Your Honor," I said, "if I don't get somewhere with this line of questioning, I will gladly spend yet another week in jail. But please let me finish this line of questioning." I was about to embark on a fishing expedition of major proportion. But sometimes you have no choice. And my guess was, if I could pull it off, there was one hell of a fish down there somewhere. If I could just get my hook close enough to it.

Evola looked ready to blow his stack. He glared at me for a long time. "Make it quick. Objection overruled, pending some payoff for this line of questioning."

I continued the questioning. "You're a tall man, Mr. van Blaricum. How tall?"

"Six-three. And a half."

"And your hair, it's white, correct."

Van Blaricum snorted. "Obviously so."

"When did it start going gray?"

Van Blaricum looked at the jury as with obvious irritation. "When I was in my late twenties, I suppose."

I turned to my client. "Mr. Dane, would you mind standing?" Miles stood slowly. "Mr. van Blaricum, how tall is my client."

"How should I know?"

"Okay, but you'd concede that he's a short man, yes? Would it surprise you if I said he was five-six?"

"Nothing would surprise me at this point."

"His hair, it's brown isn't it? He's well into his fifties, and it's just got a fleck or two of gray in it, correct?"

"Yes. But don't ask me his shoe size because I don't know it."

There was some laughter from the jury. I smiled obligingly then handed him a picture. "Can you identify the man in this photograph?"

He pulled out a pair of reading glasses. "It's a criminal mug shot. I don't know, but I'm guessing that it would be Blair Dane."

"You are correct, sir. What color is his hair?"

"It's gray."

"And behind his head, there's a measure on the wall. How tall is Blair Dane?"

"It says seventy-six inches."

And then, suddenly, I was there.

"Hair color and height, so far as you are aware, these are things that are all genetically determined, correct?"

"I suppose."

"Passed on through your DNA, right? The genetic code?"

"Yes."

"Which is found in your blood, right?"

Stash Olesky stood. "Please! Your Honor! These are obvious stall tactics."

"I swear, Your Honor, I'm almost there," I said.

"You'd better be," Evola said.

"Blair Dane discovered something odd when he had Miles Dane's blood tested, didn't he?"

"I really wouldn't have the slightest idea."

"Oh, yes you do. What he found out was that Miles Dane, in fact, is not his father at all."

"How could I possibly have any knowledge of that?"

"Because, Mr. van Blaricum, you're Blair's real father. Aren't you?"

The room was dead silent.

The left side of van Blaricum's face worked furiously, while the right remained calm. After some struggle both sides went calm, and both sides of his face smiled. "No. That's ridiculous, that's scandalous. I am not Blair Dane's father."

"Your son Blair figured out the truth, didn't he?"

"That's a lie!"

Stash stood up. "Objection. There's been no evidence introduced to support these outlandish and sick allegations."

"Give me a moment, Your Honor," I said. "I'm getting there."

Judge Evola wanted to sustain the objection so badly he could taste it. But he was petrified of looking biased in front of that camera in the back of the room, or worse, of having the biggest trial of his career reversed on appeal in the middle of a future political campaign. "Pending some sort of proof," he said through clenched teeth, "I'll let you take this one step further. But if you fail to offer hard evidence supporting these allegations, I am going to sanction you in the harshest kind of way, Mr. Sloan."

I had, of course, no such evidence at all. Unless . . . I thought back to my one previous meeting with Roger van Blaricum. And suddenly something struck me. There are times—rarely, I admit—when it pays to be somewhat less than a neatnik. But this was one of those times. I reached into the pocket of my rumpled suit—the same suit I'd worn on my trip to New York, the same suit that hadn't been dry-cleaned since November—and there it was. I pulled out a wadded handkerchief, held it up in the air. "Do you know what this is, Mr. van Blaricum?"

He stared at it. "It's a handkerchief," he said in a sarcastic tone.

"Let's get a little more specific. Could you read the initials embroidered there in the corner?"

He stared at the handkerchief for a long time.

"Mr. van Blaricum?"

"RVB," he said quietly

"Big R. Little V. Big B. The initials on this handkerchief stand for Roger van Blaricum. Correct?"

Stash stood up, "Okay, okay, okay. Objection. This whole thing is going out of bounds. Here we go with more alleged evidence to which the state has not been privy. I'd ask that it be excluded."

"Your Honor," I said, "this evidence is being proffered solely for the purpose of impeachment. I had no obligation to disclose it to Mr. Olesky."

"You're impeaching your own witness?"

I shook my head. "This man is the state's witness. They simply opted not to call him."

Evola stared at me furiously. I was glad I wasn't in a dark alley with him. I probably wouldn't have walked out alive. Evola slowly brought himself under control. "Subject to your making a nice, crisp point, I'll allow it."

"Thank you." I turned back to van Blaricum. "We've established that you met with my daughter. I believe it was in the Oak Bar at the Plaza Hotel in New York City."

"So?"

"Do you recall dropping a glass of scotch that day? You made a grab for it as it shattered, and you cut your hand?"

He shrugged.

"Yes or no?"

"I suppose."

"And you bled, didn't you?"

"When one is cut, one bleeds."

"And you wiped the blood off on your handkerchief. Correct?"

"Maybe."

"Mr. van Blaricum, there's no maybe about it. That's what happened. Look at the stain." I waved the handkerchief in the air, showing off a large brown splotch. "You wiped the blood off on your handkerchief. This handkerchief."

"I suppose that's possible."

"And minutes later, when you found out who Lisa was, that she worked for me, you threw this handkerchief in her face, didn't you?"

Van Blaricum just glared at me.

"You might be interested in knowing, Mr. van Blaricum, that we tested that blood for DNA. We also tested Mr. Dane and his alleged son, Blair. Guess what we found, Mr. van Blaricum. The man who left his blood on this napkin is the father of Blair Dane."

Van Blaricum's face went white as a sheet.

Stash Olesky stood. "Your Honor, counsel is testifying! None of this is in evidence. None of this was produced to the prosecutor's office prior to trial. Move to strike this entire line of testimony."

I ignored Stash. I picked up a piece of paper off the table. "Mr. van Blaricum, I'd be happy to show you the test . . . unless you'd prefer to just skip straight to telling the truth."

"Let me see this alleged DNA test," Judge Evola demanded.

"Actually Your Honor, if Mr. van Blaricum would just tell the truth, I probably won't bother introducing it," I said.

"Give me that DNA report!" he snapped. "Now!"

I handed him the paper I was holding.

He stared at the sheet of paper through narrowed eyes. It was just a blank sheet of paper. When Evola looked up at me, he was smiling. His smile was tight as a drumhead as he turned to the jury. "Ladies and gentleman of the jury, Mr. Sloan has testified—there's no other good word for it—that he has a DNA test proving Mr. van Blaricum is the father of someone named Blair Dane. Apparently he has lied. No such evidence exists. I'm asking you to do something fairly difficult. That is, to purge your minds entirely of these spurious and outrageous allegations made by Mr. Sloan in which he has implied that Mr. van Blaricum had some sort of incestuous affair with his sister."

Then he turned toward me and his smile broadened in triumph. "And you? You know better. So congratulations, Mr. Sloan, I'm now going to file a recommendation to the state bar to have you disciplined and your license suspended. Please continue with your examination. But if you mention anything about incest or any other spurious irrelevancies, I'll declare a mistrial, and we'll do this whole dance over next week."

It was a horribly tantalizing moment. I'd reached the point where I finally believed that I understood the case. But now I couldn't go the last yard.

"Mr. van Blaricum," I said, "you came to Detroit back in October, didn't you?"

Van Blaricum's eyes burned into me. "No," he said.

"You came to Miles Dane's house on the night of October 20, didn't you?"

"That's absurd." A little smile of ugly triumph licked at the corner of his mouth.

"You're lying."

Stash hopped up. "Objection. Badgering."

"Did you or did you not come to Miles Dane's house on the night of October 20?"

"Asked and answered," Stash yelled.

"Sustained," the judge said. "Move on, Mr. Sloan."

And there I was. Stuck. No evidence, no corroborating witnesses, no way of impeaching what I knew in my heart to be lies. Behind me somebody cleared their throat loudly. I turned. It was Lisa.

And she was alone.

"Your Honor, could I have about thirty seconds with my paralegal?" I said.

Evola looked up at the clock. It was twelve on the nose. "I think this might be a good time to take lunch," he said. I could see in his eyes that he thought that an hour of lunch would cool everybody down, kill my momentum, and derail my entire examination. Fortunately for me, he couldn't have been more wrong. "Any objection, Mr. Sloan?"

I put a look of annoyance on my face and stood there for a while like I was debating whether or not to make a stink. "I suppose," I said grudgingly.

"Lunch it is."

Fifty-nine

W HERE'S BLAIR, LISA?" I said.

"He's outside. He's sitting in the car. Trying to decide what to do."

I rubbed my face in my hands. What to do? All along I'd thought that Blair was the guy. But now, suddenly, I was convinced I'd been wrong.

"Tell you what," I said. "Forget Blair for the moment. There's something else I need you to do . . ."

T HEN I WENT in and sat down with Miles. "Remember what you said? You said that when you walked into the room with Blair and Diana at ten o'clock, Blair said, 'I guess he's not coming,' or something to that effect. What if he was talking about Roger?"

"Roger?" Miles shook his head in disbelief. "Jesus H. Christ. I never even thought of Roger! I thought for sure that . . . Oh, my God."

"There's something else I need to know . . ." I said.

A FTER LUNCH I put van Blaricum back on the stand.

"Mr. van Blaricum, I'm giving you State's Exhibit 59. Can you identify this for me?"

Van Blaricum looked sullenly at the book I'd handed him. "It appears to be one of Miles's books. The title is *How I Killed My Wife and Got Away with It.*"

"Interesting reading, wouldn't you say?"

Van Blaricum seemed very much in control of himself now. "I wouldn't know."

I feigned surprise. "You've never read it?"

"I wouldn't read his trash if you paid me."

"There's a paper clip on one of the pages in the book there. Could you turn to that page and read me what it says? The highlighted portion?"

Van Blaricum flipped the book open, looked at it for a long moment.

"Cat got your tongue Mr. van Blaricum?"

His voice was low and cold. "It says, 'My special thanks to Roger van Blaricum, who gave me both the original idea for this book and the implement that inspired the murder weapon itself.'"

"So you gave him the idea for this book," I said acidly. "But you didn't actually read it?"

"The book is about a man who hated his relatives. I presume that's what he meant."

"So you have read it."

Van Blaricum saw his mistake and tried to correct it. But it was a little late. "I *haven't* read it." His voice went defensive. "I *haven't.* I just heard on the news what the, ah, what the plot was about."

"No doubt." I laughed derisively. "Earlier you testified you had studied martial arts in Japan. What was the name of the martial arts style called again?"

"Muto Ryu."

"I'm not a martial arts expert," I said. "Is that like karate or kung fu or what?"

There was a long pause. "Swordsmanship. It's a style of Japanese swordsmanship."

"You practice that with a real sword?"

"Generally, no."

"What *do* you use?"

One side of his face twitched a couple of times. "A bokken."

I lifted the presumed murder weapon. "Like this one?"

He spread his hands slightly. "Similar, I suppose. But . . ."

I waited.

"But what, Mr. van Blaricum?" I said finally. "But . . . no, I didn't frame my brother-in-law? But . . . no, I didn't sneak his bokken out of his office while he was in the bathroom? But . . . no, I didn't kill my sister? No, I didn't use Miles Dane's book—the book I myself served as an inspiration for—as a road map for helping me frame an innocent man? Is that what you were going to say?"

"Objection to form," Stash said.

"Sustained."

But van Blaricum answered anyway. "This is perfectly ridiculous. I was in New York when he killed her. I can prove that."

I was about to break into a nervous sweat when the back door of the courtroom banged open and Lisa literally ran into the room, a triumphant smile on her face. She thrust a piece of paper into my hand.

"You were right," she whispered loudly.

I smiled at her, scanned the piece of paper she had given me, then turned back to the witness stand.

"Your Honor, I've got another piece of evidence which hasn't been disclosed to Mr. Olesky. Again, this is for the purposes of impeachment."

"Show me."

I showed it to him. He winced. "This has no foundation. I'm extremely reluctant to admit this." He scratched his head furiously. I could see the wheels turning. If Miles was really innocent; if this was what it looked like; if Miles got convicted when he should have gone free; and if the whole question resolved itself on appeal rather than in trial—then his face would be on TV about a million times, with every legal correspondent in America saying that his flawed decisions had put an innocent man in prison for life. "Very well," Evola said, sighing. He handed the paper to his clerk. "Mark it, please, Mrs. Wilson."

I took the piece of paper back from the clerk, set it gently on the edge of the witness stand.

"Could you read the lines I've marked with my pen?" I said.

Roger van Blaricum looked at it.

"It says, 'Record of Travel. Northwest Airlines. Flight 921. Date: October 21. Departs 11:05 AM. Arrives 1:25 PM. Ticket type: One-way. Origination. Detroit. Destination. New York-La Guardia. Payment, cash. Passenger name, colon . . .'" He looked up at me, eyes wide. "This is . . . this is . . . this is someone else."

"Keep reading."

"Passenger name, colon, van Blaricum, comma, Roger."

Suddenly there was a lot of noise in the courtroom. It took a few seconds for the hubbub to subside.

"Earlier, Leon Prouty testified he saw what he called an 'old guy' leaving the house at around midnight. That was you, wasn't it?"

Roger van Blaricum blinked, then stared around the room in shock. He didn't answer.

I heard the door in the back of the courtroom open a second time. I turned and looked. A tall young man with prematurely gray hair and scary blue eyes was standing in the back of the room. "There he is, Mr. van Blaricum. I've been instructed to avoid the issue of paternity. But that man back there has run the blood tests. He knows the truth, and will testify to it when I put him on the stand. I'm sure he has copies of the tests, even if I don't. Are you prepared to continue perjuring yourself? Or do we have to hear it from him?"

Van Blaricum said nothing.

"All we want is the truth."

Van Blaricum stared angrily at the man in the back of the courtroom. "Alright," he said finally. "Alright. I made a terrible mistake one time in my youth."

"Say it plain. The truth. Everything."

Van Blaricum continued to glare at the gray-haired young man in the back of the courtroom. "I suppose, yes, I suppose he is my . . . offspring. But—"

"Your son."

Long hesitation. Van Blaricum couldn't seem to bear looking at the tall man in the back of the room. "My son," he finally whispered, one side of his face twisted in disgust.

"Look, here's your choice, Mr. van Blaricum. Right now, before Mr. Olesky gets mad and embarrassed, and charges you with first-degree murder, you can feel free to make a confession. If your confession shows that you killed her in the heat of passion, then Mr. Olesky will be obliged to charge you with manslaughter. Which, I might add, carries a *substantially* lower penalty than first-degree murder. So I'll ask you again. Did you kill your sister?"

The courtroom was dead silent. Stash could easily have objected. Judge Evola could easily have called a halt to the proceeding, too. But I guess they wanted to know the truth as badly as I did.

Van Blaricum's gaze shifted from the man in the back of the court over to the defense table. He pointed a shaking finger at Miles. "This is all his fault. Miles was nothing before he met her. A cheap, poor, chiseling, worthless little Midwestern nobody. If it weren't for *her* contacts, *her* strength of character, *her* assistance, *her* money—why, he would still be hitchhiking around America telling people in third-rate saloons that he was working on a novel and, gosh, he sure hoped he'd get it published someday."

"Tell us the truth," I said again. "You killed her."

Slowly van Blaricum's eyes went down until he was looking at the floor. "Yes, I suppose I did."

With that, Blair Dane walked slowly down the aisle toward his father.

"I suppose I'm capable of anything. After all, I spawned *that*." Van Blaricum looked at his son with disgust. "A criminal, a drug addict, a convict with tattoos on his knuckles. He is nothing. He is less than nothing. And *I* did that."

"Hi, Dad," he said brightly. "Great to see you, too. Thanks for all your love and support over the years."

Then Blair raised a small silver .32 Smith & Wesson—the one he'd taken from the top drawer of my desk—fired once, and hit Roger van Blaricum just above his right eye. Roger slipped out of the chair, stone dead, and hit the ground before the deafening crash had ceased to echo.

Blair Dane just stood there, staring with his empty eyes at the blood splashed on the wall next to Judge Evola's chair.

"Drop it!" It was the bailiff—the same big aggressive guy who'd restrained me when I attacked the dummy in the back of the courtroom. The bailiff's muscular arms were extended, chin on his shoulder, his automatic pistol leveled at Blair Dane's chest. Perfect form, just like they taught in police training school. "*Now!*"

"Some people are born to go out easy," Blair said to the bailiff. His voice sounded casual, almost sleepy. "Me, from the day I arrived, I was born to go out hard."

"*Drop it!*" The bailiff said, still pointing the gun. In his eyes you could see it: He was the kind of guy who'd been looking for this moment ever since he pinned on his badge. Itching for an excuse to pull that trigger.

And Blair gave it to him—raising his gun slowly toward the bailiff, a bitter smile on his face. I could see the crude green tattoo on his hand. GO DOWN SHOOTING. "There's no fighting fate, man," Blair said.

I dived under a table, pulling Lisa with me. There were two small cracks from the .32, and an uncountable number of the loud, terrifying *wham-wham-wham-whams* from the bailiff's big automatic. When the sound stopped, I poked my head up. The bailiff was still standing, eyes wide with adrenaline. Blair Dane lay on the floor groaning.

The room was utterly silent for what seemed a long time, though it was probably only a second or two.

Finally, someone broke the silence. Me, actually.

I stood, tugged at the lapels of my jacket, and said, "Your Honor, the defense rests."

VERDICT

Sixty

OKAY, OKAY," LISA said after we had walked out of the courthouse, waded through the forest of microphones. "You've convinced me. I'm going back to law school." Her face was glowing with the cold, the excitement, and the horrible triumph of the moment.

"I didn't say a word, Lisa." I held up my hands in mock surrender.

Behind us Miles Dane stood in the middle of a circle of cameras, boom mikes, and journalists waving their pocket recorders. He was thanking the judge for the wise and fair handling of the case, thanking the prosecuting attorney for having the guts to dismiss the charges in such a complex and high-profile case, thanking his friends, thanking the marvelous and courageous Charley Sloan, lawyer *extraordinaire*.

"Yeah, but you planned it, didn't you, Dad? This whole trial was just a ploy, wasn't it? Just to make me go back to law school."

I laughed for a minute, then looked out at the river. The wind off the water was frigid, and yet I felt hot as a radiator, like I could warm the whole county.

"So you ever going to tell me what happened back there in New York?" I said. "Why you dropped out? Why you fell off the wagon?"

Lisa's face fell. She looked at me thoughtfully, then finally stood on her tiptoes and kissed me on the cheek. "If there's anything I've learned this week," she said, "it's that some things are best left in the past."

Then she walked away, whistling the theme to some old TV show. *Perry Mason*, I think it was.

Sixty-one

"IT'S FUNNY," MILES said, "the things that come over you sometimes."

I frowned, not sure what he was getting at.

"I was always good at writing under pressure," Miles said. "I came up with the whole plot to *Fisticuff* in ten minutes. Every twist and turn just appeared full-blown right there in my head—ten minutes, tops."

I had asked Miles a simple question just minutes earlier. His reply seemed, as we lawyers say, nonresponsive—as though he were answering another question entirely.

It was a few months after the trial, and Miles and I had gotten together for a drink, sitting out by the boardwalk over behind the Pickeral Point Inn. Miles was looking good. Ten pounds heavier, tanned, fit. All the publicity surrounding his trial had revived his career to an almost unimaginable degree. *How I Killed My Wife* was being made into a movie with Mel Gibson; his latest book was hanging doggedly at number two on the *Times* best-seller list; and he was working on a made-for-TV screenplay about his experience as a falsely accused person. The tentative title—*Blindside*.

Sitting on the table between us was a yellowing, fragile old copy of *How I Killed My Wife and Got Away with It*. Miles had given it to me after the trial, signed and addressed to me personally. Lisa tells me that signed copies of the original—not the reprint—are going for upward of two grand on eBay. Recently I had found something odd in my copy, something I had felt compelled to ask Miles about.

"Okay," I said, "but what I asked you is this: I was looking at this copy of *How I Killed My Wife*. Right? And there's no dedication in it. That whole thing—thank you, Roger, for giving me the idea for this book, blah blah blah, it's only in the reprint, not the original. So what I'm asking is how do you account for that?"

It was the second time I'd asked the question, and still Miles seemed intent on not answering the question.

"She told me that night," Miles said.

"Told you what?"

I had been nursing my soda water while he sipped on a double of some obscure and expensive single malt with an unpronounceable Scottish name. It was a warm May day, sunny, with just a hint of coolness in the air that you only felt when the wind picked up.

"I went to bed that night. She was waiting up. Diana. She told me about everything. She told me that Blair had come to visit. That the results of the blood test had come back, and she wanted to tell me herself. About . . . whatever you want to call it . . . the incest thing with Roger. That her child—Blair—that he wasn't mine. That she'd always known the baby was Roger's. She told me that she had been young and scared. She told me that she knew she had to get away from her family or her whole life would have ended up a ruin. She told me that when she married me, she had done it mostly because she hated her family so much—and Roger in particular. She said marrying some hick striver like me had been the most malicious thing she could possibly do to her brother."

Miles looked out at the river. The surface was smooth and tranquil in the late-afternoon sun. His gray eyes, reflecting the blue of the water, looked luminescent, like smoke caught in a shaft of sunlight.

"Yeah, she told me she had made a truce with fate. She said that she knew I was attracted to her money. She said she knew that even if she couldn't give me her love, fair's fair, she could at least support my little writing career with her dough, and try to make me happy. Her freedom for my happiness."

I made one of those uncomfortable murmurs that you use when you really have no idea how to respond to somebody.

Miles laughed mirthlessly, a sharp exhalation of breath. "I couldn't believe, after all these years, that she'd got me so wrong. I never gave a damn about the money. Never! I just loved her. *Worshiped* her." His eyes closed briefly. "And I thought she felt the same way about me."

"But she didn't?"

The sad smile lingered on his lips. "She told me this: She said, 'I've always been alone, Miles, even when I was with you.' I asked her if she loved me, if at least she had grown to love me, if she had *ever* loved me, and she said, 'You're a decent man, but I don't think I ever learned how to love anyone . . .' "

He finished his scotch in one swallow.

"Up on the stand? When Roger said he killed her? That wasn't really a confession. What he meant when he pointed at his son and said he'd killed her was that by siring Blair—the guy who, by that point in the trial, he believed had *actually* killed her—that in that sense he was responsible for her death. 'I'm responsible.' That's what he meant. Not, 'I did it.' But then Blair shot him, and the bailiff shot Blair before anyone could clarify that point."

I wrinkled my brow. "You're getting me all confused," I said. "Are you saying *Blair* killed her?"

The light off the river made shadows come and go in the brightness of his eyes. "No. I'm saying that's what Roger believed, once he'd heard the evidence. In his heart, Roger knew I loved her, so he figured, okay, maybe it wasn't me after all."

"Oh," I said.

There was a long silence. "But, of course, Blair didn't kill her either."

I felt goose bumps rise on my skin.

"I loved her more than you can possibly imagine," Miles said. "I mean—God!—I can feel it in my bones. Even now, even after all these years and everything that's happened."

A big steamer slowly slid into view from the north, heading down toward Detroit.

"When she said she had never loved me?" He shook his head slowly as though puzzled by something. "I felt like everything had fallen apart, like my whole life had come to nothing. I had set out from this crummy little town with such big dreams. Money, success, love, family, fame . . .

I wanted all of that. But mostly I wanted love. And where was I now that I'd reached the end of my life? Broke, childless, forgotten, career in the crapper. And where I'd thought there was love, there was nothing at all. Just some kind of good-mannered patrician toleration."

He sat for a long time.

"I had nothing left, you see, Charley? I was right back where I'd started when I left this town forty years ago—minus all the hope and all the possibility. When she said those things, it all just kind of bubbled up in me. That's what I'm saying: Strange, you just never know what you're capable of."

He finished his scotch and set it on the table.

"After it was over, I stood there looking at Diana, and I realized what a horrible thing I'd done, that the person who really deserved punishment was not her. It was Roger. And that's when it came to me."

"What did?"

"Act Two, you might say."

"I don't follow." My voice had gone low and soft.

"Like I said earlier, I always came up with ideas real quick. It just came to me." He snapped his fingers. "In one second I saw how I could avoid being punished and how I could get back at Roger at the same time, for the terrible thing he'd inflicted on Diana, on me. Even on that poor bastard Blair."

Suddenly, I was having to concentrate on my breathing. The air seemed to have gotten dense as mud.

"It always bothered me," I said finally, "that Roger only bought a one-way ticket from Detroit to New York. Why not a round-trip? That didn't make any sense to me."

Miles nodded. "Sure. I had to run down to the airport and buy a ticket with cash. That's why the body was already cooling by the time I called you. That's why the timing didn't make sense. Couldn't buy him a round-trip ticket *to* Detroit, obviously. It was too late by then. But I figured if I bought a return trip, that would be enough. Then I opened the book of Japanese erotic woodblock prints on the living room table. Then went out and planted the clothes in Roy Beverly's boat."

I prodded the copy of *How I Killed My Wife* with one finger. "So that's it then. That's why there's no dedication in the original."

Miles nodded. "I had to call Bob Gough's assistant at Elgin Press from the jail and have her add that dedication in the new edition. She was the only person who even knew I'd added it—just some lowly kid, two months out of Haverford or Bryn Mawr or whatever. The general theory was that I'd try to make what happened to Diana fit the crime out of *How I Killed My Wife*. I figured that if it totally matched up with something out of a book, that the whole thing would be too perfect, too easy, too crisp and unnatural. And so everybody would eventually conclude that someone was trying to frame me." He laughed, a brief and mirthless sound, like the cracking of a stick. As the late-afternoon light failed, his gray eyes had gone flat and dead, like roofing nails driven into his face.

My hand was shaking slightly. I felt sick. Not quite nauseated; it was more that clammy, weak feeling that comes over you when a high fever is just about to break. "What about those splinters of ebony?"

"I planted them, too. Right in the wound. Why do you think that tool mark woman, Helen Raynes, said they were snipped off at the end? Raynes may have been a flake, but she was right on the money: I chipped the splinters off the bokken with a Swiss army knife. Like I say, I wanted the crime to match up point by point with that stupid book. Remember how he almost got caught in chapter fifteen because of the splinters? But then he turned it around, used it to incriminate his friend Horace, the guy with the boat?"

"So you didn't kill her with the bokken at all?"

He shook his head. "No. Like I said, I just got mad. Crazy mad. I grabbed what came to hand. A lamp. It's out there in the river some-where. That's why the blood spatter didn't quite match up. JoEllen Flynn was right too: The lamp was shorter than the bokken." He smiled without warmth. "I guess I got too cute, huh? It really came down to the wire. I kept thinking you'd catch on that it was supposed to be Roger who did it. You almost didn't make it, did you?"

"And Leon Prouty?"

"I ran into him at the lockup the day I was arrested. Promised him five hundred bucks to tell you that story. He was supposed to tell you about Blair coming in the old Lincoln, then, oh by the way, there was this rental car that came later with some tall, white-haired old guy in it. That moron. He forgot all about the second half of the story. Until trial anyway. Nearly blew the whole thing."

The big steamer sounded its foghorn—a low, dismal note that hung in the air, then slowly died into nothing.

"Why not just say you saw Roger do it?"

He shook his head. "I had to make you work for it. If I had come out at the beginning and said it was him, they'd have dug around, found that he had an alibi, so on, so forth. No, the ideal situation was for it to come out in trial, way late in the game. That way there wouldn't be any time to check on his alibis or anything like that."

He picked up his empty glass, then set it back down.

"There were a bunch of other details, Charley, little clues I planted that were supposed to point toward Roger. But you never really picked up on them. Like I say, I got too cute. Real life ain't an Agatha Christie novel. It's too messy, isn't it?"

A big breakbulk steamer came and went, carrying wheat down from Canada. The bow waves spread slowly across the channel, lapping noisily against the pilings of the boardwalk. I wanted to stand up and walk away, but I was pinned to my seat—maybe out of horror or maybe because I had one more question I wanted answered.

"Why did you tell me this?" I said after a while. The air was growing chillier now, the sun working its way down toward the horizon. "Do you want me to do something about this?"

He breathed out heavily. "No. No, not really. But you wouldn't have asked me about the dedication if you hadn't suspected something, am I right?"

After a moment I nodded.

"You're a bulldog, Charley. That's why I hired you. So if I'd tried to bullshit you, you'd have poked around until you turned up more inconsistencies. I figured I'd save you the trouble."

My hand was still shaking a little.

Miles shrugged slightly. "Anyway, as soon as you called, I knew you were on the road to figuring it out. I could have dodged you if I'd wanted to." He looked out at the water. "Truth is, I guess I just wanted it off my chest. Confessional instinct, or something? Or maybe I wanted to gloat, let somebody know I got away with murder." He made an ironic grimace that suggested this was not the reason at all. "Tell something like this to a priest or a psychiatrist, who the hell knows what'll happen. But a lawyer?" He cocked his head slightly. "There's only one thing you can trust a lawyer to do."

"What's that?"

"You sons of bitches'll take a client's secrets right to your grave."

Then he stood and walked off down the boardwalk, past the pretty maples and the amorous couples lying in the grass, growing smaller and smaller in the dying sunlight until finally I couldn't see him anymore.

I wanted to feel angry, but I didn't, quite. What I felt—aside from the weak, shaky, feverish sensation that had settled over my body—was a terrible and general sadness that only deepened as the sun sank away and the river went dark.

MILES PUT 221 Riverside Boulevard on the market a couple of days later, sold it to a sixteen-year-old rap star from Detroit, then moved out to LA. I saw him a couple of times on TV—*Entertainment Tonight*, that sort of thing—squiring bosomy young actresses around at movie openings.

Then last week, page three of the *Free Press*: "Controversial Author Dies of Self-Inflicted Gunshot."

He told me he'd gotten away with murder. But who knows, maybe there's no such thing—not in Miles Dane's world anyway. As Daniel Rourke said on the stand: In the end, Miles Dane's creations always got their just deserts.